WE
OWN
THE
SKY

WE OWN THE SKY

LUKE ALLNUTT

PARK
ROW
BOOKS

PARK
ROW
BOOKS

Recycling programs
for this product may
not exist in your area.

ISBN-13: 978-0-7783-1473-8
ISBN-13: 978-0-7783-1362-5 (International Trade Paperback Edition)

We Own the Sky

For questions and comments about the quality of this book, please contact us at CustomerService@Harlequin.com.

ParkRowBooks.com
BookClubbish.com

Printed in U.S.A.

For Markéta, Tommy and Danny

WE
OWN
THE
SKY

PART 1

1

She read up a storm before she left. In her favorite hard-backed chair; in bed, propped up on a mound of pillows. The books spilled over from the bedside table, piling up on the floor. She preferred foreign detective novels and she plowed through them, her lips chastely pursed, her face rigid, unmoving.

Sometimes I would wake in the night and see the lamp was still on: Anna, a harsh, unmoving silhouette, sat with a straight back, just how she was always taught. She did not acknowledge that I had woken, even though I turned toward her, but stared down into her book, flicking through the pages as if she was cramming for a test.

At first it was just the usual suspects from Scandinavia—Henning Mankell, Stieg Larsson—but then she moved on: German noir from the 1940s, a Thai series set in 1960s Phuket. The covers were familiar at first—recognizable fonts and designs from major publishers—but soon they became more esoteric, with foreign typesetting and different bindings.

And then, one day, she was gone. I don't know where those books are now. I have looked for them since, to see if a few of them have snuck onto my shelves, but I have never found any. I imagine she took them all with her, packed them up in one of her color-coded trash bags.

The days after she left are a haze. A memory of anesthetic. Drawn curtains and neat vodka. An unsettling quietness, like the birds going silent before an eclipse. I remember sitting in the living room and staring at a crystal tumbler and wondering whether fingers of vodka were horizontal or vertical.

There was a draft that blew through the house. Under the doors, through the cracks in the walls. I think I knew where it was coming from. But I couldn't go there. I couldn't go upstairs. Because it wasn't our house anymore. Those rooms did not exist, as if adults with secrets had declared them out of bounds. So I just sat downstairs, in that old dead house, the cold wind chilling my neck. They had gone, and the silence bled into everything.

Oh, I'm sure she'd love to see me now, tucked into this gloomy alcove in a grubby little pub—just me, a flickering TV, some guy pretending to be deaf selling Disney key rings that glow in the dark. The front door of the pub has a hole in it, as if someone has tried to kick it down, and through the flapping clear plastic I can see some kids hanging around in the car park, smoking and doing tricks on an old BMX.

"I told you so." She wouldn't say it out loud—she had too much class for that—but it would be there on her face, the almost imperceptible raising of an eyebrow, the foreshadowing of a smile.

Anna always thought I was a bit rough, could never quite shake off the housing project. I remember what she said when I told her my dad used to spend his Saturday afternoons in the bookie. Polite bemusement, that smug little smile. Because no one in her family even went to pubs. Not even at Christmas? I asked once. No, she said. They might have a glass of sherry after lunch, but that would be it, nothing more. They went bell-ringing instead.

It is dark now, and I cannot remember the sun going down. A car revs outside, and headlights sweep around the pub like a prison searchlight. I go back to the bar and order another pint.

Heads turn toward me but I don't make eye contact, avoiding the stares, the inscrutable nods.

A burly fisherman is perched on a stool, facing toward the door as if the pub is his audience. He is telling a racist joke about a woman having an affair and the plucking of a lone pube, and I remember hearing it once after school, in an East London alleyway where people dumped porn mags and empty cans of Coke. The regulars laugh at the punch line, but the barmaid is silent, turns away from them. On the wall behind her, there are pinups of topless models and framed newspapers from the day after 9/11.

"Four pound 10, darling," the barmaid says, putting the beer down. My hands are shaking and I fumble around in my wallet, spilling my change out onto the bar.

"Sorry," I say, "cold hands."

"I know," she says, "it's freezing out. Here, let me." She picks up the coins from the bar and then, as if I am a frail pensioner, counts out the rest of the money from my open hand.

"There you go," she says. "Four pound 10."

"Thank you," I say, a little ashamed, and she smiles. She has a kind face, the type you don't often see in places like this.

As she bends down to unpack the dishwasher, I take a long swig of vodka from my hip flask. It is easier than ordering a shot with every pint. It marks you as a drinker, and they keep their eyes on you then.

I go back to my table and I notice a young woman sitting at the far end of the bar. Before, she was sitting with one of the men, one of the fisherman's friends, but now he has gone, screeched away in a souped-up hatchback. She looks like she is dressed for a night out, in a short skirt, a skimpy, glittery top, her eyelashes spiky and dark.

I watch the barmaid, checking I cannot be seen, and then take another swig of vodka and I can feel that familiar buzz, that sad little bliss. I look at the woman sitting at the bar. She is doing shots now, shouting at the barmaid, who I think is her friend. As she laughs, she nearly topples off her stool, only just catching her balance, her breath.

I will go over to her soon. Just a couple more drinks.

I flick through Facebook, squinting my eyes so I can see the screen. My profile is barren, without pictures, just a silhouette of a man, and I never "liked" or commented or wished anyone happy birthday, but I was there every day, scrolling, judging, scrolling, judging, dank little windows into the lives of people I no longer knew, with all their sunrises and sunsets, their cycle trips through the Highlands, the endless stream of Instagrammed pad Thai and avocado toast, the unfathomable smugness of their sushi dinners.

I take a deep breath, then a swig each of beer and vodka. I pity them. All those tragedy whores, with their tricolors and rainbows, changing their profile pics to whatever we are supposed to care about today—the refugees, the latest victims of a terror attack in some godforsaken place. All their hashtags and heartfelt posts about "giving" because they once helped build a school in Africa on their gap year and kissed a beggar's brown hand with their pearly white mouth.

I change my position at the table so I can see the girl at the bar. She has ordered another drink and is laughing, almost cackling, as she watches a video on her phone, pointing at it, trying to get the barmaid's attention.

I go back to my phone. Sometimes I force myself to look at the photos of other people's children. It is, I suppose, like the urge to pick at a newly formed scab, not letting up until there is a metallic blush of blood. The stomach-punches of new arrivals, gap-toothed kids starting school, with their satchels and oversize blazers; and then their beach holidays, with their sand castles and moats, and ice creams dropped in the sand. Big shoes and little shoes, lined up on the mat.

And then the mothers. Oh, those Facebook mothers. The way they talked, as if they had invented motherhood, as if they had invented the womb, telling themselves they were different from their own mothers because they ate quinoa and had cornrows in their hair and ran a Pinterest board on craft ideas for the recalcitrant under-fives.

I walk back to the bar and stand close to the drunk woman. With enough drink inside me, I feel better now and my hands have stopped shaking. I smile and she stares back, wobbling on her stool, looking me up and down.

"Would you like a drink?" I say, cheerfully, as if we already know each other.

In her glazed eyes, there is a flicker of surprise. She forces herself to sit up straight, so she is no longer slumped over the bar.

"Rum and Coke," she says, her swagger returning, and she turns away from me, tapping her fingers on the bar.

As I am ordering the drinks, she pretends to be doing something on her phone. I can see her screen, and she is just randomly flicking between applications and messages.

"It's Rob, by the way," I say.

"Charlie," she says. "But everyone calls me Charls."

"You're local?" I ask.

"Camborne, born and bred," she says, swiveling her body to face me. "But I'm staying up here now." Her eyes are like lizard tongues, darting toward me when she thinks I'm not looking.

"You've probably never heard of Camborne, have you?"

"Mining, right?"

"Yeah. Not anymore, though. My dad worked at South

Crofty, till it were closed," she says and I notice how Cornish she sounds. The fading inflection, the soft rolled *r*'s.

"And you?"

"London."

"London. Very nice."

"Do you know London?"

"Been there once or twice," she says, looking away again to the other end of the bar, taking a deep drag of her cigarette.

She is younger than I thought, midtwenties, with red-brown hair and soft, childish features. There is something vaguely un-hinged about her, something I can't place, that goes beyond the drink, beyond the smudges around her eyes. She seems out of place in The Smugglers, as if she has ducked out of a wedding party and ended up here.

"Down here on your holidays then?"

"Something like that."

"So you like Tintagel then?" she asks.

"I only arrived today. I'll go to the castle tomorrow. I'm staying in the hotel next door."

"First time here then?"

"Yes."

It is a lie, but I cannot tell her about the time we were here before. The three of us, the end of a wet British summer, wrapped up against the wind, raincoats over shorts. I remember how Jack charged around on the grass next to the parking lot and how fearful Anna was—"hold hands, Jack, hold hands"—in case he got too close to the edge. I remember how we walked up the steep, winding path and came to the top of the cliff, and then, out of nowhere, there was a break in the weather, an al-most biblical respite, as the rain stopped, the clouds parted and a rainbow appeared.

"Rainbow, rainbow," Jack shouted, hopping from foot to foot, the leaves dancing around him like fire sprites. Then, it was as if something touched him, or someone whispered in his ear, and he stood still, looking up through the column of light that pierced the clouds, as the rainbow faded into the blue sky.

"You okay?"

"What? Yes, fine," I say, taking a sip of my pint.

"You were miles away."

"Oh, sorry."

She doesn't say anything and drinks half of her rum and Coke and shakes the ice around in the glass.

"It's all right, Tintagel," she says to nobody in particular. "I work in the village, at one of the gift shops. My friend works here." She points at the barmaid, the one with the kind face.

"It's a nice pub."

"It's okay," she says. "Better on the weekend, and there's karaoke on Tuesdays."

"Do you sing?"

She snorts a little. "Only once, never again."

"Shame, I'd like to see that," I say smiling, holding her gaze. She laughs and smiles back, then coyly looks away.

"Same again?" I ask. "I'm having another."

"Not having something from that then?" She reaches over and pats my jacket pocket, feeling for my hip flask.

I am annoyed that she has seen me and just as I'm thinking what to say, she gently touches my arm.

"You're not exactly subtle about it, mate." She looks at her watch and then realizes she is not wearing one, so instead checks the time on her phone.

"Go on then. Last one," she says, chuckling to herself, struggling to get off her stool in her tight skirt. I watch her walk to the bathroom—a journey she chastely announces—and I can see the outline of her underwear beneath her skirt, the imprint of the bar stool on her thighs.

She smells of perfume when she comes back, and she has

fixed her makeup and tied back her hair. We order some shots, and we are talking and drinking and swigging together from my hip flask, and then she is showing me videos of dogs on YouTube, because her family breeds Rhodesian Ridgebacks, and then clips of people fighting, people getting knocked out on the street on CCTV, because one of her mates from Camborne was a kickboxer but he was in prison now, assault.

Then I look up and it is all a blur, a skipping CD, the lights are on, and I can hear the harsh whine of a vacuum cleaner. I wonder if I have fallen asleep, passed out, but Charlie is still there next to me and I see we are now drinking vodka and Red Bull. I look at her and she smiles with wet, drunken eyes and she starts laughing again, pointing to her friend, the barmaid, who is scowling and pushing the vacuum cleaner around the carpet.

And then we leave, via a brief little farce where she said she thought she should go home, and then we are walking arm in arm along the deserted High Street, giggling and shushing and falling up the stairs to the little flat she has above the gift shop where she works. When we get to the top of the stairs, she looks at me, her mouth shaped like a heart and I feel a rush of boozy lust, so I pull her close to me and we start kissing, my hand reaching under her skirt.

After we finish, we lie on her small single mattress on the floor, without making eye contact, our heads buried into each other's necks. When we have held each other for what seems like an acceptable amount of time, I walk along the hall looking for the bathroom. I fumble for a light switch, but it is not the bathroom, it is a child's bedroom. While Charlie's room was sparse, unfurnished, the bedroom looks like a showroom in a department store. A light shaped like an airplane, mirrored by a giant stencil on the wall. Neatly stacked boxes full of toys. A desk with colored pencils and stacks of paper. And then, pinned to a board, certificates and awards, for football and judo and being a superstar in school.

Next to the bed there is a night-light, and I cannot stop myself from turning it on. I watch as it casts pale blue moons and stars onto the ceiling. I walk toward the window, breathing in the faint smell of fabric conditioner and children's shampoo. In the corner, I see a little yellow flashlight, just like one Jack once had, and take it in my hands, feeling the tough plastic, the durable rubber, the big buttons made for young, unskillful fingers.

"Hello," Charlie says, and it startles me and I jump. Her tone is nearly but not quite a question.

"Sorry," I stammer, suddenly feeling very sober, my hands beginning to shake. "I was looking for the bathroom."

She looks down at my hands, and I realize I am still holding the flashlight.

"My little boy," she says, a moon from the night-light dancing across her face. "He's staying with my sister tonight, that's why I'm out getting drunk." She straightens out some paper and crayons, making them symmetrical with the edge of the desk. "I've just had the room done," she says, putting something in the drawer of the bedside table. "Had to sell a lot of my stuff to pay for it, but it looks nice, don't it?"

"It's lovely," I say, because it really was, and she smiles and we stand like that for a while, watching the planets and stars dance around the room.

I know Charlie wants to ask me something: if I have kids, if I like kids, but I don't want to answer so I kiss her, and I can still taste the vodka and cigarettes. I don't think she is comfortable kissing me here, in her son's room, so she pulls away, takes the flashlight out of my hand and puts it carefully back on the shelf. She turns out the night-light and leads me out the door.

Back on the single mattress, she pecks me sweetly on the neck, as you would kiss a child good-night, and then turns away from me and falls asleep without saying a word. Her naked flank is exposed and the room is cold, so I reach over and tuck the cover under her and it reminds me of Jack. *Snug as a bug, snug as a bug in a rug.* I drink the remainder of my hip flask and lie awake in the pale amber light, listening to her breathe.

2

In the morning, it is cold but sunny and I walk down from the parking lot, past the Magic Merlin gift shop and the sandwich boards advertising King Arthur tours and two-for-one cream teas. With my equipment strapped to my back, I head down into an earthy hollow and then cross a small rocky walkway that connects the mainland to the island. To my right, there is a sloping baize of grass that leads down to the cliff edge, broken up with rabbit holes and occasional patches of sand.

I didn't sleep at Charlie's. She stirred as I was leaving, and I could imagine her, one eye open, pretending to be asleep, waiting for the click of the latch. The guesthouse was only a few doors down. It was strange to be sleeping in a hotel when I lived close by, but I wanted to be able to drink without having to worry about driving home.

I clamber up the rocky path, my head pounding, the taste of Red Bull still on my breath. Moving slowly as the incline sharpens, I climb the steep wooden steps up to the ruins, the camera bag heavy on my shoulder. Close to the edge, I can feel the spray of the sea, and I stop to rest and watch the tide coming in, quickly now, ruthlessly sweeping away sand castles and seaweed dumped by an earlier swell.

I climb farther up the hill to the site of the old lookout point. There are no tourists up here, just the wind and the squawk of seagulls. I find a piece of flat ground and place my wooden board down to secure the tripod, to add extra weight so it is not easily dislodged. I fix the lens and then attach the camera, testing to see if the rotation is smooth.

The conditions are perfect. The sea, sand and grass are so vivid, unreal; in the morning light they look like the colors of a child's rainbow. With my back to the sea, I can see the natural camber of the hills, the slow descent into the valley, down toward the bric-a-brac town. It is an incredibly visceral place. From up here, you could almost reach out and run your hands over the land, feeling the bumps and indentations as if reading braille.

The wind is slowly picking up, warm gusts that blow up white crowns on the waves, and I know I must start soon. I set up the first shots for the panorama, looking northeast toward the headland, and then slowly rotate the tripod disc, stopping at regular intervals to take bursts, until I have gone round the full 360 degrees.

When the camera has stopped its gentle whir, I check the little LCD screen to see that all the images are there and then pack up my equipment and walk back down to the parking lot.

The house is about an hour's drive down the coast. The village is deserted as I drive through. The corner shop is still closed, shuttered down for the off-season. I drive past the church and then along the winding road across the dunes, past the National Trust information center, and then up the unpaved track toward the edge of the cliff and the house.

It wasn't just the cottage's solitude that attracted me, but it was the way it was exposed, utterly at the mercy of the elements. Perched on an outcrop of rock, across the bay from St. Ives, it is the only building in sight. There is no shelter, no valley to break the ferocious Atlantic wind. When the rain lashes at the windows, when the sea winds refuse to let up, the house shudders, and it feels like it is crumbling into the sea.

As soon as I am in the door, I pour a large glass of vodka. Then I go to my office upstairs, sit at my desk and stare through the dormer window that looks out across the bay. I log in to my profiles on OKCupid and Heavenly Sinful to see if I have any messages. There is one, from "Samantha," a woman I was messaging a few weeks ago.

Hiya, you disappeared. Still interested in meeting?

I look at her pictures, skipping through the tedium of patent shoes and discarded umbrellas and plane wings and hearts on cappuccinos, and there is one of her on holiday somewhere, and I am reminded that she is pretty, a slight, mousy brunette.

I thought it was you who disappeared! And yeah would love to meet...

I connect the camera and start downloading the Tintagel images. When the download is finished, I flick through the photos, happy to see they are well-aligned and won't need much retouching. I load them into the rendering program I have written, and the software starts stitching the images together, the pixels fusing like healing skin.

You can never predict the light. Some days, when I am out with the camera, you think it is just right, but then the shots all end up looking grainy or overexposed. Today, however, it is perfect. The sea shimmers, the grass on the cliffs is as green and tight as snooker cushions. In the distance, I can see the faint outline of the moon.

When the program finishes processing the panorama, and when the images are joined together like a miniature Bayeux Tapestry, I encase the final image in a layer of code, so that people can zoom in and out and spin around. When all that is finished, I upload the image to my website, *We Own the Sky*.

I am surprised that the website has been popular. It started as a hobby, something to break up my afternoons. But the link was quickly shared on amateur photography forums. People wrote to ask me about my technique, the equipment that I used. The website was mentioned in a Guardian piece on panoramic photography. "Simplistic and beautiful," the writer wrote and I felt a rare swell of pride.

People ask me sometimes, in the comments, in the emails they send: "What does *We Own the Sky* mean?"

"Is it a reference to something?" And the truth is, I don't know what to tell them. Because ever since I left London, those words have been bouncing around in my head, and I have no idea why.

When I am out for a walk on the dunes, or sitting at my desk looking out to sea, I whisper those words to myself—"we own the sky, we own the sky." I wake to the sound of them, and before I fall asleep I can hear those four words, as if they were a mantra or a prayer that was drummed into me as a child.

The image has now finished uploading and I look out of the window, drinking my vodka, waiting for the ping. It takes a little longer than normal. Ten minutes instead of the usual five. And then there it is. A comment—always the first comment— by the same user every time.

swan09
Beautiful. Keep up the good work.

The comments are always like that—"Beautiful."
"Lovely."
"Take care of yourself"—and always so soon after the image

has been posted I assume that the user has set up some kind of alert.

The night is closing in and, before bed, I pour myself another vodka. I can feel the pull of sleep, the anesthetic effects of the alcohol, and I want to hasten it, bring it even closer.

Sometimes, I like to think it is Jack who is commenting on the photos. I know that he will recognize them, because they are all places he has been, views he has seen with his own eyes. Box Hill, the London Eye, a lookout point on the South Downs. And now, Tintagel.

Just to be sure that he remembers, that he doesn't forget the places we have been, I leave him messages, paragraphs of text hidden in the code, invisible to browsers, readable only to the programmer's eye—and, I hope, to his. It is, I suppose, the things I would say to him if I could. The things I would say if she hadn't taken him away.

TINTAGEL

---

do you remember, Jack, when we got back to the parking lot and you had fallen in the brambles and done yourself an injury. both hands, daddy, both hands, little red welts on your palms. so i kissed your fingers to take the owies away and you wrapped your arms around me, carefully planting two kisses on my neck. i remember, i can never forget. your kisses, like secret whispers. the gingerbread freckles on your face. your eyes, warm like the shallow end.

PART 2

1

"You don't look like a computer scientist," she said.

A little tipsy, I had started talking to her at the bar in a student pub in Cambridge. It was in that postexam, preresults purgatory, a lazy, sun-kissed time, squeezing out the last of our student days.

"Because I don't have a briefcase and a Lord of the Rings T-shirt?"

She smiled, not cruelly, but knowingly, as if this was the type of joke she had heard about herself. As she turned back to the bar to try to get a drink, I stole a glance at her. She was petite with black hair neatly tied back off her face. Her features were sharp but softened by her pale skin.

"I'm Rob, by the way."

"Anna," she said. "Pleased to meet you."

I almost laughed. She sounded so formal, and I wasn't sure if she was making a joke. "So what are you studying?" I fumbled, trying to think of something to say.

"Economics," Anna said, squinting at me through her glasses.

"Oh, cool."

"Actually, you're supposed to say I don't look like an economist."

I looked at her neat hair, so black it was like looking in a mirror, her bag stuffed with books, the strap secured to the leg of the stool she was perching on. I smiled.

"What?"

"But you do a little," I said. "In a good way, I mean."

Her eyes sparkled, and she opened her mouth as if she had thought of something to say, something that amused her, but then thought better of it.

I knew she was friends with Lola, the person whose birthday we were celebrating. They seemed unlikely friends. Hippy-dippy Lola, who loved to tell everyone that she was named after that Kinks song and would always sing it on request. Lola, who was known around town as the girl who got naked at the summer ball.

And then this Anna, with her sensible clothes and sturdy shoes. I had seen her around campus, often with a musical instrument strapped to her back. Not casually slung over one shoulder, but carefully and firmly attached. She always seemed to be walking with pronounced intent, as if she had a very urgent appointment.

"So what will you do with computer science?" she asked.

I was flustered, looked toward my friends at the quiz machine, not sure how to answer a question I thought was normally reserved for people who studied ancient history. There was something almost Edwardian about Anna—her puckered vowels and pristine consonants. She spoke with the precision and bearing of a character in an Enid Blyton novel. A little bit of a Goody Two-shoes.

"Maps," I said.

"Maps?"

"Online mapping."

Anna didn't say anything. Her face was blank, unreadable.

"Have you heard of this new Google Maps?"

She shook her head.

"It's been in the news a little recently. I'm writing some software connected to that."

"So you'll join a company then?" Anna asked.

"No. I'm going to start my own."

"Oh," she said, lightly touching the rim of her empty glass.

"That sounds ambitious, although, in fairness, I don't really know much about such things."

"Can I see your phone?"

"Sorry?"

"I can show you what I mean…"

Anna looked confused, rummaged around in her bag, and produced an old Nokia.

I smiled.

"What?" she said, her grin revealing two almost symmetrical dimples on her cheeks. "It does everything I need."

"I'm sure it does," I said, taking it from her, my hand brushing her fingers.

"So…imagine in the future, you'll have a much bigger screen here, perhaps even a touch screen, and somewhere here you'll have a map. People, anyone, will be able to add things to the map, restaurants, their running routes, whatever they want. So I'm working on some software that lets you do that, where you can add things, customize the map how you want it."

Anna looked bemused and touched the blue screen of her Nokia. "It sounds interesting," she said, "although I am something of a Luddite. Will I still be able to send texts?"

"Yes," I said, laughing a little. She was so dry, so straight-faced, I couldn't tell if she was joking.

"Good. That's a relief. So are you friends with Lola, as well?"

"Yes, a little bit," I said. "I knew her in the first year. She lived on my floor."

"Ah," Anna said. "So you're *that* Rob."

That Rob. I thought back. Had I done something when I was drunk? I remembered talking to Lola one night at Fez a few semesters ago. She went on about her upbringing in Kensington as if it was a curse, a leper's bell around her neck. I found her tiresome, a bit of a bore, but I didn't think I had been rude.

"That Rob?" I asked, smiling nervously.

"Oh, no, just Lola mentioned you," Anna said casually, trying once again to get the bartender's attention. "She said you were some kind of computer genius, a whiz kid, and from public housing to boot." She gasped as she said "public housing" and contorted her expression into one of mock outrage. "She said it was wonderful that you got a chance to come here like the rest of us," Anna said with a little giggle.

"That's good of her," I said, smiling. "The boy done good."

"Sorry?"

"The boy done good."

"What do you mean?"

"Oh, it's a football reference."

"Ah, sorry, I don't follow the sports," she said, as if it was a category in Trivial Pursuit.

The pub was filling up, and we were pushed closer together, our bare arms occasionally touching. On the side of her neck, she had a small birthmark shaped like a heart. I was lost for a moment, looking at the gentle grain of her skin, when her eyes caught mine.

"So how do you know Lola?" I said, quickly looking away.

"We went to school together," Anna said vaguely, as if she was thinking about something else.

"To Roedean?"

"Yes."

I had figured Anna was posh, but not Roedean posh. "And what about you?" I said.

"What about me?" she said. She sounded terse, suddenly defensive.

"After we're finished with this place I mean."

"Oh, I see. Accountancy," Anna said without pause. "I have five job offers in London, and I'll decide by the end of the week which one to take."

"Wow, cool."

"Not exactly cool, but it's what I do. Or rather what I will do." She smiled weakly. "We're never getting a drink, are we?"

"No. Especially not now." I nodded to a group of men in rugby shirts. One of them was just wearing underpants and protective goggles.

"Quite," Anna said, and looked away. She seemed suddenly uninterested, and I could imagine her weaving her way back to her friends and then never seeing her again.

"Would you like to go out sometime?" I said.

"Yes," she said almost instantly, and her reply was so quick I didn't think she had understood.

"I mean that..."

"Sorry," she said, "maybe I'm confused. I thought you were asking me out."

"I did. I was," I said, leaning a little closer so I could hear her above the music.

"Very well," she said, smiling again, and she smelled of soap and newly washed hair.

"Sorry, it's loud in here," I said. "So can I have your phone number or email or something?"

Anna took a small step back, and I realized I was leaning into her. "Yes, although on one condition."

"Okay," I said, still thinking about her "that Rob" comment. "What is it?"

"You give me my phone back."

I looked down and realized I was still holding her Nokia. "Oh, shit, sorry."

She smiled and put her phone in her bag. "Okay," she said. "It's Anna Mitchell-Rose at yahoo.co.uk. All one word. Two *l*'s in Mitchell, no full stops or hyphenation."

A week later, the cinema. Watching the trailers, I could feel the warmth of her body and I wanted to reach out and touch her, to put my hand on her bare leg. I glanced at her a few times and hoped she might turn toward me and our eyes would meet, but she just stared at the screen, her back straight as if she was sitting in church, her thick-framed glasses perched on her nose. The only movement she made was to silently take sweets from her bag of pick 'n' mix. I had watched her count them out when she bought them: five from the top row, five from the bottom.

I fidgeted through the movie, about an insufferable drifter who hitchhiked around North America and then died in Alaska. I couldn't wait for it to end. Anna, however, seemed to be enjoying it—judging by how still she sat, how her eyes never left the screen.

When the movie ended, I thought that she might be one of those people who sit in a reverential silence until the last of the credits rolled, but the moment the screen turned black, she stood up and picked up her coat.

"So what did you think?" I said, as we hurried down the stairs toward the cinema bar.

"I hated it," Anna said. "Every single minute of it."

"Really?"

"Yes. It was absolutely awful."

In the little lobby bar, we sat down at a table next to an antique piano. "It's funny," I said, "I thought you were enjoying it."

"No, I hated it. I found him to be very unpleasant. Traveling all over the place, not letting his family know. He didn't give two hoots about anyone but himself."

Two hoots. I imagined for a moment introducing her to my friends back home.

"You didn't think it was cool when he renounced all his possessions and burned his money?" I said, enjoying egging her on. Anna took her glasses off, wiped the lenses with a small cloth, then put them in an ancient-looking case.

"What on earth was 'cool' about that?" she said, her cheeks flushing. Then she squinted a little, as if she needed to put her reading glasses back on. "Oh, you're joking," she said, smiling. "I see. But really, though. His family worked hard for what he had and he gave it all up, because of…because of what, some tedious teenage philosophy. He was utterly, utterly self-indulgent." She suddenly seemed a little self-conscious and stopped speaking as the waitress brought over our drinks.

"Did you like it then, the movie?" she said, when we were alone again.

"No," I said. "I absolutely hated it."

Anna beamed. "Good. I'm so glad."

"What was it he was always telling people? 'Make each day a new horizon.'"

"God, yes," Anna said. "Preachy New Age rubbish."

"And you know what was funny?" I said.

"What?"

"The one thing—the only thing really—that he wanted to do, which was live in the wild, well, he wasn't very good at it, was he? He failed."

"Exactly," Anna said, laughing, her blue eyes flashing in the dim orange light of the bar. "God, you're right, he was even rubbish at that. The thing is, if he had actually listened to advice from those who knew better, people who had experience living in the wilderness—wilderness experts, for example— then he might still be alive."

"Wilderness experts?"

"Yes, wilderness experts," she said, looking at me sternly. "I believe that's the official name for them."

I looked at Anna as she took a sip of her drink. She really was beautiful, her mouth always on the cusp of a smile, her eyes sparkling like a promise. She was too good for me. She would go to London and end up with the type of guy who was invited to her high-school dances.

"And what about you, where do your parents live?" Anna said, and I realized I was staring at her.

"My dad still lives in Romford."

Anna hesitated, took a sip of her drink. "Are your parents divorced?"

"My mom died. When I was fifteen."

"Oh," Anna said. "I'm very sorry."

"It's okay," I said, "it's not your fault." It took her a moment to get my little joke, and I grinned and she smiled back, a little more at ease.

I didn't like talking about that morning, when Dad was waiting for me outside the school gate. For some reason, he was wearing his best suit. He didn't say much. He didn't have to. Mom had collapsed at work, he said, a massive stroke. They had always joked that he would be the one to go first.

"So where's home?" I asked Anna.

"Oh, the main house is in Suffolk, but we've not really been there enough for it to feel like home."

"Ah, the hard life, so many houses…" I didn't know why I said it. It was meant to be flippant, a quip, but it just sounded petty and unkind.

Anna scowled at me and took a hurried sip of her drink as if she had to leave. "Actually, Rob, if you must know, I was on scholarship at Roedean, and my parents don't have two pennies to rub together."

"Sorry, I didn't mean…" I stammered. She was frowning, and I could see she found it hard to disguise her annoyance.

"And before you try to out-poor me, Rob, my parents were missionaries and I spent most of my childhood living in Kenyan slums that would make your public housing complex look like Cheam."

She angled her body away from me, and we both silently sipped our drinks.

"Sorry again. I didn't mean it like that, I really didn't," I said.

Anna sighed and nervously fiddled with the menu. Then she smiled and looked at me again. "Sorry, I probably overreacted a little. Evidently you're not the only one to have a chip on your shoulder."

That night we kissed as soon as we closed the bedroom door. After a few breathless minutes, Anna stopped and I thought she was having second thoughts. But then she started to undress, as if she was alone in her own room, and I watched her and I didn't think she minded me watching her: the angular bones of her hips, her neat little breasts, her pale delicate arms. When she was naked, she folded her clothes and left them in a tidy pile on my desk.

Since I had been a teenager, sex had always been an exercise in caution. A gradual testing of the waters, a constant expectation that my probing hands would be quickly brushed away. Anna was nothing like that. She was hungry and uninhibited, so unlike the prim and proper way she carried herself. Her desire was single-minded—a quality then, not really knowing women, I found curiously masculine. We stayed awake until the early hours, shuttered behind hastily drawn curtains, our bodies wet with each other, until finally we slept.

I waited for her out on the court, feeling a little uncomfortable in my West Ham United football shirt and Umbro shorts. The court smelled of rubber and fresh sweat. I wanted to impress on her that I was sporty, that I didn't just spend my time in front of my computer. So we agreed to a game of squash, which Anna said she had played once or twice at school.

Finally, after what seemed like an eternity, she came out onto the court. In her flappy men's shorts and regular blouse, she looked like a 1920s tennis star.

"What?" she said.

"What, what?" I said, stifling a laugh.

"Well, your clothes aren't exactly regulation either. With your football jersey."

"I didn't say anything," I protested, smirking and looking away from her.

"Right. Shall we play then?" she said, awkwardly holding her racket with two hands.

We started warming up, slowly hitting the ball back and forth. Except Anna wasn't really hitting the ball, but flailing, struggling to connect even when she was serving.

"I'm not so good without my glasses," Anna said, as she scooped the ball up toward the ceiling.

We carried on like that for a while, not having anything that would resemble a game.

"Okay, I admit it. I lied," Anna said, after she missed the ball yet again while attempting to serve.

"You lied?"

"I've actually never played squash."

"Oh," I said, once again stifling a laugh.

"I asked Lola and she said it was easy. She said that anyone could do it. Apparently not."

I wished then I could have taken a picture of her on that squash court. She looked so beautiful, her dark flannel shorts accentuating her pale legs, her dimpled cheeks flushed with exercise.

"Have you really only played a few times?" Anna asked.

"I don't know, four or five. At school."

Anna was quiet, bit her lip. "Well, the truth is, I hate sports."

"I thought you wanted to play?" I said, putting my arm around her cold shoulders.

"Not really. I thought you wanted to," she said, gently tapping her racket against her leg. "I only did it because, well, I didn't want you to think that I was sedentary."

I smiled when she said that. Sedentary. It was a very Anna word. After another five minutes of pretending, we gave up and went outside.

It was sweltering in the sun. We sat on a small wall that overlooked an enclosed field hockey turf. Children, mostly infants and a few older teenagers, were running around at some kind of sports camp.

We had both decided that we would stay the summer in Cambridge, living off the rest of our student loans. Anna said she wanted to do all the touristy Cambridge things she had never done because she had been working so hard to get her first-class honors. So we went punting and walked around some of the colleges and spent an afternoon in the Fitzwilliam Museum and a morning in the botanical gardens. Much of the time we just spent in bed.

As the summer went on, our friends gradually left. They went off traveling: backpacking in Australia, a camper van across South America. While I felt a pang of regret when they left, a sense that I was missing out on something, Anna and I were both agreed that traveling wasn't for us. We hadn't gone to Cambridge just to piss it all away "finding ourselves" somewhere in the Andes. Besides, I had my maps to think about, the software I was writing, the company I wanted to start.

The real reason, though, was that we didn't want to be apart. We were inseparable, like love-struck teens whose parents and friends can see are headed for a fall. Whenever we tried to spend just one night alone in our own rooms, we were miserable and antsy. We broke, usually within an hour. There was a line in an old Blur song that we both liked: collapsed in love. And that was what had happened. We collapsed in love.

People thought Anna was closed, a cold fish, but she wasn't like that with me. One evening, without probing, she told me about her life in Kenya and her missionary parents. In these careful, considered sentences, she talked about her father, his affairs, his estrangement from the church. She talked about her mother: how she would not accept her father's wrongdoing; how she channeled her love into her good works.

It was like a flood, an epiphany, to find out that this person that I thought was so guarded actually lay entirely open, exposed, and the one she wanted to let in was not her father, or Lola, or one of her housemates, but me.

The sun was getting hotter, and we sat on the wall drinking some water that Anna had brought in a thermos.

"Do you want to go and play squash again?"

"No," Anna said. "I think I've humiliated myself enough today."

"I enjoyed it."

"Yes," she said, "I'm sure you did."

"You do look very cute in your shorts."

She smiled and dug me gently in the ribs. "God, it's hot, isn't it," Anna said, wiping her brow.

The momentary respite of breeze had gone and it felt like it was 100 degrees. "We could go in the shade over there?" I said, pointing to an awning on the other side of the field.

Anna looked up. "We could, but we'd have to cross the field," she said. "And look."

We hadn't noticed before, but a group of animals—adults in furry suits—had joined the children on the field. A lion, a tiger, a panda, they looked like the grubby leftovers from a Disney parade. There was some kind of awards ceremony, and the children were waiting in line for their prizes.

"What are they doing?" Anna asked.

"Getting medals, I think."

"Right, I get that, but why the animals?"

I shrugged and Anna squinted, trying to get a better view.

"I don't like the look of them," Anna said.

"The animals or the children?"

"The animals."

I looked over at them. In a certain light, they did look quite sinister, their furry mouths locked into perma-smiles.

"There's a lot of them," I said.

"Indeed," Anna said warily.

"Shall we risk it then?" I said, getting up off the wall.

"No," Anna said indignantly. "We can't just run across the field, Rob. It's some kind of school function."

"We're not going to get arrested."

"We might," she said.

"Well, I'm going," I said, looking back, expecting her to follow. "It's better than sitting here and dying in the sun." I started running across the pitch, but Anna stayed on the touchline, looking sheepish, as if she was gathering the courage to jump into a swimming pool.

Now safely in the shade on the other side, I waved at her to come across and she cautiously started to move. In an attempt to appear less conspicuous, she decided to walk, but there was something about her nervousness that made her stand out. The master of ceremonies on the microphone stopped talking, and the heads of the children, the parents and the animals all turned to stare at Anna.

She smiled politely, aware that all eyes were on her, and then broke into a hurried little trot. In her gym shorts and blouse, she could have passed for a teenager, which was probably why a large orange tiger intercepted her in the center circle, linked arms and then dragged her into the line of children. I started to laugh, thinking she would make a break for it, but Anna—polite, diligent Anna—stayed in line, waiting for her prize.

After receiving her medal, Anna had to walk down a greeting line of animals. Even from here, I could see the flicker of fear on her face. With her medal round her neck, she moved down the line, being embraced by each animal one by one. Despite the animals' advances, Anna didn't hug back. She even pulled away when a bear tried to rest its head on her neck.

When it was all over, when the children had gone to greet their proud parents, Anna walked sheepishly back to where I was standing in the shade, her cheeks bright red, little bits of animal fur stuck to her blouse.

"Oh my God," I said, still laughing. "What were you doing?"

Anna started to giggle and wiped the sweat off her brow. "I panicked. I didn't know what to do. The tiger cornered me."

"Why didn't you just leave?" I said, handing her the thermos of water.

"I don't know. I was in the line and then…it was too late… Stop laughing," she said, frowning at me. "It's not funny."

"It is."

"Well, maybe a bit. And anyway, it's your fault."

"How?"

"For making me cross that pitch. You're an absolute idiot," she said, sipping the water. "It's literally my worst nightmare. Being hugged in public."

"And by animals."

"Well, quite."

We sat for a moment, cooling off in the shade, and I knew then that I couldn't possibly love her any more.

We were sitting by the River Cam, with a bottle of wine and some sandwiches. It was another sweltering day. Heat haze hugged the banks of the river like a dogged morning mist, and tinkles of jazz piano floated across the water from a café on the shore.

"Are you ever going to put that away?" Anna said.

I had spent the rest of my student loan on a digital camera and some extra lenses. "Yeah, yeah," I said, fiddling with the settings, trying to work out how to change the shutter speed.

"Seriously, stop pointing it at me. I feel like a model or something."

"You look like a model," I said, and took a photo of her. She stuck out her tongue and turned toward the water, stretching her legs out on the riverbank.

"So any progress?" Anna said casually.

"On what?"

"The job hunt, I mean."

"Oh, that," I said. "I sent off a few CVs but I haven't heard anything back yet. Do you want more wine?"

Anna put her hand over her plastic cup and shook her head, and I poured myself some more.

"You seem pretty relaxed about it all."

I shrugged. "I'm not going to worry."

Anna puckered her lips, something she did when she didn't agree. "Well, you've only sent off a few CVs. I sent off about fifteen applications and only got five job offers."

"What happened with the other ten?" I said.

"I don't know," she said, looking a little forlorn, not realizing I was making a joke. "It's annoying that they haven't responded. I don't understand why."

She had become a little agitated in recent weeks, suddenly concerned about my career plans. Anna had a job lined up, with an accountancy firm in London, and had started asking questions. What would I do next? Would I join her in London and look for a job?

My heart wasn't really in the job search, because all I could think about was maps—maps that were alive and dripping with data, maps that could be created by a teenager with a Myspace account and a laptop.

"I'm still hoping my maps idea will pan out, to be honest," I said, pouring more wine into my cup and stretching out my legs.

Anna's face tightened. "So what is the maps thing again?" she asked, pulling her sunglasses off her face. "You never really explained it."

"I thought I did."

"Well, maybe you did. But I still don't understand it," she said, and she seemed angry and I couldn't figure out why.

"Well," I said, sitting up and turning to face her. "It's still early days, but the software basically allows the user to customize their own maps. So, for example, you could map out your cycle route or where you went for a jog. Or you could upload your photos on a tourist map for other people to see."

"You'd put the photos on the map?"

"Yes."

Anna pouted. "That seems rather strange, doesn't it. Why would anyone want to do that?"

"I don't know," I said, beginning to feel a little annoyed. "Because they can."

We sat in silence for a little while, and Anna started to pack away the picnic things into her backpack.

"Anyway, you don't know the first thing about maps, do you?" Anna said. "I mean, people study for years to be cartographers. A cousin of my father was a cartographer. It's an incredibly skilled profession."

"Why are you being so weird about this?"

"I'm not, Rob. I'm just asking."

"Nothing's changed, Anna."

"What do you mean?"

"I'm still coming to London, if that's what this is really about."

She snorted a little. "It's not about that. It's nothing to do with that."

"So why does it bother you so much?"

She didn't answer, continued packing away the picnic things. I knew why it bothered her. It was my plan to go it alone. She saw it as a risk, a deviation from the proper course. To her mind, I should be applying for a job, with benefits and a pension plan. That, after all, was why we had gone to Cambridge, why we had studied so hard.

"You're exasperating sometimes," she said, staring out across the river. "You're always so absolutely certain you'll get what you want."

"And what's wrong with that?"

"Because it doesn't always work like that."

"It has so far."

"What do you mean?"

"Well, everything I've worked for, I've got so far."

I knew I sounded arrogant, but I felt under attack. Anna turned away angrily and smoothed down her skirt. "Well, as long as you know what you're doing."

"Why does it bother you so much?" I asked.

"It doesn't."

"Yes, it does. You're pissed off now."

She reached across me and poured herself some wine. "It just seems impulsive, as if you haven't thought it through. You've just graduated at the top of your class, Rob, companies would be begging to employ you, but you want to do this thing with maps."

"Right, because I think I can make it work. And besides, I don't want to work for a company."

Anna exhaled deeply. "Yes, you've made that quite clear," she said.

We had reached an impasse, and we both sat and watched

the punters on the Cam. Apart from a few minor squabbles, it was the first argument we had ever had.

"It is about that," Anna said after a while, her voice barely audible.

"About what?"

"What I said earlier. I said it wasn't about London, but it is. I just want to know you're coming."

I looked at her. She was so beautiful, her knees chastely tucked up to her chest, her hair peppered with tiny dandelion seeds.

"Of course I'm coming to London," I said, moving close to her. "But there is one thing."

"What?"

"I want us to live together. I know it's not been long, but I want to live with you."

2

"Anna, can you talk, you're not gonna fucking believe this." I was standing outside a meeting room in an office on Old Street.

"Is everything all right?" she said.

I was trying to keep my voice down as the corridor walls were thin. "They want it. The software. They want to buy the fucking software."

A pause, a faint crackle on the line.

"This isn't one of your jokes, is it, Rob?" Anna said.

"No, not at all. I can't talk for long, but they're in the room now, looking at the papers. I didn't even have to pitch it. They just want it. They get it."

The company, Simtech, had been recommended by a programmer friend. A start-up run by someone called Scott, who had been a few years ahead of me at Cambridge.

"That's absolutely fantastic, Rob. Brilliant news," she said, but it was as if she was waiting for me to tell her something else.

"And guess how much they want to pay for it?"

"I don't know, um…"

"One and a half million."

Even Anna couldn't contain her excitement. "As in sterling?"

"Yes, pounds. I still can't believe it."

Anna took a deep breath, and I could hear a shuffling sound, what sounded like her blowing her nose.

"Anna, are you okay?"

"Yes," she said, sniffing a little. "I just… I just don't know what to say…"

"I know, me too. We have to celebrate tonight."

"Yes, of course," she said, a note of caution in her voice. "I don't understand, though. So what actually happened? What did they..."

I could hear the scraping of chairs on the floor of the meeting room, the sound of people standing up.

"Anna, I've got to go, I'll call you in a bit..."

"Okay," she said, "but don't do anything hasty, Rob. Don't sign anything, okay? Say you need to discuss everything with your lawyers."

"Yeah, yeah... I've got..."

"I'm serious, Rob..."

"Okay, okay, don't worry. I'll call you later..."

The grimy heat hit me as soon as I left the building. For a moment, I just stood, blinking into the sunlight, watching the lanes of traffic hurtle around the roundabout, the happy, dirty din of London.

The last nine months hadn't been easy. Living in Clapham in a rented ground-floor flat that Anna paid for. While I worked late through the night—caffeine-fueled coding binges—Anna got up early for work. We didn't see much of each other, a wave in our bathrobes on the landing—her getting up, me turning in. It was just for a while, we agreed. It would be better when her training period was over, when I had finished writing my software.

Anna loved her job, working in a department that audited the bank's adherence to financial regulations. It was perfect for her: a stickler for the rules, she knew where the bank could trip up. And because she knew the rules, she also knew how to get around them, the legal shortcuts and back doors, the get-out clauses that lurked in the small print. Her talents were recognized, and she was promoted and fast-tracked for management in just her first six months.

I was still buzzing and didn't know what to do with myself, so I started walking toward Liverpool Street, the skyscrapers eclipsing the sun. I tried to call Anna but her phone was switched off, so I ducked into a pub for a beer.

I knew I was right. All those twenty- and thirty-hour coding sessions, sleeping under an old blanket on the floor. I told people smartphones would change everything, and they rolled their eyes. But it was true. Maps used to be static, something we kept folded up in a backpack, or in the glove compartment of the car. Now they would always be with us, customized, dynamic, on our phones, in our pockets.

The beer began to have a calming effect, and it felt like a great weight had been lifted. It hadn't been the plan—Anna paying the rent and lending me the money to buy a new suit. She didn't say it outright, but I knew what she thought. That I should do a business course, an internship at a gaming company, that I should put my silly maps idea on the back burner for now.

It grated. Because everyone always thought that it would be me, that I would be the precocious wunderkind dripping in cash. Because I had a track record. I told people I would graduate at the top of my class—and I did. I told my disbelieving tutors I would win the annual Cambridge hacking competition—and I did, every year. But London hadn't been like that. While Anna flew off to Geneva every two weeks for work, I sat on the sofa in my boxer shorts watching *Countryfile* and eating leftover rice from Chicken King.

My phone rang. It was Anna.

"Hello."

"You're in a pub, aren't you?"

"How did you guess?"

"I had training and I've finished early. Do you want to come and meet me at Liverpool Street?"

It was a bustling Thursday night. The streets were packed with commuters in suits, and you could hear the buzz of the workweek coming to an end. I got to the pub before Anna and stood in the crowd of people waiting for a drink.

I saw her walk in. Even though we had lived in London for nine months, I had never seen her on her territory and it made me fall in love with her all over again: the cautious way she approached the bar; the calculations I knew she was making about the best place to stand; the way she fiddled with her new work glasses, which she said made her look like a secretary in a porno movie.

"Hello," I said, and she turned around and smiled. For a moment, I thought she was going to hug me, but she just stared, intently, blinking as if the light was hurting her eyes.

"I owe you an apology," she said.

"Why?"

"Because sometimes I wasn't that supportive, of your idea, your software, and I'm sorry."

"That's not true, Anna, and you've essentially funded the whole thing by paying the rent..."

"Yes, but that's not what I mean. It's a horrible thing to say, but I think I doubted you. I'm very sorry. I feel very ashamed about it."

She swallowed, and suddenly looked very sheepish. "It's okay, Anna," I said, putting my arm around her waist. "I understand that sometimes it's difficult to recognize genius."

She poked me in the ribs and removed my arm from around her waist. "Don't get cocky. Wait, what on earth am I saying? You're the cockiest man I've ever met."

"Harsh. Shall we get drinks?"

Anna looked wistfully toward the bar. "I'm trying, although my plan of attack isn't working."

Suddenly, she turned to me and awkwardly kissed me on the cheek. It was chaste, like the kiss you would give an elderly aunt, but for Anna a rare display of public affection. "I promised myself I won't cry," she said, "and I keep my promises, but I wanted to say how proud I am of you. Really, Rob. You've worked so hard, and you deserve all your success."

I was just about to say something when I saw Anna tighten the strap on her laptop bag. She nodded toward the bar. "Let's go," she said. "We have an opening."

"Did you tell your dad?" Anna asked, after we had found a table and I had gone over everything that had happened at the meeting.

"Over the moon, son. That's footballer's wages, that is," I said, mimicking my dad's East London vowels. "No, he was really pleased. You know how sentimental he gets."

I could tell Dad was trying not to cry when I told him. He was still at the taxi stand, waiting for a call out. "Fuck me, son," he kept saying. "Fuck me."

When he had caught his breath, he told me how proud he was. "I still can't believe it," he said. "First Cambridge and now this. Taxi driver and a cleaner—no idea where you got it from, son."

Anna took a notebook out of her bag. "I am very pleased of course, but I do have some questions."

"Uh-oh. You've made a list, haven't you?"

"Of course I have." Anna flipped a page and I could see a numbered list in her improbably neat handwriting.

"Oh my God, you really did."

She blushed a little. "It's a big opportunity for you, Rob. I'm not going to let you waste it."

"It's a big opportunity for us."

Anna fiddled with the salt shaker and took another sip of her drink. "Seriously, can we go down my list? I'm getting nervous now."

"We should order some champagne first."

Anna slowly and demonstrably shook her head.

"What, really? C'mon, let's celebrate."

"I'm not being a killjoy, Rob. It's just that we'll pay the absolute earth here."

"Jesus, Anna. I just made one-and-a-half-million pounds."

"I know and that's good," she said, hushing her voice in case anyone was listening. "It also brings me onto my first question."

"You're so sexy in your new glasses," I said, raising an eyebrow.

"Thank you. That's very kind of you. But Rob. Please." She wiped some dust off the page. "So will they pay you a salary?"

"What?"

"On top of the money, will they pay you a salary?"

I thought back to the meeting. It was all a bit of a blur, but they did say something about a salary. "They will actually. They want me to run the company for them."

Anna beamed. "Oh, I'm so glad."

"Wait, you're happier about that than what they paid for the software?"

"Yes, I am in a way. You'll think me strange, but yes, the regular income does mean more to me."

"Wait, what?"

Anna suddenly looked very solemn, her client face. "Really, it does. Look, the windfall is great, but it's just a pot that will keep getting smaller. Whereas your regular income is a pot that, over time, keeps getting bigger."

"That makes sense I suppose."

"One of the many benefits of having an accountant as a girlfriend," Anna said, smiling and turning the page of her note-book. "Now, can I get through the rest of my list?"

There was a strange musty smell in Anna's parents' house: it reminded me of Werther's Butterscotch or the jasmine-scented handkerchiefs old people put in their drawers.

We sat and ate in near silence, just the doom-laden tick of the clock, the scratch of cutlery on bone china. The food was a turgid affair of frozen turkey, mushy overcooked vegetables, and a glass of sherry, which Anna said had been brought out in my honor.

"And how is your father, Robert?" Anna's father said, putting down his fork. He was wearing a suit, a gray three-piece that was worn and tattered around the edges.

"He's fine, thanks. Yeah, still driving his cab. Although his health isn't so good at the moment. Problems with his diabetes."

Anna's father didn't say anything and looked down at his plate.

For the last three Christmases we had been to my dad's. For proximity, we told Anna's parents. Romford was much closer and Dad was all on his own. But this year, out of Anna's sense of duty more than anything else, we decided to stay with them in their little village on the Suffolk coast.

"And will he be spending Christmas alone?"

"Nah, he's going round his best mate's…best friend Steven's for dinner."

"Is that Little Steve?" Anna said with a slight smirk. It amused her, she said, how I tried to sound refined around her parents.

"Yep, Little Steve. He'll be fine, though. He treated himself to a big flat-screen TV, and we got him a new Sky Sports subscription so, yeah, he's like a pig in…" I nearly choked on my sprout. "So yeah, he's really happy…"

At the other end of the table, Anna stifled a laugh and took a dainty sip of sherry.

"They're expensive, aren't they, those new televisions," Anna's mother said, wiping her mouth with a napkin. As always, she was dressed in her plaid two-piece, like a stern, passed-over governess. For some reason, she had served the food wearing rubber gloves and her hands underneath were a pale white, as if they had been scrubbed clean with a Brillo pad.

"Oh, he's paying in installments," I said. "He got one of those zero percent interest deals for Christmas."

Silence. We all listened to the ticking clock, the wind and rain hammering on the windowpanes.

"We've never been in debt, Janet, have we? Never had a mortgage or bought anything on credit. Africans can teach you a lot, in that regard."

I smiled politely. Well, I wanted to say, that's because the church gave you the house and because you haven't bought as much as a new shirt in thirty years.

He had been brilliant once, Anna said. Mercurial. Daktari they called him in Swahili, the doctor. In the village, he was a priest first and a doctor second, but also an engineer, a judge, a mediator of disputes. In all of the villages they lived in across Kenya, he was treated like nobility.

There had been troubles, though, Anna said. That was the word she used. *Troubles.* Affairs with the locals, the daughters of God. In the end, the church couldn't turn a blind eye anymore and, very quietly, they asked the family to come home.

"Well, he's enjoying watching his football on it and all the movies," I said, and Anna's mother mumbled, "that's nice" and something else I couldn't hear.

I kept thinking about what Dad would be doing now. Sitting down to dinner with Little Steve and his wife. The queen's speech and a game of party bingo.

"And how about you, Robert?" Anna's father said, finally breaking the silence. "Are you working much at the moment?"

I wasn't really, but I couldn't tell him that. When I sold the software and was taken on by the company, I had imagined it differently. I thought I would be living off the interest, coming in to a board meeting every now and again, riding around on a little scooter and playing pool with some of the programmers on a break.

It wasn't anything like that. Simtech didn't have an office anymore. There was no need, Scott, the investor, said. We could just outsource most of the programming to a company in Belgium. So two or three times a week, I sat in a conference call with Marc in Brussels. For everything else, we used email and Google Chat. I never really had enough to do. I spent most of my day writing comments on programmers' forums and playing fantasy football.

"Oh, you know, bits and pieces, stuff with the company."

I expected Anna's father to say something, but he just nodded, staring past me at something on the wall. He didn't approve of my career, thought I had got lucky, as if making money was a magician's trick.

It annoyed me that he thought we were extravagant. We put the money mostly into the house, a tall Georgian town house right at the top of Parliament Hill. There were new clothes, a car, but we weren't jetting off to the Bahamas every week.

"Well, jobs aren't easy to find these days, that's for sure," he said, as if I was unemployed, as if I was incapable of bringing any money home.

"And how about you, Anna? Your work, I mean," he said stiffly, and it was unfathomable to me that they were father and daughter.

"Fine, yes," Anna said, and I expected her to go on, to expand, but she didn't. She was silent and stared at an African wood carving on the sideboard.

Before I met them, Anna had warned me about her parents. She said they were cold, strange and they had never been very close. The problem, she said, was that they loved Africa and their missionary work more than they did her. When times were good, they were like honeymooning lovers, and Anna felt like an appendage, a third wheel. When things were bad, when her father was away on one of his "trips," her mother resented her, as if his insatiable lust for village girls was somehow Anna's fault.

There was a story she told about Nairobi, which, no matter how she spun it, I could never understand. Her parents would sometimes take in girls from the parish, the destitute or the troubled. Anna was expected to wait on them, not just make them welcome—she was more than happy to do that—but serve them tea, turn down their beds, bring them a towel after they bathed. She understood, she said, the need to help the less fortunate. That had been drummed into her since she had been a child. But sometimes it was as if they were the daughters, she said, and not her.

That evening at Anna's parents', I huddled under a blanket in my room reading an old James Herriot novel. Even though we were now married—an impromptu wedding on a beach in Bali—we were still given separate bedrooms. The room was sparse: a bed, a bedside table and a Bible. There was no Wi-Fi or phone signal, just a single shelf full of old beige hardbacks, their titles worn away. Our sleeping arrangement was punishment, Anna thought, for our unplanned and unannounced wedding, a union that hadn't been blessed by the church. That was the difference between them. My father couldn't have been happier, thrilled by the surprise, telling us it was our wedding, we could do whatever we liked. Anna's parents just smoldered.

I heard a soft knock at the door, and Anna came into the room, wearing her coat. "I can't take this anymore," she said. "We need to find a pub."

We said we were just going for a quick evening stroll, but instead marched the two miles into the nearest town. The breeze on our faces had never felt so sweet. So intent on finding signs of life, we barely spoke as we speed-walked along the dark country road.

The little seaside town of Southwold was dead. Only the lighthouse seemed alive, incongruous and towering over the town, its beam of light dueling with the moon. All we could hear were our footsteps and the soft sound of the sea.

"Everything's going to be closed, isn't it?" I said.

"We've got to keep looking, we must," Anna said, as we turned into yet another dark cobbled street.

Just as we were thinking about giving up, or trying to get a taxi to the next town, we turned the corner and light spilled out onto the street. A hotel that doubled as a pub.

As we opened the door, it was like easing ourselves into a steaming hot bath. We stood in the doorway and took it all in: the warm glow and chatter of the bar, the flicker and ping of the slot machines. In the corner, there was a loud group of locals wearing Christmas sweaters and Santa hats.

"What do you want?" I asked Anna at the bar, having to shout above the noise.

"A pint of something, and I think I'll have a double of something."

"A what?"

"A double. I'd like a double. A double measure of spirits."

I started laughing. Anna didn't drink a huge amount, and I had never seen her drink spirits.

"Er, okay. I'm just having a beer."

"Very well," Anna said, sounding a little like her father.

She was looking at the optics above the bar. "Gin. I think I'll have a gin."

"Okay," I said, trying to catch the bartender's attention. "A beer and a gin."

She nudged me. "But Rob, it has to be a double. Two of them in one glass."

"Yep, I got it, sweetheart," I said, smiling.

We sat at the bar, on two stools facing each other. Anna drank her gin down in one and winced a little, her cheeks flushing red. She let out a sigh of relief.

"I'm sorry," she said, chasing the gin with her beer. "About them I mean. I realize it's not easy."

"It's fine," I said.

Anna shook her head. "It's not fine actually. They're so strange, the older they get. And the thing is, this is actually them being nice."

"Really?" I said, nearly spitting out my lager.

"Really," she said. "They just don't like it here. In England, I mean. They're unhappy and it shows." She took a long sip of her drink. "I much prefer it with your dad. It's a horrible thing to say, but I wish we could go there every year."

I knew now why Anna was so keen to spend Christmas in Romford, at our little row house, which Dad decorated with reindeer lights and a giant blow-up Santa in the front yard.

I had been nervous the first time I had taken Anna back home for Christmas. Since Mom died, Dad didn't really want to celebrate. One year we ordered Chinese; another we ate our Christmas lunch in the pub.

But with Anna coming, Dad said he would do the full works, just how Mom used to do it. He got Little Steve's wife to show him how to do the turkey and roast potatoes. He got the artificial tree down from the attic and bought some crackers from

Tesco. And for the first time in his life, he bought a brown sliced loaf of bread instead of his usual white.

From the first moment he met her, Dad said Anna was family. I always thought he might joke—got yourself a high-class lady, son—but he never did. That first Christmas, they spent most of their time chatting in the living room. He loved hearing about Anna's time in Africa and her stories from boarding school. And she loved his tales of the taxi stand and watching football at West Ham.

When the drinks were flowing later in the afternoon, Dad got out the photo albums and we all scrunched up on the saggy, worn-out couch.

"And that's your mom, Rob?" Anna said, pointing to a photo of her in a sun hat on Brighton beach.

"Yep. When was that, Dad?" I said.

"Oh, I don't know, son. That's when you were about seven or eight I reckon..." Dad said, his voice cracking a little.

"She's beautiful," Anna said suddenly, and we all stared at the photo of her again.

"Yeah, she is..." Dad's choice of tense was deliberate because he had never accepted that she was gone. "Look," he said, turning the pages. "There's a nice one here. That's us at Christmas. Your mom just had her hair done."

"She looks absolutely lovely," Anna said. "Goodness and look at you," she said, pointing to awkward pubescent me. "You're so skinny."

"He always was. Don't know where he gets it from. Certainly not from me," Dad said, laughing loudly.

That afternoon, I didn't think I had ever seen Anna look more relaxed, more at home, her feet up on the coffee table, a can of Carlsberg in her hand. After that, we went to Romford for every Christmas, our family traditions rejuvenated by

Anna's presence. She loved those traditions, the things she said she had never had. The midmorning sparkling wine and ceremonial opening of the giant tin of chocolates. The pub for a pint while the turkey was cooking. The bingo. The party hats that Dad made us wear from dawn until dusk.

In the afternoon, Dad would get overemotional on the bubbly and would tell me and Anna how much he loved us, how she was like the daughter he never had. And then, at almost exactly the same time every year, he would fall asleep on the sofa, just after the traditional sing-along of "Hey Jude" on the PlayStation karaoke.

"We could all spend it together, my dad and your parents," I said, putting my hand on Anna's arm. "Although I can't imagine your mother doing the karaoke."

"Ha," Anna said and suddenly she leaned over and kissed me, full on the lips, and I felt a wave of lust, a pent-up desire like that urge to fuck after funerals.

"Wow. Be careful, Anna. Definitely a public display of affection there."

She sat back on her stool. "It's the gin, I think. I'm being serious, though. I don't want to come here for Christmas again. I know they're my parents, but I don't want that." Anna lowered her head, almost as if she was embarrassed by what she had said. "I missed you last night," she said.

"In your teenage bedroom?"

"Yes. It made me feel quite randy actually."

"Really? Well, I could always come to yours."

"No," Anna said quickly and then looked around her conspiratorially. "But, I will come to you."

I started laughing. "Are you drunk?"

She giggled. "A little actually. It's the Christmas cheer. But seriously, Rob, I forbid you to come out of your room. It's much easier for me. I know the times they fall asleep, you see. I know which floorboards squeak on the landing. I know how to close the door without making the latch click."

"I'm impressed."

"I'm not quite as square as you think, darling."

"But what if we make a noise?" I said, half joking, happily buzzed from the beer.

"We won't. Or at least I won't."

I looked at her quizzically.

"I went to boarding school, Rob. I learned how not to make a noise." She smiled at me mischievously and finally got the bartender's attention.

"Could I possibly have another gin?"

The bartender nodded.

"A double, please."

We were a little drunk walking home. For safety, Anna made us walk, single file, facing the oncoming traffic. When cars approached, she pulled me into the shoulder to let them pass.

On the final stretch, there was a sidewalk and we strolled along arm in arm.

"Are you still coming to my room?" I said.

"Yes, of course. We have an agreement," she said, almost solemnly. She then stopped, I thought for another car, but the road was empty.

"Maybe we should try..." she said.

"Try what?"

"To have children."

"Are you drunk?"

"Tipsy," she said.

"Really?" I said. We had never really spoken much about children. We were happy with our childless London lives: Anna's career; Star Wars marathons and pop-up food festivals on the weekends. Boating in the park, museums on rainy days, lazy afternoons in pubs. It was the London life we had always imagined. A world with children was still in the distant future, a future that was no more real, or no more ours, than a future that would have us living in Peru.

I watched Anna whenever she was around children. She didn't seem to coo and caw like other women. I saw her hold the baby of a friend once, and she cradled the infant so awkwardly, like a careless Mary in a nativity play. After she had returned him to his mother, I saw her discreetly wipe some of the baby's saliva on the back of her trousers.

"Yes, really," Anna said, biting her lip nervously. "During lunch today, I was thinking about your dad and how much I love going there for Christmas. Just that warmth of being in a family. And I really want to have that, as well, to make that my own."

I pulled her close to me and kissed the top of her head. Loving Anna was like a secret that no one else knew. A secret you kept close to you, that you would never reveal. Because I was the only one, the only who that she let in. We stood like that for a while, on the side of the road, gently swaying in the moonlight.

I think we conceived that night, or perhaps the morning after when Anna's parents were at church. A couple of weeks later, Anna called me into the bathroom. She was sitting on the side of the bath, examining, up close, in various angles of light, the clear blue line on the pregnancy test. I read the instructions, to check that we were reading it right. Yes, it was really there, irrefutable, a thick blue stripe.

"I can't believe it," I said.

"I know," Anna said. "Let's not celebrate yet, though. We still don't know for certain."

She saw my face drop and put her hand on my arm. "This

brand, by the way," she said, "has the lowest rate of false positives on the market. I chose it precisely because of that."

I didn't say anything, and she put her arms around me and buried her face into my neck. "I just don't want to get too excited, okay?"

"Okay," I said, and we stood and looked at the strip, the blue line now brighter and clearer than ever before.

DURDLE DOOR

—

it wasn't the water, you said, that made the big hole in the rock. it was batman with his batarangs and his blaster. we looked down at the cliff jutting into the sea, a rubber boat full of kids going under the arch, and then you started running and jumping through the grass, dodging the rabbit holes, shouting at the top of your voice, so I started chasing you, trying to catch you, and we were laughing so hard as we ran and ran, kicking up rainbow showers in the leaves.

3

A blue line. In the end that was all it was. I remember the doctor's pause. I thought that the ultrasound monitor had frozen, because the little gray-white shadow wasn't moving. I could feel Anna next to me, holding her breath, trying to decipher the shadows on the screen above her.

"Hmm, I'm afraid I'm not picking up a heartbeat, right now," the doctor said, moving the wand across Anna's belly. Where we had once seen a heartbeat, an electronic wobble, a quiver of white, now there was nothing.

She began to measure the size of the fetus. Has it grown, I said? It's small, eight weeks, the doctor said, but Anna was ten weeks gone. So it's small, I said, because I didn't understand these things. He's underweight?

Anna did understand these things. Without prompting, she wiped down her stomach with a piece of paper towel and sat up on the side of the bed, her eyes fixed on the monitor on the wall.

The second time Anna miscarried, it was at thirteen weeks.

"I'm sorry," the doctor said. "We're just not seeing the growth we would have expected at this point." This time, it wasn't just a little cluster of amniotic cells, but it had a human form, with limbs, a heart, a mouth. The baby had eyelids. That child, which had to be evacuated from Anna's body, could have been held in the palm of a hand. Even though we didn't know the sex, Anna later told me she had named her Lucy.

Anna grieved silently. She didn't tell her mother; she didn't tell Lola, who wore her own miscarriage on her sleeve. Because that was Anna's way, that was how she had been taught. Stoicism, above all.

Growing up in Kenya, a latchkey kid in a poor, dusty parish, the locals greeted her every morning on her walk to school with stones and insults, calling her a white devil and a smelly buffalo cunt. When Anna told her parents, they said she was complaining, spoiled, was not prepared to suffer for the Lord.

We kept things to ourselves. Our lost babies were our secrets. They bound us together. Yes, those secrets were devastating, but they were ours and ours alone.

She told me everything, even the feelings she said were shameful. She thought she was being punished, but she could not say for what. She said she could not bear to go to the supermarket and see young moms because she thought they had taken her babies away. She said she did not believe there was anything wrong with her eggs, the fetus we had created together, but the fault was in her ability to carry the child. She thought she was damaged, that her body had a mechanical defect. Mis-carriage. I had never thought of it that way, the carriage part.

Anna, however, wasn't to be deterred. She applied herself to having a baby in the way she had got her first-class honors. We went to see specialists on Harley Street and they ran tests, tests galore, but they found nothing wrong with her. Just one of those things, better luck next time.

So we kept on trying, refused to give up, because that was how Anna saw the world: as a fight, your guard up, backs against the wall. It was where we converged. The kid from Essex public housing and the scholarship girl, who both felt like we had something to prove, because we didn't have rich parents or a proud lineage.

At Anna's suggestion, I went to a clinic and, in a toilet stall with a handrail and an emergency cord, jerked off over some ancient pornography. But there was nothing wrong with my sperm. Top notch, the doctor said. Pristine.

We were not surprised when Anna got pregnant for the third time, because conceiving had never been the problem. We approached the pregnancy with a sense of fatalism. At around the eight-week mark, we expected the same: Anna's strange cramps, the feeling she described as an emptiness, even though both times the child had been there, living and dying inside her. But, no, there it was on the monitor: a heartbeat. And not just any heartbeat, but a strong heartbeat. There were hands and feet, the delicate outline of ribs. There were eyes, a half-formed pancreas. There were eyelids.

In the second trimester, they told us that the chances of losing the baby, even for a high-risk pregnancy, were slim. We didn't believe them. It was inappropriate, I said to Anna, but it felt like we were on *Who Wants to Be a Millionaire?*, where the questions were getting harder and we were pushing our luck by staying in the game.

"Your analogy doesn't work," Anna said, "because we can't cash out. If you could cash out with a baby, it would work."

It was at the start of Anna's third trimester when I noticed them. I was in the backyard one day, and there were two sunflowers that hadn't been there before. Anna hated gardening. It was a chore, she said, and she had never planted anything in her life.

I went into the kitchen and she was standing at the sink, in her apron, washing some coffee cups.

"I like your sunflowers," I said. "Did you do that?"

"I did," she said, looking pleased with herself. "They're nice, aren't they?"

"They are. I'm just surprised. I thought you hated gardening."

"Oh, I do, don't worry about that... It's just..." She swallowed and put down a coffee mug. "You'll think me silly, but I just wanted to do something. You know, for the little ones. I know that's not the sort of thing I do, but I thought it would be nice." Then she turned away from me, because she didn't want me to see her cry, and I put my arms around her, and she buried her head into my neck.

"The woman in the garden center said they were robust, good in all weathers."

I was sitting on the floor of the bathroom, watching Anna in the bath. She was reading a book, propped up on a wire bridge that held the soap, like something I remembered from my grandmother's house. Absentmindedly she twisted her hair around in her fingers, and I watched as the bubbles attempted to navigate her bump.

I was amazed at how much skin could stretch, her belly like a taut drum, the outer layers almost translucent. I was nervous about touching her. I wanted to, but I was worried that I would press the wrong place, that my inexpert hands would damage what was inside.

I watched as she read. Her pink razor was placed on the side of the bath and, even after all these years, there was something comforting about that. I remembered that feeling from the very beginning, when we started living together in my room in Cambridge. I used to love seeing her collection of gels and shampoos in the shower; her book on the bedside table; her earrings carefully placed in a saucer on the chest of drawers. Yes, it was a territorial advance, but one that only ever felt like a liberation.

"Oh, I was going to tell you," Anna said, putting her book down and swishing her hands through the water. "I joined this group on Facebook—Babies & Tiny Tots."

"What's that?"

"The clue's in the name, Rob. Babies and Tots. It's some kind of mother's group."

"Is it useful?"

"Well, I only just joined, but, in short, no, it's awful. Lola made me join."

"Is she still doing her raw food thing?"

"Doing it? She is it, Rob. She has her blog, the *Raw Food Mamma*, and she's working on her first cookery book."

"God. Poor India."

"I know. She swears India likes it, though. Says her croup has completely gone since she went raw."

"Lola's on Twitter, by the way," I said. "Do you know what her bio says?"

"Mmm, let me guess..."

"Hold on." I pulled out my phone. "Lola Bree-Hastings. Mother, daughter, sister, friend, fire dancer, yogi, raw food evangelist."

"Goodness. That is very Lola," Anna said, pulling on a strand of hair. "And she needs a hyphen between raw and food. In that vein, do you know what she has listed as her job on Facebook?"

"What?"

"CEO of cuddles and chief feeding assistant."

"Oh my God," I said, starting to laugh. "So how is this Babies and Tots thing awful?" I poured myself a glass and offered Anna some of the Bobby Bubble "kids champagne" she had been drinking.

Anna shook her head. "I've had enough of that stuff to last me a lifetime... Anyway, I thought it would be people, first-time mothers like myself, asking questions about breastfeeding or how the baby will sleep, but, goodness, these people are just so strange."

"How do you mean?"

"This Miranda, one of the admins, sent me a list of the acronyms they use in this group and, really, I'd never heard of any of them."

"Like YOLO?"

"What does that mean?"

"You only live once."

"Oh. Why would someone say that?"

"I don't know, if you're going bungee jumping or something. Like, YOLO!"

Anna shook her head and narrowed her eyes. "Anyway, I just found some of these acronyms to be utterly bizarre."

"Was it all DD, DS and DH?"

"What?" Anna turned toward me, mock outrage spreading across her face. "You know this?"

"Everyone knows it. Dear son, dear daughter, dear husband."

"Well, everyone doesn't know it," Anna said. "Okay, cleverclogs. EBM. What's EBM?"

I thought about it for a moment. "Expected breast manipulation?"

"That's actually quite a good guess. You got the breast at least."

"I always do."

Anna raised her eyebrows. "You're not funny, you know."

"Not even a little bit," I said, touching her back and tickling her arm.

"Don't, please don't," she said, giggling. "It hurts when I laugh, with all this extra weight."

"So what is it then, EBM?"

"Expressed breast milk."

"Aha," I said, turning away from her, surreptitiously checking the West Ham score on my phone.

"There's this woman," Anna said, "I think she might be one of the admins. She constantly shares all her craft ideas, all the a-maa-zing things she does with her kids. Today she posted, asking where she could find polystyrene beads because she needed to fill her handmade breastfeeding pillow. That led to a discussion about whether the chemicals in the polystyrene could infuse her breast milk."

"What was the conclusion?"

"Lentils and dried beans. Cheaper and safer."

"Of course."

Anna looked down mournfully and stroked her bump with the tips of her fingers. There was a line of moisture on her top lip and brow.

I put my glass down, inching closer to her on the bathroom floor. "Shall I do your back?"

"You might have to." She leaned forward, and I watched little drops of water scurry down her back. Her skin felt hot and smooth, like a wet waterslide in the sun.

Anna got out of the bath and walked back into the bedroom. She waddled a little: tiny, slow penguin steps, as if she was walking over pebbles. She didn't have the careless confidence of other pregnant women. When she slept, she would only lie on her side. If she bumped her bump, she would agonize about it for days.

I understood why. Because even now, a few weeks until he was due, I felt like we were living on borrowed time. I expected his heart to stop beating. A black hole on a scan. An evacuation. We didn't like to talk about names.

I sat next to Anna on the bed. Without warning, she started to cry and nuzzled her head into my chest.

"Are you okay, sweetheart?" I said, stroking her hair.

"Yes," she said, wiping her eyes and sniffing a little. "I think I'm just a little hormonal. That stupid Facebook group got me all worked up."

"How do you mean?"

"I'm just worried I won't be good enough. Be a good enough mother, I mean. Because I'm just not like these women, and I don't want to be like these women."

I touched her arm, and she angled her body toward me.

"But then," she said, "I suppose it's nice to worry about that, instead of what we usually worry about."

We lay next to each other in bed, her lips inches from mine, staring into each other's eyes. That was what always drew me in. Her eyes. The soft pump of her pupils; her eyelids, as thin as sugar paper, fluttering with each beat of her heart.

"I can't wait," I said, my voice cracking. "I just wish Dad was here to see it."

Anna pulled me closer and stroked the back of my neck. "I know. It's just so unfair. He would have been so proud."

Dad died of a heart attack two days after we told him the news. Little Steve, who had a spare key, found him in bed, as always sleeping on Mom's side. Next to him, on the bedside table, was the ultrasound photo we had given him.

I didn't thank him enough. All those night shifts he did in the taxi to buy me a computer so I could learn to code. All those wonderful afternoons at West Ham. All the times he stayed up late, nodding off in the living room, making sure I came safely home. All the love.

Anna looked at me, her eyes still a little damp. "I can't wait," she said. "To see his little face."

"Me too."

"I can't believe that it's real," she said. "When you want something so badly, when you wait so long, and then finally—finally—it's actually happening, I just…" She couldn't speak, her words trailing off into tears.

I was outside in the garden, experimenting with my remote-control helicopters. My toys, Anna called them, although they were anything but. I had a new one, a trainer flyer, with coaxial blades, and I had welded a little digital camera to the underside. I managed to get the helicopter up in the air, but the camera added too much weight and it crashed into the rose trellis.

I listened, thinking I might have heard a shout. Any day now, any day. Waiting for the other shoe to drop. Anna was upstairs, resting on the bed. She was a week overdue now and, as we had been told, the waiting was the worst part.

I picked up the helicopter and tried one more time after the wind had died down. It took off and I managed to keep it steady, hovering alongside the French windows, but then a gust of wind smashed it into the glass, snapping off one of the rotors.

"Rob," I heard Anna shouting, just as I walked back into the living room.

"Yeah?"

"Can you come up?"

I ran upstairs and found her sitting, with her legs apart, on the end of the bed.

"Shit, are you okay?"

"I think I've had contractions."

"Really? Are you sure?"

"Yes," she said, steadying herself by putting her hands on her knees. "I timed it. And it's definitely unlike anything I've felt before." She checked her watch, a chunky Casio that she praised for its night-light and accuracy.

"How long have you had them?" I said.

"I don't know. Forty-five minutes maybe."

"Jesus, Anna, you should have called me…"

"I wanted to be sure." She looked terrified, ashen-gray. "I think we should go."

"I'll get the bag."

"It's the day one."

"Okay, sweetheart," I said. "Shall we go down?"

Anna had two separate bags packed and they were both sitting in the hall with luggage labels tied to their handles. One said "Day," the other said "Night."

"Right," I said as we stood at the door, me holding the bags, Anna going through a mental checklist in her head. Just as we were leaving, I reached for my camera bag from the side table.

"Don't even think about taking that, Rob."

I looked at her face. Now definitely wasn't the time to argue.

The doctor had just left when Anna screamed and my first thought was that she had lost the baby. I pressed the emergency bell, but already a tuft of hair, the beginning of Jack's head, had begun to emerge. The doctor came running back and called for a nurse but she was elsewhere, on her break.

Anna was still screaming, so the doctor shoved her legs into the stirrups and then thrust a tray of instruments into my hands. She barked something at me but I didn't know what, so I just stood at the end of the bed, holding on to the tray for dear life, as Anna screamed out her pain and screamed out Jack.

We joked at first that he wasn't human—our little alien, we called him. Because even when I saw his slick dark hair emerge, his tiny body encased in gunk; even when I heard his screams pierce the cold matronly air, as he lay on the antique mechanical scale, I could not believe that he was real.

I would never forget the way that Anna smiled at him, when she held that little snuffling body in her arms and put him to her breast, so naturally, as if she had been taught by a heavenly midwife. Her smile was so natural, so unguarded, and I didn't think I had ever seen her smile like that at anyone before.

"Do you want to hold him, while I stitch Mom back together?" the doctor said.

I cradled him in my arms, gently, afraid I would crush him. He was wrapped up as tight as he was in the womb, straitjacketed, his eyes swollen slits. I was glad he was now getting some comfort away from the cold scale, the doctor's coarse hands.

In the baby books I read, they said it would take time to develop a bond, that while Anna would feel it, with me it would take time. It wasn't true. I felt it instantly, and it was like a lightning bolt down my neck, my spine, a feeling that everything, everything had been for this.

That we could produce this—this—a little bundle who squawked and cooed; no, it couldn't be true. That the two of us could create another person, with fingers and toes, a brain, a soul. That we could create a life. That we could create Jack.

4

It was hot for spring, and Hampstead Heath was full of runners, day-trippers, families with strollers. The grass was a patchwork of picnic blankets and hampers. The regulars, the elderly men who came up here every day, sat on their usual benches holding up small radios to their ears. A girl and boy kicked a football around with their mother: big run-ups, little kicks, the ball pinging around in the wind.

Jack had just got a new Spider-Man bike, with a windshield and cannons on the side, and he wanted to try it out. It was difficult to find somewhere flat around Parliament Hill, somewhere without a busy road, so, as we always did, we came up to the heath.

I watched Jack as he marched up the hill, the bike still too big for him. How quickly the contours of our world had changed. He was five, a proper little boy, as my dad would have said. Gone was the bow of his toddler's legs, the babyish lilt of his speech. Now our world was library books and parents' evening and trying to persuade Jack that the after-school drama club was cool.

"How about here?" I said, as we got to some flat ground.

"Okay," Jack said, putting his leg over the crossbar.

"Boys, no," Anna said. "It's far too steep here. I thought we were going to the flat bit."

"This is the flat bit," I offered.

"It's okay here, Mom," Jack added.

Anna thought about it, looking up and down the path. "No, I don't think so. It's too steep."

Jack sighed and rolled his eyes, something he had learned in kindergarten.

"C'mon, Jack," I said, "let's go to that bit up there."

"Okay," Jack said, starting to push his bike up the hill.

When we got to the top, to the plateau of flat ground, we watched a boy on a tricycle, his father anxiously running behind him.

"Should be okay here," I said.

Anna looked perturbed, a little flustered, as if she thought she was somewhere else. "Okay," she said, checking out the terrain, "but you go carefully, Jack."

He secured the strap on his helmet like a fighter pilot and then pushed himself down the path, weaving in and out of the walkers. I ran alongside him, smiling, brimming with pride, and it was like an old home movie shot on Super 8, the trees whizzing by, the lens-flare in the blinding light.

I felt something touch my arm and realized that Anna was by my side. At first I thought it was out of nerves, that she was ready to swoop in and save Jack, until I realized she was smiling, happily letting him trundle down the hill.

Jack slowed a little, now facing a gentle incline, and I ran behind him and gave him a push, my hands on the back of his saddle. I remembered the feel of my father's hands, the powerful thrust as he pushed me, his cheers of pride as I rode my bike for the first time on our street.

"There is one more present," Dad said that Christmas, and I remembered Mom smiling, her cheeks flushed with wine. "But you gotta close your eyes, son."

That December, I thought Dad was working a lot on his car. After I had gone to bed, I could hear him, tinkering in the garage, the radio on low, the occasional *ptush* as he cracked open a can.

Mom tied one of her old scarves over my eyes, and they led me out to the garage.

"Are you ready?" they said and I squealed, barely able to contain myself.

They pulled the scarf off and I opened my eyes, and there it was, what Dad had been working on every night. A little BMX, but not just any BMX, but one that had been tricked out, with five-spoke mag wheels and chrome pedals and pegs.

"Fifteen quid, it cost," Dad said proudly. "Everything donated or from the scrap yard." I didn't think I had ever seen him look so pleased.

"You did brilliantly, Jack, well done," I said as he expertly slowed to a halt.

Jack got off and started to make sure the bike's plastic cannons were still working.

"He's really got the hang of it," I said to Anna.

"He has, hasn't he?"

"Can I go again?" Jack said, tightening his helmet.

"Of course you can."

Jack got back on his bike and practiced riding around in circles, weaving in and out of some tree stumps on the grass. Anna and I were talking, not paying attention, when Jack, instead of turning, rode straight into a tree.

Anna let out a scream and we both ran over. He was lying on the ground, a dazed look in his eyes.

"Are you okay?" I said, kneeling down next to him.

He nodded vaguely, as if he didn't know what happened.

"Are you hurt?" I said. "How many fingers am I holding up?"

Jack smiled at me. "A million."

"Can you remember your name?"

"Jack."

"Can you remember my name?"

"Mr. Piggy Face," he said, starting to giggle a little.

"Good. I think you'll be fine."

I helped Jack to stand and picked up his bike from the ground.

"What happened, poppet? Are you okay?" Anna said, dusting off his jacket and trousers.

"I'm okay," Jack said, still looking confused.

"What happened, mate?"

"I don't know. I was just on the Spider-Man bike and then I… I don't know… I felt all funny and then did a big crash into the tree…"

When we got back to the house, I sat with Jack in the living room, drinking hot chocolate and watching *Final Score*. Jack listened, mouthing the names of some of the teams. Accrington, Chesterfield, Blackburn. He tried to say the more difficult ones out loud: Gillingham, Scunthorpe, Shrewsbury.

As he was listening, Jack started to go through the photos he had taken on his camera, his little point-and-shoot. It had been a present for his fifth birthday, and it never left his side. He always gripped it tightly with two hands, just like we had shown him, because it wasn't a toy, Jack, it wasn't a toy. After he had finished taking his photos, he would wipe the screen with a piece of toilet paper and put it back in the case.

"Daddy," he said, carefully putting the camera on the coffee table, "can I have special cheese toast?"

Special cheese on toast was butter, Marmite and a few slabs of cheese melted in the microwave.

"Of course you can. I think Mommy is making it right now."

"Are you having it too?"

"No," I said. "I'll just eat all yours."

"Nooooooo." Jack looked at me and crossed his eyes. "If you
do, I'll do something bad to you."

"Like what?"

"Hmm." Jack put his finger to his lips. "You will have to go
to bed and...and..." He thought hard and I raised my eyebrows.
"And...and you can't watch football," he said triumphantly.

"Ah, okay," I said, scratching my chin. "You win. I won't
eat your special cheese on toast then."

Jack beamed, and I went into the kitchen to see if it was
ready. Anna was cutting the toast into little squares.

"Is he okay?" she said.

"Yes, he's absolutely fine."

"I still don't understand what happened."

"Anna, he just fell off his bike. It's completely normal."

"But it was like he blacked out. He said he felt funny."

"He just lost his concentration. It's a new skill, a lot to take
in."

Anna didn't look convinced. She handed me the plate, and
I carried it in to Jack.

It was the only thing my dad could ever make. He did everything around the house but never learned how to cook. When
Mom was out cleaning offices downtown that was what he
would make for my dinner. He knew how to get it just right.
Lightly browned toast, the butter spread as soon as the toaster
popped. A layer of Marmite and then thin slabs of cheese. He
always put it in the microwave for thirty seconds but would
watch, bent over the kitchen counter, waiting for that perfect
cusp just before the cheese started to bubble.

I made him special cheese on toast after Mom died. He
would sit silently at the kitchen table, Mom's place mat, her
knife and fork, laid out next to him. Every night he sat and
cried, and all I could do was make him his dinner, as my mom
had always done.

"Thanks, beautiful," he said, when I put down his plate, be-cause that was what he always said. In front of my friends or at West Ham, it was always "handsome" or "son." But when we were alone, it was always "beautiful."

So that was what I did, that was all I could do. For a year, I made Dad his favorite frozen pizzas, his Crispy Pancakes, his Fray Bentos pies. When he came home after his afternoon shift on a Friday, I always had it there waiting for him, his treat: two rounds of special cheese on toast with ketchup on the side.

I watched Jack eat, little dabs of tomato sauce around his mouth. He was still watching the football results, mouthing the names of the teams. Sometimes, I could really see Dad in him. The careful, considered manner in which he ate. The way he would hold his head to the side when he was listening, as if he was hard of hearing.

I daydreamed sometimes, imagining them together. How Dad would let him sit on his belly, as I had done as a child. How one day, when Jack was old enough, the three of us would all go to West Ham. How he would let him sit in the front of the taxi and speak on the radio to the dispatchers. Dad would have glittered with Jack.

"Seriously, mate, not the drones again. Please, God, not the fucking drones."

I was sitting with Scott in The Ship, our impromptu of-fice. It was always quiet in the afternoons, the big tables empty enough for us to stretch out with our laptops. The wood pan-eling made you feel like you were on a ship; the stained glass like you were in church.

"The thing is…" I started.

"No."

"But I've made progress, Scott…"

"Jesus, Rob, please not again…"

"I'll buy all your drinks if you allow me five minutes to talk about drones."

Scott laughed and slapped the table with his hand. "There is literally nothing you can buy me that would make you talking about drones worth it."

"Fuck off."

Although Scott grew up a few streets away and went to Cambridge, we never met until I walked into Simtech's meeting room on Old Street. Parallel lives, we always joked. Scott was the only Cambridge graduate I had ever met who bought his underwear at Romford market and had a West Ham birthday cake every year until he was eighteen.

"On another subject, though. I really need that code," Scott said.

I checked my phone, as if I had just received an important email. I was supposed to have written some scripts for a Chinese mapping company, but I was stalling and Scott knew it.

"I'm on it, Scott. I'm on it. It's just more complicated than I thought."

"So give it to Marc."

"It will be complicated for him, as well." Scott had wanted to outsource it to our team of programmers in Belgium, but I insisted on doing it myself.

"Right, but there's six of them," Scott said.

"Right, but it doesn't always work like that in programming."

My trump card. Blind Scott with science. He was rich, a brilliant businessman, but he couldn't code. He sighed and swiveled around on his chair.

A few worry lines had appeared on Scott's face. I knew he was thinking about selling the company. He had taken a hit after the crash and was "moving a few things around." That was why he wanted me to write the code: to impress a potential Chinese buyer.

"Rob, look, you're a mate, and we've been working together for a long time. I've always tried not to micromanage you, but I've gotta draw the line on this one. I need that code by the end of the week, okay?"

He looked out of the window, and I noticed his foot was tapping on the base of the chair. I didn't want him to sell. I would lose my salary, something that petrified Anna. But more than that, to get my drones idea off the ground, I needed Simtech. I needed their name, their pedigree, Scott's contacts in the finance world. Without them, I would be right back to where I was, in the suit that Anna paid for, presenting my scribbled-out business plan.

"If I get you the code by Friday, can I talk about drones?"

"For fuck's sake, Rob," Scott said, laughing, his accent thick, as if he was selling shoes on Romford market.

"Juan," he said, looking at the bartender, his Spanish pronunciation flawless, "can you get us a couple of beers when you have a minute?"

Juan nodded and dutifully pulled a couple of pints and brought them over.

"Go on then. I'm all ears," Scott said, taking a deep gulp. "But promise me you'll get me the code by Friday."

"Promise."

Scott smiled and shook his head. "Right then. Drones. My favorite subject."

"So," I said, "we've talked before. You know what I think. It's the future. The hardware is cheap, and people are going to use them everywhere. They'll deliver us pizza, our Amazon orders. Builders will use them to deliver cups of teas on their..."

"Rob, spare me the preamble," Scott said. "I've heard it a

million times before. You'll tell me about the search-and-rescue teams next…"

"Right, but there's something new, and this is what I wanted to talk about."

"Okay, go on."

"Personal drones."

"Personal drones?"

"Yes. Ultracheap, ultralight and ultradurable."

"Okay," Scott said. "And what do these personal drones do?"

"Take photos mostly."

"Take photos?"

"Yeah, you've seen those selfie sticks."

"Unfortunately, yeah."

"Well, that's exactly what these little drones will do, all controlled from your phone. So just imagine: You're at a wedding and you need that big group shot. Or you're hiking in the mountains and want to show people just how high you are, how amazing the scenery is… Or you're in a crowd at a football match. These were things that only pros could do a couple of years ago. Now anyone can do it with a five-dollar bit of plastic."

Scott thought for a moment, stroked his stubble. "Look, I get it, Rob, there's something there and maybe you're on to something. But it's just too…"

"Too?"

"Too niche, Rob."

"That's what they said about selfie sticks."

Scott's phone beeped and he looked at his watch. "Fuck, I've gotta go."

"Meeting?"

"No, new lady."

"Oh."

"She's Russian. Lovely, but a little demanding."

"You'll be bored of her in six months."

Scott looked down at his laptop. "Bit harsh, mate," he said, scooping up his car keys off the table.

"Sorry, was only joking."

"Probably true, though," Scott said, waving goodbye to Juan. "And anyway, you prick, I could say the same about you. You love the chase, building the new project, but then you get bored."

"Touché."

"All right," Scott said, downing the remains of his beer. "Don't worry about the tab. I got it. And please, my little beauty, please get me that fucking code, okay?"

HAMPSTEAD HEATH

———

it was the first time you'd seen snow so we went sledding, up on the hill where the big boys were and i just remember hurtling down, you crammed between my thighs, snow spraying up into our faces like the warp-speed millennium falcon. the only thing i would have changed jack is that i could have seen your face, that i could have seen your face as we were going down.

5

It was spitting with rain as we stood at the base of the Monument. We looked up at the column, the gray-beige stone blending into the rain, the only color we could see, the crop of golden bird feather at its peak.

We began to make our way up the spiral steps, Jack in front, going as fast as he could, his camera case strapped to his back. As we got halfway up, I could feel the chilly wind blowing down the steps, the pale ginger light beckoning from above.

For as long as we could remember, for as long perhaps as Jack could speak, he had wanted to be up high. At first it was the top of the stairs, the attic, but then it was tall buildings, hills, cliffs—wherever he could see the view from the top.

We would go up to Parliament Hill and look out across London. Jack would sit on my shoulders, banging his little heels on my chest, and I would point out all the buildings on the skyline: the Telecom Tower, the Gherkin, Canary Wharf.

When he got older, he printed out pictures of skyscrapers—the Burj Khalifa, Taipei 101, the Shanghai and Petronas towers—and stuck them to the wall around his bed. He said he was going to go up them all.

At the top of the Monument, we were the only ones on the viewing platform, and I was surprised by how narrow it was up here, a circular alleyway enclosed by a wire mesh, the walls daubed with a crumbly white plaster.

"So how was school today? Did you learn anything?"

He was still wearing his gray school trousers and green Amberly Primary polo shirt.

Jack didn't answer, too busy trying to peep over the barrier. "Jack?"

He sighed like a teenager. "Math, reading, writing and PE," he said rapid-fire and then looked up at me. "Daddy, why is it called Monument?"

"Do you remember I told you about the big fire in London?"

"In the olden times?"

"Yes, in the olden times."

"So they built this to remember the people."

"Why?"

"Because that's what people do sometimes. They build things to remember people."

"Why was there a fire?"

"Well, it started close to here, just around the corner, and in the olden days lots of the houses were made out of wood."

"And they build all the houses again?"

"Yes."

"That's cool."

Jack tried to peep over the barrier again. *Cool.* Ever since he had started school, everything was cool.

"Do you want to go up in the air?" I asked. "That way you can see something."

"I'm not too big now?"

"You're big but not that big," I said, lifting him onto my shoulders. I could feel him turn his head, moving his little hips, his heels on my chest.

We moved closer to the edge and looked east down the river. Amid the gray, there were just a few dashes of color: a smudge of green trees along the river; a red asphalt children's playground squeezed between two buildings.

"Look, Daddy, I can see Tower Bridge."

"Wow, yeah, you can. Do you want to take some pictures?"

He nodded solemnly, and I could feel him tug at his bag and carefully take out the camera.

Jack started to take photos, and I could feel him swiveling his hips, trying to get the best possible view. He liked to take photos from up high, and we printed out some of his best ones to add to the collection around his bed. The morning sun taken from his bedroom window. A weekend in Dorset, a white light-house against a purple sky. Raindrops against the windowpane taken from the top of Canary Wharf.

Jack had stopped moving and sat motionless on my shoulders, and I thought something might be wrong so I looked up at him but he was just still, staring out over the city, like an old yeoman surveying his land.

London was all Jack had ever known. His dragons were Tube trains, and he knew the bears would eat him if he stepped on the cracks in the pavement. He went to Chinatown for dim sum when he was two, and he could name all the bridges that crossed the Thames. He loved it all. Watching the summer sunset from the South Bank. Jumping the fishy puddles in his rain boots at Billingsgate. The throaty warm wind at the entrance to the Tube. The grime that feels a part of you.

We stood like that for a while, a four-armed giant, listening to the police sirens in the distance, the gray hum of traffic, the static of the city, a sound you would only notice when it was gone.

Jack was quiet on the Tube on the way back. I knew he was counting the stops, a trait he had inherited from Anna. She still did it, every time she got on. A quick little glance up at the map, and then the gentlest quiver of her lips as she ran through all the stations in her mind.

She memorized all of her journeys when she got to London. I

used to test her, give her a little quiz. Without pause, she could tell me how to get from Piccadilly Circus to Camden Town or the fastest route from Lancaster Gate to Regent's Park. Sometimes it was easier to consult Anna than a map.

It was still raining when we stepped out of the Tube. We were going to the play center in Hampstead, the one that offered mother-and-baby yoga where you could only get organic bhajis and Sumatra-roast coffee. As Jack headed toward the ball pit, I found a table and ordered an Americano. I listened to two women at the next table talking about another mother, whose child refused to eat, who had her wrapped around her little finger. That was what happened, they agreed, if you bottle-fed and gave them all that processed rubbish.

I drank my coffee and checked email on my phone. There were pitches for start-up investments, some paperwork from our accountant. I had been asked to speak at a tech-incubator event, something about nurturing a new way of thinking in virtual reality.

Jack had come out of the ball pit and was now charging through a plastic tube with another boy, I thought someone he might know from school. The two women were still talking, about their depressed nannies and how it must be a Slavic thing, and I knew why Anna couldn't stand it here. It was better if you were a man. They left you alone.

My phone chirped. It was Scott.

I thought you were sending me that code

At play center can we talk later?

A pause, a thinking pause. Then I could see that he was writing again.

Rob please call me I'm getting pissed off now

Will do later no probs.

I wasn't going to write that code. The Chinese company was huge, flush with cash, and would snap us up. They had their own people, their own infrastructure. Simtech would be dead as we knew it—and with it my chance of launching my drones.

I looked for Jack. With another boy, he was trying to get inside a plastic car through the windows, *Dukes of Hazzard*-style. I put down my phone and watched him. Since he had been small, I loved to see him play with other children, his first fumbling efforts at making friends: how he would cautiously smile and raise his eyebrows, his attempt at an opening; how he would try to woo his suitor by showing them all of his things, his colored pencils, his toys, the picture on his T-shirt.

I felt in my pocket for the shopping list Anna had given me. Her lists always made me laugh. Their neatness, their specificity, how she would state the particular brand of cherry tomatoes, her starred annotations, instructions on precisely which asparagus tips to choose. I used to keep her old shopping lists in my wallet and read them on the train, the bus, whenever I was sat somewhere waiting for her to arrive.

"Please turn over," she wrote once, "for the cheeses to buy if they don't have Gruyère." On the back of the paper, there was a neat numbered list of seven cheeses, with a parenthetical note to say that they were in descending order of importance.

I looked up from the shopping list and suddenly couldn't see Jack. I stood up, slopping my coffee on the table, but he wasn't in the ball pit, or inside the Toytown car. Then I spotted him, in the corner on the edge of the mat, lying motionless on the floor.

I ran over to him and he was still in the same position, lying on the floor, looking up at the ceiling.

"Jack, Jack, are you okay?"

He looked at me, his eyes glazed. It was as if he had just woken up and didn't know where he was.

"Did you hurt yourself?"

"No," Jack said, "I just fell over."

"Do you have any injuries?"

Jack narrowed his eyes. "I feel… I feel funny…"

"Funny how, beautiful? Like dizzy?"

"What's dizzy?" he asked.

"You know when you're on the roundabout in the playground?"

"The big playground or little playground?"

"The big playground."

Jack nodded.

"So you know when you go really fast on the roundabout and then you jump off and you feel funny. That's dizzy. Is that how you feel?"

"Yeah, I think so."

"And have you had it other times, when you're at school?"

Jack considered what I had said.

"I was on the jumping pillow with Nathan, and it felt like spaceships flying through my head."

"And can you feel the spaceships now?"

"No, Daddy, don't be silly," he said, sitting up, the color returning to his cheeks.

Ever since he had fallen off his bike in the park, Anna was sure that Jack's balance was off. I wasn't convinced. It was just clumsiness or overexuberance, I told her. It was normal for kids to bang into things. But she was insistent. It wasn't just when he was running around, she said. She noticed it when he was walking to the bathroom before bed.

"Can I go and play with my friend again?"

"Are you feeling okay now?"

Jack tapped his head and patted down his stomach and legs. "Yes, I'm fine."

"Go on then, but be careful," I said, looking him up and down.

He ran off and found his friend. I watched him, as he navigated the tunnels and climbed inside the police car and then, with his new partner in crime, started to pelt the playhouse with rubber balls.

"How was your day?" Anna asked when she got home. She'd had a meeting with a client and ditched her laptop bag and sensible shoes for heels and makeup.

"Was good. Pretty quiet," I said, folding the risotto over itself.

"Are you okay?"

"Yeah, fine, just a bit tired."

"Where's Jack?"

"Upstairs in his room."

"Ah, okay. I'll go up."

She filled her glass with some tap water, leaned back against the kitchen counter and kicked off her shoes. I knew she didn't find it easy, to be working at the bank while I did the school runs and looked after Jack. Even though she had gone to a progressive school, where girls were taught to be independent and empowered, she still found it hard to come home and find me cooking Jack his dinner, joking with him about the things we had done that day—things that, deep down, she felt that she should be doing.

Anna, though, was never one to allow a feeling to get the better of her. She found a way. When she came home, instead of putting her feet up, she spent all her time with Jack, doing his bath and his story, the little bits of homework he now had. After working all day, it was Anna who made sure that Jack's water glass was filled, that his bedroom door was at the right angle, that Big Teddy and Little Teddy were standing guard.

She put her arms around my waist and nuzzled my neck. "Are we having kids' food or adults' food tonight?"

"Adults' food."

"Really?"

"You want fish fingers and beans again, don't you? No, I've made a risotto."

"Ooooo, fancy."

"Are you disappointed?"

"No, risotto sounds great," she said. "How was playtime by the way?"

"It was good. Jack loved it, made some friend. Oh, and I think I saw one of Lola's friends there."

"Who?"

"The snooty one."

"Well, that's a big help."

"I don't know. With a scarf. Big Mommy trousers."

Anna shook her head. "You've just described all of her friends."

I started to chop up some chives, wondering how to broach it. "Nothing to worry about, but he did fall over again."

"Really," Anna said, turning to face me. "Was he okay?"

"Yeah, absolutely fine. He fell over and then said he was feeling dizzy."

Anna turned pale and started scrunching her fingers into her palm. "I knew it, I knew something was wrong."

"Sweetheart, you always do this," I said, putting my arm around her.

"Will you take him to the doctor tomorrow?" Anna said, pulling away from me.

"Of course I will, but do you really think it's nec—"

"Yes. It's necessary, Rob. This has gone on long enough."

"All right, I'll take him. They have a walk-in clinic after school. It's probably just a little ear infection or something. Do you remember he used to get them when he was little?"

"So you think it is something?" she said.

"Jesus, Anna. No, not at all. I'm just saying that I really don't think you should worry..."

As we were speaking, we watched Jack climb onto the back of the sofa and then do a tightrope maneuver along one arm.

"Look at him," I said. "There's nothing wrong with him."

"I hope so," Anna said. "He does get quite tired, doesn't he, with school."

Jack had now climbed down from the sofa and was attempting to do a headstand on the floor.

"Seriously, sweetheart. He'll be absolutely fine."

6

"Now, I don't want you to worry, but there is something here I think we should have a little look into," the doctor said, regarding the report. Next to me, I could feel Anna wince and then lean forward in her seat.

Two weeks ago, I had been here in this same doctor's office with Jack. The doctor watched him walk in a straight line, shone lights in his eyes, tested his reflexes with a rubber hammer. He was fine, the doctor said, absolutely fine. But what Jack was experiencing did sound a little like epilepsy, so as a precaution they would need to do some blood tests and a CT scan.

We all went together for Jack's scan. We told him there wouldn't be any pain, and they were just going to take a picture of his head. We promised him that if he managed to lie very, very still—as still as a statue, Jack—then we would all go to McDonald's for a Happy Meal and ice cream.

"So," the doctor said, "the scan does show a little something on Jack's brain. Now, we don't know exactly what this is yet, but just to be extra cautious, we do need to get you an appointment with a specialist."

"A little something. What does that mean?" I asked.

"Well, first of all, don't panic. These things almost always turn out to be nothing. It could be several things—some kind of growth, a cyst. And, in a very small number of cases, a tumor. But even if it was that, they mostly turn out to be benign."

Tumor. I thought of Jack, outside in the playroom.

"And there's nothing more you can tell us?" Anna asked.

The doctor looked at his screen, moving his lips as he read. "No, nothing more I'm afraid. Just that there is a lesion, and it requires further investigation."

Anna took a deep breath, and I could see her pinching the skin on her hand.

"So what happens now?" I said. "Will he need an operation?"

The doctor pressed his hands together. "Goodness, let's not talk about that yet, Mr. Coates. We don't even know what it is yet. It's probably absolutely nothing. But, to be on the safe side, I have referred Jack to a specialist, so we don't lose any time."

"Is it possible to see them this week?" Anna asked.

The doctor took a deep breath and looked down at his calendar. "I can get you in on Wednesday, if that suits."

"Thank you," she said.

A specialist? Why did Jack have to see a specialist, when there was probably nothing wrong? It didn't make any sense. "And you really can't tell us any more?" I asked the doctor.

"I'm sorry, I really can't. Dr. Kennety will be infinitely more qualified to make a judgment on the scan."

"Right," I said, "I understand that. But surely you can say something from your experience..."

There was a photo on the doctor's desk, facing away from us, and I wondered if it was his children.

"If it is a tumor," the doctor said, "then at Jack's age, he would certainly need an operation. But we just don't know, and it would be unethical and unfair of me to speculate. As I said, if it is a tumor—and that's a big, big if—mostly they turn out to be benign. So I know it's difficult, but please try not to worry."

Benign. Mostly benign. My legs felt shaky as we left, and I was just about to confer with Anna, when Jack charged toward us wearing some sort of cape.

"Can we go to McDonald's?"

"Of course we can," I said, ruffling his hair, smoothing down his cape.

In McDonald's, while I nabbed a table, Jack walked to the counter with Anna. He was wearing his *Angry Birds* sweatshirt and blue jeans. His hair was a little too long, his blond curls looping behind his ears. He came triumphantly back from the counter holding his Happy Meal box.

Jack sat at the table, carefully deconstructing his hamburger. We watched him as he methodically removed the gherkins, scraped off the sauce and then ate in a dignified silence. When he finished, he smiled, dabs of sauce around his mouth, and asked if he could have another one. There was nothing wrong with him. There couldn't be. Just look at him!

"I don't want to go, Rob."

"I know, but it will take your mind off things."

"Right," Anna said, looking away. "And why you do want to go so much? You normally hate this kind of thing."

It was a launch party for Lola's *Raw Food Mamma* recipe book. "Admittedly, it's not my favorite thing in the world," I said, "but if we don't go, we're just going to sit and worry."

Anna looked at me from across the kitchen table. "I just... just, God, I can't, I don't even want to think about it..."

"Sweetheart," I said, reaching across the table and putting my hand on her arm, "I know what you're doing, but you can't think like that. Remember what the doctor said. Only in a very small number of cases, it would be a tumor. And even then, it would most likely be benign. They're just being careful, that's all."

Anna didn't respond, and I could see that she was grinding her teeth. "C'mon, we should go. Jack's looking forward to seeing India."

"You're right," Anna said after a pause. "It will take my mind off it."

★ ★ ★

"Hello, poppets," Lola said, as we walked into the converted warehouse in Hackney Wick. We were standing under a wrought iron staircase that didn't lead anywhere. Next to us, two men wearing pipe-cleaner glasses were sitting on a sofa that looked as if it had been rescued from a dumpster.

Lola was wearing a jungle-print onesie. "Oh, wonderful, you brought Jack. India will be delighted."

"Hello, Auntie Lola," Jack said.

"Well, if it isn't my favorite boy," Lola said. She bent down to kiss Jack's head and next to me I could feel Anna flinch. "You all look so well. Right, let me show you through. Now, you won't be surprised to hear that everything on offer tonight is all my own creations. It's all raw, all organic—of course—and there are absolutely no chemicals in anything."

I smiled, wondering whether I should interject with my standard response that everything was a chemical. Our bodies, Lola, your onesie, your amber necklace, your free-range apples, your tarragon orange sliders, are all made of chemicals.

"Thanks for coming, Rob," Lola said, squeezing my arm. "I know it's not exactly your thing."

"I don't know, Lola. Maybe it might be. Don't knock it until you've tried it and all that, right." Lola looked pleased, still holding on to my arm. "And besides," I said, taking a chipped antique glass of champagne from a wallpaper table, "we can always stop at McDonald's on the way home."

"Don't you bloody dare," Lola said, but she was already looking over my shoulder, ready to greet the next guest.

Jack ran off to play with India, and Anna and I stood next to a table loaded with food and drink.

"You okay?" I said.

"Yes, I'm fine."

"You sure?"

"Can you stop asking if I'm okay?" Anna snapped.

"Sorry, I just…"

She turned away and took something from the table that looked like a patty made from compressed oats.

"Do you want a drink?" I said.

"I'm driving, Rob."

"You don't have to drive. We can get a taxi back and leave the car."

"I'm not so desperate to have a drink that I'm going to leave the car in Hackney."

"Okay." I went over to look at a painting on the wall. There was nothing I could do when she was like this. When I came back, Anna was still eating. The patty was falling apart, crumbling into little bits in her hand.

"Is it good?"

"No," she whispered, moving closer to me. "It's horrible, like eating sawdust."

I sniggered, spluttering my champagne a little.

"I want to get rid of it, but I don't know how."

"Isn't there…"

"No, I've looked. There's nothing, no trash cans, dirty plates, anything. How can they have no plates?"

Anna was still looking for somewhere to put her patty and her face was taut, a deathly pale, and I remembered that face from the days after the miscarriages. The tightened skin on her forehead; the slight movement of her cheeks as she ground her teeth.

"I'm going to check to see if Jack's okay," Anna said.

I stood for a while next to the table, not really knowing anyone and not knowing what to do.

"Ah, and I thought you were trying to avoid me," I heard as I was getting another glass of champagne. I turned to see Scott, standing with a tall woman with brown hair.

"Hello, mate. I didn't know you'd be here," I said, smiling at him and his friend. "I was going to call you tonight."

"Right," Scott said.

"Didn't know this was your sort of thing," I said brightly. "Raw food..."

"I get out and about, Rob..." I hadn't seen him like this before. He was openly hostile. He had called and emailed a few times about the code I was supposed to be writing, the little script that he hoped would seal the deal with the Chinese company and end his money troubles. But I had ignored him, fobbed him off, bought time—and now with everything with Jack, I hadn't given it a moment's thought.

"Well, seems like a good party..." I said, trying to break the silence.

"This is Karolina by the way," Scott said, nodding at her.

"Hello," she said frostily and with a thick Slavic accent. Then she looked wistfully at a group of young people on the other side of the room.

"This is Rob," Scott said.

"Uh-huh," Karolina said, and I expected her to say something else, but she just nodded to herself.

"Look, Scott, I'm sorry," I said. "I've had a lot going on, some family problems. But I was hoping we could meet to talk..."

"I'm going to sell, Rob. I've made up my mind. I just asked you for one thing..."

"I know, I'm sorry. But it's not as simple as that..."

Scott took a deep breath, looked into the mingling crowd. "Rob, let's talk tomorrow. I'm not going to bother to ask you to send the code because I know you won't. As I said, I've made up my mind."

We stood in silence for a moment, picking at our food. "Have you tried the food, Karolina?" I said after a while.

"It's okay," she said without looking at me. "Nothing special." I nodded, swallowed, trying to think of something to say, when Jack and India came running up.

India was eighteen months older than Jack. When she was little, she used to call Jack her doll. She would play with his hair, putting his curls into bunches, trying to fashion his locks into a ponytail. Jack was besotted by her, the older sister he never had.

"Hello, Uncle Rob. How are you?" India was six, but spoke like a twelve-year-old.

"I'm fine, India. How are you?"

"Very well, thank you."

"Are you both having a nice time?"

Jack nodded enthusiastically. "There was a spider on the floor, so we came here."

"Oh. Do you think it's still there?" I asked.

"I think it's gone now, Jack," India said, and Jack blushed a little, just like his mother.

"Shall we go and see if my mommy needs any help?" India said.

Jack nodded so vigorously his ears wobbled.

"Did you see Mommy, Jack?" I asked. "She said she was coming to find you."

Jack shook his head. "No. Maybe Mommy's gone home."

"No, she's here somewhere," I said, looking around again.

"Come on, Jack." India took Jack's hand in hers and led him off to the play corner. I could hear her telling Jack about the nutrients, how the food was much cleaner this way.

"Is that your children?" Karolina asked, when I turned back to her and Scott.

"Just the boy. The girl is Lola's daughter."

"Who's Lola?"

"She's the host, babe," Scott said, checking if anyone had heard. "The raw-food woman."

"Oh, her," Karolina said. She turned to look at me, and I found her intense, unnerving. "He looks tired, your son."

It was a strange thing to say, and I didn't know how to respond. "He probably is a bit," I said, a little flustered. "It's been a long day."

"He's got these—how you say, Scottie?" She turned to Scott, and with her finger made half-moons under her eyes. "These black *krug*, circles, here."

"Yes, well, he is a bit tired at the moment," I said, trying to temper the annoyance in my voice.

"Sometimes it means problem with liver or kidneys, it's connected," Karolina said.

"Excuse me for a bit," I said, and as I walked away, I could hear Scott raising his voice.

I went to the bathroom and sat inside a cubicle and Googled "brain tumor dark circles" on my phone. One million two hundred fifty results came up in 0.59 seconds. Shaking, I clicked on one, *The 5 Warning Signs of Pediatric Cancers*. There it was. The neuroblastoma symptoms to watch out for: bulging eyes, dark circles, droopy eyelids.

I sat in the cubicle listening to the dripping of a pipe. Outside in the gallery, I could hear the sound of speeches, of Lola on the mic. I Googled some more, clicking on link after link. There were other symptoms—glassy eyes, a worsening stutter, sensitivity to bright light. Jack didn't have any of those things. I was just getting myself worked up, so I took a deep breath and headed back to the party.

Lola was still on the mic at the other end of the gallery, but I couldn't see Anna. I looked around and then found her outside, sitting in the car with the light off.

"I'm sorry, I know I'm being rude. I just can't be in there

right now," Anna said. "I just keep thinking about it, and I can't smile and pretend that everything's normal."

"I know," I said, putting my hand on Anna's shoulder. "Why don't we leave? I can make some excuse."

"Would you mind? I just can't go back in there."

"Don't worry, I'll make something up."

"I'm sorry, I shouldn't have come. It was a mistake."

"It's okay, sweetheart. I'll go and get Jack, all right?"

"Thanks." Anna looked broken, as if she was shrinking into the seat. I went back inside and told Lola that Anna wasn't feeling very well and went to look for Jack. He was sitting with India under the champagne table. They had taken their shoes and socks off and had laid some paper plates out on the ground.

"We're having a picnic," Jack said, pretending to drink out of his shoe.

"I can see that. It looks yummy."

"Can we play more, Daddy?"

"We have to go, I'm afraid. Mommy's not feeling very well."

"Oh, Dad-dee."

"But you'll see India very soon."

Jack reluctantly put his trainers back on and then kissed India goodbye.

"Bye-bye, Jack," India said formally. "I enjoyed playing with you today."

As we were leaving, Jack kept turning around to see India, to see if she was still waving goodbye. He fell asleep as soon as he got into the car. We drove home in silence, listening to the hum of the tires on the tarmac.

"Are you okay?" I said as we pulled into the drive.

"Yes, sorry. I know I'm being unpleasant, but I just can't stop thinking about it." Anna checked that Jack was still sleeping and lowered her voice. "Thinking what if, what if, and I know it's stupid but I can't…"

"I know," I said, wanting to tell her what Karolina had said, but I knew it would only worry her more. "You can't think like that, you just can't," I said, putting my hand on her leg.

We took Jack up to bed when we got home. He was sleepy, but we managed to stand him up, so we could get him in his pajamas and brush his teeth. When Anna had gone to get him some cream for a rash, I looked into his eyes to see if there was a droop, if his eyelids were bulging, the symptoms I had read about online. I looked from both sides, turning him toward the light, but I couldn't see anything unusual.

We tucked him in together, putting his things—the cookie-tin lid, Darth Vader's ripped cloak—on the end of the bed and then putting his favorites—Little Teddy and flashlight—next to his head, so he could find them in the night.

I sat on the end of the bed, looking at his photos and the pictures of skyscrapers on the wall. Sometimes, after I had kissed him good-night, I watched him through the crack in the door. He would lie on his back and then shine his flashlight on the pictures, whispering the names of all the buildings, the places he had been, the skyscrapers he was planning to climb. Tonight, though, he was quiet. Tonight, he just slept.

7

We did not speak in the taxi to Harley Street nor in the waiting room. Anna sat upright in her chair. She did not move, or read or check her phone. A woman, covered by a burka, was sitting opposite us. I knew she was ill. I could tell by the way she gently rubbed her thumb and forefinger together, the way her husband paced, his prayer beads wrapped round his knuckles.

The secretary called our name and led us through to Dr. Kennety, a small man sitting behind a large desk, like a child wearing his father's clothes.

"Hello, Mr. and Mrs. Coates," he said, clearing his throat as we sat down. "Thanks for coming. Did you come from far?"

"No, just Hampstead," Anna said softly.

"Oh, lovely, I live quite close." He looked at us and then down at his papers. "So let's talk about Jack's scans. Before we start, please bear in mind, I am just one doctor. Another doctor may well see the situation differently, and I always advise my patients, and the parents of my patients, to get a second opinion." The doctor looked at us, raised his eyebrows, and I didn't know if he expected a response. "So that's my usual preamble. Now, from looking at the scans, it does seem clear that Jack has what we call a glioma, which is a type of brain tumor."

I could hear a car alarm, hushed talking in the waiting room. Out of the window, a pigeon walked along a shit-splattered sill. The doctor paused, waiting to see if we would react, but we were still, silent. It was as if the doctor's words were being spoken to someone else, as if we were watching a drama unfold on the stage. I stared at a Disney World paperweight on his desk that contained a photo of a child wearing a *Finding Nemo* T-shirt.

Dr. Kennety looked up from his papers, a stray hair protruding from one nostril. "Should I give you a minute?" he said.

I tried to speak, but my throat wouldn't open, as if it was clogged with soot. I didn't know what Anna was doing. I could only feel her stillness, the sound of her breathing, next to me.

"I'm sorry," the doctor said. "I'm sure this is quite a shock. However, it does appear—and this is the good news—to be slow growing."

I managed to sit up in my seat, to catch my breath again.

"Now, some of these tumors don't grow. They are essentially benign and just sit there for years, and you'd never know about it. On the other hand, some of them start off benign and can then turn nasty. In Jack's case, it does appear to be in the early stage, but we would want to take it out, to prevent it from growing into anything unpleasant.

"Here, look," Dr. Kennety said, taking a scan of Jack's head out of his folder. Anna and I both leaned in. "Can you see this lighter part here?" We bent over and nodded. I had expected the tumor to be more spherical, better defined, but it was just an amorphous shadow, as if a photograph had been overexposed.

"It looks like Jack has a tumor called an astrocytoma, and his more specific type is called a pleomorphic xanthoastrocytoma. Quite a mouthful I know, so we call these PXAs."

The room started to spin and I wanted to rewind, to play the doctor's words back, because nothing he was saying made any sense.

"Let's talk about the next steps," he said, writing something on his pad. "Now, I do want to focus on the positives—and there really are many positives here."

Dr. Kennety pulled a plastic model of a brain out of a desk

drawer. "So," he said, putting it down in front of us. "Here are the two temporal lobes on the side. And here on the left side is where Jack's tumor is. Now, the harder-to-reach tumors are much deeper in the brain, but that doesn't appear to be the case here. That means it will be much easier for the surgeon."

"So he will need to have an operation?" Anna asked, the first words she had spoken.

"Sorry, yes. I'm jumping ahead of myself here. Yes, surgery to remove the tumor."

"And would that be it?" I said. "He wouldn't need any more treatment?"

"Hopefully, that would be it, yes," the doctor said. "In the cases where there is a complete resection—meaning where the surgeon manages to get out all of the tumor—we're looking at a cure rate of 80 or 90 percent."

Eighty or 90 percent. One in five, one in ten.

"And if the surgeon doesn't?" Anna said, her voice clinical and clear.

"Well, that gets a bit trickier, but let's not think about that now," he said, clasping his hands together. "From the scans, it looks like it would be no problem getting it all out."

"That's good," I said, and it was, but the words still felt like razor blades in my throat.

"I know the waiting is horrible," Dr. Kennety said, "but we'll know so much more after the operation."

We both nodded because what else could we do?

"I'm going to book you an appointment with a neurosurgeon. Her name is Dr. Flanagan, and she's really the best in the business. Of course, you're welcome to do your research and find someone else, but this is who I would recommend. And I will of course need to see Jack to give him a thorough neurological exam."

Dr. Kennety looked from side to side, demonstrably making

eye contact with us. "Okay then," he said softly, and I watched his hands, small and childlike, pecking at his keyboard like a hen.

We walked quickly down Harley Street toward Oxford Street. I crossed the road without looking, powering ahead of Anna. You didn't normally notice life going on around you—it was just a hum, a murmur in the background. You could unsee it, push it from your mind. But suddenly, now, it was shrill, like a dog whistle in my ear. Schoolgirls in split skirts eating potato chips, swigging from Coke cans; delivery drivers shouting instructions, angry that something was late, that someone was in their way; a slick of Soho advertising types guffawing outside a wine bar.

We just kept walking, quick strides, as if we were racing, but we didn't know where. My head was full of numbers, percentages, 80, 90—the chance of my son staying alive.

"Can you wait? Can you please wait?" Anna said.

I stopped. We were standing on Cavendish Square, in the gardens under a bronze statue, and it had started to rain.

"I just can't believe it," I said. "I don't understand. Does he look like he's got a..."

"No," Anna said. "No, he doesn't." She shook her head, and her chin began to dimple and then quiver and then, in the afternoon drizzle, she began to cry.

"I wish it were me, I just wish it were me," she said, and I put my arm around her and pulled her closer, and she rested her head on my shoulder and we stood like that, her tears wet on my shirt, listening to the sounds of the city, the sounds of other people's worlds.

"We should get back," Anna said suddenly, her face a ghostly white. The rain was beating down now, gasoline rainbows in the gutters, a dark blanket of cloud suffocating the city.

I needed to see Jack. To take him in my arms and feel his warm skin on mine. I didn't want him to be alone. Once, when he was three or four, he said that he was sad because *Peppa Pig* didn't want to be his friend. It broke my heart. I could not bear to imagine Jack's loneliness, like the feeling, as a child, of wetting the bed in someone else's home.

Jack ran toward us when we got home. I picked him up and swung him around. He looked so alive that evening, boisterous, oversugared by his grandmother.

Anna's mother could see it in our faces. "So how was it, any news?" she said.

"We can talk about it later," Anna said quickly. Janet narrowed and then widened her eyes, like a puppy wanting a treat, and I wanted to scream at her, *can you just wait, can you just fucking wait.*

"Well, Jack has been a very good boy," Janet said, ruffling his hair. "We've been reading stories."

I resented Janet being here, in our home, in London. A woman who had spent her life between rural Suffolk and Kenya, who always said that city life wasn't for her. After Anna's father had suddenly upped and left for his beloved Africa, Janet said there was nothing for her in Suffolk anymore. Her husband's abrupt leaving, a month before Jack was born, was rarely discussed. He had a calling, Janet said, a desire for solitude, to be closer to God. A desire to be closer to the village girls, Anna said, although she could not say such a thing to her mother.

The church arranged the flat for her. A little place above a Lebanese barbershop on Praed Street, just a few doors down from the drop-in center where she served goulash to the homeless in return for a book of prayer. She tried, but she could not hide her pain, her shame at being abandoned. You could see it in the slight hunch she had developed in her shoulders, the sag of skin on her face that had nothing to do with age.

"We did a story about Daniel," Jack said, "and they throwed him in with the lions but they didn't eat him because they would get in troubles."

I didn't like Janet teaching Jack Bible stories but now wasn't the time. "Ooo, I know that one about the lions," I said. "That's a good one."

Janet smiled at me approvingly.

"Right, beautiful," I said. "Let's get you to bed."

We took longer that evening with Jack's bedtime routine. We both read *Shark in the Park*, and then we tucked him in, doing *snug as a bug in a rug*, once, twice, three times. How could I reconcile all this, the way he lay down, clutching Little Teddy and his flashlight, tucking his knees up to his chest, with what we had just been told?

When I got downstairs, Anna and her mother were sitting in silence, rigid, their familial response to crisis.

"I am very sorry to hear the news," Janet said, looking up at me.

"Thank you, Janet."

She shook her head. "Poor little mite," she said. Little mite, like a helpless Victorian child, Tiny Tim but worse.

"I will be praying. For you all, every day," Janet said, looking down into her lap. Anna remained still. She had not moved a muscle since I entered the room.

"I don't think Jack needs prayers right now," I said. She was acting as if he was dying. "This is something that can be cured. That's what they've said."

Anna's mother nodded sympathetically, but there was something robotic about her reaction, a rote response, as if she was counseling a wayward drunk at the drop-in center. She kept shaking her head. "Of course, of course, but what a terrible thing. And so young. Just a child."

I couldn't listen to her anymore and left the room, taking refuge in the office upstairs. There was something about her response, a smugness, almost as if she had always known this was going to happen. Poor little mite, as if Jack was forsaken, done-for already.

After Janet had gone, we sat in the living room. Anna, still pale, sat in silence, watching the finance channel. Later, we looked at a list of pediatric neurosurgeons that Dr. Kennety had already emailed us. When she went up to bed, I sat downstairs and heard her pause outside Jack's door and then go into his room. In a little while, she came out again and I could hear her start to cry.

I went to check on Jack. I could see the light of his flashlight through the half-open door. He liked to sleep with his flashlight so he could find his way to the bathroom. Every night, he said, it was like having an adventure.

I watched him through the door. He was lying on his side, looking at his Pokémon trading cards. They were spread out, organized in rows and columns as if he was playing solitaire. He got it from Anna. The classification. The need to order things. Her color-coded Tupperware. Her spreadsheets and lists.

He inspected each card with his flashlight, turning it to see every detail, before placing it down on the bed. I could hear him whispering to the cards—"you go there…there you are… you sit down there with him…" He liked to organize them into teams, dividing them by color, by type, by whether they lived on the land or in the sea.

"Hello, beautiful," I said, as I walked into his room.

"Hello, Daddy." He pointed to his Pokémon cards. "I'm putting them in teams."

"That's cool," I said, sitting down on the bed.

"This is the naughty team," Jack said, pointing to one pile of cards. "And these are the good ones. And tomorrow, in the morning, they're going to have a big fight."

"Wow," I said, "and who's going to win?"

Jack considered the question. "The naughty ones," he said, and then laughed loudly.

"C'mon, you should sleep now."

"Okay," he said, picking up the cards and putting them on his bedside table.

He settled back on his pillows, and I tucked him in again. "How do you feel, Jack? You don't feel dizzy or anything?" I looked at the left side of his head. The temporal lobe.

"No, Daddy," he said, his eyes beginning to close, and then quickly he was asleep. I watched him as his breathing began to deepen, little question marks of hair wrapping around his ears, the light brown moles on his nape. A little me, Anna always said. A little me.

I kissed his forehead and sat for a while on his sofa with the sprinkles of stars and dancing comets. I stilled myself, trying to slow down my breathing, so I could listen to him. But it was not enough: I could still hear my breathing, my heartbeat. So I held my breath for as long as possible—ten, twenty, thirty seconds—and then finally, all I could hear was Jack, the sound of him breathing, the occasional snuffle and murmur, the only sound in the world I wanted to hear.

THE GHERKIN

———

we raced up in the elevator, as fast as a space rocket, and then the doors opened up into a huge glass room and you said it was like stepping out into the sky. and it was jack, it really was, because we could see right across london, as far as the south downs, nearly as far as the sea. we walked around, looking up and down, left and right, like timothy pope with his telescope and i will never forget that day jack for as long as i live. your laugh like chocolate as you danced with the shadows, the tinkle of rain on the glass.

8

I woke early, before sunrise. Anna was turned away from me, her legs tucked up to her chest just like Jack, the cover pulled around her neck. I looked for Jack, but he was not there. He was an early riser and would often creep into our bedroom before we woke, sitting on the floor at the foot of our bed, whispering to himself, ordering and reordering his Pokémon cards.

I went downstairs and sat at the kitchen table with my laptop and started Googling "pleomorphic xanthoastrocytoma."

"Treatments for childhood brain tumors."

"Child brain tumor prognosis." I read National Health Service fact sheets, Wikipedia pages, a long interview with a doctor from the American Brain Tumor Association.

I varied my searches, digging into the third, fourth, fifth pages of results. Everything I found confirmed what Dr. Kennety had said. They were grade 2 tumors, rare, especially in children. And as the doctor had said, the overall survival rate was high, as much as 90 percent.

I heard the sound of little feet and saw Jack standing at the bottom of the stairs. He looked so young, so lithe in his Spider-Man pajamas. Still sleepy, he climbed into my lap and wrapped his arms and legs around me. I could feel his breath on my neck.

"Daddy, can I have cheese toast?"

"Of course you can."

"Special cheese toast."

"Special cheese toast?" I said with mock outrage. "Really?

In the morning? Well, I don't know about that. What will you give me in return?"

Jack thought about a possible bargain. "I'll give you a kiss," he said, smiling.

"Only a kiss. Hmm, anything else?"

Jack looked around him and then ran over to a wicker box of toys. He rummaged around inside and came back with something clenched tightly in his little fist.

"I'll give you a present too." He opened his hand and it was the broken arm of a Transformer.

"Bumble Bee's arm?"

"Yes." Jack nodded, and then started laughing.

"It's a deal. Can I have my kiss now?"

Jack nodded, and as he planted a neat kiss on my face, I heard a small sob, a sharp intake of breath, and saw Anna standing at the bottom of the stairs, her hair still wet from the shower. She quickly turned and went back up the stairs.

"Where's Mommy gone?"

"To the bathroom."

"Why?"

"To do a wee-wee probably. Shall we make the special cheese on toast then? But first, I'm just going to check that Mommy is okay."

"Can I watch the iPad?"

"Sure, you can." Jack smiled, took the iPad off the shelf and sat down cross-legged on the sofa.

"But don't watch those stupid toy videos, okay?"

"Yeah, yeah, Mr. Piggy."

"Jack. I mean it."

Upstairs, Anna was in the en suite bathroom, and I could hear the sound of running water.

"Anna?" I said gently through the door.

"Yes," she said, her voice hoarse, distant. "I'll be out in a minute."

I sat and waited for her on the bed. "You okay?" I said, when she emerged and sat down next to me.

She shrugged, her face wet with tears, her eyes red.

"We're going to get through this," I said, putting my arms around her.

She nodded and turned away from me, not wanting me to see her tears.

"Really, we are. Remember, 90 percent cure rate," I said, stroking her back.

"I still can't believe it," Anna said. "I couldn't bear it if something happened to him, I just couldn't bear it. I just want..." Her words trailed off and she wiped her eyes.

"We're going to fight it and beat it, okay?" I said. "When Jack's at the play center, let's do some more research on the neurosurgeons."

Anna chewed on her lower lip and shook her head. "I don't want him going to soft play today," she said.

"Why?"

Anna looked at me, narrowing her eyes. "We can't... I don't want to risk anything."

"Anna, have you seen him this morning? He's charging around downstairs. We have to carry on as normal."

Downstairs, I could hear the voice of Ryan from Ryan's Toys videos on Jack's iPad.

"I've told Emma he can't go."

"You spoke to her already?"

"I texted her."

"You didn't tell her, did you?"

"No, of course not."

"But Anna, we have to carry on as if nothing is wrong. For Jack's sake. I don't want him to know that he's ill."

"I agree, but he's not a baby anymore," she said. "We have to tell him sometime. He's going to wonder about all the doctors' visits and why he's feeling poorly."

I went into the bathroom and got her a tissue to dry her eyes. "He's not feeling poorly now," I said, sitting back down next to her and putting my hand on her leg. "He wants his cheese on toast. Special cheese on toast."

Anna laughed sadly, sniffed and wiped her face. "I just don't want him to bang his head," she said and she started to cry again, and this time no amount of tissues or hugs or words would stop the tears. I pulled her close to me, feeling her body tremble, her frantic little breaths.

"Why is Mommy crying?" We turned around, and Jack was standing at our bedroom door.

Anna wiped her eyes with her sleeve and sniffled a little.

"Well, sometimes people get upset, just like you get upset sometimes," I offered.

"Did you do something bad to Mommy?" Jack said to me, moving closer to Anna.

"No, not at all," I said.

"Are you angry, Daddy?"

"No."

"Is Mommy red with anger, like the man in the fireman book?"

Anna laughed a little, her sobs subsiding.

"Daddy, can I show you something?"

"Okay, let's go and Mommy will come down in a bit."

We walked downstairs, and on the table there were bits of broken bread, torn off from the loaf, topped with hard clumps of butter and a large uncut block of cheddar.

"I made special cheese toast."

"You did," I said, ruffling his hair. "That's impressive, Jack."

"Are you happy, Daddy?"

"I'm very happy, Jack," I said. I watched him eat his bread and cheese, the morning light making columns of glitter dust, halos in Jack's hair.

In the afternoon, the doorbell rang. Jack was napping and we were sitting in the living room. I looked out of the window and could see Lola's little Fiat parked outside. "Did you tell her?" I asked Anna.

"No, I didn't."

"So what's she..."

Anna stood up. "I don't know. You know sometimes she just pops by."

"Can you tell her to..."

Anna was already opening the door. "Hello, poppet," Lola said, and I could hear the sound of her air-kisses and then silence. "Goodness, why the glum face, darling?"

Anna didn't say anything, and I could imagine Lola trying to read her, the girl she knew so well, adjacent beds at boarding school, roommates in Halls.

"Hello, Rob," Lola said as they walked into the living room. She looked at me quizzically, her eyebrows raised almost as an accusation.

"Where's Jack?"

"He's napping upstairs," I said.

Lola looked at Anna, who was stone-faced, motionless. "Anna, darling?" she said and then looked back at me, and I thought I could detect a slight annoyance in her face, as if she felt she was being excluded. Lola always had to know everything.

I swallowed and took a deep breath. "We had some bad news yesterday, with Jack," I said, my voice beginning to shake. "He's been having a few problems with his balance, so we went to get it checked out. There is something on a scan that they think is…is a…" Tumor, tumor. I couldn't say the word out loud. "…a lesion, yes. He has a lesion…"

Lola looked confused. "A lesion. What do you mean? Like a tumor?" Of course, that word meant nothing to her: it was just vowels, consonants, not something that was growing in my little boy's brain.

"Yes, they think it is."

"Oh, God, poor Jack. Will he need treatment?" Lola moved next to Anna on the sofa and put her arm around her.

"Yes," I said, steeling myself. "He will have surgery to remove the…you know, to get everything out, and then we'll know more. But the doctor thinks that will be it, he won't need any more treatment…"

"And then he'll be okay, right?" Lola said, looking at Anna and then me.

"Yes, we hope so," I said.

"God, how terrible. I can't imagine what you're going through." Lola took a deep breath and started speaking again to break the silence. "There was a little boy at India's nursery who had something similar. He had the tumor removed, and he's absolutely fine now. Made a full recovery…"

Lola pulled Anna closer to her. "Oh, sweetheart, I hate seeing you like this. It's all going to be okay, I promise."

Anna nodded, stiff in her arms, and Lola didn't know what to say. She looked around the living room, as if, for a moment, she thought other people besides us were there.

"Actually, there's a woman I follow on Twitter, and she was diagnosed with a brain tumor, and then I think another cancer. Well, she turned to alternative remedies, I forget what exactly, but she's completely cancer-free now. I can send you the link to her blog if you like."

Lola's words fluttered by like dandelion seeds in the wind.

"Thank you, Lola. We're looking into everything at the moment."

Just then, Anna stood up and walked out of the room. I could hear her quick little steps padding up the stairs.

"Should I go and see her?" Lola said, looking crestfallen.

"No, it's fine. Best to leave her now."

"Scott."

"Hey."

His tone was cold, unsparing.

"Would you have time to meet today?" I said.

"I thought we were supposed to meet a week ago. You know, to discuss the sale."

"Sorry," I said, "something's happened."

"Right, it always does, doesn't it? Mate, you're my best friend, but I can't deal with this at the moment."

I was quiet, didn't know what to say, could feel the tears welling in my eyes.

"Rob? Are you still there?"

"Could you meet now?" I said, my voice cracking. "In The Ship?"

"Yes, of course." Scott's tone had softened. "Is everything okay?"

I didn't say anything, couldn't say anything.

"I can be at The Ship in about fifteen."

Scott was already there when I arrived, sitting at the bar, scrolling through something on his phone.

"I ordered you a pint and a cheeky one," he said, pointing to a whiskey. "Sounds like you need it."

"Thanks."

Scott took a long swig of his pint. "So what's up, mate? Trouble with the Mrs.?"

I downed my whiskey in one gulp, and the ice rattled around the glass. "It's Jack," I said, taking a deep breath and pinching the backs of my thighs. "They've found something, some kind of lesion in his brain."

"A lesion? What's a lesion? Is that a tumor?"

"Yes."

"Fuck, I'm so sorry. That's awful."

Scott indicated to the bartender we wanted more whiskeys. "And what did the doctor say?"

"Well, he'll have to have an operation first, and then they'll know more," I said, picking up my pint. "And hopefully that will be it."

Before he could answer, Scott's phone rang and he looked at the screen. He shook his head as if he didn't want to take it. "Sorry, hold that thought. It's Karolina, and I'm in the doghouse…"

He stepped off his bar stool, and I noticed he was wearing new brogues and skinny jeans. "Hello, babycakes," he said as he walked away. He stood at the other end of the bar, laughing and whispering. I stared at a clock, a barometer, a ship in a bottle.

"Sorry, mate," he said, coming back to the bar and sitting back down on his stool. "She's so demanding at the moment. Anyway, you were saying about the treatment… I mean, they caught it early, right?"

"Yes," I said, but suddenly I wasn't so sure and couldn't remember exactly what the doctor had said. "He has to have an operation, and they think they can take it all out."

"Well, that's good news. Really happy to hear that."

"Thanks," I said, pinching my thighs again, so hard it made me wince. "I just don't understand it, because…because, he's so well, he's so active and…and…well, normal, I just don't…"

"God, Rob, I'm so, so sorry," Scott said, and I didn't know why he was apologizing until I realized his phone was ringing silently, throbbing on the bar.

"Sorry, sorry," he said, declining the call but then the phone lit up again, and we both stared at the flashing screen.

"So what's the next step then? What happens now?" Scott said, when Karolina had finally hung up.

"Well," I said. "In the next few weeks, he'll have an operation to remove the...you know, to get everything out. And then hopefully that will be it."

"I'm sure it will, mate," he said, touching my whiskey glass with his. "And please, keep me in the loop, let me know if I can help. By the way, I do know some Harley Street types from the golf club, so I could ask around about the best people for this kind of thing." Scott started scrolling through his phone. "Yep, here we go. This guy, Dr. Khan. Indian guy. Very clever. I'll give him a ring later if you want?"

I was sweating and could feel cold trickles run down my back. "I've got to go," I said, suddenly feeling a bristle of panic.

"Okay, mate," Scott said, taking a leisurely sip of his pint. As I was leaving, he put his arm around me, I think an attempt at a hug, but I didn't respond, my body stiff.

"Seriously, let me know if there's anything you need. Your Jack's a fighter, especially if he's anything like his old man."

Anything we need, I thought as I walked back up Parliament Hill. Anything we need? Maybe not being on the phone to your new girlfriend. Maybe not staring at the barmaid's breasts when I'm telling you my son has a brain tumor.

Anna was in the living room when I got home, sitting on the sofa with the laptop on the coffee table.

"Is he still sleeping?" I said.

"Yes, I just went up and he's out like a light... Sorry about before. I know Lola means well but I just couldn't..."

I sat down next to her. She had done her makeup and tied back her hair. "I've gone through the list of neurosurgeons and put all the contact info into a spreadsheet. I printed one out for you. We can just split it up and work our way down the list."

I looked at the spreadsheet: doctors, their addresses and phone numbers, a note on their area of specialization.

"I'll get started."

"I was thinking back to the appointment with Dr. Kennety," she said, "and it's all just a blur. I'm kicking myself that I didn't write things down. There are so many questions I wish I had asked but it was like this fog came over me..."

"Yeah, I know. I was thinking about that earlier."

Anna sighed and I put my hand on her knee.

"We'll be ready for the next meeting," I said. "With lots of questions. We're going to fight it, okay?"

My words felt feeble, but Anna squeezed my hand. "Yes, we will. We have to," she said. "Lola sent me a very sweet message, by the way. She was worried she'd upset me. How was Scott? Did you tell him?"

"Yeah."

"And how was he?"

"Oh, just Scott being Scott."

Anna was about to say something, to probe further, but she stopped, bit her lip. "Okay," she said, standing up. "I think I'm missing a page."

I looked at her, confused.

"Of the spreadsheet."

As she went to the printer, I opened the laptop so I could research the doctor that Scott had mentioned. In an open browser window, there was a page of search results. Anna had been Googling "miscarriages and brain tumors in children." In another tab, there was a story from *The Huffington Post*: "How My Miscarriage Caused My Child's Cancer."

I didn't read it, but just looked at the stock photo of a woman, her head bowed, clutching her stomach.

★ ★ ★

Anna had always done her Christmas letters, a tradition she inherited from her mother. I had teased her about them in the past. They were awful, I said, from another age. Middle-class humble-brags: "Jonathan has had another fantastic year at Oxford, but sometimes we wish he would spend as much time on his studies as he does on his rowing and fraternizing with members of the opposite sex!"

They don't have to be like that, Anna said. Hers weren't like that. And besides, it was a good way of keeping in touch. So every year, despite my mocking, she carefully folded a sheet of paper into her Christmas cards.

I had not been sure about sending the email. I was worried we would have to spend our time answering messages of support, fending off friends armed with food baskets at the door. But Anna convinced me. It was better this way, she said. Let everyone know together, and then it would be easy for us to manage. Her word bothered me a little—"manage"—as if it was one of her clients, a crisis at work where everyone had to be on-message.

Subject: Jack
Sent: Mon May 12, 2014 2:00 pm
From: Anna Coates
To: (Undisclosed Recipients)
CC: Rob

Dear Friends,
We hope you are all well and apologies for the mass mailing. We wanted to let you all know that Jack has recently been diagnosed with astrocytoma, a type of brain tumor.

He will soon have surgery to have the tumor removed and the doctors are optimistic that he will make a full recovery.

This has obviously been a tremendous shock, but we are hopeful and positive we will get through this. We thank you all for your support.
Best Wishes,
Anna and Rob

I had added the "positive we will get through this" part. It was true, I told Anna, and, besides, we didn't want people to worry unduly, to think that Jack was going to die.

I didn't understand her at times. Her genetic impulse to look on the negative side of things. She got it from her parents, handed down like a cursed heirloom. The glass–half-empty family, she used to joke.

The replies came quickly. People wrote to say they were sorry, shocked, saddened. They told us stories: mothers, fathers, friends of friends, who had taken on cancer and won. They told us about little children they knew who were diagnosed with the same—or something similar—and were now doing very well. They told us to stay positive because that, they said, was the most important thing. They told us they would pray, that they would carry Jack in their hearts and be thinking about him from morning until night.

I read and reread Anna's note. A full recovery. That was what she wrote. So why did they all act like he was dying? Did they know something we didn't?

9

I sat at my desk, buzzed with caffeine, my fingers twitching as I checked my email. I preferred to work on the sofa, or in bed, anywhere I could position my laptop on my knee, but Anna made me set up the home office. We went to choose a desk and a comfy office chair and she bought some organizers and stationary. It was important, she said, for my state of mind, so I felt like I was going to work.

I scrolled through my in-box. The tech-incubator organizers were still chasing me, now offering to pay my expenses plus a speaker's fee. Marc wanted some input on one of the programmers. There was something from Jack's nursery, which I couldn't bear to open, and then, hidden between an advertisement for a garden center and a PayPal receipt, an email from Scott.

Subject:
Sent: Wed May 21, 2014 1:05 am
From: Scott Wayland
To: Rob Coates

hello mate just wanted to say sorry about the other day in the pub. I know you're going through so much right now and probably wasn't as attentive as I should be.

btw, I spoke to the doctor friend of mine, pulled a few strings and he said the best in the business is dr. kennety on harley st. he really knows his stuff apparently. lemme know if u want to go down that road and I can hook u up...

regarding other stuff, I still desperately need to talk to you about the China thing, selling I mean. they're pestering me and I don't want to lose the window on it. time to chat about it? if you don't want to come by the office we could meet at The Ship or I could pop by the house.

in other news, Karolina broke up with me and ive taken it pretty hard, so not going through the best time myself at the moment...

anyways, chin up mate. hope to see u soon.

Sent from my iPhone

Chin up, mate, as if West Ham had been crushed at home. Did he not realize how he sounded? With everything that was happening, was I really supposed to care that Scott's latest Slavic fuck-buddy had moved on to better, richer things?

After I had calmed down, and made more coffee, I started to do some more research. As I was searching for "PXA treatment options," I clicked on a link that led me to a forum called *Hope's Place*. On the front page there were yellow-winged butterflies dancing across a baby-blue-and-pink sky. In one corner, underneath a giant rainbow, was a picture of Hope: a seven-year-old girl in a *Glee* T-shirt.

I clicked on Hope's picture and it led to a discussion forum for parents of children with brain tumors. I dug deeper and found a thread for Jack's tumor type, PXA.

I read quickly, scrolling through the posts. From what I could tell, removal by surgery was the preferred treatment option, but some of the children were given radiation therapy, and I didn't know why. Was that for children with more serious tumors? An option we should consider for Jack?

Can anyone help us?
by Rob» Wed May 21, 2014 8:45 am

Hello, everyone, I'm new to Hope's Place. We have recently received the news that our 5-year-old son Jack has been diagnosed with pleomorphic xanthoastrocytoma.

In a few weeks' time, Jack will have an operation to remove the tumor and then we will know more.

Apart from this, Jack is in very good health. He has some balance issues, which prompted us getting him checked out, but you wouldn't know he was ill at all. He is still very active and sharp.

The doctor was very hopeful that Jack could be cured, but we realize there is still a risk that he may not. They have recommended just surgery, but I see some children have also had radiation as well. What would be normal in our son's case?

Also, I have been reading on this board about Gamma Knife and Proton therapy. Would these be things we should be looking into?

Any information would be very much appreciated.
Best Wishes,
Rob

I heard Anna come home, the door gently close, the rattle of her keys on the hall table, but I couldn't hear Jack, his usual greeting of "Hello, everyone!" I rushed to the door and found Anna standing in the hall, with Jack slumped over her shoulder.

"He fell asleep in the car," she said, removing her second shoe. He seemed to sleep a lot now, nodding off when he was watching cartoons or even the shortest car journey.

I took him in my arms and carried him up to bed. The midafternoon sun was strong, so I closed his curtains and laid him down on his bed. He stirred, turned to his side and pulled his knees up to his chest.

When I got downstairs, Anna was staring into space, a glass of wine in front of her on the coffee table.

"You okay?" I said.

"No, I'm not actually," she said. The skin on her neck and chest was red, a rash that appeared when she got angry or nervous.

"What happened?"

"God, I'm fuming right now. Stupid fu—" She stopped herself. For as long as we had been together, I had never once heard Anna swear. "Stupid, stupid people everywhere."

She took a large sip of wine and put the glass back on the coffee table. "I was in Costa, the one at the bottom of the hill, and it was quiet and Jack was in the play corner drawing. And it was nice, because we haven't had time alone for a while, and he had a chocolate milk shake and he was an absolute delight. Then I saw this woman, Joanna. Do you remember her? From Jack's Little Gym thing."

"Joanna, yeah, it rings a bell. Oh, the woman who was always going on about her divorce?"

"Yes, that's the one. Well, she sort of sidled up to me, in this really creepy way, and said hello and I knew she knew because she had this weird nervous grin. Then she said, 'I'm so very sorry' and she looked over at Jack and said, 'poor little thing,' and he was right there, right there next to her. And then she said, 'I suppose you're making memories now.' Making memories. She actually said that. And I just didn't know what to say, so I said, 'well, Jack is going to make a full recovery,' as if I had to justify myself. To her. As if it was any of her damn business. And then you know what happened?"

"What?"

"She hugged me. She hugged me right in the middle of Costa Coffee."

"Oh my God."

"Quite. Well, you know how freakish I am about such things, even with you. It was awful. I didn't think she'd ever let go."

I started to giggle, the thought of Anna in Costa Coffee, stiff-bodied, not hugging back.

"It was one of those situations where afterward I was kicking myself, because I really wished I had told her just how rude, how insensitive she was being, but I couldn't because Jack was there, and anyway, what would have been the point?"

"That's awful," I said. "Some people are just assholes."

I went to the kitchen and poured myself a glass of wine and joined Anna on the sofa. "It's silly to get so pissed off at this stuff," I said, "especially with everything that's happening, but I got so angry the other day over this fucking Facebook post."

"Who was it?"

"Just this girl from school. It was this long, long post about how she had had some growth on her neck, and she was worried that it was cancer, and she thought she was going to die. So they cut it off, and of course it turned out not to be cancer. Then she went on and on about this doctor who looked her in the eyes and said, 'Now you should stop worrying and go and live the rest of your life.' And then all these hashtags. Hashtag positive. Hashtag cancer. Hashtag fuck off."

Anna laughed, and I couldn't remember the last time I had seen her smile. This was what we used to do. Our wine-fueled rants about friends and colleagues. Happy conspirators, sitting up late into the night.

"I'm going to talk to my boss tomorrow," Anna said, "about taking a leave of absence around the time of the operation."

"Okay," I said.

"I just think I should be with Jack when he's recovering."

"Do you think they'll go for it?"

"I don't know. They do offer compassionate leave in some situations, but that's for, well, you know... I know some people have taken unpaid sabbaticals, so I was thinking I might be able to do something like that."

"Right, that could work, I suppose."

Anna narrowed her eyes. "So you don't agree?"

"No, I do, yes... I haven't really thought about it to be honest. But are you sure it's necessary? I'm going to be here every day, when he's off school after the operation. And there's the money, as well. Would we manage without it?"

Anna looked at me sharply, her cheeks flushed with the wine. "I don't know, Rob. I hope so. And if you're so worried about the money, maybe you should speak to Scott. Because if he sells, that's half our income gone."

I didn't say anything, choosing my words carefully. I knew what she thought. That I was being lazy and irresponsible, that I wasn't doing enough to convince Scott not to sell the company to the Chinese. She had always worried about money, even with us both earning. London was expensive, she said, and we were living beyond our means. We weren't saving, and now Jack's school fees were mounting up.

"So have you spoken to him about it?" she asked.

"Yes, of course I have, but I'm not sure there's much I can do. I don't have the energy to argue with him anymore."

"Great," Anna said, looking away. "You don't have the energy." She shook her head. "You're amazing sometimes, Rob. You don't work and I do, and all I want to do is to take some time off so I can spend more time with Jack, and then you make me feel guilty about it."

"Sorry," I said. "I really didn't mean it like that."

Anna stood up and took a pair of Jack's trousers off the radiator. "Anyway, maybe you're right, maybe we can't afford it."

"I'm not giving up on Scott yet, though," I said.

"How do you mean?"

"Well, it's not the best time to talk to him about it, but I've made a real breakthrough on the drones thing. In fact, I think that this Chinese company might be able to help."

Anna sighed and picked up the pile of clothes.

"What?"

She rubbed her forehead as if she had a migraine coming on. "Please don't start on about the drones thing again. You know I support you, but it's been more than five years now, and you still don't have anything to show for all the work you've put in."

"I get that," I said, her words stinging a little. She was like this about the maps, overly cautious, convinced it was a fool's errand. "These things take time. And do you remember how it was with the maps? Nothing for ages, and then suddenly I got money. So I'm not going to throw in the towel with the drones yet."

Anna shook her head and sat down next to me on the sofa. "You always think that everything's going to be okay," she said, half smiling, shuffling closer to me.

"Sure," I said. "What's the alternative? Thinking that everything is going to be shit?"

"True," she said, putting her feet up on the sofa and then resting her head in my lap.

She slept like that once, our backs against the promenade on Brighton beach. A dirty weekend in a guesthouse near the sea. Still so new to each other, we spent most of our time in bed that weekend. It had started to get dark when we dragged ourselves out to eat fish 'n' chips and cotton candy on Palace Pier. Afterward, we went clubbing, some cheesy indie night where we danced to The La's and the Happy Mondays.

That night, we were fearless on the dance floor, without shame, our hands everywhere, and it was as if we were back in the guesthouse, tingling with lust, our bodies damp with each other. We walked out at 4:00 a.m., the air chilling the sweat on our backs, laughing and stumbling, drawn back to the sea.

Anna wanted to watch the sunrise, so we went and sat on the beach and talked for a while, about London, where we might live. We joked—the way new couples do—about the kids we would have one day.

Just as the sun was coming up, Anna began to fall asleep and rested her head in my lap. Some things you never forget. The waves gently shuffling the pebbles; the birds awakened by the red dawn; the warm, salty wind. Anna was happily oblivious to it all. I watched her sleeping, locked into our bliss, our endless summer, her chest rising and falling in perfect time with the sea.

That evening, I logged back in to *Hope's Place.* There were already fifteen responses to my post.

Re: Can anyone help us?
by dxd576» Wed May 21, 2014 10:34 am

I cant help you with your particular condition or recommend any surgical stuff or anything but we are now eighteen months out from our daughter's diagnosis. We have been juicing and our little one (and all the family) have moved to an all vegan all raw diet. While we can't say what is round the corner our little Jade is doing well and we know that is to do with the changes to our diet and less with the drugs that the doctors have been giving her.

Re: Can anyone help us?
by Chemoforlifer» Wed May 21, 2014 10:58 am

Rob,
Sorry you're dealing with all of this. It must have come as quite a shock. While of course it is a brain tumor (and no one likes

to hear those two words), do take comfort from the fact that PXA is a very treatable and survivable cancer.

(Just FYI, as you're new here. I lost my only daughter, Hope, to glioblastoma multiforme five years ago when she was eight years old. I started this forum in her memory to try to help other people. I am a research scientist by trade.)

So, regarding concrete advice. I would highly recommend, if he hasn't already, that your son get genetically tested. Even though you are looking at surgical resection as a cure, it's always good to have things in the armory, in the unlikely event the tumor did recur.

Please feel free to ask me anything. I am always here to help. Best Wishes,
Chemoforlifer
Admin

Re: Can anyone help us?
by Trustingod» Wed May 21, 2014 11:44 am

Sorry to hear this Rob, although, as you say, there is much to be hopeful about. We are in a similar position, although our baby was diagnosed a few months ago. We have found that our faith has been such a comfort to us in these difficult times. May God put his healing hands on your little boy. I will be praying for you and your family.

I stopped reading. These people weren't us. They were the desperate parents you read about in magazines, who watched as their children slipped away. We had nothing in common, because Jack was so alive; the doctor had said he would be cured. Suddenly I needed to see him, to touch him, and recently these moments had become more frequent and painful, like crippling attacks of gout.

I was just about to close my laptop and go downstairs when a little mail icon pinged to let me know I had received a private message through the forum. It was from someone called Nev.

Subject: Hello
Sent: Wed May 21, 2014 10:16 pm
From: Nev
Recipient: Rob

Hello, Rob. I'm sorry to hear about Jack's situation, although it sounds like you have a huge amount to be hopeful about.

I wanted to tell you my story, in case things don't work out as planned. My son Josh was diagnosed with glioblastoma three years ago, when he was six. The doctors basically wrote him off. After they removed the tumor, they said there was nothing they could do, that it would definitely grow back and all they could offer was chemo and radiation as palliative care.

That was when I found out about Dr. Sladkovsky. Before you stop reading, hear me out. This is a legitimate clinic based in Prague. It's not a cactus juice for a thousand pounds a pop cancer clinic. This is cutting edge stuff and utilizes all the latest treatments, in particular what's called immuno-engineering.

Going to Prague was a risk of course. But we took it and our Josh underwent a variety of treatments. To cut a long story short, six months later, the tumor was gone and it hasn't been back since. He is now a happy nine-year-old, living a normal life, and cancer is beginning to become a distant memory.

I have been banned from posting links to Dr. Sladkovsky on Hope's Place (the software doesn't even let me send them in private messages) so all I can say is Google Dr. Sladkovsky in Prague and you will find everything you need to know.

If you want to find out more about Josh's treatments, please check out my blog at nevbarnes.wordpress.com or feel free to message me.

I wish you the best of luck. I'm crossing fingers and legs and toes and everything really. PM me if you want more info.
Nev

Nev sounded like a con man. I put the name "Sladkovsky" into the search field on *Hope's Place* and hundreds of results popped up.

PLEASE READ re Sladkovsky Clinical Trial
by Chemoforlifer» Mon Jan 26, 2012 6:03 am

Dear All,
Regular users of the board might have seen several posts by Nev about a proposed clinical trial run by Dr. Sladkovsky. These posts no longer exist and have been deleted by the moderators. They were deleted because they explicitly violated the "no solicitation or promotion" rule.

There have been extensive discussions of Sladkovsky's clinic on this board. One of the threads is here, for new users who maybe are not familiar with the clinic's "work."

forum.hopesplace.topic/article/1265%444

Dr. Sladkovsky's clinic is not reputable. He has never allowed his immuno-engineering treatments to be evaluated in an independent, accredited clinical trial, nor has he ever shared the results of his work with other researchers. Every reputable cancer-treatment watchdog has concluded that his "immuno-engineering" treatment is a scam.
Best Wishes,
Chemoforlifer
Admin

I was angry and considered writing this Nev back, telling him what I thought about people preying on the parents of sick children, peddling fake cures over the internet. I read his message again. He was convincing and seemed to believe what he was writing. That, I supposed, was how he reeled people in. I logged out of *Hope's Place*, closed my laptop and went to find Anna and Jack.

10

It was early evening and Jack could not sleep. It was a side effect of the steroids, which reduced the swelling from the fluid around the tumor. The operation was now only a week away, and Jack was antsier than ever. We tried to tire him out, reading him stories, letting him watch cartoons, but sometimes the only thing that would work was going out for a walk.

"How are you feeling today, beautiful?" I asked, as we walked along one of the winding paths up the hill to the heath. "How are your injuries?"

We had told him that he had an injury in his head and would have to go to hospital to take it away. Jack wasn't remotely concerned. He seemed to think it was nothing more serious than a grazed elbow or a funny tummy. Last year, he had fallen off our backyard wall and had to go to hospital for stitches in his chin. Would it be the same? he said. Even better, we replied. He would be asleep and wouldn't feel a thing.

Jack patted his head, as he did now, now that he knew something was wrong. "I think it's fine, but..."

He dithered, scuffed his shoe along the path.

"But what, Jack?"

"It's difficult sometimes, in school, to think."

"Yeah?"

"We did sums today with Miss Jackson and I..." His words trailed off.

"And did you find it difficult?"

"Yeah. Adding up and doing sums and…and… I had for-gotten my numbers."

"Well," I said, putting my arm around his shoulders. "Add-ing up is difficult. You've not been doing it long."

Jack nodded and looked up at me with his pale blue eyes. "We did letters, as well, and I got a sticker."

"Really?"

"Yeah, look." On the lapel of Jack's coat, there was a small star that said *Good job!* "I put it here so it won't get broken."

"Well done. You're doing really well, Jack. And don't you worry about school, because we're going to take all the inju-ries away, okay?"

"In the hospital?"

"Yes, in the hospital."

"And I'll be asleep? They'll take away the injuries when I'm asleep?"

"Exactly, beautiful."

Jack beamed. He was excited about staying overnight in the hospital.

"Daddy, will I be there for a long, long time ago?"

I smiled, pushing his hair out of his face. "No, just a few days, the doctor said, maybe a week. And, Jack, you don't have to say a 'long, long time ago.'"

"Why?"

"Because you don't need it. You can just say a long time. You don't need to say the 'ago.'"

Jack didn't look convinced. "But in the stories they always say 'a long, long time ago.'"

"Right, but…"

Jack looked up at me and fluttered his eyelashes.

"Never mind, son," I said, pulling him closer to me.

We walked back through the heath toward home and Jack seemed content but solemn, as if something was on his mind.

He was narrowing his eyes, the way he did when he was trying to solve a puzzle or do one of his jigsaws.

"Daddy, will I get better, after I'm in the hospital?" he said suddenly.

"Of course you will," I said, smiling cheerily at him. "That's why you're going to the hospital, so they can make you better."

Jack looked up at me, but then bowed his head again, as if he was watching where he was walking.

"Daddy," he said, looking down at his shoes. "You know Jamie Redmond?"

"I don't think so."

"He's in my school. He's in first grade, but he does some of his lessons with us."

"Is he your friend?"

"Nooooo," Jack said, stopping on the pavement, as if I had just said the most preposterous thing. "Jamie Redmond isn't friends with anyone!"

"Oh. Well, you be nice to him if he doesn't have any friends."

We walked in silence, and I could tell he was thinking about something.

"So why did you mention this Jamie Redmond?" I asked after a while.

Jack thought for a moment and looked sheepish, as if he was in trouble. "Because Jamie Redmond said I was going to die. He said I had an injury in my head, and everyone with injuries in their heads dies."

Jack didn't sound perturbed, as if dying was of no consequence, like falling asleep or finishing early at school.

"Well, Jamie Redmond doesn't know what he's talking about. You're not going to die, Jack, and you're going to get better. Okay? He shouldn't be saying things like that."

"It's okay, Daddy, I told him he was a silly-billy," Jack said. "I told him that everyone dies one day, and everyone knows that."

"Good," I said.

"Actually, Daddy, there's lots of things Jamie Redmond doesn't know. Maybe that's why he's in first grade, but he has to do our lessons."

I sniggered a little. "You didn't say that to him, did you?"

"Noooo," Jack said.

"Good, because even if he's mean to you, you don't want to be mean to him."

Jack nodded. "I didn't say it to him because Jamie Redmond is very big, and he hits people. He's even bigger than you, Daddy."

"Good," I said, squeezing Jack's shoulder. "Is he bigger than the Incredible Hulk?"

"Don't be silly. Nobody's bigger than the Incredible Hulk."

Dr. Flanagan's office couldn't have been more different to Dr. Kennety's, with its high Georgian ceilings and oversize antique furniture. Dr. Flanagan's office looked like a children's ward, with painted murals and tiny furniture and a play corner with a ball pit tucked inside a large alcove.

"Hello," Dr. Flanagan said, coming out into the waiting room. In her yellow smock and bright orange Crocs, she looked like a preschool assistant. Don't let her appearance deceive you, Dr. Kennety had said. Julia Flanagan was the best in the business. We had read about her online. Parents called her a miracle worker: the pioneering brain surgeon who had dedicated her career to saving children's lives.

"And this must be Jack," she said, as she led us into her office. "I like your T-shirt," she said, pointing to the bats flying around the dinosaur's head. Jack blushed and smiled.

Dr. Flanagan turned to us as we sat down. "Before we start, one thing for Mom and Dad." She suddenly seemed very businesslike. Don't let the smock and Crocs deceive you, people said about her on *Hope's Place*. She was blunt, did not have much of a bedside manner, but she would do everything for your kids.

"I'm sure you saw it on my website, but I have a rule. I don't allow any of my consultations to go over twenty minutes, and I'm a brutal timekeeper. It's very important for me to keep to this. That way I can see as many patients as possible."

"Yes, of course," I said. We had read about her strict appointment times. People on *Hope's Place* said she would cut them off midsentence, pointing to her watch.

"Good," she said, turning to Jack. "Now, I've got some lollipops in my desk. Would you like one?"

Jack nodded nervously.

"I thought you would. But to get it, you have to help me, okay?"

"Okay."

"Right, Jack. Can you close your eyes and count for me, from one to as high as you can go?"

Jack closed his eyes and started to count. "One, two, three, four…" He had been able to count to twenty since his third birthday, but now when he got to eleven he paused. "One and two, one and four," he said and then stopped, looking ashamed as if he had done something wrong.

"Well done, Jack, good boy," the doctor said. "Now, can you come around here and try to find the lollipops? They're in my desk somewhere." Jack walked toward her and started looking around the desk, touching Dr. Flanagan's paperweight, her calendar. She was watching him intensely, how he walked, what he did with his hands.

"You're very close now. Maybe it might be somewhere here?" she said, opening up her drawer.

Jack's face lit up when he looked inside. "Wow, there's so many."

The doctor reached into the drawer and held out a red lollipop. "There you go. Now, can you tell me what color it is?"

"Red," Jack said quickly.

"Excellent," she said. "Now, can you remember what we call these? What is this, Jack?" she said, holding the lollipop under his nose.

Jack looked at the lollipop, thinking it might be a trick question. "It's a lollipop."

"Well done," Dr. Flanagan said, giving Jack the lollipop. He beamed and put it carefully into his pocket.

"Now, Jack, can you see this line?" She pointed to a taped line on the floor covered with little fish stickers. Jack nodded. "I want you to walk along the line, okay?"

Jack didn't move. He looked at Anna and me for encouragement and we smiled at him, urging him on. He dithered, chewing his fingernails, and it was as if we were asking him to walk along a precipice. Finally, he slowly started walking, but he couldn't keep straight, weaving his way along the line like a drunk.

"Well done," the doctor said. "Now, the last thing. Can you stand here, Jack?" She touched him gently on both cheeks and then examined his head, the little bumps that had appeared under his skin.

"Wow, you're an amazing little boy. Would you like to go and play with Suzie out in reception?"

Jack didn't move, looked nervously at me and Anna.

"We have a PlayStation," the doctor added, "and no one's playing right now."

"Really?" Jack said, his eyes lighting up.

"Really," Dr. Flanagan said, and she held out her hand and led Jack outside.

"It always gets them," Dr. Flanagan said, when she came back to her office. "My nephew has one, and it's like we don't even exist half the time." She looked at her watch. "Right, we have eleven minutes left. So I have looked at all the scans and the reports, and I do agree with Dr. Kennety's and the radiologist's assessment. It almost certainly is an astrocytoma. However, looking at the shape on the images, I think the tumor might be a little more advanced."

I felt breathless, like that first meeting in Dr. Kennety's office. Despair in the pit of my stomach, like feeling homesick as a child. "So it could be a more advanced tumor? A glioblastoma?" I asked, my voice shaking. I had read about glioblastomas on *Hope's Place*. They were the astrocytoma's uglier cousin, a tumor so complex, so aggressive it could kill people in weeks.

"No, I don't think so," the doctor said, picking up one of Jack's scans from her folder. She typed something on her computer and then turned the screen toward us. "That's what glioblastoma looks like. There, you see all those white areas around the outside. Now compare that to Jack's."

We looked at the image. There were no white parts, just an amorphous black blob.

"No, I'm almost certain it's an astrocytoma. It just might be more advanced than we thought."

"And could that affect Jack's prognosis?" Anna asked.

The doctor paused, which was unusual for her. "It could, but I don't want to speculate or talk numbers until after the surgery. Believe me, I do understand the need—your need to know—but really, it doesn't help anything."

I wanted to say something, but my vocal cords had seized up. Dr. Kennety had said 80 or 90 percent. He had said that Jack would be cured.

The doctor looked at her watch. "Right, time is getting tight now, so how much did Dr. Kennety tell you about the operation?"

"A little," Anna said. "We've both read up on it since. He gave us some handouts."

"Good," she said. "So the goal is to remove everything. That's the best chance of a cure for Jack. And from looking at the scans, the location isn't toooo bad, although I am a bit worried about this part," she said, pointing to one of the shadows.

I felt that fog descend again, the sense that I was here but not here, that I was floating, looking down on myself. I had been secretly hoping for good news from Dr. Flanagan, that the tumor was in fact benign, or that it wasn't a tumor at all. I wasn't expecting to hear that Jack's prognosis might be worse.

A faint alarm beeped from somewhere within Dr. Flanagan's desk.

"I know it's easy for me to say," she said, as she was showing us out, "but please do try to stay positive. These are very survivable tumors, and there's a reasonable chance that we'll get it all out and that will be it. Please try to remember that."

"Thank you," we both said, but her words sounded empty, as if they were merely an afterthought.

"Good. So I will see you on Tuesday for the operation. You need to sign some forms regarding Jack's hospital stay, but Suzie will take you through it on reception."

We shook hands with the doctor and went back to the reception. Jack was in the kids' corner playing Super Mario Cart. He was leaning into each corner, nearly falling off the beanbag.

"You okay, matey?" I said, when he had finished his game.

"Yeah, the driving's really good."

"It looks cool," I said. I couldn't stop thinking about what Dr. Flanagan had said, her concerns about the shadows on the scan.

Jack looked up from the beanbag. "Daddy, why do you look so sad?"

I smiled and reflexively wiped my eyes. "I'm not sad, I'm very happy."

Jack looked skeptical and then handed me the controller. "Do you want to play the driving game? Maybe it will cheer you up."

"Okay," I said, sitting down on the beanbag next to him. "They have two-player mode so we can race if you want."

"Cool," Jack said.

We played a few games, and I forgot for a moment that we were in the doctor's waiting room. I turned around, looking for Anna, and she was sitting on a chair, watching and smiling at us both, patiently waiting for us to finish our game.

EPSOM DOWNS

do you remember that day, jack? mummy was at work and we braved the traffic to go to epsom downs and you took your pictures, practicing zooming in and out, and then we ate our packed lunches in the car, looking out over the city. you've probably forgotten what happened on the way home, but you needed to pee and wouldn't do it by the side of the road because you said you'd get in trouble with the man and go to prison, so you just held it in, all the way home. you were so funny, jack, grimacing a little, your legs crossed, complaining every time i went over a bump.

11

We had gone out to get some supplies: Jack's favorite cartons of orange juice, Jaffa Cakes, his superhero magazines. We had left him with Anna's mother and when we came back, she was sitting on his hospital bed, leaning back on the pillows, with Jack cuddled up next to her.

"Can we do the whale again?" Jack asked.

"You like that one, don't you?"

Jack nodded, and Anna's mother began the story again, how Jonah had angered God and brought on the storm before the sailors threw him into the sea. And then it was God, in all his righteous mercy, who sent the whale to save him.

Since we had got to the hospital, there had been a constant stream of visitors to Jack's bed: surgeons, junior residents, various nurses. Jack was examined and reexamined and prodded and poked. They took his blood, swabbed under his tongue, hooked him up to an ECG. This morning, they took him for an MRI to map his brain and he emerged, his head shaved, with little doughnut-shaped stickers attached to his scalp to guide the surgeons.

"That was very nice of God after Jonah was naughty," Jack said.

"Well, that's what God is like," Janet said, with an eye in my direction. "He will always help you. He helps everyone. And that's what He does in heaven."

I looked at Anna with incredulity, expecting her to say something, to tell her mother to stop, but she was silent, thinking about something else.

"Janet," I said quietly, as the nurse was busy with Jack. "Please don't talk to him about these things. These Bible stories about death and heaven."

"Why on earth not?" she said. "He loves the stories."

"He might do," I said, lowering my voice, "it's just that we don't want to talk to him about heaven or anything like that…"

"Well, Anna never said anything," she said, avoiding my gaze. I looked at Anna, but she was tidying Jack's bedside table, mopping up some spilled drops from the water jug.

In the last few weeks, Janet had been making noises about Jack getting baptized. Now was the time, she said, cautiously at first, feeling her way, but then, as she saw Anna wavering, her lobbying became more intense. I thought Anna would eventually falter, the daughter of missionaries, all those years spent at Bible class and Sunday school, but she didn't. Absolutely not, I had said, expecting an argument, but to my surprise, even though I knew it still gnawed at her, Anna acquiesced.

As I was thinking how to respond to Janet, Lola walked in with India and a huge bunch of balloons. Jack's face lit up, because they weren't just any balloons, but plump and swelling as if they were about to burst, in a rainbow of carefully assorted colors, with bespoke, plaited wool strings. Emblazoned on the side of each one was #JackStrong.

"Hello, darlings," she said, kissing Anna on both cheeks. "And hello, lovely," she said, kissing Jack on the head.

"Hello, Auntie Lola."

Anna smiled. She always seemed to relax when Lola was around.

"Now, they're all for you, Jack, but would you like to choose one to hold?"

Jack's face flushed with joy. He had always loved balloons. He sought them out on the street, the ones given out for free by phone companies and campaigning politicians. At children's parties, he would ask if he was allowed to take an extra one home.

"So here's the thing," Lola said, after Jack had chosen a red one. "I've done the balloons with the hashtag, #JackStrong, and I've started a little campaign on Twitter, just for well-wishers really, and we already have some retweets, someone from that Essex program and that nice Scarlett girl from Gogglebox."

"What's Gogglebox?" Anna said.

"Oh, you have to see it. Terribly funny. Anyway, I thought it would be good to raise awareness about Jack's illness, but sometimes getting these celebrities involved on Twitter can be a real game changer. Trips to Disneyland, balloon rides et cetera, et cetera."

She was speaking about him as if he was dying. Everyone was speaking about him as if he was dying.

"India," Lola said, placing all the wool strings into her daughter's little clenched fist, "do you want to give Jack the rest of the balloons?"

India hesitated. For a moment she was uncharacteristically shy, but Lola nudged her forward, and she stood next to Jack's bed, in her little pink dress and woven headscarf. She presented the balloons one at a time, Jack making sure they were securely in his hand.

As we were watching Jack and India, there was a knock at the door. A nurse walked in and handed Jack a parcel.

"Is it for me?" Jack said.

"Is your name Jack Coates?"

Jack nodded excitedly and stared at the box, feeling it, gently shaking it, the way he would do with the Christmas presents under the tree.

With Anna's help, he opened the package, neatly tearing off the paper, then folding it and putting it on the bed. Inside was a scrapbook and on the cover it said "Dear Jack, From All Your Friends In 1A."

Jack opened the scrapbook as if each page were made of the most precious, delicate petals. On the first page, the words were written in an assortment of big and small letters, drawn by the hands of different children:

> Jack, we know how much you like tall buildings. So we wanted to do something special for you… We hope you get well soon and can't wait to see you again!

Slowly he began to turn the pages. Pasted onto the rainbow-colored paper were pictures of his classmates on top of tall buildings, up on cliffs, looking out to sea. The Telecom Tower, Canary Wharf, the lighthouse at Beachy Head. The children were all holding signs saying "Get Well Soon, Jack."

"You're The Best, Jack."

"We Love You, Jack!"

I had never seen him look like that before. It was as if he had unwrapped the world. He savored each and every picture, every single message on every single page. Then he paused for a moment, lingering on one photo. It was his best friends at school, Martin, Tony and Emil on the top floor of a skyscraper somewhere in London. They were grinning and holding a sign that said: "Jack Coates: Pokémon Collector and Superstar." Jack's bottom lip started to quiver and then, for the first time since all of this began, he started to cry.

On the day of the operation, Jack cheerfully sat upright on the gurney, his surgical gown making him look like a little elf. As we descended into the bowels of the hospital, the bright yellows and reds of the children's ward turned to sullen greens and browns as we entered the complex of vestibules and waiting rooms where we would eventually leave Jack.

We kissed him and told him we'd see him in a bit, not wanting him to think he was going anywhere for long.

"Bye-bye," he said, unphased. "Kiss Little Teddy," he added, holding up his bear, whose arm had been bandaged by a nurse.

★ ★ ★

We sat on a bench in a park for hours that day, waiting for Dr. Flanagan's assistant to call. To think that once, we were so worried about a rogue mole, a tiny lump that appeared on the side of Jack's neck. To think that once we used to agonize about his milestones, wondering why he hadn't yet started to walk, why he had no interest in stacking more than three blocks at a time. To think that we were worried about all that, when Dr. Flanagan was now cutting into Jack's skull with a circular saw. A neat cut, like a cartoon ice hole. Another human being's hands inside my child's brain.

That afternoon, we sat in the park and tried to ignore the trudge of time. When you lived in peace, when your concerns were minor and mundane, time was invisible: it flowed, ebbed, like an app quietly running in the background. But now time was impossible to ignore: it was menacing, counting down, the second hand on a giant Orwellian clock.

I didn't know what to do, so out of habit I opened *Hope's Place* on my phone and saw that I had a number of private messages.

Subject: Best Wishes
Sent: Mon Jul 7, 2014 1:58 pm
From: Camilla
Recipient: Rob

Hi Rob, I see from your posting last week that today is Jack's operation. I just wanted to wish you well and let you know that I'm thinking of you all. I'm a long-time veteran of Hope's Place. My daughter was diagnosed with PXA in 2009. She has been healthy and happy ever since and lives a normal life. I know it might be hard to hear now, but you have so much to be hopeful for. Take care.

"Look," I said, handing Anna my phone. "From someone on

Hope's Place." Without her glasses, Anna squinted as she read. "How lovely," she said. "Do you know that person?"

"No, not at all. I asked something on the forum this week about recovery time, and I said Jack's operation was this week. There's more, look." I opened another one.

Subject: Good luck!!
Sent: Mon Jul 7, 2014 5:16 pm
From: TeamAwesome
Recipient: Rob

I have to be quick because I am just off out the door but wanted to wish you the best of luck for today. We have a little tradition around here on Hope's Place of sending good wishes on op day...so just to say that I'm thinking and praying for you all. I know just what a lonely, heartbreaking, nerve-racking time this is. My son was diagnosed eight years ago and is now a happy healthy teen, who manages to find a million ways to drive me mad! I am telling you this as I remember just how much I needed to hear stories of hope, not from doctors but from real people, people who had gone through the same. So that's my story of hope. Do post to let us know how it went (if you feel like it). All your friends on Hope's Place are cheering you on.

"Goodness, people are so kind," Anna said, scrolling through the message again.

"Are you okay?" I said, squeezing her shoulder, pulling her closer to me on the bench.

"No, not really. I'm just so, so..." Her words trailed off, and her eyes followed an old couple strolling with a bag of bread crumbs for the birds.

"Me too," I said, and took a deep breath, letting some air into

my lungs. I went back to my phone and started to read the rest
of the messages, stories of hope from strangers on the internet.

Jack had woken up, and we went to see him in intensive care.
One half of his head was covered with a dressing and net. Occasionally his eyes would flicker open but then quickly shut
again, and we sat on either side of him, each holding a hand.

"I'm sorry," a nurse said, when we asked her if the operation
had gone well. "I can't tell you that, but the doctor will let you
know more. She's in the waiting room, the one at the end."

I knew something was wrong as soon as I walked into the
room. Dr. Flanagan was sitting down, still wearing her green
scrubs, frantically checking something on her phone. It made
sense now: how the nurse averted her eyes, a more secluded
meeting room at the end of the corridor.

"So," Dr. Flanagan said, putting down her phone. "It's good
news." I waited, too scared to breathe. "The operation went
very well. Everything is out. No complications. And Jack did
brilliantly."

"You managed to get all of the tumor?" I said, feeling the
pump of my heart, the quickening of my breath.

"Yes, we got all of it," the doctor said, taking her surgeon's
hat off. "It was simpler than we anticipated. Some tumors are
complicated, tangled up with blood vessels, but that wasn't the
case here. We'll have to do a scan to confirm this, but I'm confident that we're looking at a gross total resection."

Gross total resection. We knew those words. We had read
them on *Hope's Place*, in the medical literature. It was the gold
standard for children who were cured. All visible signs of cancer removed.

"So this…this," Anna stammered, almost gasping for breath.
"This might mean he's cured?"

"Yes, it might," Dr. Flanagan said quickly. "Officially I'm

not allowed to say that. We doctors are very nervous talking about cures but, in Jack's case, the surgery did go incredibly well, and I really expect him to make a full recovery. However, to be fully straight with you, there is always a risk that it will come back. In Jack's case, that would be a very small risk, but a risk nonetheless."

A risk, a very small risk. But there were always risks, crossing the road, playing rugby at school.

"And will he need any more treatment?" I asked.

"So," the doctor said, looking at her watch, "in the coming days we'll do another scan to make sure that the resection was total, that there are no signs of cancer. And if that scan confirms what we think, no, Jack won't need any more treatment."

"Thank you," I said, "thank you so much."

"Well, it's nice to be the bearer of good news," the doctor said, standing up and walking toward the door. "But if you'll excuse me, I need to prepare for another operation."

Suddenly, Anna stood up and flung her arms around the doctor. Their embrace was awkward, two people who didn't know how tight to squeeze or how long to hold on. But Anna wouldn't let go, her arms tightly wrapped around the doctor's body, as if she was clinging to her own child. They stood, gently swaying next to a fire extinguisher, as Anna whispered "thank you, thank you" into Dr. Flanagan's neck.

12

I listened to the waves lapping against the shore, with the occasional crash, the wake from a distant boat. Anna was reclined on the chaise lounge, reading her book. Jack sat on his beach mat, flicking through his Pokémon cards. His hair was beginning to thicken with salt and sand, his nape tinted blond with the sun.

We loved watching his hair grow after the operation, back to how it was when he was young, when the barbershop was an ordeal. Anna wanted him to grow it long, to let it curl and flop into his eyes. She didn't want him to ever cut it again.

Dr. Flanagan had been right. The MRI showed that she got it all. Jack soon regained his strength. He started school again. He went up the London Eye with his class. He even started football training with Hampstead Colts. Did we dream it all? *Look at him, look at him,* I thought as I watched him play football or jump into the swimming pool. Does that look like a boy who had a brain tumor?

It had been Anna's idea to come to Crete, an apartment her colleague had recommended. It was a penthouse suite, a terrace with an unbroken view of the sea. The apartments were at the quieter end of the beach, away from the boat trips and Jet Skis, the hawkers selling dresses and coral necklaces and salted corn on the cob.

Suddenly, Jack shrieked, jumped off his beach mat and ran to the water's edge, dodging and weaving, leaving wet footprints in the sand. We jumped up, thinking something was wrong, and then we saw the butterfly dancing around his head.

"It's chasing me, it's a wasp," Jack said, waving his arms around, his little feet jumping in the sand.

"It's a butterfly, Jack. It's not going to hurt you," I said.

"How do you know?" he said. "Butterflies can eat people sometimes." He walked toward me, holding out his hands like a dinosaur. "Really, Daddy. How do you know?"

"Because I'm very clever."

"Ha," he said, twisting my toe, "you're not as clever as Philip Cleaver."

"Is he clever then?"

"He can read and write and do all the sums, since he was a baby."

"Wow, do they call him Clever Cleaver?"

"What?" Jack said, his hands bolshily on his hips. "His name isn't Clever, it's Philip."

Anna laughed. "It's okay, Jack," she said. "No one gets Daddy's jokes. By the way, is it too early for a beer?"

"It's 11:05," I said, looking at my watch.

"That's acceptable on holiday, right?"

"I thought we had decided 10:30 was the acceptable cutoff."

"Ah, then one beer, please, and some of those little chocolate pretzel things." Anna stretched out on the chaise longue, her legs turning a light shade of brown.

"Anything else?" I said.

"No, no," she said, "that will be all, although you could do my back before you go?"

Anna sat forward and handed me the cream, and it was nice to touch her again, to feel the soft purchase of her skin.

"So nice," she said, sighing a little too hard, as if we were alone after Jack had gone to bed.

"It is nice."

"But you should stop, otherwise I might do something inappropriate."

"Okay," I said, laughing and rubbing in the last bit of sun cream. "Right, matey," I said to Jack. "Shall we get some ice cream?"

"Again?" Jack asked. "Is it the weekend?"

"We're on holiday, Jack. We can have ice cream every day."

We walked along the beach to the bar, Jack running ahead with a stick he had found. His camera strap was slung over his shoulder, and it reminded me of how Anna used to carry her viola case around campus.

As the beach curved into another bay, we stood on a little outcrop and looked out to sea.

"It's beautiful here, Daddy."

"It is, isn't it? Look, can you see the little fish jumping in the water?"

I pointed to the ripples and bubbles on the surface. "Fishies, fishies," Jack said, hopping up and down. "Why are they jumping, Daddy? Are they playing?"

I tried to think of an answer but didn't really know why. "I think so, or maybe they're looking for food."

Jack began to take his camera out of the case.

"You going to take some pictures?"

Jack nodded, carefully holding his camera with two hands as we had shown him. He then pointed it toward the fish and started snapping away.

I watched him, crouching down, getting as close to the water as he could. The weather was perfect, the sun beating down, not a cloud in the sky. In the distance, there were yachts out on the open sea, their masts twinkling in the sunlight.

"Daddy, Daddy, look," Jack shouted excitedly. He was holding out his camera. I looked at the little screen, and there was a close-up of a fish jumping out of the water, its silver skin shining, its mouth agape.

"Wow, Jack, that's amazing. That could win a competition or something. You'll have to show Mommy."

Jack beamed. "I'm going to show my teacher when we go back to England."

The bar was a little round shack, Hawaiian-style with palms and wicker, reggae blaring out from a little speaker. I lifted Jack up onto one of the bar stools and sat next to him.

"Hello," the bartender said, in what sounded like a Jamaican accent. "Let me guess. Two beers, one fizzy orange and nothing else." He winked at me and then bent down into the freezer. "And definitely no ice cream or anything for this little boy."

Jack giggled, as he did every day with the ice-cream man. The bartender took out a cone and scooped out some vanilla and chocolate and then held it behind his back.

"Definitely no ice cream for this young man…" he said again, shaking his head from side to side, and then suddenly he produced the ice cream, now covered with sprinkles and a Flake, and Jack squealed, and we still had no idea how he did it.

We sat for a while at the bar, the sun on our bare backs, nothing more important in our little world than the beach and the sea. I watched Jack as he ate his ice cream, methodically, just like Anna would, evaluating where the drips and flows were the most precarious.

"Can we go and see the fishies, Daddy?" Jack said, as we were walking back to Anna.

"Of course. We'll just take this beer back to Mommy and then we'll go, okay?"

I could see Anna was watching us from behind her sunglasses, waiting for us to emerge on the grass that backed onto the beach.

"I thought you'd got lost," she said.

"Ice-cream emergency," I said.

"And Daddy drank a beer. That's his second one."

"Thanks, Jack."

"You're welcome, Daddy," Jack said in a singsong voice, and I dug him gently in the ribs.

"Sorry we took so long," I said, handing Anna her beer.

"It's okay. I was happy with my book to be honest."

She closed her book and put it down on her towel. Anna had always been a reader. On those long, empty African days, when her parents were busy with the church and her school friends lived a few villages away, she sat on the veranda and read. She devoured Gerald Durrell and Willard Price. She could recite passages by heart from James Herriot novels because she had read them so many times. After she had worked her way through her parents' collection, she found a library in a nearby township and began to read through the centuries: Jane Austen, Daphne du Maurier, Virginia Woolf.

We finished our beers and then walked along the shoreline, past the big hotels and discotheques, until we came to the public beach, a wide expanse of unsullied sand. There were just a few local families, sitting up closer to the road and grilling lamb on a little barbecue.

The three of us waded into the rock pools, where Jack liked to see the fish.

"Be quiet, Daddy," he said, standing very still. "Look, there's the fish." Jack had his bucket and was trying to catch the little minnows, but they moved too fast, their reactions too quick, changing direction before even a fingertip touched the surface of the water.

"There they are," Jack shouted, pointing and kicking up clouds of sand. So we tried and tried, first targeting the lone ones that had become separated from the pack. Then we tried the schools, dipping the bucket like a dragnet, but they always evaded us, and we waded back to the beach empty-handed.

"They're too fast swimming," Jack said, shaking his head. "They're turbo fish."

"Right, I'm going to show you how it's done," Anna said suddenly, adjusting her bikini and taking off her sunglasses.

"Mommy! You're going in the water?" Anna wasn't much of a swimmer. She always said she preferred dry land.

"Yes, and I'm going to catch all the fish."

"Noooo, you won't," Jack said.

"Just watch me," she said, picking up the bucket.

Anna waded slowly into the water, a look of concentration on her face, as if she were a hunter spearing fish. She pounced and Jack squealed, but the fish were too fast and she just scooped up a bucketful of sand.

She wasn't to be deterred and assumed her pose once again, staring down into the rock pool, waiting for her moment. Just as she was about to strike, she lost her footing on a rock and went under, kicking up mushroom clouds of sand.

We couldn't stop laughing. "What are you doing, Mommy?" Jack shrieked, as she tried and failed to get up out of the water. Finally, she managed and wobbled back to us, drenched, wet sand caked over her face.

"It's not so easy, is it?" she said, wiping the sand away and catching her breath. "I think that's enough for now."

The three of us sat sunning ourselves on the edge of the rock pool. Sandwiched between me and Jack, Anna gently stroked our legs with her fingertips. "Look at you both. My beautiful bronzed boys."

I smiled at Anna, as we watched Jack making spiral patterns with his toes in the sand.

"Although I'm putting sunscreen on both of you, the minute we get back to our towels," Anna added.

I didn't know how long we sat there, staring out across the azure sea, the mountains looming in the haze. The only sounds we could hear were the shouts and cries of children playing, the distant whir of Jet Skis. What we had, what we so nearly lost, suddenly crushed me, as if someone was standing on my chest. I took a deep breath and looked at them both, Anna counting out seashells into Jack's palm. The life we had now was sacred. I could never let myself forget that.

Anna was reading and Jack was napping on the sofa, so I sat outside on the terrace and went through the email on my phone.

Subject: Hello again
Sent: Wed Aug 13, 2014 12:16 pm
From: Nev
To: Rob

Hi, Rob. It's Nev from Hope's Place. I messaged you a few weeks ago. Don't worry, I'm not here to bug you about Dr. Sladkovsky's clinic. I just wanted to ask how Jack's operation went. I know what a horrible time that can be and sometimes friends and family don't get it, so if you ever want to talk... I hope everything went well.
Take care,
Nev

Nev, the crank from *Hope's Place*, who was promoting the shady clinic. I was just about to swipe and delete his email, but for some reason I hit Reply. Perhaps I had misjudged him. At least he had made the effort to ask about Jack.

Subject: Re: Hello again
Sent: Wed Aug 13, 2014 2:26 pm
From: Rob
To: Nev

Hi Nev, thanks for the note and for getting in touch. Very kind of you. Actually, some very good news. Jack had his operation about a month ago now and had a complete total resection. The neurosurgeon managed to get it all and no further treatment is needed. He will obviously have to have it monitored but for now the news is good. We're actually on holiday in Greece at the moment. Thanks again for being in touch and I wish you and your son well.

Sent from my iPhone.

Nev's reply was almost instant.

Subject: Re: Hello again
Sent: Wed Aug 13, 2014 2:27 pm
From: Rob
To: Nev

Hi Rob,
That's so great to hear. Big congrats from me, I'm sure it's a huge relief. Have a great holiday.
Cheers,
Nev

Jack had fallen asleep holding his camera and it looked like it was about to fall to the floor, so I crept into his room, pried it out of his hands and took it outside. I sat down and began to scroll through his photos. His first shots from the holiday were pictures of the seahorse-patterned floor tiles, his little sofa bed, his Spider-Man suitcase. Then the choppy sea, the beach at night, and an abandoned ice cream covered in sand.

It was fascinating to see how Jack saw the world. A picture of a plant, but not the flowers or the stem, but the soil, the cracks on the pot. A garbage can on the heath he thought looked like R2-D2. A picture in a magazine of a cow sitting down.

As I scrolled on, I saw some pictures Jack had taken from our terrace here in Greece. At first I thought they were simply repeats of the same shot, as if the camera was stuck on burst. But then, when I looked closer, I saw that each shot was taken from a slightly different angle.

I clicked through them, and then I saw what Jack was trying to do. Standing on a chair, he had rotated himself like a tripod, methodically going around 360 degrees, capturing the sea, the sky, the mountains rimmed with wisps of cloud. Shot after shot—endless photos of the sky. I smiled, a little awestruck. Jack was making a panorama.

Jack had woken, and Anna was sitting by his side, stroking his hair.

"Hello, sleepy," I said.

"Hello," Jack said drowsily. "Is the holiday finished?"

"No, not at all. We've got five more days."

Jack perked up, wiping the sleep from his eyes.

"Monday, Tuesday, Wednesday, Thursday, Friday. Five days," he said, counting on his fingers.

"Exactly," I said, sitting down next to him on the sofa. "I saw your photos, by the way, on your camera. All the ones you took of the sky outside. They're really good. Do you want to take some more with me? I can show you how to use my big camera."

Jack nodded solemnly. "I was trying to make a circle, like a circle of photos." He suddenly looked very sheepish. "And I'm sorry, Daddy."

"Why are you sorry, Jack?"

He bit his lip. "Because I stood on the chair when I was taking the photos, and you and Mommy told me I shouldn't stand on the chair."

I ruffled his hair. "That's okay, you don't have to be sorry. But next time you do it when we're there. So do you want to try to do a panorama with the big camera?"

"What's a panorama?"

"A panorama is what you were doing, taking lots of photos in a circle."

Jack sat up and smiled. "Can we do it now?"

I went to get my camera and tripod, and we all went up the spiral staircase to the roof terrace. It was siesta time and the sun was relentless, only softened by occasional gasps of breeze.

I extended the tripod and Jack watched me, carefully noting each step, the methodical way his brain worked.

"That's the tripod, Jack. Now we just need to attach the camera. Can you help me?"

Jack nodded excitedly, and I pulled over the white plastic chair. He climbed up and the chair wobbled a little, and I saw a flicker of concern on Anna's face. I stood behind him so he couldn't fall and then showed him how to clip the camera onto the tripod.

I looked through the viewfinder at the bay curving away into the haze, and I could feel Jack's eyes on me, intently watching what I was doing.

"I've only actually tried this once before, but we'll give it a go," I said. "Look through here."

Jack bent down and looked through the viewfinder. "Wow, it's amazing, Daddy."

"And press this button here. But be careful, just press it lightly."

"Like that?" Jack said and I could smell the tang of salt and sunscreen on his skin.

"Exactly. Good boy. Now listen to the camera."

WE OWN THE SKY

Jack bent down so he could hear the camera's little whir. "It's like an airplane."

"Right, because it's doing what we call a burst. So it's taking lots and lots of photos."

"Like a million?"

"Well, not quite that many. But hundreds maybe."

"Wow, that's a lot."

The whirring had stopped, so I flicked the dial on the tripod and then set the camera's frame rate again. "Now, we're going to turn it a little—will you help me?"

Very gently, Jack helped me move the tripod into place. "It's going to take more photos, and then we'll move it around again, and then we'll have a picture of everything."

"The whole world?" Jack said.

"The whole world."

Anna put her arm around my waist. "He's doing really well, isn't he?" she said. We watched as Jack methodically turned the camera and then looked through the viewfinder, making sure he wasn't missing anything, making sure he was capturing it all.

13

"Where's Jack?" Anna said. We were at the Amberly Primary fireworks night, and it seemed like the entire school was scurrying through this particular corridor.

"He went to the bathroom," I said.

"Yes, I know, but about five minutes ago."

"Shall I go and check?"

"Could you."

It was strange being back in the boys' bathroom. Everything was so small. Lowered urinals and sinks; tiny little cubicles.

I looked along the row of sinks and then turned the corner to where the cubicles were, but there was nothing, no children, no sounds.

"Jack." No answer. "Jack," I said again, feeling a slight panic, like the feeling of losing sight of him in the playground.

I went back to the corridor, thinking that perhaps he had come out and I had missed him, but I couldn't see him, just throngs of parents and children walking past. I went back in the bathroom and paced around, sure that I hadn't seen him come out, and then I heard a snigger coming from one of the cubicles. I opened the door and there was Jack with a boy I didn't know, both with a fan of Pokémon cards in their hands.

"Jesus, Jack, don't do that. I was worried where you had gone."

"Sorry, Daddy, we were playing Pokémon, but Sasha doesn't have any energy cards so I gave him one."

Sasha looked nervous, as if he was in trouble.

"Shall we go and watch the fireworks? They're starting soon."

"Okay." Jack had a quick shuffle through his Pokémon cards and carefully took one out. "This is for you," he said to Sasha. "Porygon is very strong and he will protect you, but you have to take him into your bed at nighttime."

Sasha nodded seriously, carefully putting the card into his coat pocket.

I herded the boys out and Anna was standing outside. "Is he okay?" she said, looking relieved.

"Yeah, he's fine. He was playing Pokémon with another boy."

"Ahh. C'mon, we should go. The fireworks start in five minutes."

The playground smelled of late autumn—wet leaves and roasting chestnuts—and we could hear the crackle of the bonfire in the air. The Friends of Amberly Primary were running a burger stand, and the smell of fried onions reminded me of going to West Ham with Dad.

Dad loved that smell. Best smell in the world, son, he always said. I remembered the last time I went to the football with him. We walked his usual route along Green Street and then onto Barking Road. He knew everyone, my dad, waving to all the Bangladeshi shopkeepers, who always gave him their little mangos, the only fruit he'd ever eat. They all loved Dad, in that little part of East London, because he was the cabbie who'd pick you up at any time of day or night. "The Ambulance," people called him, because he always took people to hospital for free.

"Hello, Jack," children said as we walked through the playground toward the fireworks, older kids from grade 3 or 4.

"Are they your friends?" Anna asked.

Jack shrugged nonchalantly. "We play Pokémon sometimes."

We were glad that Jack had stopped being known as the brain

tumor boy. The sickly child they prayed for in assemblies. The boy who received the giant Get Well Soon card, signed by the whole school. Now he was known for his Pokémon, his cards meticulously ordered by strength in his folder, his duplicates kept in an old cookie tin.

We found a good place to watch the fireworks and looked around for anyone we knew, but could see only shadows, ghostly faces occasionally lit up by the glare of the bonfire.

"Can I go up in the air?" Jack said.

"Aren't you too big now?"

"Nooooooo," Jack said, with as much outrage as he could muster.

I lifted Jack up onto my shoulders, and it used to be a smooth move, like a weight lifter's clean and jerk, but this time I struggled, wobbling a little.

"Are you okay?" Anna asked.

"Yep, just lost my footing a little. I'm not quite the power-house that I once was."

"Right, darling," Anna said, smiling to herself and turning away to watch the fireworks.

The first bars of the *Star Wars* music began, and I could feel Jack kicking his heels and excitedly holding on to my ears. He loved the fireworks, screaming "wow" after each fizz, flinching at the bigger bangs. When it was finished, gunpowder pungent in the air, he clapped and cheered, looking up into the night sky, waiting, hoping for more.

After the fireworks, there was a little autumn show, and Jack's class had been chosen to sing the closing hymn. It was "Jerusalem"—one of Anna's favorites—and I was surprised, thinking it too patriotic, or too Christian, or too socialist, for Amberly Primary.

I watched Jack, his little halo of blond hair lit up by the stage lights, my heart melting as he struggled to remember the words.

I could see him blinking into the glare, looking out for us in the audience. And then, suddenly, he wasn't there anymore. I thought perhaps it was a trick of the light, but, no, there was now a gap where he had been standing, as if he had been excised from a school photo. Just as the children started to sing "And did the countenance divine," I heard a shriek and then the screech of the piano. We both ran through the audience and jumped up onto the stage. Jack was lying crumpled on the floor, still clutching his book of hymns.

He probably just fainted, the EMTs said, even though we told them he'd had a brain tumor. Nah, don't worry, they said, as if we were telling them he had a nut allergy. It was hot in there; kids fainted all the time.

We went in the ambulance with Jack, the sirens blazing, much to Jack's delight. I looked at Anna. I knew what was going through her head. Dr. Flanagan had said there was a 14 percent chance that the tumor would come back. I knew how her brain worked. Fourteen percent. With a reasonable margin of error, a little bad luck, that was 2 in 10, or 1 in 5.

She sat with one arm over Jack's blanketed legs, and I knew that she knew. I could see it in her dulled eyes, the way that she hung her head.

In the hospital, I was watching a Pokémon cartoon with Jack on his iPad when Dr. Flanagan walked in.

"Hello," Jack said, and smiled sweetly. We didn't expect her, didn't know she would be coming to this hospital in a different part of London.

"Hello, Jack," she said, smiling. "How are you? I hear you've been throwing yourself around on the stage."

Jack smiled and shyly looked down at the iPad.

"And how do you feel now, Jack?" the doctor asked.

Jack tapped his head and then his torso and legs. "Okay, no injuries. But I lost some of my Pokémon cards. They fell down on the floor."

"Don't worry, angel," Anna said. "I promise we'll find them."

Jack nodded, unconvinced.

"Excellent," Dr. Flanagan said. "Now, I want you to try to get some sleep, Jack. You're going to stay here tonight and then go home in the morning."

I felt a flush of relief, that perhaps it wasn't serious, just a minor complication from the operation. Dr. Flanagan looked at Jack's chart and then nodded at us, indicating she wanted a word outside.

She led us into an unoccupied waiting room. We all sat down at a table on some plastic chairs, and the harsh light made it feel like an interview room at a police station. The doctor took a sip of coffee and she seemed nervous, a state we had never seen her in before.

"So," she began, trying to look at both of us across the table. "From what we can tell, Jack has had another epileptic seizure." She paused, swallowed, and I noticed that her lips were dry. "I'm very sorry, but from the scan we've just done, it looks like there has been a recurrence of his tumor."

I didn't understand what she was saying. They had got it all. Dr. Flanagan told us repeatedly they had got it all. An 86 percent chance he was going to get better.

"Jack's... Jack's tumor?" I stammered. "But I thought you got all the tumor out. It was gone, you said it was gone."

Dr. Flanagan swallowed again, unsettled. Anna sat rigid in her chair, her hands clasped in front of her as if she was praying.

"We got out everything we could see," she said, "everything that could be seen on the scan, but I'm afraid in a small number of cases with astrocytoma, this does happen. There are microscopic tentacles that grow into the surrounding brain tissue..."

"And that's what Jack has?" I said.

Dr. Flanagan took a deep breath. "From its appearance on the MRI, it does now look like a glioblastoma."

We knew about glioblastoma. We saw the parents on *Hope's Place*. They posted for a few frenzied weeks and then never came back.

"But...but...it can be removed, right, as before?" I said. "There are treatments..."

Dr. Flanagan shook her head. "I'm so sorry. There is absolutely no easy way of telling you this. The MRI showed many, many tiny microscopic lesions all over Jack's brain."

I didn't understand. It didn't make any sense. He had been swimming, playing football every day. I looked at Anna, expecting, wanting her to say something, but she was silent, unmoving, her hands locked together.

"And it's not possible to take these lesions out?"

The doctor shook her head. "I'm afraid not. There are just too many. Even if we could take them out, given how aggressive the tumor is, they would just come back." She exhaled, rubbed her hands together as if she was applying hand cream. "I really am so very, very sorry."

I looked at Anna next to me. Her head was bowed, her hair draped over her face.

"And is there any treatment to...to...?"

"We need to talk about this, of course. But first we need to do some more tests."

Slowly Anna lifted her head up, her eyes glassy, her face gray and pale. Her voice was small but filled the silence of the room. Where I stammered, stumbled over my words, her enunciation was considered and clear. "And does this mean that Jack can't be cured?"

Dr. Flanagan held her gaze for a moment, calibrating her response. "I'm sorry, I just can't tell you that now. But I promise you we'll know more tomorrow."

We woke and listened to the sounds of the hospital waking up. The chatter from the nurses' station, the orderlies discussing last night's football. The tyranny of other people's lives.

We sat in chairs by the bed, without speaking, only interacting with Jack. The world existed, but it existed somewhere else. It felt like I was swimming underwater with only a vague impression of what was going on above the surface.

Knowing what we knew now, how could I even look Jack in the eye? To keep such a secret from him, as he sat in bed eating toast, expecting that tomorrow he would go back to school. How could we betray him like that?

"First of all," Dr. Flanagan said, as we walked into her office that morning, "no twenty-minute restrictions today. We will take as long as you need. Okay?"

We nodded as we took our seats, too scared to speak. "I spoke to the multidisciplinary team this morning. That's the radiologist, Dr. Kennety, another neurosurgeon, and we are all in agreement that an operation would not make any sense."

The doctor waited for us to speak, but we sat, silent, motionless. "What we were all agreed on is to start some chemotherapy, to see if we can shrink the tumor."

"And could this..." I said, trying to steady my voice. "Could this get rid of the tumors, I've read that sometimes..."

Dr. Flanagan waited for me to continue, but I couldn't finish my sentence. She leaned forward over her desk and looked at us both. "I'm so sorry, there really is no easy way to tell you this, but any treatment that Jack has will only be palliative. It will just be a matter of trying to prolong Jack's life."

Palliative, the word's horrors hidden behind the softness of its vowels. Hospice and rose gardens. Busybodies who brought in their dogs for the dying to pet. A place where old people spent their final days listening to Muzak and well-meaning lay preachers. Palliative: not a word for a child.

It was Anna who asked. I was glad that she did, because I could not.

"So how long?" she said. "How long does Jack have left?"

Dr. Flanagan took a deep breath. "It's impossible to say exactly," she said. "A typical time frame might be a year, with treatment. Perhaps less. Just so you know, we do have counseling services available if you're interested. But for now, as heartbreaking as it is to say, it might be best to focus on enjoying your time together."

Enjoying our time together. The implication that Jack was no longer infinite. A year. How could she say that? Had she seen him, just three days ago, kicking a football around in the backyard? Surely it was a mistake. They were just going on pictures, images on a scan.

"I really am so sorry," the doctor said. "I know parents hate to hear this, because they think it means that we're giving up, but now it's just about making Jack as comfortable as possible."

Comfortable, like an ailing aunt who desired no more than a good pair of bed socks and some chamber music on the radio.

"And is there anything experimental?" I asked. "Clinical trials, new drugs that we could try?" I could hear my voice tremble.

Dr. Flanagan made a note on her pad. "I have looked and will keep looking," she said. "But at the moment there doesn't seem to be anything that's appropriate for Jack. There is one, though, at the Marsden. It's actually for leukemia and melanoma, a phase 1 trial, but I think Jack might fit the genetic profile. I will check with them today and let you know, although I think there is only a very small chance they would take him."

"Thank you," I said, and there was something I wanted to ask, but I grappled with my words, trying to find the right way to say it. "I just don't understand why... I thought he was cured...you said...a 90 percent chance that he would be fine."

The doctor leaned forward again, and I thought for a moment she was going to grasp my hand. "I'm afraid Jack was one of the unlucky ones," she said. "What happened, his tumor transforming like that, is really very rare."

Rare. We had heard that word before. His tumor was rare. It was rare that he was diagnosed so young. And now it was rare that his tumor would mutate and become malignant. Did they tell us all that to soften the blow? As if it was a freak accident, something that was beyond our control.

We took a taxi back from Harley Street to the hospital. After seeing our stony faces, how our bodies were angled away from each other, the taxi driver was silent on the way back to Hampstead. We listened to the click-clack of the blinker, the rain beating down on the roof of the car. I took out my phone and started to search for the clinical trial the doctor had mentioned, struggling to keep the screen straight as we went over bumps in the road.

I turned to Anna when we were stuck in traffic. "I've been researching that Marsden trial," I said, "the one that Dr. Flanagan recommended."

Anna looked at me but didn't say anything, her face a ghostly white.

"From what I read, it seems like it might be something worth trying."

"She said it was for kids with leukemia and melanoma." Anna's voice sounded robotic, without emotion.

"Right, but it's also Jack's genetic profile."

Anna turned away to look out of the window again. I saw the taxi driver staring at us in the mirror and then quickly look away.

"It's as if we were listening to different conversations," Anna said, still looking out of the window.

"What do you mean? This was something she recommended. That's what she said."

"It wasn't something she recommended," Anna said. "It's something she said she would ask about. She said there was a very small chance they would take him."

I saw the taxi driver's eyes flicker toward us in his mirror. He reminded me of my dad, the way he used to recline his car seat as far back as it would go. His drinks lined up, his little TV wedged into the dashboard.

I thought back to what Dr. Flanagan said about the trial, but it was just a blur. "So you don't think we should do it?"

"I'm not saying that, Rob." Anna paused, her eyes dipping down toward her lap. "Let's just wait for what the doctor says."

I nodded, and we did not speak for the rest of the journey. It was as if we were magnets of the same polarity, repelling, pushing each other apart.

The taxi driver was solemn when he dropped us off back at the hospital. I held out a twenty to pay him, but he shook his head. "This one's on me, mate," he said, and I could see tears in his eyes.

Sometimes love comes from the strangest places. People don't realize how much they can break your heart.

Later that day, we took Jack home. We tried not to be solemn, so we put our faces on, we playacted, stopped for ice cream on the way home.

We all stayed up late watching television. As a special treat, we said he could watch anything for as long as he wanted. We made him special cheese on toast, fed him chocolate and more ice cream. What else could we do?

After Jack finally fell asleep and we carried him up to bed, I opened a bottle of wine and started Googling. There had to be something out there: a caveat to the survival rates, a new treatment, a clarification on something we may have misunderstood. I found studies, forum posts, discussions on Yahoo Answers and Quora, but it was of little use.

What was I looking for anyway? A reprieve? A different prognosis? An academic paper in the ghettos of the internet that would tell me the doctor was wrong, that Jack had a chance, that my beautiful boy would live?

Can anyone help us?
by Rob» Thu Nov 6, 2014 9:20 pm

Hello, everyone, I posted on Hope's Place a few months ago, after our five-year-old son was diagnosed with PXA. He subsequently had a resection and was doing well. We have just received the devastating news that his tumor has come back and is now glioblastoma multiforme.

We met with his neurosurgeon today and she said that a cure is out of the question and all they can do is give Jack palliative chemotherapy. We asked the doctor how long Jack has left and she said probably a year at the most.

We just don't understand what is happening. Jack still seems in such good health. Are there really no other options?

The doctor said there was possibly a clinical trial and is looking into that. (We're based in the UK but can go anywhere.) Does anyone know about anything else on the horizon for glioblastoma multiforme? Or does anyone have any experience with new or even alternative treatments?

Any information would be very much appreciated. We are devastated and desperate and just don't know what to do.
Rob

I looked around on my desk and found Jack's imaging report and started to search some of the medical terminology on the forum. An old thread from 2012 came up about a clinical trial and, as I read down the page, I felt a flush of excitement, exhilaration. It was a wonder drug, vaunted in the press, for children who had exhausted all other options.

I clicked on a user profile of someone whose son had taken part in the trial. Her last visit to the forum was 2012. Her signature at the end of each post read:

Clinical trial Oct '12, Damon joined the angels 23/12/2012

I clicked on a few more profiles. None of the posters on the thread had visited the forum since late 2012. Their children were all gone.

14

There was a moment when I woke. A second, a millisecond, or perhaps less. In that fuggy world between worlds, it was just another morning, of sunshine and school, of late breakfasts and happy squabbles. And then I remembered and I wished I could go back, to wake once again, because even that miniscule fraction of a second, that half breath, that flicker of the eye, felt like paradise.

Anna was still asleep, her breathing deep and regular, so I reached for my phone and opened *Hope's Place*.

Re: Can anyone help us?
by SRCcaregiver» Fri Nov 7, 2014 1:20 am

Hello Rob so sorry to hear about your situation. My daughter had a similar diagnosis and it hit her very hard. Hers spread so quickly that hospice was the only response in the end. Cancer is a terrible disease ill be praying for you...

Re: Can anyone help us?
by Camilla» Fri Nov 7, 2014 1:58 am

I am very sorry to hear about Jack's diagnosis. You are very welcome here and will find lots of support. We never know when or where the finish line is, so please just love the journey.

Re: Can anyone help us?
by LightAboveUs» Fri Nov 7, 2014 7:30 am

Holding you in prayers Rob. You might not like to hear this right now but you have to focus on the time you have left. Cancer really can be a gift. It has allowed me to appreciate what is important in life and taught my family how to live. My daughter lived for much longer than anyone thought possible and she made the most of her time. I will be praying for you on your journey. Much love.

Was that it? The consensus? That we were to enjoy the time that we had left with Jack? That we were to celebrate every sunrise, every dew-dappled morning? Because Jack was a "survivor" now, on a "journey." Oh, how I had already come to hate those words.

It was evening, Jack had gone to bed, and Anna was reading in the living room, her legs over one arm of the chair, a glass of wine in her hand. I watched her as she read. There was a small mole on the side of her cheek, which she'd had since she was a girl. A hair was now growing in its center. At first I thought she hadn't noticed, that she had simply been preoccupied with everything, but the hair had now started to curl, growing to the length of a fingertip.

If, before, you had said to me: imagine yourself in this situation. How would you react? How would you spend each day when you have been told your child is going to die? I didn't know what I would have said. Perhaps I would have imagined long evenings of tears, of beating our fists on our chests, of begging, cursing God on our knees, and praying, praying, praying for a miracle.

It wasn't like that. It was the mundanity of it all that crushed me. The way that things that once glittered were now rotten, steeped in tarry grief. I could not watch Jack pushing his fish fingers around on his plate or see him mouthing along to *Peppa Pig* without feeling an inordinate sense of loss.

It was the little things, always the little things. Seeing food in the freezer that I had made when Jack was healthy. My antivirus program asking if it should run a full-system scan, because who cared if I had a computer virus now. Sullen old people in the street, scowling as they lugged their tartan grandma carts up the hill. Did they not realize what they had? The luxury of old age.

Anna had taken leave from work and Jack was off school, and we waited on him, played board games, made endless rounds of cheese on toast. Surely, surely, there was more than this? Fish fingers and *Peppa Pig. Shark in the Park.* Marathon sessions of Guess Who and Hungry Hippos. Shouldn't we be doing something, anything, not this?

As I opened the laptop, there were some tabs open in the browser, one of them a Google results page. The string was still in the search box: "How do you tell a six-year-old he is dying."

I read it out loud, almost without thinking, and Anna glanced up from her book, a puzzled look on her face.

"Your search."

"Right," she said.

"So is that what you think we should do?" I said softly. "Tell him he's dying."

"I don't know, Rob, that's why I was Googling it."

I tapped my fingers on the arm of the sofa. Could she not even discuss it with me? Sometimes she was so infuriatingly straightforward about everything. "I don't think we should tell him anything," I said, "especially when we don't know anything for certain. There are still options. We can't just give up on him."

"We're not giving up on him, Rob," Anna said, turning her

body away from me. "But we have to face reality. And you keep talking about options, but what options are there?"

"Well, there are cancer clinics all around the world, places I've been reading about. And then there's the trial Dr. Flanagan mentioned..."

"Please, please, don't start on about the Marsden trial again. We've spoken about it, and I don't know what else to tell you."

"I wasn't going to actually, Anna," I said, my face and neck prickling with heat. "What I'm saying, if you'd just listen to me, is that I still think there are options out there. I think we've only really scratched the surface with the doctors we've seen. There are other kids out there who've had what Jack has and have been cured..."

"Don't say that word," Anna said, looking at me angrily. Her eyes were dark, opaque. "There is no cure, Rob, there is no chance of a cure, not in cases like this. You don't think I've been researching this, as well? I've also read about the new drugs, and the trials, and at the moment there is nothing—nothing, Rob—to suggest that any of this would work for Jack."

A deep crimson flush spread across Anna's cheeks. She turned sharply toward me, nearly spilling the wine in her glass.

"And before you interrupt me again and tell me I don't know what I'm talking about, that's not just me saying that. It's the doctors, Rob. And before you accuse me of not caring, or 'giving up,' I'm happy to go for a third and a fourth and a fifth opinion if that's what you want, but they're going to tell us exactly the same thing."

"But we can't know that."

"We can't know that? Well, we can't know anything can we, Rob? Dr. Kennety, Dr. Flanagan, they're two of the leading specialists in the world on pediatric brain tumors, and they have both told us the same thing. God, Rob, Jack isn't something you can program. He's not a machine you can hack. You can't just waltz through this like you do with everything else..."

"Why are you even bringing that up? It's not about that..."

"Yes, it's not, it's about Jack. It's about Jack's quality of life now. It's about making sure he doesn't suffer on some trial that has almost zero chance of working. Just so we can make ourselves feel better, that we did something."

Anna saw the rage on my face and stopped and took a deep breath. "Sorry, that wasn't fair. I didn't want to imply that you would do anything to hurt Jack. I just don't see any other way. There's nothing they can do, Rob. It breaks my heart just as much as yours, but we have to listen to the doctors."

Listen to the doctors. Anna always had an inordinate amount of respect for the professions. The doctors, lawyers, teachers of the world—the type of person you would ask to countersign a passport photo. Because in those people, she saw herself. Hard work, prudence, judiciousness. There was, she thought, a nobility to these professions, and to question them was unthinkable. Where I grew up in Romford, those people were often the enemy. They didn't get a free pass.

"I'm sorry," she said, touching my arm. "I don't want to argue. I just think that all we can really do is enjoy our time together."

"Enjoy," I said, cutting her off. "How are we going to enjoy any of this? We're just sitting around, doing fucking nothing."

The muscles in Anna's neck stiffened, and she put her wine on the side table. The glass rocked slightly on the mat. She picked up her book and left without saying a word.

I went to check on Jack, and he was sound asleep. I tucked the covers under his body, cocooning him, and put Little Teddy in the crook of his arm.

In our bedroom, I could hear the faint sound of water running, of Anna in the shower, so I went downstairs and poured myself a whiskey and stewed at my desk.

I logged in to *Hope's Place*—now an almost hourly ritual—and there was a new thread at the top, already with pages and pages of posts. The son of one of the forum members had died and they were honoring him, replacing their profile pictures with his, a little boy, his face lopsided, as if he had suffered a stroke. He was courageous, they said, a warrior. Heaven had gained an angel.

I couldn't read any more. They were just wasting time, with their sunset photos, their Thankful Thursdays and Welcoming Wednesdays, their ruminations about "gratitude" and "mindfulness." Because all their talk of being "brave" and "blessed" was a delusion, a ruse, which sugarcoated the unpalatable truth that their children were dying and they were doing nothing to save their lives.

Then I remembered Nev. What was the name of his son again? I pulled up my email and found his note from a few months ago. Josh, that was it. His son had had glioblastoma and been treated at the clinic in Prague.

I read Nev's email again and started researching the clinic and the doctor he had recommended. Dr. Sladkovsky's website was sleek, easy to navigate, and I began reading about the clinic's patented immuno-engineering treatment. Patients had their blood drawn and their T-cells reengineered with a vaccine. The blood was then injected back into their bodies. It was, according to Dr. Sladkovsky, beautifully simple. Just a case of enhancing the body's natural immune system rather than destroying it with chemotherapy.

I started to watch video testimonies of patients who were treated at the clinic. Kirsty, twenty-three, had pancreatic cancer. They filmed her soon after she arrived. She looked hollow, her head wrapped in a scarf, a scaly red rash covering her neck and face.

The voice of a solemn narrator said that under the standard of care for stage IV pancreatic cancer, she would die within six months.

And then we saw Kirsty again, now with a short crop of blond hair, sitting up in bed and talking to her father on Skype. She had good news, she said, her voice cracking, her eyes filling with tears. "It's working," she said, swallowing her sobs, "it's working, Dad." Then, Kirsty again, a few years later, whizzing around with a toddler on a roundabout, her husband in the background cradling a newborn infant.

I watched another, the mother of a boy, Ash, who had an advanced brain tumor. An American, she was filmed in her living room. The lighting was pale, and it was like a front room from the 1950s, pristine but unlived in, and I thought that the boy must have died. But then the filters changed, and it was as if Ash's mother had been made over, like the before and after shots in a trashy weekly mag. And there was Ash, gorgeous little Ash, running around, looking older, healthier, not knowing or caring why he was being filmed because there were trees to climb and creeks to jump.

It was too good to be true. There would be a catch, a caveat, something that wasn't obvious at first.

Subject: Re: Jack
Sent: Tue Nov 11, 2014 8:33 am
From: Rob
To: Nev

Dear Nev,
I don't know if you'll remember me but we were briefly in touch a couple of months ago.

I'm afraid we've had some bad news. Last time I wrote to you, Jack was doing well after his operation. Unfortunately, his tumor has come back in a more aggressive form. Jack now has a glioblastoma with additional seedling tumors throughout his brain. The doctors have said there is nothing they can do.

I have been reading about Dr. Sladkovsky's clinic in Prague and I wondered if you could give me more information.

Also, and I hope you don't mind, but can I ask exactly what treatments Josh had? Not just at Dr. Sladkovsky's clinic but everything. And to be clear: Josh had grade 3 glioblastoma multiforme, right?

I hope that's not being too intrusive. As I said, I have read your blog detailing Josh's treatments but I want to be 100 percent sure I understand correctly.

Sorry to be writing to you out of the blue like this. I hope you understand.

Best Wishes,

Rob

BOX HILL

———

mommy was away for the weekend with work so we took a day trip, out of london and into the countryside. it was amazing that day, jack, blazing hot, and we drove up the windy road to the top of box hill and then sat at the lookout point and ate sandwiches and jaffa cakes. i remember how you liked to nibble the chocolate, jack, and then scrape the jelly off with your teeth, just like daddy showed you. chocco first then jelly. chocco first then jelly.

15

We could only ignore the phone calls, the emails, the Facebook messages for so long. The people who just wanted to check in because they had heard Jack had been taken ill. The friends who offered to pop around, just for five minutes, to catch up on our news.

Anna suggested sending another email to all of our friends. That way, she said, they would leave us alone. I shrugged, said that I didn't care either way.

The replies came quickly, filling up our in-boxes. They couldn't believe it, they said. They were crying, shaking, couldn't think about anything else. Why was this happening to us, they asked, why oh why? And was there anything they could do? Could they bring us food, help clean the house, anything really, anything, because they just felt so helpless.

And how was Jack? How was he taking it all? Such a terrible thing to happen to a little boy, because they knew how much we treasured him. They knew because they knew how much their own children meant to them. God, they couldn't even begin to contemplate what we were going through right now.

Then I saw the status updates on Facebook. Friends, friends of friends, people we didn't even know so well.

Just received some very sad news...

Devastated, blown away...

Sometimes you get reminders that life is so terribly short. Never forget to hold on to what you have.

I counted: Jack, by proxy, was the recipient of 126 likes. Just as I was thinking how to respond, the posts in my feed were no longer about Jack.

RIP David Frost.

So sad right now: RIP Sir David.

Crying now this man was a genius. RIP.

Within minutes, Jack was forgotten. Gutted, they said, absolutely gutted. Because *Frost/Nixon* had always been their favorite movie. Because they don't make journalists like that anymore, a true gent, integrity to the core, better than Murdoch and his phone-tapping hacks.

"Too soon," they all wrote. Too soon. Those two little words bounced around in my head. Too soon. He was seventy-four. He'd had his three score and ten. David Frost had probably spent more time on the toilet than my son had been alive. Too fucking soon?

Subject: Treatment
Sent: Tue Nov 11, 2014 10:59 pm
From: Nev
To: Rob

Hi Rob, really sorry to hear your news. I know what a terrible time it is and how there's nothing anyone can do to make it better.

Right, so down to practical matters. As for Josh's treatments, he was diagnosed over three years ago and, yes, with grade 3 glioblastoma multiforme. He had his tumor resected at the Royal Preston Hospital in 2009. After that he had Gamma Knife radiation therapy for a few microscopic nodules.

We were told shortly after that that there was nothing they could do and all that was left was palliative care. That was when I started looking into Dr. Sladkovsky's clinic. It's expensive but it saved my son's life. Please don't hesitate if you need any more details. Happy to talk by email or on the phone (01632 532676) any time you like.

Take care,

Nev

My phone rang and it was Scott.

"Hi, Rob." His tone was formal, awkward, his phone voice.

"Hey," I said, and for a moment he didn't speak, and I could hear what sounded like a café or bar in the background.

"I'm so sorry to hear the terrible news."

"Thanks."

Another pause, the faint sound of him chewing gum. "Please let me know if there's anything I can do," he said.

I didn't reply. Anything I can do. I had heard that phrase a lot in the last hour.

"You should have said, mate," Scott said, his tone less formal, old friends chatting in the pub. "You should have told me, maybe there was something I could have...you know. It was just the group email was such a surprise... I thought everything was..."

"Are you unhappy about the way we told you, Scott, with the email?"

"No, no," he said, stumbling over his words. "I didn't mean it like that..."

"Should I have come around and told you personally? Would that have been better for you?"

"No, mate, sorry, that's not what I meant. Please don't be like that. I just wanted to let you know that you can call anytime, or we can grab a beer or something, talk about stuff."

Talk things through. As if we were discussing Scott's latest failed relationship, or West Ham's struggles in midfield. He started to say something about a doctor he knew, someone who owed him a favor, but I hung up the phone.

Subject: Re: Jack
Sent: Thu Nov 13, 2014 8:33 am
From: Rob
To: Nev

Dear Nev,
Thanks very much for your information about Josh. To be honest, I was a bit skeptical at first about Dr. Sladkovsky's clinic. I've read lots of criticism on Hope's Place, so it's very interesting and encouraging to hear your story.

We are rapidly running out of options. Yesterday, the doctor told us that Jack hadn't been accepted on the clinical trial at the Marsden. Now they're saying that chemo is all that's left and that will only slow things down at best.

I would take his place in a heartbeat, if I could. I would give him my brain, everything, if I could. I just don't know what he has done to deserve this.

I'm very sorry for telling you all of this, Nev, as I know we don't know each other. As you've gone through all this before, I just thought you'd understand.
Take care,
Rob

Subject: Re: Jack
Sent: Fri Nov 14, 2014 10:42 am
From: Nev
To: Rob

Dear Rob,
Your little boy did nothing to deserve this and don't you ever forget that. I did the same when my Josh was diagnosed, constantly asking myself why. Why Josh? What did he do? What did I do? Was there something that could have prevented it? Was it because we lived near that cell phone tower? Was it all the chemicals they put in that baby food?

I do understand what you're going through though because I went through the same. I constantly thought about a world without Josh and it just destroyed me. I suppose that was what pushed me toward the clinic in Prague. Nothing the doctors said here made any sense anymore and I just felt like we were wasting time.

I'm so sorry about all this. Please always know that you can talk to me about this stuff any time. I'm only an email or a phone call away.
Take care my friend.
Nev

PS I'm attaching some pictures of Josh so you can get an idea of what the treatment involves. They're from when he was diagnosed and go right up to now. (There's more of them on my blog, nevbarnes.wordpress.com)

I started clicking through the photos. Josh's first chemo. Josh, now completely bald, coming out of an MRI. Josh sitting up in bed, a cannula in his arm, with Dr. Sladkovsky standing next to him.

There was one photo in particular that I couldn't stop looking at. It was of Josh sitting on a rock on a beach somewhere. His face was fuller, his hair now long, curly and blond. He was squinting, the sun in his eyes, at his feet flippers and a snorkeling mask. He looked so different to the sick, gaunt little boy from before. Josh was older. He had aged. He was alive.

A new batch of pills had arrived. Vacuum-packed, in boxes covered with space foil. They were Chinese imports, delivered in twenty-four hours from a Swiss company I found online. Hydrazine sulphate, Indian frankincense, resveratrol, zinc, an acne drug called Accutance, which recharged the immune system.

Every day I was researching, staying up late with coffee and whiskey, reading anything I could get my hands on. The information was out there, but it was hidden behind all the noise, the chatter on patient forums, the dietary advice, all the guff about butter beans and the guyabano fruit. It was there, though, if you knew where to look, on the stock-market newsletters, the oncology forums, the clinical-trial databases, which could easily be hacked.

I learned quickly. It was like becoming fluent in a new programming language. I understood now how to read between the lines of drug companies' press releases. I understood that what worked in mice didn't necessarily work in humans. I understood that even if Jack was denied entry to a trial, there were still options: getting medication on compassionate grounds; clinics in China that cloned leading trial drugs and offered bespoke services for clients who could pay.

Because there were children who survived what Jack had. You had to dig deeper, follow leads, links, obscure blogs. But it was all there: hyperbaric oxygen chambers, proton therapy radiation, a surgery called devascularization, which was only performed in Barbados.

They called these patients anomalies. The ones who got better, that defied the odds. The doctors talked of them as if they were a phenomenon, in the realm of the supernatural, an occurrence that was beyond the understanding of medical science.

But the truth was that the doctors just didn't know why some patients got better. One day, when the genome had been decoded and unraveled, it would all make sense. It would be as self-evident as gravity or the laws of motion.

Some things could always be hacked. In computing, if there was a problem, you build around it. You code it out, program a cheat. But to do that, you had to take a chance. I remembered at school when they locked me out of the computer room. They said I wasn't spending my lunch hours appropriately, not using the computers for their designated purpose. So I hacked the system from home, made myself an administrator, and moved like a ghost through the school's network.

Anna never really understood that part of me. She thought I was reckless, a risk-taker, even about the littlest things. For refusing to pay for travel insurance on a flight. For insisting on carrying around large wads of cash. For her, there was always protocol, a proper way of doing things. Anna's rules. Always arrive early. Always eat a small dinner. Always fold your clothes before bed.

Now I was being reckless because I wanted to save my son. *Listen to the doctors. Follow the "standard of care."* But none of that would work for Jack. If we followed the doctors' advice, Jack wouldn't stand a chance.

It felt like returning to the scene of the crime—to be walking through the gates of Amberly Primary, this time for the Christmas Fair. How different it was to the fireworks night. Then, Jack had bounded through the front doors, greeting his friends, showing us his artwork on the walls.

Today, he was withdrawn and frail. He kept close to us, and I could no longer pretend he wasn't ill. He moved slowly, with careful considered steps; his lips were blue, his face pale, like a boy with a weak heart I remembered from school. People stared at him and then quickly looked away.

As we waited for Anna to buy entrance tickets, I fussed over Jack's coat, trying to avoid eye contact with people passing by. It was strange to be out in public. It had been a month since Jack collapsed on the stage at school, and we had mostly cut ourselves off from the world, politely declining the careful and considered offers from friends. Anna was now just working mornings, so in the afternoons, if Jack was feeling up to it, we went out: to the cinema, the dinosaur park, the traveling pirate road show. Our life felt like it was on the most monstrous kind of hold.

Chemotherapy provided a new rhythm. Jack went to the hospital once a week as an outpatient and then spent the next few days recovering at home. There was a small amount of a comfort in that routine. It gave us something to prepare for, something to do. We could buy the little cartons of orange juice that he liked, or the soft candy that, sometimes, was the only thing he could stomach. We could launder and iron his Spider-Man bathrobe and make sure his hospital slippers were clean.

We both agreed it would be too much for Jack to go back to school. He said he didn't mind—he could do his reading and writing at home—but he missed his friends. There had been playdates at home, visits that were tightly supervised and controlled, as if Jack was a young prince, his servants and courtiers lurking in the background in case anything went awry. Even though I loved seeing Jack's joy at playing with his friends, I hated those visits. The awkward elliptical conversations we had with the parents, where we tried as much as possible to talk about them, about their lives. The unbearable gravity of those lingering goodbyes.

I looked at some pictures on the wall with Jack, a school project from room 1C, words stuck over interlocking rainbows. Jack traced the letters with his fingers and softly spelled out the word. *S H A R E*. Share.

Outside, the air was sweet with the earthy tang of roasting chestnuts and mulled wine. On the patch of grass where we had stood to watch the fireworks, there were now stalls selling bric-a-brac, a juggler and a ball toss where you could win a teddy bear. Children charged around from stall to stall, buoyed on sugar and the looming end of term.

Jack suddenly looked very scared and gripped tightly to Anna's hand. We walked across the playground and passed some parents from Jack's class, but they didn't say hello, their heads bowed, pretending they were on their phones. It didn't matter. I didn't want their pity, their sideways glances, the lengths to which they went to pretend that nothing was wrong.

We headed toward the tombola and the hot-chocolate stand. Jack walked with an old person's gait, carefully, as if he was on ice and he was scared to fall.

"Look, Jack," Anna said, pointing to two boys. "Isn't that Martin over there?"

Jack shrugged and tightened his grip on Anna's hand. "Do you want to go and say hello to him?" she said, as we walked past a stall selling handmade Christmas decorations.

Jack shook his head and looked away from where Martin was standing. Martin Catalan was the first friend at school that Jack had really adored. We were always amused when Jack said his name. It was never just Martin, but always Martin Catalan.

According to Jack, Martin Catalan could do everything. He could run faster, throw farther, jump higher than any human. At the age of just three, he could read, write and add up with numbers bigger than a million. He had read books—the biggest books in the whole world—and was so good at football, he already played for Spain.

I had seen Martin Catalan once at a school function, and there was definitely something about him. While the other children had their shirts untucked, their noses running, Martin Catalan was pristine: a crisp white shirt and cords, his slicked-back hair emphasizing his broad Musketeer's jaw.

"Why don't you go and say hello, Jack?" I said. "I'm sure Martin would love to see you."

Jack would normally correct me if I said Martin, insisting on the full Martin Catalan, but this time he didn't answer and just buried his face into Anna's coat.

A little later, while Anna was in line at the hot-chocolate stand, I lost sight of Jack. I had turned away for a moment to give Anna some change, and suddenly he was no longer there. I panicked, frantically looked around, until I saw him, a forlorn little figure standing under the floodlights, watching the children on the bouncy castle.

Jack stood, as still as a statue, taking it all in: the whoops of delight; the shoes haphazardly discarded on the tarpaulin; the bobbing heads above the bright yellow parapet, as the older boys pushed into each other, trying to collapse the castle's sides.

"Are you okay, beautiful?" I said, putting my arm around him as Anna arrived with the hot chocolate. "Do you want to go and sit down somewhere?" I asked, but he pulled away from me, and even in the dark I could see the glisten of tears in his eyes.

"I want to go home," Jack said, looking at the bouncy castle.

"But we just got here, Jack. I thought you wanted to see your friends."

"I don't have any friends. I want to go home."

"No, sweetheart, don't say that," Anna said. "You've got lots of friends."

Jack shook his head, defiant. "No, I don't have any friends. You're telling lies."

Just at that moment, Martin Catalan appeared beside us.

"Hello, Jack," he said and smiled, his clothes and hair immaculately groomed.

Jack turned around and saw Martin and his face lit up.

"Do you want to come on the bouncy castle with us?" Martin said.

Jack was beaming and quickly trying to wipe his tears away without Martin seeing. "Can I, Mommy?" he said, looking up at Anna.

"I don't know, Jack," she said, watching some older boys doing belly flops. "It's very rough on there, with all the big boys."

"It's okay," Martin said. "It's my brother. I will tell him he has to get off."

Without warning, Martin ran back to the bouncy castle and shouted something to the older boys. One of them, an older version of Martin, looked over toward us and then nodded and jumped down onto the mat. One by one, the other boys followed Martin's brother until they all stood in a line blocking the entrance.

"Is it okay now, Mrs. Coates?" Martin said, as he came running back. "We can go there on our own, and my brother will stand guard and not let anyone else on."

Jack looked up at Anna and then me.

"Okay," Anna said, and I knew that it petrified her, but we knew we had to let him go.

"And can Tony and Emil come, as well?" Martin said, and we hadn't noticed Jack's friends lurking behind us. "I promise we won't jump too high."

"Of course," I said, "but Jack, you be careful, all right?"

He nodded and they walked toward the bouncy castle, Martin's hand protectively around Jack's shoulders.

"I'm not so good at jumping anymore," we heard Jack telling Martin as we followed behind at a safe distance.

"That's okay," Martin said. "We can do little jumping... Look, watch this." He breathed heavily out of his mouth, making a little cloud of fog that hung in the air.

"Cool," Jack said, and he did the same, his breath glittering under the floodlights. "We're like dragons."

They joined Tony and Emil on the mat, and I couldn't hear what they were saying, but I imagined Jack was telling them about his tumor, tapping the side of his head and showing them his scars.

We had seen Jack and his friends on bouncy castles before. They would charge and dive, attempting somersaults and scissors kicks. This time they were all perfectly restrained. Martin Catalan chastely took Jack's hands, as if they were at a barn dance, and they began to gently bounce up and down. Tony and Emil did the same, resisting the urge to charge into the walls or leap over the sides.

Anna and I stood next to the boys' discarded shoes, drinking our hot chocolate and just for a second—like that moment on waking—I forgot why we were here. Because Jack was just like any other child enjoying the Christmas Fair. For a blissful moment, his world was not like an hourglass running out of sand.

After a while, the boys were starting to slow down and Martin's brother couldn't hold off the waiting children anymore. Martin, Tony and Emil helped Jack down onto the mat, fussing over him, helping him put on his shoes.

Before they parted ways, they hugged, formerly, as if they were consoling each other. The dignity of old men who had seen it all. Martin Catalan was the last to embrace Jack. They held each other for a little while, Jack leaning on Martin's shoulder, Martin's hand cupped protectively over the side of Jack's head, the side where his tumor was.

I printed off a few more articles about Dr. Sladkovsky and put them in the folder I was preparing for Anna. It was just the way she would like it: methodical, neatly bound together.

I read another interview with the doctor about what had driven his research when he was a young oncologist at a provincial Czechoslovakian hospital. It was the outliers that fascinated him the most, the patients whose responses defied explanations. The miracles. Why did they get better when others didn't? Study the outliers, Dr. Sladkovsky surmised, those rare cases of remission, and you might find a cure.

I read through more discussions about Dr. Sladkovsky and immuno-engineering on *Hope's Place*. There were more skeptics than believers. The treatments were unproven and offered no more guarantees than traditional chemotherapy. A snake pit, a money suck, they said.

But what about Josh? That was what I kept coming back to. If it worked for him, it could work for Jack. I remembered a comment that Dr. Flanagan had once made. She said that what doctors understood about cancer was just the tip of the iceberg. There was so much more they didn't know, she said.

She had meant it, I think, as a kind of salve, a way of telling us that Jack's disease was so fiendishly complex that there really was nothing we could do. But I took heart from what she said. What if Jack possessed a certain genetic mutation, one that was unexplored, uncharted by medical science? And what if that mutation enabled him to respond to certain treatments, just like Josh had?

I was normally the first to sneer at homeopathy and iridology and all that rubbish. I was a programmer. I lived by data and dreamed in code. I was always banging on to Anna about the dangers of bad science. But every time I told myself to forget it, that the Sladkovsky skeptics were probably right, that Nev was just some crank, I thought of those testimonials. I thought of Kirsty's and Ash's mother and James and Robson and the little girl called Marie who had a brain tumor at the age of eleven and was now going to the prom on her daddy's arm. These children were not a data point in a clinical trial, they were flesh and blood.

I checked online the flights to Prague. There were more than ten a day, and we could be door to door in about five hours. I was researching hotels near the clinic when my email pinged.

Subject: Re: Jack
Sent: Tue Dec 2, 2014 12:05 am
From: Nev
To: Rob

Hi Rob,
Got some great news from the hospital today. Another clean set of scans for Josh.

No signs of cancer and all tumor markers are at the lowest level since diagnosis. Of course, we do have to make sure he gets tested over the next few months and years, but every clean scan is another big step in the right direction.

We took him for his treat after the scans and went to see Star Wars in the cinema. (They're showing all the old ones in our local.) He absolutely loved it and it was so amazing to see him enjoy it like I did as a kid all those years ago.

I wondered whether I should tell you this as I know you're going through a hard time right now and didn't want to be insensitive or nothing. Anyway, mate, I'll sign off now.

There is hope, Rob. Never give up, my friend.
Nev

PS Jack's probably a bit young for Minecraft but Josh is really into it at the moment. He's just built this castle and said he wanted to send it to Jack to cheer him up. (I told him Jack was poorly.) I'm sending you a screenshot. Hope it comes through okay and Jack likes it.

I clicked on the Minecraft screenshot, an 8-bit block with turrets and a flagpole and a sign that said Jack's Castle. Looking at that castle made me cry, but not because I was thinking about Jack. It reminded me of when I started programming, writing little scripts on the old laptop my dad picked up from a garage sale.

I looked at the castle again. I could imagine Jack playing Minecraft when he was older, constructing houses, planting trees, climbing mountains that led to new worlds. Sometimes, I let myself daydream like that. The things I would do with Jack, when he was older, better. Saturday afternoons in the cinema, Jack in little jeans, trainers with wheels, carrying a vat of popcorn bigger than his head.

Oh, the things we would do together. Season tickets at West Ham. Dim sum on a Saturday morning on Gerrard Street. All those summer holidays, sitting at the bar together, as I teased him about all the pretty girls.

They weren't just fantasies. They were the things I had done with my own dad. The times he would come and watch me play football, and no matter the score, we would go afterward to The Crown for Coke and potato chips. The family TV nights, with fish 'n' chips on our laps: *Dallas* on Wednesdays, *Minder* on Thursdays. Memories were like cartilage: stubborn, tough to break.

A few months after Mom died, I was looking for a book in the Romford house. I thought I remembered seeing it downstairs, packed away in the sideboard in the living room. It was dusty inside, something that would have horrified my mother. I didn't find what I was looking for, but under some old trinkets, cookie tins full of buttons, I found some exercise books inside a plastic bag.

I pulled out the first one, and there were pages and pages of Dad's small, neat handwriting. I hesitated, not wanting to read something private, but then a sentence leaped out at me: "Cottee on fire. Goddard dire." I started to leaf through all the books, smiling as I realized what they were: Dad's match reports of every West Ham game he had ever been to.

Each entry was pristine, as if Dad had drafted them first on a rough piece of paper. They were short, but he wrote beautifully.

Jennings was stellar tonight. Paddon, on the other hand, was useless, like a trapped wasp, barely touched the ball.

Tommy Taylor up like a salmon; down, however, like a diving bell. Absolutely brilliant, though. Even got the West Stand on their feet.

I read on, into the late 1980s, the games I had been to with Dad. Beating Chelsea at home 5-3 after we'd been 3-2 down. Our glorious promotion in 1993. As I read on, I noticed that some of the entries had gold stars attached. Gold stars like you'd get in school. At first I thought it was the games we had won, but I knew we hadn't beaten Villa in 1995 because I was there. And then I realized what Dad had done. He had put a gold star for every game we ever went to together.

Was it really so much to ask for Jack to have the same? There had to be a way, there just had to be. Because if you dream it, it means it's true, my dad always said.

If you dream it, it means it's true.

★ ★ ★

I was lying on our bed upstairs and could hear Lola, her voice warbling up the stairs. I went down to the kitchen, and she was sitting with Anna on the bar stools drinking coffee.

"Hello, Rob," she said, "how are you?"

"Okay, thanks," I said, and she gave me her look of concern. A raised eyebrow, a gentle bite of her lip, that said, I know, I know.

"Lola is just showing me this Make-A-Wish foundation," Anna said, pointing to some brochures open on the table. "They do surprises and trips for kids who are ill."

"Right," I said, filling up the kettle. "I've heard of them."

Even though my back was turned, I knew Anna and Lola were looking at each other, gauging my mood.

"I wrote to them," Lola said, "and they sent me these." She was holding out another brochure.

"Look, there's this one," Lola said, flicking through the pages. "A day with Spider-Man," she said, as if she were talking to a child. "Jack would get to wear a costume and then meet the real Spider-Man, and then they all go into some kind of special playroom and bring in all the characters, the Green Goblin, The Flash, Aquaman."

"Right," I said.

"I think Jack would like that, don't you, Rob?" Anna said.

"They were very nice and accepted my application right away, and we can basically choose anything we want," Lola added. "Do you want to take a look?"

She pushed the brochure into my hands. On the front page, there was a child wearing a fireman's helmet. Underneath I could see that his head was bald and white, like a baby bird's. I flicked through the brochure, waiting for the kettle to boil.

"Look, there's this one, as well," Anna said, holding up another and pointing to a boy sitting in the cockpit of a plane. "He'd like this."

"Yes, maybe," I said.

Anna sighed softly and put the brochure on the countertop. "Well, there's lots of different things here. We don't have to decide now. Lola just thought it might be nice."

"I'll take a look later," I said, putting the brochure back on the kitchen table.

"I was just telling Anna," Lola said, "about a friend of John's at work. Well, their daughter has just been diagnosed with something similar to Jack, and I thought you might want to connect with them. I remember when my mother had breast cancer and, well, you try to say the right things, to be helpful, but I don't think you can ever really understand unless you're going through the same thing."

Lola waited for me to say something or nod my assent, but I was silent.

"It just seems to be everywhere now, doesn't it," she said, almost to herself, always unable to cope with silence. "I suppose that's the curse of modern life, the price we pay."

The boiling kettle reached a crescendo, and I heard the click of the button. "What do you mean, the price we pay?" I asked quietly.

"Oh, nothing, poppet, just me rambling."

"I just want to know what you mean," I said, my tone quiet but firm, and Anna put her head down, letting the steam from her coffee curl over her lip. "Do you think this is our fault then?"

"Oh, God, Rob, no, not at all. No, I didn't mean that in the slightest. Goodness, you haven't done anything, don't you ever think like that. No, what I'm trying to say—and as usual being a complete ninny about it—is it's us, our society, our modern way of life. It's the foods, the stress, the Wi-Fi, the pace of it all. No, goodness, poppet, it's not you, it's us, all of us, and it all adds up. Sometimes, I just think we need to slow down, take stock…"

I already knew everything Lola wanted to say. Because I had heard it before. It was always there, in person or in the emails they sent, like a malicious undertow at a picturesque beach. "And do you know why he got it?" they asked, their words stealthy, inadmissible.

"It's just one of those things," we said, or some other platitude, and they nodded sympathetically, but you could see in their eyes what they were thinking.

Because they knew. Oh, they knew. It was the Wi-Fi, the sugary drinks, those baby shampoos that were full of chemicals. They asked, not out of concern for Jack, but because they wanted to protect their own children. To make sure it could never happen to them. You could see them making a mental note to reduce Timothy's iPad time and finally write that letter to the school about the healthfulness of the lunch options.

"Fuck off, Lola," I said, staring at her right in the eye.

"Rob!" Anna said.

"What, you're just gonna let her spout all this shit, things I know for a fact you don't agree with? Or do you think it's our fault, as well?"

"I don't, Rob, of course I don't. That's not what Lola's saying. And please stop shouting."

"Please don't shout? I should be shouting a lot more, instead of talking about all…all this shit," I said, pointing at the brochures.

"Can you just stop? Can you please stop?" Anna said, raising her voice, an argument that in another time, another world, we never would have had in front of someone else.

"Can I stop? Stop what, Anna? Stop looking for ways to get my son better while we sit around choosing fucking day trips?"

"It's not about that, Rob," Anna said, starting to cry, "please don't do this, please don't." Lola put her arm around her and Anna buried her face into her shoulder.

I couldn't listen to her anymore. We were just wasting time, time we didn't have. I went back to my desk and wrote an email to Nev.

Subject: Re: Jack
Sent: Wed Dec 10, 2014 9:12 pm
From: Rob
To: Nev

Dear Nev,
Sorry to disturb you again but I wanted to ask about Dr. Sladkovsky's clinic.

I have already emailed them but do you know how quickly Jack could start treatment? Is there a long waiting list? I want to book flights right now and get out to Prague because we're just wasting time here.

I was so glad to hear that Josh's scan went well and I loved seeing the pictures of him that you sent. Not just because I'm happy for you, but because I wish so desperately that one day that could be Jack. I wish that could be Jack four years down the road, happy, loving life.

So please, keep sending them. More than anything right now, they give me hope.
Take care, Nev.
Rob

PS Please thank Josh for the Minecraft castle. I showed it to Jack and he absolutely loved it.

16

"Is he still sleeping?" Anna said, as I went outside onto the patio, holding my laptop under my arm.

"Like a baby."

It used to be our joke when Jack was small. How was he sleeping? Like a baby. Because he was a baby, you see.

Jack slept a lot, now that he was doing chemotherapy. When he was awake, he spent most of his time on the sofa, watching cartoons, surrounded by his favorite toys and books. When he slept, we watched *Poirot* and *Homes Under the Hammer*, always listening, waiting for Jack to wake.

Anna was cleaning the patio windows from the outside. The house had been spotless since Jack was diagnosed. A cleaner came once a week, but that wasn't enough, Anna said; she liked to do it herself. So every day, she scoured the bathroom and toilets. She cleaned under the sinks. She took on the oven, scraping off all the grime and then polishing it on the inside.

She kept her cleaning suppliers in a cupboard in the utility room. There was a box full of sponges and squeegees and microfiber cloths. On the top shelf, there were bottles of detergent, ammonia, white vinegar, all lined up as if they were in a trophy cabinet.

It was cold outside, even for December, and I was chilly in just a shirt. I took a deep breath and a large gulp of my coffee. "I've been looking into this clinic," I said to Anna.

I expected her to say something, to turn toward me, but she carried on rubbing the windows with a cloth.

"It's in the Czech Republic, run by this Dr. Sladkovsky." A twitch in Anna's face, a minuscule movement of her nose. I had the feeling that she was about to interrupt me, that I had to rush out my words.

"Look, I know how you feel about all of this, but please hear me out."

"Hear you out?"

"Well, yes, I know we feel differently about the treatment options."

Anna went back to her windows, targeting a spot close to the ground. "I'm not sure that's how I would characterize it," she said. "But I'm happy to listen. We make decisions together, right?"

"Right. Okay, it's this clinic in Prague—I printed some stuff out for you—that does this immuno-engineering treatment. I have researched it quite a bit, and it seems there is a good deal of science behind it. The thing is, so many children have got better at the clinic, even children with brain tumors. I've been emailing this guy Nev from the forum. His son, Josh, also had glioblastoma and was treated at Sladkovsky's. He's now three years in remission."

"Yes, Nev. I've seen his posts."

"You have?"

"Yes, on *Hope's Place*. I've seen his posts about Dr. Slad-kovsky."

"Oh. I didn't realize…"

Anna sighed. "I read the forum, as well, you know," she said.

"So what do you think then?"

"About the clinic?"

"Yes."

"I don't think much, really. I looked at the website a while back. I mean, it looks impressive with the testimonials and ev-erything. But then I read some opinions on the forum about it and some piece on this *Quackwatch* website. It said there was very little scientific evidence to back Dr. Sladkovsky's claims, and there was zero evidence that immuno-engineering worked."

I had read that long, snarky *Quackwatch* piece she was referring to, which rambled on about peer review and Dr. Sladkovsky's disregard for proper scientific method. I remembered being annoyed by the smugness and pedantry of the journalist, like one of those excruciating fanboys who picked plot holes in popular movies.

"I know, I know, I read that too. But maybe it will work. Maybe there is something in it. People—other children—do get better. I don't think these people are lying in these testimonials."

Anna shrugged, and the gesture infuriated me, like a stubborn child refusing to say sorry.

"Look, I just think it's worth a try," I said, my voice cracking. "What else can we do now?"

She looked at me disapprovingly—like Jackie Onassis in her big bug-eyed glasses.

"Do you not think that if I thought there was something in this that I would do it for Jack?"

"I know. I'm not saying that, I'm really not saying that…"

"And, regardless," Anna said, "what about the money? It's obscene to talk about such a thing, but have you seen how much the treatment costs? Even if we wanted to, how on earth would we pay for it?"

"We'll find it," I said, "we'll scrape around. There's always money."

Anna sighed. "Where is this money, Rob? Where is it? I looked on the website, and the treatment can cost hundreds of thousands of pounds. I just don't understand how you think we can pay for that. Scott is selling the company, Rob, he's selling and I'm not working. So…so what? We won't have any money coming in."

"We'll find it. I can ask Scott for a loan."

"Jesus, Rob," Anna said, snatching up her cloth and bucket. "Scott doesn't have any money. He's practically bankrupt."

She walked back inside, and I followed her into the living room. "I'm sorry, I just can't do this," she said, sitting down on the sofa. "It makes me feel absolutely sick, like I just want to die, talking about the money. And if I thought the treatment would work, I would sell everything, the house, the car. Everything. I would beg, borrow and steal to get the money."

Anna began to sob, and I put my arm around her. She felt cold, gaunt beneath her woolen sweater. "I know," I said. "It's horrible—just horrible—to have to discuss it. But I'm sure we could find a way, even if there's just the tiniest chance that it would work…"

"Will you just shut up?" Anna shouted. "Did you actually read about the treatments at the clinic in Prague?" she said through gritted teeth, trying to keep her voice down so she wouldn't wake Jack. "Did your friend Nev tell you about that? Because you know what, Rob, I've actually read the whole damn forum, and I know there are plenty of parents who have gone to Sladkovsky's clinic and had entirely different experiences. Did you read their stories, as well? You should, because then you might start seeing Nev's claims in a different light."

"Nev's claims? So you think Nev is lying about his son getting better? Look," I said, thrusting the laptop under her nose. "This is an email from Nev. Read it. Three years in remission. Three years. Josh has just had another clean scan."

"Can you please stop being so aggressive?"

I took a deep breath, tried to calm down. "Sorry, I didn't mean to… I just want to show you how the treatment can work."

"We don't know if it worked."

"What does that even mean? He had the same tumor as Jack—glioblastoma multiforme—and it's gone. It's gone, Anna."

"Right. But how do we know it had anything to do with the clinic?" Anna said. "The science is just not there, Rob. They don't publish their results from their clinical trials. It's just people's testimonies."

"So you're a scientist now, Anna? A medical expert. Doctors don't always know everything, you know."

"Goodness, you're even starting to sound like Nev. If Nev is even real..."

"If he's even real? What the fuck is that supposed to mean?"

"I don't know, that's just what some people have said on *Hope's Place*. That maybe he's paid by the clinic or something to recruit patients. How can you be so sure he's who he says he is? He's just a username, Rob."

"Aha, I see. That all seems very elaborate. Quite the ruse."

Anna shrugged. "Stranger things have happened, I suppose. Preying on desperate parents. It makes sense to me."

"Look, look at this," I said, scrolling through Nev's emails until I found the pictures of Josh.

"What am I even supposed to be looking at?" she said, as I thrust the laptop under her nose.

"Nev's son Josh."

"I know, Rob, you told me before. He's always posting pictures of him on the forum."

I looked for a flicker of emotion in Anna's face, but there was none. People said Anna was cold, people who didn't know her. I remembered her bedroom at college and how sparse it was. There were no fluffy cushions or corkboards with collages of friends at teenage parties. There was just a desk and a chair, and some thin hardback books on the shelf. Her bedspread was plain, a dull green.

Did it all come from her father? She never talked about it, but I knew she felt abandoned. She wouldn't discuss his abrupt departure for Africa, the grandson he had never met. That's just what he does, she said, and left it at that.

"Look," I said, pulling up Nev's last email. I clicked on the image file and it was Josh's Minecraft creation. "It's this Minecraft game. Josh made it for Jack."

Anna looked at me in disbelief. "You're talking as if they know each other, Rob. As if they're friends. You don't even know this person."

"Just because I haven't met him in person doesn't mean that I don't know him."

Anna shook her head.

"I can call him now if you want," I said, raising my voice.

"Do whatever you like," Anna said.

We sat on the sofa, not touching, our bodies angled away from each other, and the house had never felt so quiet, so cold.

"What is happening to us?" I said. "We can't even have a normal conversation anymore."

"Our son's dying, that's what's happening to us," she said. Already, Anna's lexicon was different to mine. Whereas I struggled to say the word hospice—with its soft, beguiling hiss—Anna would use words like "terminal" or "dying."

"Right," I said, trying to not get angry. "I know it's horrible—it's the most horrible thing imaginable—but we're on the same side in this."

"On the same side?" Anna said. "You've barely spoken a word to me in days. It's like you can't even look at me anymore. You're obsessed, Rob, with this Nev guy, with this... this false hope that you're clinging to..."

Anna went back to cleaning the patio windows, trying to get rid of the smears. At that moment, the only thing I could think to do was to call Nev. It wasn't just for Anna, it was also for me. Yes, he wasn't asking for money—"only $25 to kick cancer to the curb!"—or asking me to sign up for his healing-the-holistic-way newsletter, but I still had my doubts. Little things that didn't add up. I had once asked Nev about his wife or partner, but he didn't answer. In another email, I asked him where he lived. Nothing.

There was something else that made me wary. Nev was very public with his support for Dr. Sladkovsky. He was active on the forums, but there was never a testimonial from him on Sladkovsky's website. A boy cured of glioblastoma, one of the most aggressive and devastating childhood cancers. Why wasn't Josh a poster child for Dr. Sladkovsky?

One night, to put my mind at rest, I did a little research. I wasn't going to fall for a scam, like some lonely groomed teen. I did a reverse image search on Google, but all the photos of Josh led back to Nev's photo album. I ran the photos through a little script I had written, to scrape and analyze the image's metadata, to see if it showed when and where the photos were taken, but there was nothing. No data. Nothing at all.

"Hello," I could hear a voice, a northern voice. "Nev speaking."

For a moment, I was speechless, surprised that anyone had answered, a lingering suspicion that perhaps Anna was right.

"Hello," the voice said again. "Can you hear me?"

"Yes, hello, Nev. It's Rob."

A pause.

"Hello, Rob, very nice to hear from you." I knew Nev was from the north because Josh had been treated at the Royal Preston Hospital, but I was surprised by the thickness of his accent. In the background I could hear what sounded like children playing.

"Hold on one second," Nev said. "Can you take your shoes off?" There was a muffled sound in the distance, a banging noise. "Sorry about that. Just come in from the park. So how are you, Rob? How are things going?"

"Not too bad," I said, and it was strange thing to say, an odd platitude. "Actually, Jack isn't doing very well, I'm afraid."

Another pause. The line sounded faint, as if we were calling long distance. "Well, all I can say is that I'll be thinking of you all. I can remember just how terrible that time was."

"Thanks." I struggled to find my words. "Look, the reason why I called. I was just speaking with my wife about the treatment at the Prague clinic..."

Anna looked angrily at me, shaking her head. She quickly stood up and walked out of the living room.

"She's reluctant, you see, has read bad things about the clinic."

Nev was silent.

"Are you still there?"

"Yes, I'm still here," Nev said, the warmth gone from his voice.

"I didn't mean to, you know..." I stumbled.

"No, no, it's fine," Nev said. "I know a lot of people feel that way. I understand. Look, Rob, I'm not a medical man, I'm an engineer by trade. I can't convince you that the clinic is right for your Jack. That's up to you. I would never ever try to convince or persuade you—or anyone—what to do. I can only tell you what happened to my son. That's all I can do."

The phone was quiet for a second, and in the background I could hear what sounded like children's cartoons.

"Thank you, I appreciate that. As you can understand, it's a difficult time."

I looked up and saw Jack slowly walking down the stairs, Anna holding his hand. He was a little unsteady on his feet and was clutching Little Teddy under his arm.

Looking at Jack, I didn't know what else to say to Nev. It all seemed ridiculous. Should I ask him if he was lying about his son's health, as Josh sat a few feet from him watching cartoons?

"I'm really sorry, Nev, but I'm going to have to go. Jack has just woken up."

"Of course, Rob, of course," Nev said, his voice warm once again. "It was nice to chat, Rob. And please, please, if ever you want to talk more—about anything—just give me a buzz."

"Thanks, Nev, I really appreciate that."

I waited for him to hang up, listening for the click, but it didn't come, and for a few seconds I listened to Nev breathe on the other end of the line. Just as I was about to put down the phone, I heard a child's voice in the background: "Daaa-deee, Daaa-deee," and then Nev shout, "Coming, sweetheart." I stayed on the line, listening to the muffled voices, the sound of things being moved around, until finally I hung up.

The silence was corrosive as I entered the bedroom. Anna was reading and didn't look at me when I got into bed. After the phone call with Nev, we hadn't spoken, avoided each other in the house.

"I'm sorry," I said. "I wasn't fair to you and I lost it a bit. I'm sorry, okay?"

Anna put her book down and smoothed the sheets with her hand. "I'm sorry too. I didn't handle it very well. I know you're trying to help Jack, I get that, but I just think…"

She stopped herself, not wanting to retread old ground, and then looked at me cautiously, almost like a child in trouble. "I feel ashamed even saying this, because it feels so selfish, but I feel like I'm losing you," she said.

I understood the shame. To think now about ourselves, about our relationship, seemed somehow grotesque.

"You're not," I said, turning to her and rubbing her leg. "Why do you say that?"

Anna shrugged. "We've just been so distant from one another. I'm not blaming you. I've been the same. I suppose it's inevitable."

"Yeah," I said, looking down at the patterns on the duvet, pulling on a small piece of thread.

"We used to talk about everything, didn't we?" Anna said. "Do you remember after we lost the babies and we would sit up late and talk about it? Till one or two in the morning. It was sad and horrible, but it felt good somehow to talk, because we suffered together and we understood each other. I felt I had so much to say. But now, with this, with Jack, I just can't, I can't find the words."

The room was dark, just the low glow of Anna's lamp. It felt like a hotel room, a room that wasn't ours.

"I know," I said. "I feel the same."

"I don't want to lose you," Anna said. "Because that's what happens when…" She stopped herself, found her words again. "And I don't want that to be us."

I knew what she had meant, what she stopped herself from saying. Because that's what happened to couples when their children die. We had seen it in the movies. Anna had read about it in her novels. We knew how it went with those wretched couples. Every time they looked at each other, every time they heard each other's voice, they would be reminded of what they had lost. The child that had once bound them together now ripped them apart.

Anna started to cry, and even though we had become experts in each other's tears, this time they were new, undiscovered, like nothing I had ever heard before, as if they came from another place, another age. Her tears just weren't hers anymore.

I pulled her toward me, and her face was dripping with tears and snot.

"It's my fault, I know it's my fault," she said, over and over again.

I held her tighter because I was worried she wanted to hurt herself, to pound her fist into her face. "It's not your fault, please don't say that. How on earth could any of this be your fault?"

And then as quickly as she had begun, Anna stopped crying. Her voice was insistent, strangely serene. "It is, I know it is."

"Sweetheart, how? What do you mean?"

Anna swallowed. "The miscarriages."

"Anna, no, don't think…"

"I couldn't hold on to them, and I can't hold on to Jack," she said. "It's my body. It rejected our babies, and now it's rejecting Jack."

"No, Anna, no," I said, starting to cry. "That's just not true, and you know it's not true. The two aren't connected, and you know that. Please don't do this to yourself."

There was nothing I could say or do. The horror of watching someone perform a clumsy and unanesthetized surgery on themselves. I could hold her frail body and let her tears and snot drip onto mine. I could pull her close to me, stroke her neck and back, but it would not be enough. It could never be enough.

"I love you," I said, and those words now felt bitter, laden with guilt.

"I love you too," she said, and we lay for a while in silence. I wanted to speak, to remove the wedge that had come between us, but I couldn't find the words, as if I was struck dumb before a crowd of people.

It was strange to hold her in my arms again. We hadn't touched each other for a long time. Once, all we wanted to do was touch. How quickly, back in Cambridge, I came to know her: every inch, every nook and fold of her body; every scent, every dimple and mole on her face and back.

Our compatibility never had to be learned; it was always just there, from the beginning. There were no learning curves or proficiency tests. It was our shared mother tongue.

We had managed to keep it over the years, that thrill of the touch. But then as quickly as it once came, it was now gone. We were strangers again, our bodies utilitarian, perfunctory, places to be lived in but not explored.

I knew why we did not, could not touch, why perhaps we had even began to repulse each other. Because it felt like a betrayal. A betrayal of Jack. Everything was now tainted. To experience joy, to experience anything he could not, felt like a stab in Jack's back.

That was why I reached under the duvet and started stroking Anna's legs, my hands gingerly moving around to her crotch. I was trying to get something back, something we had lost. I thought she would resist me, because now most certainly wasn't the time, but she didn't and instead angled herself toward me, slightly raising one leg, and I could feel her wetness on my fingers.

I kissed her and then shuffled down the bed, putting my head under the covers, like a child's game. I lifted up her nightie and then buried my head into her, feeling her flinch and buck, her legs thrusting and then wrapping around my head.

Subject: Re: Jack
Sent: Fri Dec 12, 2014 10:42 am
From: Rob
To: Nev

Dear Nev,
Thanks for your info regarding the clinic. I gave them a call and mentioned your name and they were very welcoming. They talked about some payment options and I think we'll be able to manage it, at least for the first few treatments.

I went ahead and booked flights to Prague for the three of us. I haven't told my wife yet. We have spoken about it repeatedly but she has made it clear that she won't allow Jack to be treated in Prague. I'm still trying to change her mind.

Time is running short. I can see it in Jack's eyes. It's like we're treading water, knowing that we're going to drown. I will keep you updated.

Rob

They did their best to make the chemo ward a happy place, especially before Christmas. There were multiple trees around the ward, professionally decorated, surrounded by stacks of donated presents. The nurses wore red noses and Christmas hats, and the cleaning and kitchen staff dressed as Santa's little elves.

I watched as the nurse tweaked a valve on Jack's cannula. He winced a little, but sat still. He was an expert at sitting still, now.

"Is Steven here, Daddy?"

"I don't think so, not today, beautiful."

"Oh," Jack said, "He's probably with his mommy and daddy."

"Yeah," I said, stroking Jack's hand. "Maybe he'll be here next time."

Steven had leukemia and often had his treatments at the same time. They quickly became friends, passing things from bed to bed, their toys and sticker books. They made silly noises and faces to each other when the nurses weren't around.

One afternoon, we got talking to Steven's parents and, when the boys were napping, went for a coffee in the hospital canteen. Knowing, I think, how ill Jack was, Steven's father was diplomatic and only told us bits and pieces about his son's diagnosis and treatment.

I knew, though. I knew. Steven was expected to make a full recovery. His treatment wasn't about extending life, about hustling for a few extra months. His leukemia was curable.

Quite why Steven's tumors were lying dormant, sinking back into the blood and plasma from where they came, while

Jack's spread, mushrooming through his brain, I didn't know. Was it in my and Anna's genes? A defect, a crack that went unnoticed in our own bodies, but in Jack's was a fatal flaw. A product of the two of us: a mutation born of our union. A flaw forged by us.

I was glad Steven wasn't here today because every time I saw him, I wished it were him. I wished they could swap places, so that it was Jack's cancer that was seen by the doctors as just a blip. And for that, I would accept the bargain. Gladly, in a beat of my heart, I would accept, no, welcome, beg, that Steven—kind, thoughtful Steven—be given the brain tumor instead.

The pump started once again and its rhythm reminded me of *Ivor the Engine*. Jack was quiet, watching cartoons on my laptop and sipping juice. I sat back in my chair and read the email on my phone. There was a new message from Nev.

Subject: Re: Jack
Sent: Sun Dec 14, 2014 8:17 am
From: Nev
To: Rob

Dear Rob,
I'll be blunt with you because I know you're running out of time. If I had listened to the doctors, my Josh wouldn't be here now. I think you're making a good decision about Prague. Yes, there are no guarantees, but at least you have a chance.

I don't want to push anyone and I respect that every parent makes their own choices. But sometimes, I have to speak up. How many of these lives could be saved? Every day it's like watching planes crashing. Planes full of children that don't have to die. I will not be a part of that.

Are you sure you can't persuade Anna about the clinic? If

you want I could talk to her. If that's an imposition, I apologize. I just want to help.

Nev

PS I'm sending a video of me and Josh that we did for Jack. I hope he likes it.

I clicked on the video and, there, sitting at the kitchen table were Nev and Josh, dressed up as Batman and Robin.

"Hello, Jack," they both said, waving into the camera. And then Nev, in that thick northern voice: "We know you've been feeling a little poorly, Jack, so we wanted to say, from us both, Batman and Robin, get well soon."

"Get well soon," Josh shouted, and his Robin mask slipped down and I saw his face, confident, alive, his school tie loosely slung around his neck.

"See you later, Jack," they both said in unison, Josh waving with one hand, pulling up his Robin mask with the other. Then Nev reached forward into the camera and the screen went blank.

"Hey, Jack," I said, "look at this." I held out my phone and started playing the video.

"Who is it?"

"It's Josh, you remember I told you about Josh. He did the picture of the castle for you."

"The boy who had the injuries like me?"

"Yes."

"And now he's better?"

"Yes," I said, putting my arm around him, careful not to nudge his cannula.

"Can we watch it again?"

Jack watched the video a few more times and then touched

my arm and looked at me. "Daddy, am I sleeping in my bed tonight?"

"Yes."

"At my house?"

"Yes, beautiful, in our house."

"Will Mommy be there?"

"Yes."

"And Daddy?"

"Yes."

"Everyone?"

"Everyone, Jack."

He was tired, his eyes beginning to droop, and in a few seconds he was asleep. I pulled the blanket up around his neck and watched the rise and fall of his breath. It still didn't make any sense. How could Jack be dying? There were mistakes being made, I was sure of it.

I looked at his hands, chastely resting on the tray-table. He seemed so indelible. His fingers, made of skin and bone, gripping onto the white plastic ridge of the tray. His slender legs and thighs, wedged into the soft fabric of the seat. If I leaned close, I could feel his breath on my neck. How could any of that not exist?

That night, after we got home from hospital, Jack was sick in his bed. I carried him, limp in my arms, to a chair, and then stripped down the sheets. He was shivering, his teeth beginning to chatter, so I wrapped him up in towels.

I looked at him, sitting in the chair. The whites of his eyes were no longer white. His skin had become pallid, like the skin of an old man. His hair was lank and limp. The chemotherapy was eating away at him, hollowing him out, like a body scoured with bleach. As he shivered, his little broken body convulsed, spewing out every ounce of himself, every last drop of moisture.

I lifted him out of the chair, put him back under the fresh

sheets, and he quickly fell asleep. I remembered a holiday to Cornwall, in a trailer with my parents. I was fourteen, and one night I went out with some local kids and came home drunk. I vomited in the bathroom and all over the kitchen floor. My mother was angry, gave me a whack, said this wasn't what she came on holiday for.

In the morning, shamefaced, Mom gave me another dressing-down. "You should thank your dad," she said, angrily doing the dishes, "he stayed up with you all night to make sure you were okay. He set his alarm to go off every fifteen minutes, so he didn't fall asleep."

After Anna came in to relieve me, I lay awake until my alarm went off in three hours' time. Jack was sleeping soundly and I watched him—happy that he had found some temporary relief.

His peace didn't last long. I could hear his stomach gurgle, and then the sound of him beginning to retch. I shook him awake, getting the bucket in place, and he vomited again and again, his body so weak and broken now, his stomach distended, his legs and hips so lean.

He was shaking now, his lips chapped and peeling, his eyes sunken into dark sockets, and he was still retching, but nothing would come out, just bile and foamy spit, and I held him in my arms, my beautiful, beautiful boy, and I could do nothing except empty bucket after bucket of sick.

As I was helping him lie down again, Jack leaned close to me, and I could smell the vomit on his breath. He looked me in the eye and said his words with such clarity that I knew that I would have to honor them.

"Dad, please, Dad. I don't want to be ill anymore."

It was the landline that broke the silence, a rare occurrence these days, and we listened as the ring echoed around the house.

Anna wiped her eyes and walked over to the hall table. "Hampstead 270-6296."

"Yes, that's me, yes, Anna Coates..."

I watched Anna listening, her face turning pale, ever so slightly moving her lips.

"Oh, God... Is she..."

Her face was now a ghostly white, and she put her hand on the sideboard to steady herself.

"Yes, of course...thanks for letting me know."

Anna put down the receiver, her face white and drawn. "It's my mother," she said without looking at me, staring out of the window. "She's had a heart attack."

"God, is she..."

"Yes, she's alive," Anna said quickly, her voice starting to quaver. "But it's touch and go, apparently, and it doesn't look good. The hospital thought it was best if I came."

"Which hospital is she in? I can drive you."

"She's up in Norwich."

"Norwich?"

"Yes, that was her friend Cynthia. She was visiting her and collapsed at the train station." Anna swayed a little on her feet and quickly sat down.

"Are you okay?"

"Yes, sorry. I just feel a little faint."

I went to the kitchen and brought her a glass of water. A little bit of color had come back to her face.

"You should go," I said.

She looked up at me, her brow heavy, tears in her eyes. "How can I go now?" she said.

"It will just be a day or two," I said. "I know it's the worst time, but you won't forgive yourself if you don't say...well, you know..."

"Say goodbye," Anna whispered, and I went over and took

her in my arms. I could feel her heart beating on my chest. I knew she had to go now, otherwise it would be too late. But that wasn't what I was thinking about as I stroked her hair. I was thinking about Jack.

THE SEVEN SISTERS

———

sitting in that café at the top of the seventh hill and you had got yourself cold because the weather had turned and mommy was getting worried, so we went inside, out of the wind and the rain, the spray from the gnarly sea, and we played rock-paper-scissors to warm up. you introduced dynamite, which beat everything, you said, and you just kept winning and winning and laughing so hard, your cheeks glowing red like the embers in the fire. we stayed there for a while that afternoon, happy in the cozy warm, drinking our hot chocolates with marshmallows on the side.

17

"Where are we going, Daddy?"

"We're going on holiday, beautiful."

"Is Mommy coming?"

"No, she can't."

"Why?"

"Because she's with Granny."

Jack was sitting in the entrance hall in his parka and hat, his *Finding Nemo* backpack looped over both shoulders. He was a little better now that his last weekly round of chemotherapy had left his system, and I had given him some strong painkillers. But he was still pale, his body emaciated and weak. He walked slowly and gripped tightly on to my hand, visible lumps of accumulated fluid now growing on the back of his head.

"We're not going to Granny's?"

"No, not now. Granny's not feeling very well."

Jack was quiet, thought about what I had said. "Are we going in the car?"

"Well, we're taking a taxi to the airport and then we're getting a plane."

"Really? Can we take photos from the window?"

"Of course we can."

"Cool," he said, beaming. "Where are we going?"

"We're going to Prague."

"Is Prague the beach?"

"No, it's a city, like London." The taxi beeped again outside, and I shuffled Jack out of the house.

Just before I closed the door, I put an envelope addressed to Anna on the hall table.

Jack loved the plane journey and didn't once look at his iPad or his books. He sat, his body angled away from me, with his nose glued to the window, looking out at the clouds, the spreading sky. We landed in the sunlight, the fields around us covered with snow. The airport was clean and bright, and we were efficiently swept through passport control, our bags already waiting for us. Outside, I braced myself for taxi bargaining, but there was a fleet of bright yellow cars and a dispatcher who spoke English.

"Did Mommy call?" Jack asked as the taxi pulled away from the terminal.

"She didn't. But remember, she's with Granny, and Granny's not feeling very well."

"Granny has injuries, like me?"

"Yes. Anyway, we're going to get your injuries better."

Jack didn't acknowledge what I had said. "When is Mommy coming?"

"She's not coming now, Jack. She has to be with her mom."

"Her mom?"

"Yes, Granny is Mommy's mom."

"Oh," Jack said.

The taxi sped through the tidy, suburban streets of the Prague outskirts. I had expected rows and rows of drab apartment buildings and graffiti-strewn bus shelters, my impression from a business trip to Katowice years ago, but at least this part of Prague looked like Austria, with large Cubist villas, expansive gardens, the flags of foreign embassies blowing in the wind.

The taxi driver was speaking on his phone, and I listened to him speak Czech. It was unlike any language I had heard before: there seemed to be an absence of vowels, but it was still soft, precise, as if you were being counseled. Jack was happily absorbed, looking out of the window, taking pictures of the snow.

We passed a small château and some shuttered food stands and there, nestled behind some trees, was Dr. Sladkovsky's clinic, a modern prefabricated building made with huge blue tiles and large square windows.

It was cold, about three degrees below freezing, but the sun was strong and the clinic sparkled like an upmarket spa. A few patients were sitting outside, reading books and magazines, wrapped up in coats and blankets. As we got closer to the entrance, I could see the garden, with a small pond glistening with ice and a winding path, which the website said was designed for barefoot walking.

Inside, the clinic was a warm fusion of glass and soft wood. There were green pod-like chairs and large soft rectangular sofas in the waiting room.

"Where are we, Daddy?" Jack said.

"We're here to see the doctor, Jack. The doctor who might be able to take some of your injuries away."

Jack pulled on my hand, and I could see a flash of fear in his eyes. "Daddy, they're not giving me the medicine, are they? The chemo medicine?"

"No, they're not, Jack. Don't worry."

I gave the receptionist my name, and we went to sit on two of the pod chairs. There was a waiting list at the clinic, but Nev was still on good terms with the receptionist and had managed to pull a few strings to get us fast-tracked. Through a glass door, I could see a café where some of the patients congregated. The patients were gaunt, but with their grooming, the expensive shawls thrown over their shoulders, they looked like they came from money.

"Like spaceship chairs," Jack said, his legs dangling from the pod.

"You look like a turtle," I said.

Jack smiled. "You're a turtle."

In the doctor's office, there were black leather couches, bookcases packed with medical tomes and antique surgical instruments. On the wall, embossed awards and certificates hung alongside pictures of the doctor. Sladkovsky on a hunting expedition; Sladkovsky shaking hands with various dignitaries; Sladkovsky hiking in the mountains, a floating ledge of cloud behind him.

When the doctor entered from a side door, he looked younger than I expected. His face had a healthy crimson hue, a mustache hiding the remnants of a hare lip, and he was wearing a tailored white coat, with his initials, Z.S., embroidered on the left breast. There was something vaguely plastic about his complexion, a waxy variegation of his skin, as if parts of his face were coated with TV makeup.

"Mr. Coates, how are you?" Dr. Sladkovsky heartily shook my hand, and his hand felt unusually dry.

"And you must be Jack. Hello, Jack." Jack smiled weakly and huddled closer to me on his chair.

"Do you like ball pits, Jack?"

Jack nervously nodded.

"Well, that's good. Because we have an amazing one out there. Do you want to go with Lenka? She might even give you some candies."

I looked up, and a tall blonde woman had appeared through

a side door. Lenka smiled and held out her hand, but Jack stayed in his seat, unsure whether to go.

"It's okay, Jack," I said. "Why don't you go and play with the nice lady?"

Jack cautiously slipped off his seat and put his hand in Lenka's.

"Thank you for coming, Mr. Coates," the doctor said, when Jack and Lenka left the room. I noticed for the first time his Slavic accent. There was something avuncular about it, like an elderly Polish watchmaker.

"We are so very glad to have you with us. Thanks for sending me everything. I've looked through Jack's notes and scans at length and, while his disease has progressed quite far and looks to be aggressive, I think it would be worth trying some treatments."

He smiled, and I noticed just how thin his top lip was when it wasn't hidden under his mustache.

"I assume you have an idea of our treatment here, Mr. Coates?"

"Yes," I said, "I've read a fair bit and Nev—his son, Josh, was treated here for a brain tumor—has told me a lot about it."

"Ah, yes, Josh. Such a nice little boy. Last I heard he was doing very well. They always send me his scans," Sladkovsky said. I noticed that he hissed on certain words, the remains of a lisp, studiously curtailed over the years. He scratched his chin and looked down at his papers.

"As I think you discussed with one of our practitioners on the phone, in Jack's case, we would offer you a complete course of immuno-engineering. We would also want to do more extensive genetic testing, to see what additional treatments he could be given. We have had some good results with patients like Jack."

"When you say good results, what do you mean? Could Jack be cured?" I said.

"Yes," he said quickly, holding my eyes with his. "Cured."

"You mean children with glioblastoma?"

"Yes."

"But high-grade glioblastoma, like Jack's."

"Yes, of course."

Dr. Sladkovsky looked at me, so intensely I thought he was going to grasp my hand across the table.

"Look, Mr. Coates, for all the time I do this job, I don't ever find these consultations easy. Your little boy, he is certainly very ill. I would say it breaks my heart, but no, because I don't let it. I try to keep the professional distance, but it's hard sometimes because I also have children." He clasped his hands together, and I noticed a large signet ring on his right hand.

"So if I will be honest with you. I have had children come to me with glioblastoma and survive. And I have had many who have not. I offer you no guarantees of a cure for Jack. It would not be ethical for me to do so. However, other oncologists will, how you say, write off their patients, but I won't do that. So all I can say—and please forgive me my English—is if you decide that Jack would undergo the treatment with us, then I could offer you no promise, but we could at least give you chance."

"Can I ask you something?" I said.

"Of course."

"Would you treat your own children with immuno-engineering? I mean, if they had cancer."

"Yes," he said. "In a beat of my heart. I would push them to the front of the line. They're my children, and I would do anything for them. Who wouldn't?"

Sladkovsky tapped his pen lightly on the desk. "Is it just you? Is Jack's mother here, as well?"

"Not yet. But she's coming. Her mother is very ill at the moment."

I felt a prickle of sweat on my back, imagining Anna coming home to find the note on the hall table.

"Okay. Please think on it. If you decide that Jack will undergo treatment with us, then we would like to start as soon as possible. Just so you know, this consultation is at no charge, should you choose not to stay with us…"

"Will it hurt?" I said suddenly.

Sladkovsky furrowed his brow. "The immuno-engineering, the treatments you mean?"

"Yes. Jack has gone through so much, the chemo, the recovery from the surgery. I don't want him to be in pain."

"Well," the doctor said. "I will be truthful with you. It affects people in different ways. Some patients have almost no side effects, and with children we often find that is true. But according to medical ethics, I must tell you that in perhaps 30 percent of our patients, they do experience side effects, some of them severe. Vomiting, sweating fevers, much of what you might see on chemotherapy. But I would add that we are very used to controlling these side effects. We have many, many new drugs. Was Jack scheduled for more chemotherapy in the UK?"

"Yes, next week."

"Believe me, it will be no worse than that."

The phone on Sladkovsky's desk rang. "Sorry, I will be one minute. I'm afraid I have to take this."

He picked up the receiver and, after saying a few words in Czech, pulled out a notepad on his desk. I watched as he listened, nodding, occasionally touching the end of his pen to his lips. I remembered someone on *Hope's Place* calling him Dr. Sleaze. They said he tried too hard with the smart suits and doctorly bow ties, his attempt at an English upper-class accent. But as I watched him now, writing down numbers on a blank page, professorial in his trim white coat, he radiated nothing but composure.

"So you have decided?"

"When can we start?"

Dr. Sladkovsky looked at me and scratched his chin. "I'm glad you would like to go ahead with the treatment, but we do have to take a few steps to check that Jack is eligible."

"Of course," I said.

"This is standard practice," he said. "Nothing to worry about. We are bound by European medical law to make sure that we are doing Jack no harm."

"Yes, of course, I understand."

I followed Dr. Sladkovsky out of the office and down a corridor until we reached an atrium with a glass ceiling where we found Jack throwing a ball back and forth with Lenka.

"Hello, Jack," the doctor said, but Jack didn't smile back and clung to my trouser leg.

"So I'd like to take Jack for his checks. Is there a suite free now, Lenka?" the doctor asked the receptionist.

"Of course," Lenka said, and smiled.

"Jack," she said, "do you want to come with me?"

"Am I having the medicine?" Jack asked.

Lenka paused, not knowing what to say.

"No, Jack," I said, putting my arm around him and guiding him out of the atrium. "Just a couple of tests. Nothing that will hurt, I promise."

"Okay," Jack said. "Is there a TV?"

"There is," Lenka said. "A big TV."

Lenka led us into a private room, and Jack lay down on the bed. A nurse came in and checked Jack's heart rate and then took some blood. I held his hand when they put the needle in, but he didn't even flinch. As we waited for the doctor, I remembered the checks we went through before Jack's operation in London. The questionnaires, the endless medical tests and pre-op assessments. There was nothing like that here. It was all so quick. Could they really gauge his fitness from a quick blood test?

After a little while, Dr. Sladkovsky came into the room and looked at Jack's charts and then asked to see me outside. I felt a familiar sense of dread, a shiver as I remembered sitting with Anna on fireworks night in that cold London waiting room.

"All good to continue," he said. "His vitals are excellent. He's a strong boy, and we think he would be an excellent candidate for immuno-engineering."

"Thank you," I said, and it was almost like he was telling me that Jack's cancer was gone.

"Good. We just need you to sign some paperwork," Sladkovsky said, as he led me down a corridor and into a busy office. "Our secretary will bring you the consent forms and all the payment information. I'll be doing my rounds now, but if you would like to chat about anything, any concerns you might have, please talk to Lenka and I can find the time later."

"Thank you," I said, and we shook hands.

I read through the papers, embossed with the clinic's logo. It was mostly paragraphs of legal jargon that highlighted various sections of the European Medical Code. If Anna were here, she would have been reading the small print, cross-checking paragraphs of the law.

It was too late now. This was the only chance Jack had. I signed the papers and filled in the payment information. It was expensive, but I had the credit cards and was in the process of emptying a savings account. There would be ways of finding the rest. We could remortgage the house or raid Anna's pension plan. We would find a way.

"Look at all the lasers, Jack," I said, after the nurse had come to take his blood. In the private room, where Jack would have his first infusion, there were white instruments, machines that looked like space cannons, but Jack wasn't looking at them. He was staring down into his lap.

"Daddy?"

"Yes."

"Am I having the medicine?"

"Well," I said, hesitating, "it's a different medicine. But it's going to help make you better."

Jack was silent, didn't look convinced.

I started showing Jack something on the iPad, when Dr. Sladkovsky came into the room. He walked over to a cart, shook out a pill from a bottle and put it in a small medicine cup.

"Now," he said, "we would like to give Jack a light sedative, if that's okay. But I do need your permission for that. It just makes the process more relaxing for the patient. Is that okay? It's extremely fast-acting."

"Of course," I said.

"Good. Jack, will you take this little pill?" the doctor said, holding out the cup and a glass of water.

"Okay," he said, expertly putting the pill on his tongue and swallowing with a quick sip.

"Wow, what a skillful boy," the doctor said, and Jack smiled proudly. "Now, we're going to start. You can be my helper if you want, Jack. Or you can be the doctor and I can be your helper. Would you like that?"

Jack shrugged and looked at me as if I had an answer. A nurse came in and they put a cannula into his arm. Jack stared at a calendar on the wall with beach scenes from Thailand. A woman wearing a long white dress looking out to sea.

I looked at my phone to see if Anna had called or texted, but there was nothing. Perhaps I should tell her now. Instead of her discovering the note on the hall table.

"Okay, Jack, that was the worst part. You won't even feel it going in now," Dr. Sladkovsky said, taking off his gloves.

"So," he said, turning to me. "First of all, we're going to do a little injection of the blood."

"This is the blood that has been engineered with the vaccine?" I said.

"Yes, that's right."

"From the blood that the nurse just took?"

"Yes, exactly. We don't want to keep pricking him, so we just use the blood we took when we did the readiness tests."

"It…it just…it all just seems so quick," I said, and I was sure that I had once read something about that on *Hope's Place*, about how quickly the clinic accepted patients.

Dr. Sladkovsky shrugged. "We treat over one hundred people a day. It's very normal for us."

A nurse wheeled in a drip stand with three large bags of a urine-colored liquid.

"And this is the second part," Dr. Sladkovsky said, wheeling the cart closer to him. "These are the various compounds and minerals that allow the blood to settle and disperse properly."

"It's a lot of liquid," I said, unable to imagine it all going through Jack's body.

"Yes, it is. Don't be alarmed, though. We have found that patients tolerate it better when it's more diluted. As Jack is being infused, you will find that he needs to go to the bathroom a lot…

"Jack," the doctor said, picking up two syringes full of blood from a cooling container.

"Is that mine? Is that my blood?"

"Yes, it is, and this is what's going to help you get better. Now, it might feel a little cold but it won't hurt. I promise."

"Ooo, it's cold. The blood is cold," Jack said excitedly, as Dr. Sladkovsky injected the first syringe into the cannula.

"And does it hurt?"

"No," Jack said. "Doesn't hurt."

"You see, I told you," the doctor said. "It's not like that nasty chemotherapy."

Soon Jack had fallen asleep, and I listened to the sound of the pump, imagining his T-cells rallying, steeling themselves for one final battle.

I looked at my phone again, but there was still nothing from Anna. I wasn't sure what she would do when she found out. I hoped she would come to Prague, that she wouldn't call the police or get the embassy involved. That wasn't her style, though, to make a fuss, to make a public show of things.

What else could I do? After all those endless conversations, I knew she wouldn't change her mind. But if she were here, forced by my hand, she could meet Dr. Sladkovsky, she could see how the clinic worked. In London, it was an option too abstract to be considered.

I wouldn't tell her yet. I would wait just a little longer. I needed more time, to get Jack properly started on the treatment. I looked at my phone again. It was seven o'clock in Prague, and the UK was an hour behind, so I texted her:

Everything is fine here. Jack is happy, taking a nap now. How is your mom? x

I waited for a response but it didn't come. It had always been a joke between us: how quickly Anna would respond to text messages. Why wait? she would say. You only forget to answer. Jack was still sleeping, so I checked my email on my phone and there was a message from Nev.

Subject: Re: Jack
Sent: Tue Dec 16, 2014 1:05 am
From: Nev
To: Rob

Dear Rob,
Just a quick e-mail to wish you all well. Hope you arrived safely
and everything is going as well as can be expected.

I told Josh that Jack was going for treatment in Prague and
he drew him a little picture. I scanned it and am attaching it
to this email.

Take care of yourselves and let me know if there's anything
I can do.
Nev

I opened the attachment. There was a drawing of a little boy,
with a bandage around his head, sitting in a hospital bed. Next
to him, two dinosaurs dressed as nurses were carrying a tray.
All of this was happening outside on the grass, under a blazing
yellow sun.

Jack stayed the night at the clinic for observation. It was a precaution, they said, something they did with all their new patients.
Anna had called last night and I closed Jack's door, in case she
would hear the unfamiliar sounds of the clinic in the corridor
outside. Jack was in bed asleep, I said, which wasn't actually a lie.

The next morning, I woke in a chair next to the bed, still
drowsy and stiff, and saw Dr. Sladkovsky standing over Jack,
his finger pushing a pill onto his tongue.

"Good morning," the doctor said. "Just giving Jack his morning medications."

I turned to Jack, who was smiling, sitting up in bed, a blood-
pressure cuff still around his arm, a plate of toast next to him
on a tray-table. "How are you feeling, beautiful?" I said.

"Fine," Jack said. "I had cheese toast, but not special cheese
toast. They don't have that here."

"That's great, Jack, you've done really well."

Just then, my phone chimed and it was a text message from Anna.

Mom's still in intensive care and not very responsive. I miss Jack so much and want to come home, but I can't leave her now. How is he doing? Will call in a bit. x

I gazed at Jack. I had not seen him look so well in a long time. His cheeks were rosy; his hair had regained its shine. When he spoke, there was a sparkle in his eyes.

Dr. Sladkovsky, who had been busy filling in Jack's chart, turned to me and lowered his voice so Jack couldn't hear. "I do have some good news for you," he said. "While it's quite early, it seems that Jack is undergoing an extraordinary response to the treatment. His protein markers are excellent. We've not seen anything like it for a long time."

The doctor took out a piece of paper and traced a line on a graph with his finger. "Yes, these are very good. His GML and CB-11."

"These are the blood proteins, right?" I said.

"Yes, blood proteins, exactly. They're very sensitive indicators. It's one of the ways we track how well the treatments are working. Put simply, it's a measurement of how well his immune system is fighting the cancer."

I was breathless, the hairs prickling on the back of my neck. In all of the consultations with Jack's doctors, we had never once received even a slither of good news.

"I... I... I didn't know that you would be able to tell that it's working so soon."

"Actually, Mr. Coates, this is what I wanted to talk to you about. You see, with immuno-engineering, it's like riding a wave and it's all about maximizing that wave as much as possible. Do you see what I mean?"

"I'm sorry, I'm not sure I do."

"My apologies, please forgive my bad English. Let me try to explain it to you another way. Jack's body is fighting hard now. Very hard. You see his red cheeks, how he has become more engaged, alert. Well, that's his body working overtime, what we call an immune response. This is good, a very excellent sign. Now, in previous patients we've found that now is a good time to boost and to give him another infusion."

I looked at Jack again, playing a game on the iPad, a game that a week ago he had lost interest in. Dr. Sladkovsky was right. Something had happened. He was more alert, unrecognizable to the boy he was before. Jack looked up at me and smiled, his eyes as big as saucers, the dark shadows that had eclipsed them were now almost gone.

"So move the next treatment forward you mean?"

"Yes, exactly, Mr. Coates. He was due his next round in three days, but we would recommend doing another today. It would mean him staying here today for observation."

"I understand," I said, taking out my phone. "But, if you can give me a second, I just need to check something."

"Of course," the doctor said, averting his eyes as I logged into my banking app. The savings had already been transferred.

"Okay, let's do it," I said, and Dr. Sladkovsky smiled and nodded to the nurse.

"Excellent," the doctor said, as the nurse handed him a clipboard. "I do, however, need you to sign another consent form. We are bound by EU law on dosage procedures and are required to get your compliance for the shortening of time between doses."

After I signed the form, I went outside into the corridor, lined with photographs of Sladkovsky's survivors, and felt a tingle up my spine. What if Jack was really getting better? It had worked with Josh. Why not Jack?

I knew that I had to call Anna. If she came here and saw him, she would change her mind. I wanted her to see the color in his cheeks, to see how he mouthed along to Trevor the Train. I wanted her to see how, for the first time in weeks, he happily and absentmindedly devoured a piece of toast.

"Hi, darling," Anna said, picking up the phone.

"Hi. How's your mom?"

"Well, she's actually much better. It was touch and go before, but it seems she's making a miraculous comeback."

"Oh, that's good news," I said, and I knew now I would have to tell her.

"Yes, she's now sitting up in bed, ordering the nurses around. They think she'll make a full recovery."

"Ah, I'm glad," I said.

"And how's Jack?" Anna said, and I could feel my heart beating faster.

"He's very well, playing on his iPad."

"Really, that's good, he's not been doing much of that recently, has he?"

"No, actually, that's what I wanted to talk to you about…"

I paused, my mouth suddenly incredibly dry.

"Rob, is everything okay? Is everything okay with Jack?" I could hear the panic in her voice. "Rob? Rob? Speak to me."

"Anna. There's something I need to tell you."

"Oh, God, it's not Jack, is it."

"Anna, he's fine. It's just…just…"

"Just what? Rob? What's happened?"

"We're in Prague."

"You're in Prague," she said. "What are you talking about? I don't understand. What do you mean, you're in Prague?"

Static on the line, an inhalation of breath. And then a pause, a rustle, and the sound of a chair being dragged across a floor.

"Oh, Rob, please tell me you're not at that clinic."

"Anna, please, just hear me out." My voice was shaking, and I was pacing up and down the corridor. "I know I shouldn't have taken him, it was wrong, but please, please listen to me. He's doing so well, Anna, he's responding to the treatment and he's never been better. There's color in his cheeks, he's laughing and joking like never before... It's unbelievable, you have to see him."

"Wait, what? I can't believe what you're telling me. You mean, he's already doing the treatment? Please tell me he isn't, Rob, please tell me that's not true."

"I'm sorry, I know I should have told you. He's just started, but already they're seeing results—already. These proteins they use as markers are way up. It's amazing, you can actually see it in him, how his body is fighting this. Anna, please, you have to come and see it for yourself. I'm so sorry I took him, but it was the only way and it's working, Anna, it's really working."

"Is this for real, Rob?" Anna asked, and her voice cut like a cold knife. I could hear the spittle, the anger. "I just can't believe you would do this, I just can't believe it..."

"Anna, I know you're angry, and you have every right to be, but please, please, I'm begging you, just come. Please come and see how well he's doing."

Anna did not speak, and I listened to her short, rapid breaths. "I just don't know what to say. You have kidnapped our son, our dying son, when you are supposed to be looking after him."

"Please, Anna, just come, you need to."

"Don't you dare tell me what to do. I've a good mind to call the police, but of course you know very well I would never do that. How long have you been planning this, Rob? A week, a month? I bet you couldn't believe your luck when my mother fell ill... I forbid you to allow any more treatments, do you hear me, Rob? Are you listening? I forbid you. I will be on the next flight over to bring Jack back home."

I tried to speak but she interrupted, her voice shaking with rage. "I will never ever forgive you for this, Rob. Never," she said, and then put down the phone.

I took a deep breath, feeling my chest tighten, and went back into the room to see Jack. He was smiling to himself and watching something on the iPad. Anna would be on her laptop now, booking the next available flight. I looked at Jack, hungrily stuffing bits of banana into his mouth. When she saw him, I knew she would understand.

Jack was waiting by the window and saw Anna's taxi arrive outside. We had stayed the night in a flat connected to the clinic and were given an emergency number to call if Jack experienced any side effects. The flat was clean and bright, like an upmarket city hotel, with modern white furnishings, a space-age kitchen, and a flat-screen TV.

"Mommy!" Jack shouted as we opened the door.

"Jackie," she said, holding out her arms and embracing him. "Oh, I missed you so much. Come on, let's go inside. It's freezing."

"Was the flight okay?" I said as we walked up the stairs, but Anna didn't answer, would not meet my eyes.

She looked around the flat, as if she was inspecting it, and then sat down with Jack on the couch, and he showed her some little Matchbox cars we had bought at the airport.

After Anna went to read Jack a story and he fell asleep for his afternoon nap, she came back into the living room and sat on a curved plastic chair in the corner.

"I am so angry right now," she said quietly, in a breathless tone I had never heard before. "You take our terminally ill son on a plane to Prague and you don't tell me. I can't believe you would do that."

"I'm so sorry I didn't tell you, but it was..."

"Are you an idiot, Rob? I could have called the police. I would have been well within my rights to do that. And did you not think about Jack? About the impact this could have on his health?"

"As I said, I'm very sorry. But I did it for Jack. I did what I thought was right."

"Yes, you've made that quite clear."

"Did you see him, Anna? Did you see how well he looks?"

"Yes, he does look good and I'm glad. But he always looks well after he's finished chemo."

"God, Anna, look at him. When he's awake, really look at him," I said, raising my voice a little, causing Anna to check that the door to Jack's bedroom was properly shut. "He's like a different person since he's been here. Everything has improved. His appetite has got better, his speech is better. The doctor said both of those things can be a sign of tumor shrinkage. He's…"

"And can you tell me exactly what treatments he's received?"

"Well, as I said on the phone, he's had two rounds of immuno-engineering."

Anna held her head in her hands. "I still can't believe this, Rob. How could you even do this?"

"But he's responding really well," I said. "Much better than with chemo. There are no side effects, none at all."

"So are you a doctor now? Who even knows what he's being given."

I took a deep breath. "Look, this isn't getting us anywhere, is it? Again, I'm sorry for taking him, for lying to you. But I just didn't see any other way and you refuse to discuss it."

"Refuse to discuss it? We have had endless—endless—conversations about the clinic. We talk about it all the time. In fact, it's all you want to talk about. You're obsessed."

"Right, I'm obsessed." I went over to the sideboard and poured myself some whiskey I had bought in the duty-free shop. Anna eyed the glass and then looked away. "As I said, we think differently. I was desperate, and I'm doing what I think is right for my son."

"Oh, please don't even begin to try to make me feel sorry for you, after what you've done. All this desperate Dad stuff. Because everything, Rob, everything you're going through I'm going through, as well," she said through clenched teeth. "Do you think I wanted to leave Jack and look after my mother? Can you imagine how that made me feel, having to leave him like that? My little boy."

"All I am asking, Anna—and I am begging you—is please come and meet Dr. Sladkovsky. He said there might be a chance to cure Jack. They've seen good results with other kids with glioblastoma."

"Oh, I'm sure he did."

"Anna, it wasn't like that, believe me," I said. "Really. He said many kids with glioblastoma had died under his care, as well."

My voice cracked and I let out a sob of frustration, like the grossest injustice of childhood: not being believed when telling the truth. "He's not some miracle worker, Anna, he just said he could give Jack a chance."

"Well, yes, that's what he always says."

"What he always says? What does that even mean?"

"Rob, it's everywhere, all over the internet. There are whole forums devoted to Sladkovsky's clinic. Did you not read any of them, or did you just read all those glowing testimonies?"

Anna reached into her small carry-on suitcase and pulled out a folder. "Just in case you don't believe me, I brought these for you."

Anna handed me some printouts from a website called *The Other Sladkovsky Patients*. I flicked through, without really reading them. "Is this supposed to convince me? A few printouts from a lame WordPress site."

"Are you not going to even read them? You'll read everything on the web about Sladkovsky's. You bombard me for weeks with all this stuff, and then I show you something that might not fit your story, and you don't want to listen."

I sat down on the sofa and began to read some of the patient testimonies. The website seemed familiar, and I was sure that I had come across it before. Natalia P, Peter R, Amy T—children with vaguely Germanic or Austro-Hungarian names.

Their stories started the same way, a familiar narrative, one that I'd read many times before: a devastating prognosis with all treatment options exhausted. But these children didn't get better under Dr. Sladkovsky's care. The tumors grew back, faster, more aggressive than before, and thousands of pounds or dollars in the red, they went home to watch their children die.

"So what?" I said, dumping the papers on the sofa. "I think I've seen it already. It doesn't mean anything. Sladkovsky has repeatedly said that not everyone responds to immuno-engineering. Some do and some don't, and he doesn't claim to know why. He's been completely up front about that from the beginning. God, it's even on the liability form you have to sign. It didn't work with these kids, I get that and I'm sorry for them, for their parents, but it does work with other kids."

"Right. Josh."

Anna rummaged through her bag, looking for something else.

"What's that supposed to mean?"

"It means that I have my doubts that it worked with Josh." I shook my head in disbelief. "What are you..."

"Here," Anna said, thrusting more printouts into my hand. "It's from *Hope's Place*. You probably never read this."

Nev
by Chemoforlifer» Fri Oct 19, 2012 6:03 am
To all members of the forum:

Many of you on Hope's Place will no doubt have seen my occasional disagreements with Nev. In light of that, I wanted to share something with you all, an email I received from a member of the forum, who wishes to remain anonymous.

> Hello Chemoforlifer, I was just browsing the forum and saw something I thought was a little strange concerning one of the members, Nev. As I think you know, near the end of David's life we went to Dr. Sladkovsky's clinic for treatment. Since then, we have become very active in The Other Sladkovsky Patients group.
>
> I was very surprised to see Nev's postings about how Dr. Sladkovsky had saved his son Josh's life. We were at the clinic at the same time as Nev and I remember Josh. When we saw him, he wasn't doing very well at all and was very much in the end stages of his life.
>
> I distinctly remember this because I spoke to Nev at the clinic about what would happen if his son died in Prague and how his body would be repatriated.
>
> To be clear, we took David home when Nev and Josh were still there. So it is of course possible that Josh did recover but, from what we know about this horrible disease, that seems very unlikely.
>
> I hope you don't mind me writing to you but it's been on my mind...

I have wondered about whether to air this publicly but have come to the conclusion that it's in the best interests of the forum.
ChemoForLifer
Admin

"God, this is ridiculous. It doesn't prove anything. It's just forum drama. There are always intrigues, arguments between people. And this guy, some anonymous guy who's part of this other patients' group, so he's got an agenda, as well. In fact, nothing about it contradicts Nev's version. Nothing. He himself has said that Josh was very ill at Sladkovsky's and then got better. More to the point, Anna, I've seen Josh. I have a video, countless photos of him on my laptop."

Anna threw up her hands. "I knew it, this is pointless. No one can tell you anything, can they, Rob? And not that it matters, but how exactly did you pay for the treatments?"

"I put it on the credit card."

"Great. And the rest? How were you planning on paying for those?"

"We have options, Anna. I can ask Scott. The pension plan, the savings, there's plenty…"

"So we'll just drain everything—everything—to finance a fraud, a cheat?" Anna snorted. "You just act like we don't need the money."

"Well, do we?" I said, and I shuddered, started to sob, because I knew now that Jack's last chance was slipping away. "What do we need the money for now?"

Anna didn't answer but walked over to the sofa and crouched down next to me. She whispered, almost hissed, to make sure there was no chance that Jack could hear.

"Do you have any idea," she said, "how much these things cost?"

"What things?"

"Dying, Rob," she whispered, and I could hear the soft, controlled rage in her voice. "Making Jack as comfortable as possible, however long it takes. Paying for the best private hospice with twenty-four-hour care so he can live his last days in peace. That all costs money, Rob. And that is all I care about now. Nothing else."

We listened to the wail of a police siren outside.

"I came here for one thing," she said, "and that's to take Jack home. When he wakes up, I'm packing our things and taking him on the next flight back to London."

SOMEWHERE OVER GERMANY

———

whenever you flew Jack, you were just transfixed, your face glued to the window, and what was wonderful was how un-fazed you were by the mechanics of how we got up and how we got down. you just wanted to take photos out of the win-dow and i remember how you held the camera, gripping tightly with both hands, slowly turning it, just like daddy had shown you, making sure you got it all, the clouds, the setting sun, the endless ripples of deep dark blue.

18

It was the day before Christmas Eve, and the three of us were sitting on the sofa watching *The Snowman*. The living room was pristine, our tree shimmering with lights, Anna's intricate, woven paper chains decked along the stairs and landing. There had been so many Christmas cards we didn't have room for them, so Anna strung them up, in the porch, from wall to wall in the living room.

People made the extra effort with their cards this year. Instead of just "Merry Christmas from the Bensons!" they wished us peace and strength and said they were holding us in their hearts. There were no notes about new babies, impending marriages and Duke of Edinburgh awards.

It was Jack's first time watching *The Snowman*, and I had never seen him so transfixed, his pale, gaunt face lit up by the snow-glare of the screen. As we watched, I took a small amount of pride that Jack liked the parts that I did as a child. The places where he fidgeted, where he looked across at me and fiddled with his socks, were the parts near the beginning, when the snowman is trying on the clothes, putting in false teeth and climbing inside the glowing freezer. Those scenes had always left me cold, and it was heartening to see that Jack felt the same.

What seemed to captivate Jack were the moments of melancholy: the boredom and impatience that Christmas has not yet arrived; the urgency to get outside in the snow; and then, at the end, the singularly childish sense of loss that comes with the melting of the snow and that first heartbreaking sight of green grass.

It was our seventh and last Christmas. We prepared weeks in advance: the Christmas table, the gifts for Jack's stocking, the presents under the tree. Anna had her lists, sending me out to buy napkins, the crackers, the orange juice for the Buck's Fizz. The details weren't accidental: the sliced brown supermarket loaf, the cheap bingo set from the toy shop, the giant tin of chocolates. She was trying to re-create, for the very last time, the Romford Christmas my dad used to do at home.

I watched Jack closely at the end of *The Snowman*, when the snow had melted and all that was left was the snowman's hat and scarf on the ground. He didn't move a muscle, lost in the blizzard of white, as the camera panned away from the little boy crouched on the ground.

"Where did the snowman go, Daddy?" Jack said later that evening when Anna and I were tucking him into bed.

I didn't know what to say, because this was it, and I didn't want to fluff my lines. I thought of the little pile of snow, the scarf and hat lying on the ground.

"He's gone back to the Arctic, Jack," I said, "to see the other snowmen."

Jack thought about what I said and turned his head to the side.

"Is he having a party with the other snowmen?" he said, and I thought about the scene where the snowmen were dancing around the fire.

"Exactly, Jack. They'll be having so much fun," Anna said, dimming the light next to his head.

Jack seemed content. He stretched out and started to touch his pictures one by one: the Eiffel Tower, the Empire State Building, Taipei 101.

"Are you and Mommy sleeping in the house tonight?"

"Of course, beautiful. We sleep here every night," I said.

Jack paused. "Why are you sleeping downstairs, Daddy? Why aren't you sleeping in Mommy's bed?"

Anna and I exchanged a guilty glance. "Oh, Daddy's not sleeping so well and I don't want to disturb Mommy," I said, and it was only half the truth.

Jack thought about what I had said. "Even when I'm asleep, will you both be here in the house?"

"Of course we will," Anna said. "We'll always be here, so if you need anything, you just shout and we'll come, okay?"

"And if I go out of the house, will you come with me?"

"Absolutely," I said. "We'll always be with you."

"Even if I go to the North Pole to see Father Christmas."

"Yes," I said, tucking the cover under his body, making sure his legs weren't exposed. "It would be fun going to the North Pole. Although we'd have to wrap up warm."

"Snug as a bug in a rug," Jack said, almost to himself.

"Snug as a bug in a rug," I repeated.

Jack smiled and snuggled into his pillows. I thought he was dropping off to sleep, but he spoke again, his little voice clear and precise. "When we die, where do we go?"

He said it in a very matter-of-fact way, and I didn't know if he was talking generally or if he was asking about his own fate.

Anna and I looked at each other in the dim half-light. Did Jack know that he was going to die? It was a question I asked myself a thousand times a day. Did he twig when Spider-Man came to visit or when he received the batch of handmade cards from his classmates in room 1A?

We had read the fact sheets about how to talk to your dying child. We had spoken to Dr. Flanagan and a counselor attached to the Harley Street clinic. Jack was at a difficult age, they said, on a cusp. While he would hold certain notions about death, his conceptual understanding would be primitive and undeveloped. So do what feels right, they said, as if we were deciding whether or not to co-sleep.

We just didn't know. How could we possibly know?

"Well," Anna said brightly, and I realized then she had prepared for the question, that she knew exactly what to say. "When we die we go to heaven."

"What's heaven like?" Jack said.

"Heaven," Anna said, "is the happiest place in the world where you have all your friends and family and you can play and do whatever you want."

Jack smiled. "Will they have PlayStation?"

"Of course," she said cheerily. "They'll have PlayStation and all your favorite toys and all your favorite food."

"Will they have McDonald's?"

Anna laughed. "They'll definitely have McDonald's."

Jack grinned, but then his face turned serious. "And will you and Daddy be there, as well?"

"Of course we will," I said, trying to follow Anna's upbeat lead. I reached across the bed and held Anna's hand, our bodies creating a little cocoon. "We'll always be with you, so you'll never be alone."

Jack nodded solemnly.

"But remember, trouble, we'll be watching you," I added, softly flicking his ear and tucking the cover under him. "Making sure you do your homework, that you're not eating too many hamburgers."

Jack giggled. "I'm going to eat a million hamburgers."

"A million?"

"Really," he said, nodding proudly. He was getting tired now, his eyes beginning to flutter. "Daddy," Jack said, sitting up again on his pillows.

"Yes, beautiful?"

"You know we talked about treats?"

"Yes."

We had asked Jack whether there was anything special he wanted to do. His answers were always modest. No Disneyland to see Mickey Mouse; no trip to Peppa Pig World or Buckingham Palace to see the queen. No, he was adamant. He just wanted to go to McDonald's for ice cream.

"Can we do another thing, as well?"

"We can do whatever you want, Jack, whatever you want."

"Can we go up the London Eye again? I want to go right to the top."

Subject: Re: Jack
Sent: Wed Dec 24, 2014 3:33 am
From: Rob
To: Nev

Dear Nev,

I wrote to you before but haven't heard back from you, so I hope everything is okay. As I told you, we stopped treatments at Dr. Sladkovsky's clinic, despite the visible signs of improvement Jack was making. As soon as we got back to London and Jack went back on chemo, he started declining again.

I am still trying to come to terms with everything that has happened. There is nothing left now. No hope. I wish I could say that I don't blame Anna but part of me does. He was getting better, I could see it with my own eyes. That is a horrible thing to think about the person you love, but it is the truth.

We don't really speak about it—Jack dying that is. We don't speak about anything anymore. We just pretend it's not happening. I still can't believe it has come to this. I can't believe I will soon lose my little boy.

I hope you and Josh are well.

Rob

Bundled up against the cold, we lifted and positioned Jack's wheelchair at the edge of the cabin and then began our slow ascent up into the twilight. As soon as we rose above the Thames, the city lights glistening on the water, Jack took his camera out and started to take photos.

We climbed. I pointed out to Anna, because Jack already knew it all, the Hungerford Bridge and the South Bank Centre, which from above looked like a soulless cluster of gray chimneys. On the other bank, the wings of the air force memorial twinkled in the sun, guarding Whitehall and the Ministry of Defence. As we rose farther, we could see St. James's, Green, and then Hyde Parks, a fat royal leg stretched out across London.

It was Scott who sorted it all out. After Jack had made his request, I called the London Eye's bookings line. It wasn't open on Christmas Day and the day after was already fully booked. I pleaded with the rep, explained that Jack was very ill and asked if she could pull a few strings. She checked with her supervisor, kept me on hold, but no, she was sorry, there was nothing they could do.

I called Scott. We had barely spoken, just a couple of texts, an email around the time I had gone to Prague. He was thinking of me, he said, and I should let him know if there was anything he could do.

So I did. "You know people, Scott," I said, "all the CEOs in London you used to boast. So please help us, please help us, because we might not have much time."

Scott called back within an hour. He had a prime slot for us—at sunset on Boxing Day and we had the cabin completely to ourselves.

"Shall we move you around so you can see the other side better?" Anna asked Jack as we climbed farther.

"Okay," he said, not really listening, frantically taking photographs as if he was paparazzi afraid of missing his prized shot.

We moved him over to the opposite window, putting the brake on the wheelchair. Anna zipped up his coat and tucked in his scarf. We knew he didn't have long left. His speech had started to change. He forgot things, repeated his words. He was weak and needed the wheelchair if we were going to be out for a long time. As the doctors had warned us, he had become more detached. He did everything slowly and with such caution—walking, picking up a spoon, eating a piece of toast. It was like watching someone walk through a rock pool with bare feet.

"Look, Jack, Big Ben," Anna said, as we kept rising. We turned to look at the Houses of Parliament, lit up from below, the four faces of Big Ben hanging in the air like ghostly orbs. Jack swung himself around in the seat of his wheelchair and took more photos, zooming in and out, twisting the camera to take horizontal and vertical shots.

Making memories, they said on *Hope's Place*, and those two words had never made any sense to me. They would be our memories, mine and Anna's. They wouldn't be Jack's.

I snapped out of it, painted on my smile. Making memories, making memories. We had been at every point in the cabin now, looking down toward Canary Wharf, the Shard, the cozy huddle around St. Paul's.

"Daddy," Jack said, putting his camera down on the blanket on his lap, and his voice sounded strangely lucid—the Jack I remembered from a few weeks ago. "It's very high here."

"It is, isn't it? Do you like it?"

Jack nodded and smiled. "When I'm better, are we going to climb more tall buildings?"

"Of course we are."

"The Ivor Tower in Paris?"

"Yes," I said, putting my arm around him.

"And the one in Oompa-Loompa?"

Anna laughed gently, put her hand on Jack's shoulder. "Yes, sweetheart, Kuala Lumpur."

"Yes," Jack said, looking down the Thames. "Kuala Lumpur." I knew what he was thinking about now: all the tall buildings, the ones he had seen in his books, in the pictures on his wall.

"And the one in Dubai? Because that's the biggest one in the whole world, Daddy."

I paused, fighting back my tears, because I wouldn't, I wouldn't let him see me cry now. "We can go up all of them, Jack, every single one," I said, my voice beginning to crack.

"Because you know, Daddy, you know, when you're so high, you go up past the clouds, and it's like being in an airplane and then you can see the spaceships and the sun and all of the stars…"

As Jack's words tailed off, a bolt from the setting sun lit up the cabin, like the light from a distant, silent explosion. We crouched down and listened to the clinks and clanks of the gears, our arms wrapped around Jack's shoulders, staring at what was left of the sunset. And then, without warning, Jack slowly pushed himself up out of his wheelchair. He wobbled a little, steadied himself on the handrail, and started taking photographs again. The dim flare of city lights against the velvet-red sky. Peaks and troughs, luminous mountains of clouds. He made sure he got it all.

We decided that Ashbourne House was a good place for Jack to come to die. We had chosen it in the same way that we had chosen Jack's school. We looked through the brochures and then went to tour the facilities. We discussed the various merits of the staff, the size of the playroom, the communal dining options.

While it was a Victorian-era institution, it did not give a foreboding impression. Its brickwork was light, with a reddish

tinge; the gardens were lovingly tended, full of flowers and cu-
riosities; the corridors were light and airy, bedecked with the
residents' own artwork, wide enough for several wheelchairs
to pass each other at ease. In our room, we had a double bed
artfully separated from Jack's by a removable division. We slept
there, as a family, the way we once had when Jack was born.

Jack had mostly withdrawn from the world. As the tumor
pressed on the vital parts of his brain, he became more detached, less able to express emotions. Now there was no more
chemotherapy, his hair had grown longer, a little unruly once
again. He had a haunted, faraway look in his eyes, a look that
should never be seen on a child.

The art classes, the wake-'em-up karaoke, the superhero day,
were all lost on Jack. He didn't even recognize his pictures anymore: the buildings, the panoramas, we had taped around his
bed. It was the speed that shocked me. The cavalier way his
own body betrayed him.

Then, something else changed in Jack's brain. The tumor
shifted, or grew, or colonized a new lobe, and suddenly, while
we thought he still understood what was being said to him,
Jack could no longer speak. Now he just slept, his body already
in death's custody.

To watch a death, to see it close up, to see the pallor of Jack's
skin change, his hair mat into greasy knots despite our best efforts with a sponge. All the body's outer signs of decay—the
sourness of his breath, the flaking of his skin, the horizontal
lines appearing on his fingernails—were just prim reminders
of the horrors that were taking place within his body.

How long, how long? That was what we asked the doctors,
the ward nurse, anyone who might know, anyone who would
listen. I felt like we were betraying him.

I didn't know how I knew it was coming, but I knew. We
both knew. I put my head on Jack's chest, encasing his small

body with my arms, and then I felt Anna's arms fold around me, or perhaps Anna had been there first, and we stayed like that for ten, twenty, thirty minutes, our bodies, like wings protecting a young bird.

I would like to say that Jack held out his hand and reached over and traced the outline of mine, my knuckle, the curve between my thumb and forefinger. Or that he looked up at me with loving eyes, but he did not. His hands were like clammy ice. His eyes glassy and opaque, no longer of this world.

And then we heard a soft rasp, like an echo of a breath, and our arms tightened around him, and we waited, waited, held our own breaths so we could hear his and we waited, waited, hoping he would and hoping he wouldn't. I listened again and again, and this time I knew that his breath was not coming; this time I knew he was gone.

I removed myself from Jack's body and looked around the room. People cling to their death stories: their cozy myths of seeing the soul depart the room. But at Ashbourne House, everything was still the same. There was no beam of light or gentle rattling of the windowpane. The day was still gray outside. Jack's Minions water bottle remained undrunk on the table. I could hear the chirp of hospital bells in the distance, and I thought for a moment that their frequency, their pitch, was somehow different. I listened again. No, it was the same.

In the quietness of the room, my breathing suddenly seemed very loud. Anna was still lying on the bed with Jack, her arms cradling his head and neck. He had come from her body, and she would stay with him for as long as she could.

I looked at Jack. Sometimes people spoke of the body after death looking empty, as if it was neutered by the absence of a soul, like the discarded skin of a snake. But it was still him; it was still Jack. He didn't look to be at peace—that was just the delusion of the living—but his face was mostly without expression. The only thing I could categorically say about his expression was that it was his. It was him; it was still him.

I rang the emergency bell after that. For Anna, not Jack. Because after she pried herself away from Jack's body and fell to her knees, and after I put my arms around her, to encase her like we had done Jack, she broke away and slammed her head against the wall, again and again, so hard that her nose started to drip blood onto the yellow tiles.

The balloons had been Lola's suggestion. After the reception, just before dusk, we would all gather in the garden and let off helium balloons into the sky. Each person would write their own tribute to Jack, in colored marker, and then on the count of three, we would all send them up to the heavens.

The idea had not appealed to me. There was something ostentatious about it, cloying even. The idea that every dying child had to have something, something that defined them— as if his love for balloons was the final way that Jack would be remembered, as if that was it, that was the sum of his existence: a balloon.

Jack would definitely not approve. He would have thought that was messy, somehow improper—why would you write on a balloon like that? Balloons were not meant to be scribbled on.

"Perhaps we should do it without the messages, the writing," I said to Anna. "Or just get some from Carphone Warehouse, he always loved those."

"It's just balloons," Anna said. "It doesn't matter where they're from. And I think the writing is a nice idea."

I was sullen, silent.

Jack's funeral. I don't remember much about that day. The banal sea of people, the way they clasped my hand. Anna's mother, a specter in a wheelchair, and how I resented her presence, her very living, that she was given a second chance.

The day passed in a haze of Xanax and whiskey. A church on a hill—"lovely setting, so Jack, so very Jack"—a service where everyone, except the elderly, were expected to wear color, "because that's what Jack would have wanted." Laughs when the Spider-Man theme came on. Laughs at a little boy's funeral. "He would have loved that, Oh, Jack would have loved that."

"He loved to smile, your Jack, didn't he?" They were wrong. They knew nothing about Jack. He was frugal with his smiles, as if he thought they were being rationed. He didn't dish them out for anyone.

Jack was buried because we could not bear to have him cremated. It was a ritual fitting for the old but not for the young. And he was always terrified of fire. When he was little, we had taught him to be scared of the pot bubbling away on the stove and, dutifully, he was. He took comfort in the blinking red light on the smoke alarm in his room.

I watched as he was lowered into the ground, the earth tipped over him. All I could think was that there was Jack in that wooden box, dressed in his Spider-Man pajamas with Little Teddy, his flashlight, all of his Pokémon cards by his side. Coffins should never, ever be made in that size.

We got some lovely cards, Anna said, in the car on the way back to the house. I flicked through them, in pastels, light blues, mauves, the colors of an old woman's cardigan. In the messages, they all called Jack a fighter, a warrior. An angel in heaven. A living saint. They said he touched people's hearts. Bits of folded paper bought for 1 pound 20 from Smiths.

Oh, they loved to make it about them, didn't they? Did they think we didn't see their Facebook posts? Hug your children tonight, they wrote, spend a few extra minutes before bed. And then they posted pictures of Jack. Our Jack.

It makes you realize, they said, just how precious life is, how we have to cherish what we have. Did they not think about the implications of what they were saying? That their children were still very much alive, and they would hug them tonight and breathe them in and listen to them sing as they woke. Poor little Jack, they said. He was in a better place now. He wasn't, though. A better place was here with us. Jack was just gone. There were no playdates in heaven. He was no warrior, no angel, watching over us all. Jack did what he could and never once complained. He bore his illness quietly with a type of stoicism I had never associated with a child.

Back at the house, there were perhaps twenty or thirty people in all, family, friends, a few older children. Anna made some of Jack's favorite things and there was cake. A few others brought nibbles. Photos of Jack cycled through on the big TV screen.

When it came to balloon time, it was raining and the wind had picked up. After the adults had written their messages and the children had drawn their pictures, we counted down and then released the balloons into the sky. With black marker, I wrote:

Jack, we will never forget you, Love, Daddy.

The coldness, the brusqueness of my message was an act of defiance, so angry was I about the idea that I was being told how I should remember my son. I didn't know what Anna wrote, and I didn't want to look.

I stood next to Anna, close but not touching. Someone, not me, had put a coat around her shoulders because she was shivering. The balloons didn't go very far. A few of them never even made it off the ground and just bobbled around the backyard. Some got lodged in the eaves under the garage roof. One of them popped on the branches of the apple tree and, at that, I couldn't help smiling. Jack would have liked that.

I liked to think of Jack's death another way. In Greece, I would sometimes go for a walk with him after lunch. We walked away from the hotel, down a hidden path through the tall grass, which meandered toward the sea like a stream, until we got to the second beach, the beach with the boats and the fishmonger who always made Jack laugh.

One day, the promenade was deserted and the sun was relentless, so we took shelter under a lone tree and drank water from a plastic bottle. Jack was beginning to feel sleepy and rested his head on my shoulder.

We sat like that for a while, listening to the sounds beyond the wind. Cicadas, the rattle and chirp of a yacht's mast in the distance. New smells. Jasmine grass. Hot dust. Lamb being grilled on an open flame. Eventually Jack started to fall asleep. His eyes went, then his head slowly slid to the side. That was how I liked to imagine his death. A slow, gentle sleep. The kiss of the wind. The sound of the sea.

19

It was not wise to be a childless man around a children's playground. So I was careful about choosing my positions. A bench at an indirect angle, partially blocked by trees. A seating area in Camden where office workers ate sandwiches, directly across from some trampolines and a death slide.

My favorite spot, though, was the Parliament Hill playground, not just because I used to come here with Jack, but there was a café and it didn't seem strange to sit here, alone, without kids. With Anna now back at work, my days were empty. They offered her compassionate leave, but she said she needed something to occupy her mind.

I sat with my laptop in front of me and watched a boy, around five years old, playing on the swings. His father was leaning on a tree, one eye on his son, one eye on his phone. There was a gangly boy, tall for his age, perhaps about ten or eleven, with a shyness in his face that reminded me of Jack. He was playing with a football, occasionally smashing the ball into a wall.

I always drank Diet Coke at the café. I would buy a bottle at the counter, and then switch it with the one in my bag—the one I had already prepared, the one half-full with vodka. I started drinking more because I couldn't sleep. I would lie awake next to Anna, annoyed by the quiet symmetry of her breathing, the apparent ease with which she slept. I watched the tree branches dancing in the lamplight; I listened to the mournful howls of the neighbor's dog. So I started getting up and going downstairs, tiptoeing around in my bathrobe, stepping over the creaky stair, silently opening the latch on the drinks' cabinet. At first a few large whiskeys were enough, but then it became four or five. Soon I was taking sips from the drinks' cabinet during the day, as I had done as a teenager, taking nips from my parents' sideboard before a night out.

It had started to spit with rain, and people were leaving the playground. I needed to buy more vodka, so I walked down the hill to the Tesco Metro. I went straight to the booze counter, not allowing my eyes to wander. I could not go down the cereal aisle anymore, nor where the children's magazines were stacked. I had learned to avert my eyes as I passed the Marmite, the Babybel cheese. Once, I began to weep when I saw Jack's little pots of Petit Filous.

When I got home, Anna was somewhere in the house. We moved around like ghosts, rarely speaking, wordlessly passing each other on the stairs. We did our crying alone, in the shower, the car, at the sight of a lone robin sitting on Jack's favorite tree.

We did try to come back to each other. We attempted to eat together on the weekends, as if Icelandic scallops or an aged rib-eye steak would help us forget Jack's empty place at the table. Once, on a Saturday, we went to the cinema together, but Anna had to leave after seeing a trailer for a children's movie.

There were boxes in the hallway, things from Jack's room, things I assumed she wanted to clear out. It shouldn't have been like that. Because when your child dies, you are meant to leave their bedroom untouched. A shrine to the before. A sanctum for those quiet moments, which are now so achingly frequent. A place where you go to smell their clothes, to lie down in their rocket bed, to stack away their toys again and again.

I told her this, asked her why she was clearing out his room, but there was no point in reasoning with her. So instead, one day, when she was at work, I took the remainder of his things—his backpack, his camera, his sticker books—and snuck them away in one of the cupboards in the spare room.

I lay on the sofa in the living room, happy that Anna was upstairs, that I could drink my vodka in peace. This was now where I spent most of my days, on my laptop, my phone, staring at the wall. Scott had finally sold the company and I didn't have a job, not that it mattered anyway. I withdrew, like a wounded insect, coiling and curling into a ball. Once, I played a little mental game, to see if I could remember who the prime minister was, or where the last World Cup was held. I had no idea. Nothing. I no longer lived in the world.

I woke on the sofa to find Anna staring at me.

"Rob, we need to talk."

"Okay," I said. The vodka bottle was still on the coffee table.

"We can't go on like this. You can't go on like this."

"Like what?"

"The drinking. What you're doing to yourself."

I didn't say anything. "Sorry," I finally managed. "It's just my way of getting through it. I'll be fine."

"I know," Anna said, putting her hand on my leg. "It's a horrible time, but you can't keep on like this. You have to start doing something. Maybe doing some work again, taking on a new project..."

"I can't just jump back into work like you, Anna," I said.

She had gone back not long after Jack's funeral. A couple of weeks later, I was sitting in the kitchen listening to the news on the radio. Suddenly Anna's voice was echoing around the kitchen, talking about the likelihood of an interest-rate hike. I listened to her tone, her intonation. It wasn't the voice of someone who had just lost their son.

"And does that mean I don't care, Rob, because I went back to work? Should I do what you're doing? Sitting around drinking every day."

"Thanks for mentioning it again," I said, turning my head away from her. "What do you want me to say? Yes, I'm drinking too much. I know it's not ideal, but it's my way of..."

"Rob, look at me. You're not just having an extra whiskey at night. You think I don't notice the vodka bottles? Sometimes you can hardly stand when I get home from work. And you wet yourself the other night on the sofa."

I thought I had covered it up, invented some excuse that I had spilled a drink, but perhaps she had seen me, or noticed my wet boxers in the wash.

"What are you talking about? I told you, I spilled a drink."

"Jesus, Rob, I saw you. I came down in the night to check you were okay, and you had wet yourself. I saw it with my own eyes."

A blush of shame, and then anger. Wet yourself. It was how you would speak to a child. She was loving this, her chance to humiliate me, rubbing my nose in it.

She sighed and then chewed her lip a little, as if she was contemplating something.

"You probably don't remember what you did the other day, do you?"

"I'm sure you're going to tell me."

"You came home drunk, and you were stumbling and then you went into the backyard and urinated all over my flowers."

I felt a strange sense of relief, as I had expected worse. I smiled, more out of nerves than anything else.

"You think it's funny, Rob?"

I shrugged and looked away from her.

"It was my sunflowers, Rob. My sunflowers."

The significance, the cruel symbolism of what I had done

began to sink in. But what of it? What did it matter now? The sunflowers would be dead soon enough. They would be gone, their remains ground into the unforgiving soil.

"And you're so perfect, Anna."

She shook her head and sighed. "Of course I'm not perfect, God, far from it." Then she knelt next to me and put her hand on my chest. "Rob, I'm not telling you all this to shame you. I take no pleasure in this. I think you have a problem, and I just want to help you." It reminded me of her mother, how she spoke to the strays she was trying to save.

"It's a shame you didn't want to help Jack."

"What?"

"You heard."

Outside I could hear the caw and scratch of a magpie walking across the patio.

She stood up so she was now standing over me. "How can you say that, how can you even think that?" She started to cry, and I reached for my vodka and poured myself a glass. Could I tell her? Could I tell her now? That I thought about it every day. What if, what if? What if Nev and Dr. Sladkovsky had been right about Jack? Because Nev knew better than anyone how to save a life—in Josh, he had living proof. But Anna refused to listen, thought she knew best.

"I'm sorry," I said, "but I can't just pretend it's not there. I know you don't want to hear it, but it's the truth, whether you like it or not. Jack had a chance, yes, a small chance. But it was something. It was all he had."

Anna took a deep, resigned breath and dabbed her eyes with a tissue. "Rob, I'm not going to argue about it again. But can I ask you something? Do you not think that I don't think about it? That I don't lie awake at night, thinking that perhaps it would have made a difference, that maybe I made the wrong decision?"

I shrugged, drank my vodka.

"Well, I do, every day if you must know," Anna said, her voice cracking.

"You should," I muttered under my breath.

"What did you say?" Anna said. I looked away from her, like a sulking child.

"No, go on, tell me what you said," she said, jabbing at me with her fingers. "If you're such a big man."

"I said you should. You should feel guilty about it."

Suddenly, Anna grabbed the bottle of vodka and quickly walked into the kitchen. I jumped up off the sofa, stubbing my toe on the coffee table, and ran after her, skidding on the kitchen tiles and crashing into the fridge. She opened the cap of the vodka and held it over the sink.

"Please, Anna, please give me the bottle back."

Her chest and face were bright red, and she spoke through clenched teeth, her words a whispered hiss. "That was a disgusting thing to say. The most disgusting thing you have ever said to me. How dare you judge me. How dare you! Your father would be ashamed of you. Ashamed, Rob, because you're half the man he was."

I grabbed the vodka from Anna, but the bottle slipped out of my hand and smashed onto the kitchen floor. We watched as the vodka spread across the tiles, the splinters of glass sparkling in the afternoon sun.

Anna said her words with such poise, such clarity, I knew they must be true. "I hate you, Rob," she said. "I fucking hate you."

Maybe this was the booze talking, but you think you know a person, though you never really do. You bury the bad things, keep them out of sight. I remembered the first time I noticed Anna's coldness. A group email she had sent after her family dog had died, just after we had moved to London. A eulogy that was so awkward, so unfeeling, it was as if she had only sent the email out of a sense of duty, because she thought, in those circumstances, that was what one did.

I saw that coldness again, a few times over the years. Her curt and final "we were never that close" after her grandmother died. Her insistence that she would never give money to beggars, because there were charities for that. While her lack of empathy sometimes bothered me, it was mitigated by the fact that it wasn't ever directed at me.

Anna's intransigence. The rules are there for a reason. That's what she always said. The rules are there for a reason. Because in Anna's world, there was a proper way of doing things. You didn't cheat on your tax return, or even try to get out of a parking ticket, because what if everyone did that? You didn't sneak in to watch a second movie in the theater, when you had only paid for one. You didn't go to unregistered cancer clinics in the Czech Republic, even if it meant your dying son would be given a chance.

I cleaned up the broken glass in the kitchen and got another bottle of vodka from my backpack. Through the French windows, I could see Anna in the backyard. She was frantically digging in the flower beds with a spade. I watched her as she bent down, scooped out soil with a trowel and flung it over her shoulder.

"Can we talk?" Anna was dressed for work, in pinstripes, her hair tied back. It was two or three days since we had argued, and we had barely spoken. I nodded, confused, unable to remember what happened last night. There was a large purple bruise on my forearm.

"I made you a coffee," she said, placing a mug on the table. "Thanks."

"I wanted to speak to you now, while you're sober." She took a deep breath. "I can't do this anymore, and I'm leaving."

I did not feel anger but a sense of relief. Relief that I wouldn't have to hide my bottles anymore, that I could sit here in the living room and drink in peace.

"Okay," I said.

"We should work out what we're going to do with everything," she said, "but let's do it through lawyers. I can't deal with that right now."

"Okay," I said, and Anna bit her lip as if she had something she wanted to say but couldn't. I lay on the sofa and heard her carry a suitcase downstairs and then quietly close the front door.

Six weeks later, after I had drunk through our wine collection and our drinks' cabinet, I left. I couldn't be in that house anymore. There was nothing left; Anna had taken everything. No little shoes by the door, no dinosaurs or Lego for me to trip on in the hall. I could no longer hear the sound of Jack's songs as he sat in the bath or hear his little feet padding up the stairs.

I put our furniture and the things Anna hadn't taken into storage. The movers took my stuff to the rented house in Cornwall, a place I had chosen because it seemed suitably remote and I had been there on holiday as a child.

On the day that I left, when all the furniture was gone, I had one last drink, sitting on the floor in the empty kitchen. I finished my glass of vodka and then filled up my Diet Coke bottle for the train. Just before I left, I went into the sunroom to check that the French windows were locked. As I was looking out over the backyard for the last time, I noticed it. A third sunflower swaying in the wind.

PART 3

PART 3

The rain soaks through my trouser legs as I make my way through the long grass toward the back of Hampstead Cemetery. To get to Jack's plot, from the entrance by the church, there is a shortcut through the oldest part of the site. The gravestones here are ramshackle, resting at oblique angles, battered by the wind; the grass is overgrown.

My shoes are caked with mud but I trudge on, leaning a little into the wind. There is always one grave that catches my eye, where I have to stop and stand still for a moment. A little girl carved into stone, tortuously thin and covering her face, as if she is hiding from death itself.

As I approach Jack's grave, I stand behind an ash tree, which always seems incongruous in company, as if it should be standing alone on a Winnie the Pooh hill, waiting for lightning to strike. I peek out from behind the tree to see if Anna is here, but the graveyard is empty. I know she comes here, because sometimes there are flowers.

Jack's is a small headstone, not upright, but horizontal.

Jack Coates
10th August 2008 – 20th January 2015

Sunshine passes, shadows fall
Love and memory outlast them all

I did not like the inscription. I thought it was trite, but Anna said we had to have something. It reminded me of the condolence cards we had received, with their platitudes, their empty sentiments. Besides, I had not wanted a grave. A grave was to accept that he was gone.

It has become a monthly ritual to come here, to get the early train before dawn and to return to Cornwall around dusk. I crouch down and scrape away some leaves from the gravestone, but the wind instantly blows them back. I sit on the ground for a while, shivering in the rain, drinking from my hip flask.

I check my watch. Even though it is early, I do not want to risk meeting Anna. I kiss my hand and touch the stone lightly with my fingers and then head back to the entrance on the pebble paths, this time avoiding the long grass. There is a greater chance of meeting Anna like this, but it is wet, I am cold and I want to find a café to have some breakfast, where I can sit and wait for the pub to open.

After a sandwich in a coffee shop, I go to The Ship, the pub I used to come to with Scott. I plug my laptop into the wall and log on to the Wi-Fi, and start working on some code. I have been working for Marc, the programmer in Brussels who Scott hired. The work is boring, but it pays the bills. I work for a couple of hours, drinking pint after pint, and by the time I leave, I am drunk, unsteady on my feet. I do not want to go up our old street, so I go the long way around, trudging up past the ponds on the other side of the heath. The words "we own the sky" come into my head, as they always do when I'm alone, and I whisper them to myself with each step as I walk up the hill. "We own the sky, we own the sky."

At the top of Parliament Hill, I put my backpack on the ground, take a long drink from my hip flask and look out across London. The sky threatens in the distance, a callous, unfeeling wall of cloud. The heath is desolate. Just the occasional caw of a crow, hustling like grave diggers, flying from tree to garbage can to tree.

When the tripod and camera are calibrated, I take the first shot, down toward the Highgate ponds. The view is pastoral, a little England, houses nestled on the hill, the village spire of St. Anne's peeping above the trees. Even though I used to come up here with Jack, I have never taken a panorama from Parliament Hill.

I have been busy recently. *We Own the Sky* has been nominated for a photography award, so I have been taking more and more panoramas, traveling around the country, going farther afield. The Seven Sisters, Three Cliffs Bay, the Cheddar Gorge. Sometimes I drive, but mostly I take the train, traveling in first class, drinking Kronenbourg and vodka in the dining car. There is something cathartic about it, something that keeps me going. Visiting the places we went together; writing my messages to Jack in the sky.

I slowly move the camera around, as the hills give way to the city, and suddenly there is Canary Wharf, like a fortress, surrounded by its chunky minions. I rotate the camera for another shot, capturing the Gherkin and then the Shard, rising above the skyline like a stalagmite.

I am standing under the departure board at Paddington Station, when I see someone who looks familiar. It takes me a while, a flash of recognition, a feeling that we have met somewhere before, perhaps one of the women I have chatted with online.

I am just trying to place her, thinking that she looks rather Bohemian, a refined artiness, like a rich gallery owner, when she catches my eye. It is then that I realize it is Lola.

There is a second moment when we consider pretending that we haven't seen each other, that it was nothing more than the curious meeting of two strangers' eyes. But there is something that propels me toward her.

"Hello, Lola," I say and as I speak I realize I am slurring my words.

"Oh, hey, Rob. Wow, what a surprise," she says.

"How are you?" I say. "It's been a while."

"Yes, wow, it really has," she says, flustered. "I was at some opening last night. Bit of a late one."

She is exactly as I remember, the impression of creative chaos she so carefully nurtured, the tone and lilt of her voice, which always sounded like an air-kiss.

"And how are you, Rob?" she said, emphasizing the word *you*.

"Fine," I say.

"What are you up to then?"

"Just getting a train."

"No, silly-billy. I mean generally."

"Oh, nothing much. I'm living down in Cornwall now."

"Yes, Anna said."

"So you're still friends?"

"Yes, of course. Why wouldn't we be?"

I know I am not making much sense and I suddenly feel very drunk, like a teenager coming home and having to pretend they are sober.

"We live close by now, in Gerrards Cross," Lola says.

Gerrards Cross? I know it can only mean one thing: that Anna has remarried. I can imagine her living with an older man, divorced, teenage kids from a previous marriage.

"That's nice," I say, and I want to ask about Anna but I don't know how.

"Are you okay, Rob?"

"Yes, I'm fine," I say, speaking slowly and trying to enunciate each syllable.

"Have you been sick?"

"What?" I look down at my jacket, and there are little flecks of what looks like vomit. I try to think back and realize I can't

remember leaving Parliament Hill, or even how I got to Paddington.

Lola smiles at me, as if I am a rescue puppy she is rejecting.
"Anna said you were struggling a little with the..."

She doesn't finish her sentence, but she doesn't have to. I
know Anna will have told her everything, given her side: how
I kidnapped Jack, put him at risk. How I'm a drunk. I'm sure
she hasn't told Lola about what happened in Prague, how she
refused to allow our son the treatment that could have saved
his life. How instead of giving him a chance, she did word
searches and read crime novels.

I am just about to say something, to tell her to go and fuck
herself, when I drop my wallet and loose change spills on to
the ground. I bend down to try to pick it up, but I stumble and
my knees buckle and then I am lying on my back, looking up
at the station roof.

I can feel Lola next to me, her arms around my shoulders,
trying to help me stand up, but I can't see straight, can't seem
to coordinate my arms and legs. So I stop and sit for a while,
my head bowed, until finally I manage to stagger up and weave
my way across the platform to the train.

My jacket is wet, I think from where I have tried to clean
off the vomit in the bathroom, and I am carrying a bottle of
wine and a grocery bag full of beers. I find a seat and sit back
and stretch out my legs, watching the blurry skyline rush by.

I have Googled Anna from time to time, but there has never
been any indication that she has remarried. She had taken
up marathon running. I couldn't believe it at first. After our
aborted game of squash, it was a standing joke between us that
Anna had no interest in sports. But when I clicked on the link,
it was Anna, all right. Anna in a running singlet pictured in
a local Buckinghamshire newspaper, getting third place in a

charity fun-run. I remember the headline: 'Brave Mum Runs for Her Son.'"

Once, when I was drunk, I unsuccessfully tried to hack into her email and Facebook accounts, using every password combination I could imagine. I should have known better. Anna was always so careful about such things.

I wake. We are now a few miles past Exeter, following the path of the estuary, and I have spilled wine on the table and a couple near me have moved seats, glaring, tut-tutting as they go. The train emerges from a tunnel, and suddenly we lose sight of land and we are thrown out to sea, the train traveling so close to the shore it feels like we are tilting, then falling, into a giant pool of sea and sky.

I take out Jack's camera from my bag and look through his photos. The brilliant white lighthouse on the walk to Durdle Door; a blurry shot of his favorite robin; his makeshift panorama from the terrace in Greece. Anna might have cleared out his room, taken his things to the dump, but she wasn't having the camera. I made sure of that. I snuck it away from his bedside the day that he died, and I have never let it out of my sight.

I pass out, I think, with Jack's camera in my hand. When I wake, I see that I have missed my station and there is a damp stain spreading across my crotch. The alcohol is making me horny, and I think about getting out at the next station and trying to get to Tintagel to find the girl from the pub, but it is too late now, so I search on Facebook for Lola, squinting so I can see straight, and I find a picture of her wearing a wrap on a beach, coral in her hair. I try to click through her photos, hoping to find a shot of her in a bikini or a slinky cocktail dress, something I will dwell on when I get home, but all her privacy settings are closed.

When I get back home, after a taxi ride from Penzance, I collapse on the sofa with a vodka and switch on the news.

The Russians are still bombing in Syria, and there has been an earthquake in Pakistan. Then, something about tax credits, and I start to drift off.

I don't know if it is hearing his name or seeing his face that wakes me. But I suddenly jump forward in my seat, and I can feel my heart beating out of my chest, as if I have woken startled from a nightmare.

Dr. Sladkovsky, his face more jowly than I remember, is being led out of a villa into a haze of flashbulbs.

It takes me a while because I am so drunk, but I finally manage to rewind the report back to the beginning, unsure what I have just seen.

"The allegations are shocking," the reporter says. "Investigators have accused Dr. Sladkovsky of injecting his patients with a substance that contained human plasma."

The next morning, I reach for the bottle of vodka by my bed. Human plasma. Did I dream it? A warped fantasy from my booze-addled brain. I grab my laptop from the bedside table and see it is one of the top items on the BBC.

PRAGUE—A controversial cancer doctor has been arrested on charges of medical malpractice in the Czech Republic.

Zdenek Sladkovsky, whose clinic based in Prague attracts thousands of patients each year, was arrested on May 12 by Czech police.

Prosecutors allege that Sladkovsky was using human plasma in his controversial immuno-engineering treatments and giving patients unlicensed drugs without their knowledge. They also allege that Sladkovsky was fraudulently advertising cancer products, a violation of the European Drugs Code.

According to Jan Dundr, a spokesman for the Czech Prosecutor-General's Office, Sladkovsky has been under investigation for five years. Dundr said that investigators from the Czech Republic and the European Union started working with US law-enforcement agencies after numerous complaints to the US Food and Drug Administration about Sladkovsky's treatments.

As a result of the investigation, the European Medicine and Healthcare Regulatory Agency has banned the use of his immuno-engineering products and suspended Sladkovsky's medical license.

Dundr said that more than one thousand vials of drugs were seized in a police raid on the clinic. They said that Sladkovsky, who has declined to comment on the charges, was cooperating with investigators.

Sladkovsky has attracted controversy in the past for his expensive and untested therapies. While many of his former patients have claimed that they have been cured by the doctor, others have publicly criticized the clinic...

A prickle of cold sweat on my back and I can feel the panic rising, the palpitations of my heart, a numbness in my left arm that makes me want to crush my fist or scratch out my eyes.

I look for more online, but the stories just parrot the BBC report, so I click on *Hope's Place* to see if there has been any discussion.

It is strange coming back here again. It was a bookmark in my Favorites for so long, a place that I checked fifty, sixty times a day. I look down the list of posts and do not recognize any of the names: Motherofanangel, glioblsurvivor, strength, pleasegodhelpus. The board has a high turnover. Children die and their parents don't come back.

I start scrolling and halfway down the page, there is a thread.

Dr. Sladkovsky arrested
by Chemoforlifer» Fri May 12, 2017 7:39 pm

As some of you have no doubt seen, Dr. Sladkovsky has been arrested. I'm posting the link to the BBC news story.

http://www.bbc.com/news/europe-sladkovsky-35349861k

I am angry that so many have been tricked by this man. I am angry that children have died in his clinic, children who would have lived longer under standard medical care.

I am angry because over the years there have been many discussions about Sladkovsky and his treatments on this board. It would be nice if these people who supported him came out now and said that they were wrong—wrong to support this treatment that has cost countless families inordinate amounts of money and time that would have been better spent elsewhere. Chemoforlifer

Re: Dr. Sladkovsky arrested
by TeamAwesome» Fri May 12, 2017 9:14 pm

Disgusted to hear that but happy this man has been arrested. How can he even call himself a doctor? Just terrible.

I hope this will finally put the disagreements we have had here to rest and Hope's Place can continue doing what it does best. PROVIDING SUPPORT and COMMUNITY to everyone going through this terrible journey.

I still don't understand. Human plasma, medical malpractice? Did that mean immuno-engineering didn't work? What about children like Josh?

I read down the thread on *Hope's Place* to see if there were

any more details about the charges against Sladkovsky, but there
was nothing. Just outrage, peacocking, a stream of I-told-you-
sos, the people who said they always knew Sladkovsky's treatments were too good to be true.

But where is Nev? It is strange that he has not posted. Because on every thread concerning Dr. Sladkovsky, he was always
there, linking to academic papers or testimonials, sometimes
just posting pictures of Josh. In recent months, I have read all
of his messages again. There were nearly fifty of them and,
even though they were painful to read, I was always looking
for clues, something I might have missed, any explanation as
to why Nev suddenly stopped writing to me. Perhaps he had
just moved on, sick of being in the cancer world, fed up with
the attacks and the threats, the people who called him a liar.

I search Nev's username on *Hope's Place*, but it says "account
inactive." So I decide to do something that I haven't done in a
very long time. I hack the forum.

There is an easy exploit using Perl that should work. At Cambridge, we used it to hack into the college message boards, high
on Red Bull and vodka. We never did much: a bit of ghost
posting, a few puerile jokes.

I upgrade my Perl distribution and drop the exploit file into
the main directory. I open up the command prompt and try to
crack Nev's password. While his account is inactive, I am hoping that all his posts and private messages will still be archived.

ipb.pl http://devasc/forum Nev

Letters and numbers appear on the screen as the exploit pings
the forum, trawling through lines and lines of code. It takes longer than I remembered, and I worry that the password might be
wrapped in layers of encryption. Then, to my surprise, a hashed
password appears.

4114d9d3061dd2a41d2c64f4d2bb1a7f

The encryption is relatively simple and uses a standard algorithm. I search around on the web for a password cracker and find one I haven't heard of called Slain and Able. In about ten seconds, it gives me Nev's password in plaintext.

Grossetto

I log into the forum again, reactivate Nev's account, and reset his password. In his mailbox, there are 15,462 messages.

Subject: Can you help?
Sent: Thu Jul 10, 2010 3:27 pm
From: Htrfe
Recipient: Nev

Dear Nev,
I'm writing from Australia. In 2007, my daughter was diagnosed with a medulloblastoma that has spread to her spinal cord.
    I have been reading about your experiences at the clinic of Dr. Sladkovsky and wondered if you could help get us an appointment. The waiting list currently seems quite long and we don't have much time.

I look at the date. 2010. Seven years ago. I click on another message.

Subject: options
Sent: Mon Jan 20, 2011 3:36 pm
From: BlueWarrior
Recipient: Nev

Dear Nev,
Hi there I'm Marnie from Utah in the United States. I'm writing you because I am very interested in the protocol that your son

took and the drugs he has been given at Dr. Sladkovsky's clinic in Prague. My daughter has recently been diagnosed with...

A breeze chills the bedroom and I start to shiver. I click through the inbox, scanning the contents. There are emails from all over the world: Utah, Madrid, Arbroath, Rapid City, Bratislava.

I sit up in bed and put on my reading glasses. Did the treatment really work? That was what they all wanted to know. They had heard bad things about the clinic—but then they read about Josh. There was a waiting list, though. Could he put them in touch with someone at the clinic who could get them bumped up the list? Because if it worked for Josh, then surely, surely, it could work for...

I keep reading, trawling through the messages, refilling my vodka glass again and again. Nev wrote back to all of them. He wrote page after page, telling them about Josh, immuno-engineering, the clinic in Prague. He told them to never give up, to never take no for an answer, because what, after all, did these doctors know. He asked about their mothers, their children's schools, the troubles they were having with the in-laws. He knew the name of the family dog and the state of their lawns.

I carry on reading, and soon it is night and the moon is lighting up the room. As I click through various folders, there is something that catches my eye. In his Drafts, there are about twenty messages that look like templates Nev has used. In one, he introduces himself and tells Josh's story; in another, he gives details about Dr. Sladkovsky and the clinic. As I am reading, certain passages and phrases jump out at me and I am sure that I have seen them before.

Joan, every day it's like watching planes crashing. Planes full of children that could be saved…

I just wanted you to know, Kevin, that I'm thinking about you all and crossing fingers and legs and toes and everything really.

There is hope, John, there is always hope. Never give up, my friend.

I always knew I wasn't the only one. I knew that he wrote to other parents—he told me as much—but as I look through my own emails from Nev, I find those same exact sentences, the only difference being mine or Jack's name.

I click on another message in his Drafts.

Matilda's probably a bit young for Minecraft but Josh is really into it at the moment. He's just built this castle and said he wanted to send it to Matilda to cheer her up. (I told him Matilda was poorly.) I'm sending you a screenshot. I hope Matilda likes it.

Attached to the message is the 8-bit Minecraft image I remember so well: the blocky portcullis and turrets, the sign that, this time, says "Matilda's Castle" and not "Jack's."

I click on the next message in the Drafts folder, and it is blank except for an image. I open it and it is a drawing I instantly recognize, a drawing I think I still have somewhere on my laptop.

The drawing is of a little boy, with a bandage around his head, sitting in a hospital bed. Two dinosaurs dressed as nurses are carrying a tray. I remember how much Jack liked the dinosaurs. I remember how he asked if his bed could be moved outside, so he too could sit under the fiery yellow sun.

Anna had been right all along. Nev was a shill for the clinic, a con man preying on the desperate. I'd been had.

I am still in bed, reading through Nev's messages. I pour vodka into a toothbrush glass and drink it straight down. It stings and I retch in my mouth, but I do another shot and all I can taste is minty antiseptic and vomit.

It all seems so obvious now, when I look back, when I un-pick all the details. I never thought that I would fall for such a scam: taken in by a screen name, an avatar, like one of those poor fools who give their life savings to a foreign bride they met online.

From my bedside table, I reach for Jack's camera and I lie down, squinting my eyes so I can focus, scrutinizing every pic-ture as if I am seeing them for the first time. I can feel a vein or artery in my neck starting to pulse, but it is too deep within my body and I wish I could reach it, cut it out and touch its sinewy texture, and feel the throb of my heart.

I inhale and exhale, catching my breath. What I want now is to run outside into the inky blackness and jump from the edge of the cliff and feel my face smash onto the rocks beneath. Because grief, it smells very much like shame, and I cannot tell the difference anymore. Shame that I couldn't save him, that I didn't do enough. That I fed human plasma and God knows what to my dying son. Shame that I am still alive, that I do not have the courage to end it all.

I am trying to remember exactly what Jack looked like on the Greece holiday, with his thick blond hair and his Spider-Man shorts. But every time I try to picture him, I cannot re-member the exact contours of his skin, the constellation of his freckles, the glint and hue of his eyes. It is as if he has been pixelated out of my memory, his identity protected, like an abused child.

I can remember other things from that holiday, though: the wisp of the waiter's mustache; the code for the hotel-room safe; the convex curve of the aerobics instructor's ass. How could I think like this? To betray him like this. Every moment of every single day, I should have been scanning every line of his face, every inch of his pale skin.

You never forget, they always say. Never forget. Their touch, the smoothness of their fingers; their smile, sweet and disarming; a laugh you suddenly hear echoing around the room when you're doing the washing up. Never forget.

But you do forget, and it comes quicker than you think and in that there is shame—shame that you never really loved, that you are nothing but a fraud. Sometimes I cannot picture my dead son's face, but I do remember, in graphic detail, the breasts of the last girl that I fucked.

"Jack, Jack, Jack." I say his name out loud, over and over again, and another torrent of tears comes from deep down, beyond my ribs, my lungs, the walls of my chest. It is as if the tears are being pumped out of my heart.

"Jack, Jack, Jack." I want to open the window, climb up to the rooftop and scream his name, to write those four letters in the sky. Jack, my beautiful Jack.

I think I can see him in front of me, at the end of the bed, crouching on his knees next to his wooden garage, quietly pushing a Matchbox car up the ramp. Yes, it is definitely him. I can see strands of his unruly hair silhouetted against the light from the window. He puts his finger to his mouth and then bites his lip in concentration, just how he would when he was trying to write the letters of his name.

"Jack," I whisper, but he does not stir and continues winding up the handle of the lift, moving the cars from floor to floor.

"Can you hear me, sweetheart? Can you hear my words? Please answer me, Jack, please."

I keep on saying his name, rocking myself against the side of the bed, wringing my hands together. I want to tell someone about the lilt of his breathing as he slept, the bemused expression on his face as he woke, how he always placed his hands over his eyes to hide from me as he sat on the toilet.

I need to find someone, anyone. I want to tell them how Jack was learning numbers and could never get six, and I tried so many ways to get him to remember—drawing it like a snake and hissing out the *s*. I want to tell them how he was convinced that Batman lived in the backyard and how he babbled himself to sleep at night. I want to tell them about Jack's yogurts in the fridge, how neither Anna nor I could bear to throw them out, so we just left them on the top shelf, their lids bulging, their best-by dates long gone.

I open my laptop and go to a folder in my email called "Anna." I have written many drafts to her over the last two years, but I have never sent any of them. Some of them are particularly venomous. I call her a bitch and a whore and say she killed our son. I list my grievances against her in bullet points: how she refused Jack's further treatment at Sladkovsky's, how her pride was more important than our son's well-being.

I shiver, not from the cold, but because it is jarring to suddenly discover you are frail. That what you had thought was robust can so easily disintegrate, like an old parchment crumbling into dust. Anna was right all along. About everything. She always said Dr. Sladkovsky was a fraud, that Nev was not what he seemed. And I have cursed her for that, treated her like dirt, because I was too arrogant to listen to reason, so enthralled by my own hubris, my feeling that anything—even my own son's biology—could be hacked. I have lived in disgust for so long—repulsed by everything around me—and now I know that the only person that deserves my disgust is me.

Subject:
Sent: Sat May 13, 2017 10:18 pm
From: Rob Coates
To: Anna Coates

theres no other way to say this but im so so so sorry. I know I donyt deserve your forgiveness for what I did and I treated you and Jack terribly and I am so very vry ashamed of myself I am so sory anna.

LONDON EYE

——

watching that sunset, i wanted to tell you more about heaven, jack, but I was too scared, didn't want to say the wrong thing. i should have told you, though, but i just didn't know how. did you know where you were going, jack? i hope not. i hope you imagined yourself flying through the night with the snowman. i hope you found the winter air thick with love.

2

I lie on the sofa in my boxers and watch an American talk show. I cannot sleep at night without my usual anesthetic, so I stay up until the early hours, tossing and turning, my mind racing. I can deal, I think, with the cravings; I expected that. But what I did not expect is the constant film of sweat on my back, the needles that crawl under my skin, my heart stuttering and leaping like an old roller coaster.

I shudder, suddenly freezing, and pull a blanket up around my neck. What have I done? Perhaps the fragments that I remember are just the beginning. Perhaps I lashed out at Anna when I was drunk, or said even more unspeakable things. I remember the morning I woke up with a bruise on my arm, and I have no idea how I got it.

It is nothing, though, nothing to what I have done to Jack. Human plasma. Unlicensed drugs. "An astounding negligence of care." And now a new fear, that keeps me awake at night: that Dr. Sladkovsky's treatments might have hastened Jack's death.

Re: Dr. Sladkovsky arrested
by Rob» Sun May 14, 2017 4:39 am

Hello everyone, I haven't been on Hope's Place for a while and just wanted to reply to Chemoforlifer's post, as I am one of those people whose son was treated by Dr. Sladkovsky.

I am disgusted with myself. My wife was adamant that we shouldn't do the treatment but I went against her wishes and took my son Jack there. (Jack was diagnosed in spring 2014 and died in January 2015, not long after we left the clinic.)

I am full of so much guilt and so much pain. I have been drinking since Jack's death, drinking myself into the ground every day. I have stopped now but I just don't know how I can keep doing this anymore.

I hate myself for what I have done to my son and to my wife. I am so ashamed I feel like killing myself. I don't give a shit about anyone else other than myself. To everyone that I have hurt, I am so sorry.

Re: Dr. Sladkovsky arrested
by Chemoforlifer» Sun May 14, 2017 7:40 am

First, Rob, I hope you're okay. And please, if you want to talk about any of this, do send me a PM or give me a call (number in my sig). Please don't suffer alone and remember your friends on Hope's Place are all here for you. Regarding Dr. Sladkovsky, well, it takes guts to say that, to admit your mistake. We all live and learn. I wish you peace.

Just as I am logging out of *Hope's Place*, I receive a private message through the forum.

Subject: Re:
Sent: Sun May 14, 2017 3:21 pm
From: naws09
Recipient: Rob

Are you okay? I know I don't know you but I don't like to see someone in distress. Please don't kill yourself. There is too much sadness in this world. I lost my little girl, Lucy, a few years ago and understand exactly how you feel. I know how dark it can get and I know how long that darkness lasts. Anyway, I just wanted to let you know that you have a friend if you ever want to talk.

Subject: Re: Re:
Sent: Mon May 15, 2017 8:45 am
From: Rob
Recipient: naws09

Hello, naws09. Thanks so much for your kind note. I feel like a bit of an idiot, to be honest. I was feeling very down and detoxing from all the alcohol when I wrote that post. Sorry, didn't want to alarm you.

I was humbled by the amount of strangers, like yourself, who sent me PMs saying they were worried about me and offering their support. So thank you so much. It means a lot to me.

I think, deep down, that's what I really want—to talk—because I have kept everything inside me for so long. I remember when my wife was telling me I needed help after Jack died and I knew I needed it but I just couldn't do it, wasn't brave enough I suppose.

I hope you don't mind me asking, but how do you do it? Staying alive, I mean. Once again, thanks very much for your kind note. I really do appreciate it.
Best Wishes,
Rob

Subject: Re: Re:
Sent: Tue May 16, 2017 7:06 pm
From: naws09
Recipient: Rob

Hello, Rob, nice to hear from you and I'm glad you're feeling better now. Well done, by the way, on the drinking, or lack of drinking, rather.

You asked me how I do it. Well, I certainly don't have the formula. And I'm not sure I have any decent advice. As mundane as it sounds, I keep myself busy: I work a lot, I run, I go to the gym. I try to take an interest in things: new books, the TV series that everyone is talking about at work.

I can't say I'm happy but I'm surviving. It's only a temporary solution, though, and I have hit the bottom so many times. I have wanted to slit my wrists, jump off a bridge. I have wished terrible things, things that make me ashamed to be alive. I have wished that this happened to other children and not mine.

So, that's my story. There is one thing I do, which I think helps a great deal. I try to help people on Newly Diagnosed. It breaks my heart to see these desperate people suffering so much, so I try to help them, offer them support, just be their friend.

When I started doing this on Hope's Place, I began to notice this world of support that I never knew existed, where people were contacting each other privately and PMing each other, becoming friends on Facebook or whatever. They do it quietly, without fanfare, all these hundreds and thousands of personal connections and bonds that others don't know about. It is a small thing but it is a beautiful thing. I've become very close friends with several people from Hope's Place and it has meant so much to me. I'm not a particularly touchy-feely person and find it difficult to open up. These friendships, with people who have gone through the same, have helped me so much.

It's not going to bring your little boy back...but then nothing will.

Take care of yourself and do stay in touch.

As I am running, I watch the water hens and seagulls wade across the mudflats, drinking water from little canals in the sand. I jog past the yacht club on the estuary, the veterinary

clinic and the old Methodist church, and then start to acceler-
ate up the path that snakes along the river.

It is late spring, but the sun is blazing, hotter than it should
be for this time of year, and my T-shirt and shorts are wet with
sweat. I power into a slight incline, through a tunnel carved into
the rock, until I get to the railway bridge, a Victorian viaduct that
spans the valley. I overtake two swans, slowly gliding, their heads
pointed downward, scanning the surface of the water for food.

I come here every day now. To the bench under the viaduct.
Perhaps it is the solitude, the calming effect of the red rock, but it
is easy to think up here, without the booze clouding everything.

The world has a certain crispness now, like a morning frost,
so delicate and pristine you are afraid to take a step. I am notic-
ing things around me, details I haven't seen before: the worn-
away edge of a sideboard; the way the sun, reflected through
a lampshade, makes a rainbow of light on the carpet. Because
now, when I really listen, when I sit in the calm under the viaduct, feeling the breath of the wind, the tang of river-salt in
the air, I am feeling, seeing, hearing the world with a new hy-
persensitivity, as if a blockage has been removed from my ear
and I can hear the crash of a dropping pin.

I should have listened to my dad. He liked a drink, but hated
drinkers. It's all about them, son, he had told me, boring old
bastards, always droning on. All them clever thoughts, son, but
the boy could hardly stand. Because it gets you like that, the
booze. It makes you think you're unwrapping the world. But
you're not. The world is unwrapping you.

I come home and sit in the silence of the kitchen and drink a
glass of water. The woman I have been speaking to—naws09—
was right. Keeping myself busy has helped. Before, my whole
day was governed and punctuated by drink, propped up, like
the pillars of the church, or the call to prayer. I have had to
find things to replace that, mostly chores around the house: or-

ganizing the spoons by size in the drawer; preparing elaborate lunches; spending a week reading various review sites on the best studio speakers to buy for my laptop. I have been doing some extra work for Marc, more than I can handle, but I know I have to keep myself occupied, keep myself off the booze.

The things I have started to remember are still so hazy, I cannot be sure if what I am remembering is true. Because they tease you, memories, revealing a little bit here, a little bit there, and you are never quite sure if they are real, like an imagined spit of rain.

I remember Anna telling me how I had pissed over her sunflowers. How I pissed over the memory of our unborn children. I shudder. There are no mitigating circumstances, no equanimity of blame, but just the sordid truth of how awful I was.

I remember what she said, when things were bad at the end. How I would never live up to my father. She was right. He faced tragedy like a man. He was not weak like me. He looked after his family to the end.

For the first time in days, I feel an overwhelming urge to drink. I could get in the car and be back home in twenty minutes with fresh supplies. I can think of nothing better now than to open a bottle of vodka, or wine, and hear that glug, that little dog's cough, as the liquid is poured into a glass.

No, I will not. I will go for a shower; I will clean the filter on the dishwasher. I will not drink. It is the only thing I can do to try to make amends.

Subject: Re: Re:
Sent: Thu May 19, 2017 3:21 pm
From: Rob
Recipient: naws09

Thank you so much for your message, naws09.
I've been trying to follow your advice and stay busy and I

really think it's helping. Just having a project to do each day, even if it's organizing a cupboard or something.

I know you're right about the Newly Diagnosed thing. I would love to be able to do that, to help people in that way, but I'm not sure I can. I just don't think I have enough to give. Also, given that I took my son to Dr. Sladkovsky's, I'm not exactly the right person to advise people.

How are you, by the way? I always talk about myself but I don't know anything about you...

Subject: Re: Re:
Sent: Fri May 20, 2017 8:50 pm
From: naws09
Recipient: Rob

Of course you're the right person to help people on Newly Diagnosed. You've gone through all of this, you've lived it. You know how it feels better than anyone.

You asked how I was, well, if you must know, I have been going through a bad patch recently. Every little thing seems to be setting me off. I was watching one of those 24 hours in Casualty documentaries and there was this mother whose son was hit by a car and she was so distraught and beside herself and I had this horrible feeling of guilt that I was never like that, was never like that mother.

I'm sure there was more I could have done to make it easier on Lucy, to help her enjoy her last few months. Sometimes I am paralyzed by fear that she knew: that she knew that she was dying and she was scared and I wasn't able to take that fear away. Some days are worse than others, but I feel like I let her down.

I suppose deep down, I feel like it's my fault—that I deserve it and what happened to my daughter must have been because of something I did. That's probably just me being stupid, but it's how I feel. Thanks for asking though...

Subject: Re: Re:
Sent: Fri May 20, 2017 10:23 pm
From: Rob
Recipient: naws09

Well, of course it's you being stupid. ☺ Of course of course of course it wasn't your fault and you should never torture yourself like that. The problem is, though: I can say that, I can advise that, because objectively, as you and I both know, that's sound advice. But knowing it's a bullshit feeling still doesn't stop me from feeling the same sometimes, especially in those dark times, when it's so hard to see the light, to even imagine the light. So you're wrong to feel like that, but I understand you feeling like that, if that makes sense. (And, I know I don't know you, but I'm sure you were a wonderful mother.)

Subject: Re: Re:
Sent: Fri May 20, 2017 11:45 pm
From: naws09
Recipient: Rob

Thank you. You see, this is what I'm talking about. You're good with the advice. You should definitely help out on Newly Diagnosed. Really. ☺

   I wanted to ask you, by the way, and please don't take this the wrong way, but why did you go to Dr. Sladkovsky? There are so many parents on Newly Diagnosed going down these awful paths of alternative treatments (much worse than Dr. Sladkovsky) and I would like to help them, dissuade them, but I never really know what to say. Well, it's late now. Good night.

I sit upstairs in my little office drinking coffee. I have been trying to work today, but I cannot stop thinking about Anna. I still have not heard from her. I did write to her again in more detail, apologizing and begging for her forgiveness. I do not expect a response. I know I deserve nothing from her.

I long for her, though, and I think a part of me was always longing for her. The Anna who, with such glee, made me go to the all-night *Star Wars* marathon at the Ritzy. The Anna who fell asleep in my lap on Brighton beach. And then the time we played squash. Those wonderful Bobby Charlton shorts. The look on her face when the animals closed in.

I could watch Anna for hours, the minuscule changes she could make to the expressions on her face. How she would very slightly stick out her lower lip when she was contemplating something, a cartoon version of *The Thinker*. Or how her eyes would dart to the ground after she said something she was not sure of—a moment of modesty, insecurity—and then she would look up again and continue, somehow fortified by the slight movement of her head.

I want to look at some photos of her, but I have deleted them all. They had been everywhere, once. Digital flotsam, dormant in the memories of half-forgotten devices. Badly framed photographs, videos taken too late. But then one night, not long after I had moved to Cornwall, after I had had too much to drink, I deleted them. I remember the phone's question: Are you sure you want to delete?

I suddenly have frantic need to see those photos of Anna once again. I download some hard-drive recovery software that claims it can retrieve files that were deleted years ago, but it doesn't work. My drive has been written and rewritten so many times, the digital imprint is long gone.

And then I remember. My backups. Old habits die hard, and

I have always backed up, fastidiously once a week, connecting my computer to an external hard drive.

I open up the backup software and scroll through all the old versions of my computer on the laptop that Anna and I used to share. I choose one, from a few months after Jack died, and hear the fan start to kick in as the drive begins to restore.

I go downstairs to have some lunch and when I return, the restore is finished. I start looking through the directories, and then I find what I am looking for. Anna on the beach, her sun hat casting a shadow over her face; Anna in a Cambridge pub, poking out her tongue; Anna looking exhausted and flushed, a tiny newborn Jack held closely to her breast.

She was so beautiful, never entirely comfortable being photographed, always with a little smile as if she knew something you didn't but wasn't going to tell you.

As I am looking through the photos, I see some pictures of Josh that I must have downloaded and put on my desktop in the last few days in Hampstead. I flick through them: Josh wearing his Manchester Utd uniform; Josh at a birthday party; that video Nev had sent of him wearing his Robin mask; the picture of him sitting on a rock. Despite everything I now knew about Dr. Sladkovsky, it still didn't make any sense. Nev and Josh were not bots. They were not the creation of a Czech intern working in Dr. Sladkovsky's marketing department. They were real. I had spoken to them, seen pictures of them in flesh and blood.

I know I have to find them, to find out if Josh really died. In recent weeks, I have dug around, trying to track Nev down, and there is one more thing I have been meaning to try. I open up a penetration-testing program I have in Linux and test the URL of Nev's blog.

wpscan—URL [nevbarnes.wordpress.com]

The program looks for weaknesses, backdoors, spewing out lines of code. Nev is using an old version of WordPress, unpatched and riddled with vulnerabilities. I search for his user profiles, but they are hidden and password protected.

I guess that "Nev" is his username and try to find the password by brute force.

wpscan—URL [nevbarnes.wordpress.com] wordlist [root/desktop/Nev]<27<1

More lines of code and then a ticker, a little hourglass, as the script tries to crack his password with thousands of different combinations, all within milliseconds of each other. Then, a cursor, and there it is. I let out a little sob when I see what he has chosen for his password.

Josh2606

I log in to Nev's WordPress account and go straight to his billing information. Underneath one of his listed credit cards there is an address. I find it on Google Maps: a house in Preston.

3

There is a sheen to the red brick of the road, as if it has recently been hosed down. The mock Tudor houses, with brown beams and overwrought gables, are arranged in a semicircle around the cul-de-sac. The planners have tried to break up the monotony of the new builds, adding features to each property: a rockery, climbing ivy, a rustic wooden fence.

It is more upmarket than I imagined, not the sort of place I thought Nev would live. Too middle class, a road for real-estate agents and marketing executives, a road where people read the *Mail* and the *Times* and send their children to minor private schools.

I am tired as I park my car outside number 36. The drive, nearly seven hours, was longer than I thought, and I am glad I have booked a hotel for the night.

I walk up the drive, gravel scrunching under my feet, and then follow a neat concrete-slab path through the grass. I ring the doorbell and it is an electronic chime, a deep baritone that echoes around the house. I wait for a while, but no one comes. I am just thinking about leaving when a man opens the door. For a moment, I think it is Nev—a smarter, monied Nev— but then I look again and see that this man is older and wearing some kind of cravat.

"Hello?" he says in what I think is a well-to-do northern accent. "Can I help?" He looks at me askance, and I realize I must be staring.

"Oh, I'm sorry," I say, seasoning my accent with a little Cambridge. "I'm looking for Nev Barnes. I'm an old friend and we lost contact, and this is the last address I have for him."

My palms are sweating, and I can sense the man taking me in, my voice, clothes, furtively glancing over my shoulder at the Audi.

"Oh, Mr. Barnes is the previous owner," he says. "They left about two years ago. Him and his little one."

Him and his little one. I think about those words. Him and his little one.

"Ah, okay," I say, thinking about Nev and Josh driving away, in a car packed full of suitcases and garbage bags full of shoes. "And you don't have a forwarding address?"

"We don't, I'm afraid. It was a quick sale, and he kept saying he would send one, but he never did. I do have an email address for him, if that helps."

"No, it's fine, I have that."

"Okay," he says, looking confused and suddenly wary of the stranger standing on his doorstep.

"And you don't have any idea where he's gone?"

The man thinks for a moment, still weighing up the situation. "I think he moved to the Reeves property, as unlikely as it sounds. It's on the edge of town."

"Reeves as in *R e e v e s*."

"Yes, that's right."

"Thank you, you've been very kind. I might have a look around there."

He stares at me again, still unsure what to make of me. "Well, it's a big place. And not the sort of place you'd want to look around. Or take your car," he says, nodding at the Audi.

I laugh. "Ah, I see, well, thanks anyway. I might have a rethink."

"Yes, quite," he says. "Look, could you do me a favor? We have all this mail piling up for Mr. Barnes. It sounds like you've got a better chance of giving it to him than we have. Would you take it?"

"Yes, of course. I'd be happy to."

He disappears for a minute or two, and I stand awkwardly on the doorstep. Then he comes back with four large shopping bags full of letters. "Here you go," he says. "Evidently your friend was a very popular chap."

I put the bags of letters in the trunk and then, with the man still watching me from his door, drive back to the main road. Along the main street, most of the shops are boarded up. All that are left are a few Indian takeouts, minicab companies, a shabby office advertising "no win, no fee" legal services.

I pull in to the parking lot of a pub, a little one-story building in between two taller row houses. There is fire damage up one wall and in the row of houses, the pub looks like a broken, blackened tooth. I sit there for a while, drumming on the steering wheel, looking at the map on my phone.

As I'm thinking what to do, there is a knock on the window. Standing next to the car are two scrawny children sharing a can of superstrength lager.

"Want any bangs, mister?" says the smaller boy, as the window rolls down.

"No," I answer, not even knowing what bangs are.

"You some fuckin' pedo then, parked here?"

"Fuck off," I say.

"So what you doing here, pedo?" The older kid starts sniggering and they fist-bump and pass their can back and forth.

"I'm looking for someone actually. Can you help?"

"Why the fuck should we help you?" the older boy says, spitting on the ground.

"I'll pay," I say.

"How much?"

"Twenty quid."

"Fuck off, ya twat. I can get that in five seconds selling these wraps."

"Fifty."

The boys look at each other, eyeing each other up under their baseball caps.

"Okay. Give us the money then."

I hold a fifty-pound note just out of their reach. "I'm looking for someone called Nev Barnes. Do you know him?"

"Might do."

"Don't play silly buggers. Either you do or you don't."

"Believe it or not, pal, but I do actually," the younger boy says, "but I won't tell you unless you give us money first."

I look him up and down. "Come on then," I say, handing the cash over, but the boys just stand there, smiling at each other, lighting fresh cigarettes.

The younger boy leans in through the car window, and he smells of cigarettes and cheap body spray. "I'll tell you what, pal," he says, lowering his voice to almost a whisper. "I will definitely tell you, because I know Nev, I do. His kid goes to my school. Moved here a couple of years ago."

His kid. Him and his little one. My hands are shaking so I hold on to the steering wheel.

"You see those lads over there?" He points to some older boys on BMXs across the road, and I nod. "Right, if you don't give me another one of them fifties, I'm gonna tell those lads you just offered me fifty quid for a BJ."

He smiles a sweet cherubic smile, as if he is having his picture taken at school, and I know that I am being had, but I don't see how I have any choice, so I take out another note and press it into his palm.

He smiles and puts the money loosely into his pocket. "You're very close actually, pal," he says. "Just around the corner. It's got a red fence, and there's an old Fiesta in the drive."

"Thank you."

"Fuck off, you posh nob," he says, and they walk away laughing, swigging from their can.

The boy was right. I was about thirty seconds away, a vast rectangle of grass, surrounded on all sides by run-down row houses. On the grass, there are piles of rubbish, large industrial containers and a bonfire surrounded by a black halo. In the corner of the green, there is a bricked-off section with patches of paler concrete, where the slide and climbing frames used to stand.

I can see Nev's house, the Fiesta in the drive, the broken red fence, a St. George's Cross hanging from his neighbor's window. As I'm parking the car, some children who were playing football on the green stop and stare at me, scoping me out. I stare back, puffing myself up, so they might think I'm the debt collector, someone not to be messed with. And then, just as I am about to turn away and go through Nev's gate, I see him.

I know instantly that it is Josh. He is playing football and his blond hair flows behind him, as he ducks and weaves and spins, head and shoulders above the rest. He looks out of place in the group, hunched under their hoodies, pinching drags between goals. I cannot stop watching as he rounds three players and then fakes out the goalkeeper before effortlessly sliding the ball between two gas cans.

I have looked at his photos enough times to know the exact color of his hair, the shape of his slightly rounded shoulders. Even though he has grown, I recognize his shy smile, how his hair flops over his face as he walks back to his teammates.

I have seen that smile before. A photo of Nev and Josh standing next to the Angel of the North. I have to stop myself, but I want to walk up to him, to see and touch this miracle boy. I want to hold his face in my hands, to feel the warm flush of his skin. I wave to him, but he doesn't see me, doesn't wave back.

The gate to Nev's house is broken and needs to be lifted off the ground before it will open. I ring the doorbell and wait. Next to the door, there are some children's shoes, trainers and blue rain boots, mud encrusted on the soles. Him and his little one.

I recognize the man who opens the door. It is definitely the Nev I have spoken to, who I have seen in the photos and videos, but it is not the Nev I remember. His face is drawn, unshaved, his body gaunt, like a malnourished alcoholic. His jeans hang loosely off his hips, and there are holes in the elbows of his gray Fruit of the Loom sweatshirt. He seems thinner, older, like a man in his seventies wearing the clothes he wore when he was young. His lips are dry and chapped, and he swipes specks of dandruff from his shoulders.

"Hello, can I help?"

His accent is thick, much thicker than I remember when we spoke on the phone. I notice his eyes flicker over my shoulder, toward the kids on the green.

"Nev?"

He pauses, and I think I see a flash of fear in his eyes.

"Yes, can I help you, mate?" Maaate. Long Lancashire vowels, a reminder that I was far from home.

"It's Rob, Jack's dad," I say brightly. His face does not change, and I am not sure he remembers me. "Would you mind if we talked for a few minutes?"

Nev looks me up and down. The porch smells a little musty, like a greenhouse, and in the corner there are stacks of free newspapers and a crumpled delivery cart.

"All right then," Nev says, holding the door open.

Inside, the house is immaculate, a little oasis from the street outside. A worn but clean sofa, a fireplace and a mantelpiece, without a speck of dust. There are children's books neatly piled in the corner, and through the doors to the kitchen I can see a child's painting stuck to the fridge.

I sit down on the sofa and Nev takes a small hard chair in the corner. For a moment we don't speak. Behind him on a shelf there is a collection of marble-white figurines of angels and galloping horses. They are arranged in perfect symmetry, like a silent ceramic army.

"I don't remember you... I don't think so, I don't think I do," Nev says. He looks diminutive in the corner, forlorn, like a man captured on film by a pedophile hunter.

"It's okay. I know you wrote to lots of people. We spoke on the phone once a couple of years ago and exchanged emails. My son was Jack."

Nothing, not even a flash of recognition. I know he wrote to lots of people. But we had exchanged so many messages. I told him everything, about Jack's treatment, my relationship with Anna. And now it seems like I am talking to a different person.

"We went to Prague for treatment, but my wife didn't want to continue," I say, hoping it would jog his memory. "Jack died not long after we came back."

"Oh, very sorry about that," Nev says, but it is as if he is somewhere else, listening to a different conversation. His words were choppy, sputtered out. "How did you know where to find the house like?"

"Just asked around," I say, and Nev starts to speak but there is a shout from outside as something, a football I think, hits one of the front windows. Nev does not move in his chair, as if it has happened many times before.

"Is that Josh out there playing football?" I ask. "The blond boy."

Nev's eyes dart to the window, and then he sits back in his chair. He does not speak for a moment, and it is as if the words are difficult for him to say, as if he is trying to overcome a stutter. On the coffee table, I can see some cheaply made flyers. Nev Barnes. No Job Too Small. Painting, Gardening, Odd Jobs. Call: 01632 532676.

"No, that's not him," he says after a while. "I think I know the one you mean, though. The lanky lad."

I think about the boy outside, slotting the ball between the gas cans, sweeping his long blond hair out of his face. It was Josh; I was sure it was Josh.

Nev is motionless. One of the angels holds his attention for a moment, as if he notices that it has a speck of dust on its wing.

Suddenly, he stands up from his seat and takes a few paces toward me, and he is on edge now, tapping his legs with his hands, a red rash spreading across his neck.

"Look, I don't mean to be rude like, but what can I help you with? I... I'm very sorry about your son, but I... I... I'm not sure I can help you with anything."

"So where's Josh then?" I say, and I didn't mean it to but it sounds like a threat.

Nev walks toward me again, as if he wants to show me the door, but I don't budge, stay sitting in my seat. He is getting more agitated, pacing back and forth across the living room.

"I don't know why you've come here," he says, and he is wringing his hands together, as if he is squeezing water out of wet clothes.

"I just want to know what happened to Josh," I say, looking him in the eye.

"What happened to Josh?" Nev says, clicking his fingers and cracking his knuckles. "Why are you asking about my son?" He is standing over me, and he smells of stale sweat. "I think it's time that you leave now."

I stand up to face him. He seems smaller now, and I am nearly a head taller than him. "Where is Josh then, at school?"

He looks at me and then looks away. "That's right, yes, at school, the lad's at school," he says, and he doesn't sound as if he even believes it himself.

"You're lying, Nev. I know you're lying."

"Lying, what are you even saying now. I'm telling you, mate, he's at school, just around the corner, and he'll be home soon, doing his homework. Or he'll be out there playing football with them lads...always have to call him in for his dinner because he's football mad, my Josh..."

Nev doesn't look well. He is not pacing anymore but standing still, holding on to the mantelpiece for support. He is shaking and his eyes are glassy, as if he's had some kind of fit.

"Are you okay?" I say, touching his arm. "Perhaps you should sit down." I help him back to his chair, and he sinks into the cushions, trying to catch his breath.

"My Josh died five year ago," he says suddenly and then looks away at the wall.

I say nothing and Nev shakes his head. "He never got better, did he, poor lad. He died out there, over in Prague." He sits forward in his seat, turns away from the angels and toward me. "He also went to the clinic, Dr. Sladkovsky's clinic, for treatment but it didn't work for him either. I didn't understand it, like. I read all those testimonials about all them little boys and girls that got better. Did nothing for our Josh, though, in the end."

"What... I don't... So why, why did you say that he was alive, that he got better?" I say, the skin prickling on my neck.

Nev shrugs, and I notice that he is frantically tapping his left leg on the carpet.

"I don't understand," I say. "All your letters, your photos of Josh. We were on the phone and I heard him. I remember you asking him to take his shoes off, and I could hear the cartoons in the background. And the video of you two dressed up as Batman and Robin. I just don't understand. So who was that in all the pictures?"

Nev slumps even farther down in his chair. "The younger ones, that were my Josh. They were taken when he was over there at the clinic and around that time. But the older ones that you see, they were his cousin Tim. Same age. Everyone used to think they were brothers. It's my sister's little boy."

I swallow to try to shift something, thick like dust, in my throat. The sympathy I had for Nev a moment ago is now gone.

"So you made his cousin pretend to be Josh?"

"No, nothing like that. He knew what happened to Josh of course, and that I was involved with all these cancer groups. So when we dressed up and did all our silly videos, he thought he was just helping the little sick kiddies. To be frank with you, he liked it. Happy to help, to be honest. Look, I'm not very good at saying this, but, well, I… I am sorry, I really am," Nev says.

"You're sorry?" I say, sitting forward on the edge of the sofa. "Have you been watching the news recently? Have you seen what this man has done? To children, to families, to people like me. And you just sit here like it's nothing to do with you, like you're innocent in all of this."

"I have, yes, and I promise to God, I didn't know all that. I believed in it, I really did. Because when my Josh started going there, and he had his first treatments, they showed us all these numbers and they said it was working. These proteins, GML and that CB-11, they said it were a sign of the tumor dying. And so we kept going with the treatments, round after round. But it was expensive, you see, and we don't have much, so I borrowed money from everyone I could and then that ran out and I had to remortgage the house."

Nev sniffed and wiped his nose with his finger. "After twelve treatments, Dr. Sladkovsky said it was working, but we needed to continue. I... I didn't know how I was going to pay for it, but I signed up for four more rounds, like, and then three more. Who wouldn't, right? When it's your only son, that's what you gotta do, right? And then they kept telling me he was getting better. It's working, it's working, they kept saying, it's working. I really thought my Josh was getting better. Because he looked completely different, he really did. He was brighter and had color in his cheeks, and all the things that were wrong with him before, like his speech, his walking, they all got better. Like a new little lad. Night and day compared to how he was on that chemotherapy..."

Nev's forehead is glistening with sweat and he wipes his hands on his trousers. "I'd seen it with my wife, you see, and I wasn't going to let that happen again to my Josh."

"Your wife?"

"Yeah. She had cancer a few years before Josh. It was very quick." Nev swallows and takes a deep breath. "Yeah, we were walking out on the moors one weekend—she were a big walker, my Lesley—and all of a sudden, she had this terrible pain and had to go to the emergency room. And that was it. Cancer of pancreas. They said she had nine months, but she only lasted three." Nev nods at the angels and winged horses. "These were hers. She collected them like."

The room is silent. Just the sound of children playing and police sirens in the distance.

"That was why I went to Prague, if I'm frank with you, why I spent everything I had. It all went on the clinic—the savings, the house, money from friends. Because I couldn't bear to see my Josh go through what my Lesley went through."

I think of something someone wrote on *Hope's Place*. That we were victims in all this. Victims. Just following our own paths. Doing what was best for our kids, what any parent would do.

"I'm sorry," I say. "About your wife. But it doesn't explain why you kept promoting the treatments when you knew they didn't work."

"I... I didn't know that at the beginning, to be honest. I started promoting the clinic, talking about it on the forums when I thought Josh were getting better. They were telling me it was working, and I believed them. I was convinced by it. I wanted to shout it out from the rooftops, like. I started talking up the clinic because I really—honest to God, Rob—wanted to help the other kids."

I am sitting forward in my chair, because I don't want to miss a word. "And after Josh died?"

"Well, I kidded myself at first, didn't I, still thinking there was something to it. Josh did last longer than all the doctors thought he would. And maybe if he'd started sooner, then it would have worked. That's what I told myself, that it was my fault." Nev looks down into his lap. "It was money, as well, though. I admit that."

"Money?"

"Yes, money." Nev looks up at me. "I'm not trying to make excuses, like. I know I done wrong. I got in too deep, didn't I, just too deep. It were one of Dr. Sladkovsky's staff, who worked in the marketing department, and they saw my posts on the forums, and then they offered me a commission for every patient I brought to the clinic. I was desperate, you see, absolutely desperate. I owed so much to Sladkovsky, over a hundred thousand pounds. The house, after all the other debts were paid off, only covered half of that. Well, they said I could pay my debts off by working for them.

"I wasn't sure at first, because I knew I would have to lie about Josh, but then they threatened all this legal action and

talking about this extradition treaty. I had already lost the
house, everything like, and I was just so scared because I had
to provide for Chloe, and there's no work around here now,
nothing. And then the money started coming in from Sladkovsky and it were a lot—real good money—and I started paying off the debt, and we were able to move out of me mum's
and come down here..."

"Chloe?" I say.

"Oh, sorry, yes, I'm jabbering away, aren't I. Chloe is Josh's
sister."

The little rain boots at the door, the pictures on the fridge,
the cartoons in the background. Him and his little one.

"I knew what I were doing was wrong, but I couldn't let
Chloe down, you see. She lost her mom, her brother, and I
didn't want her to see her dad go away to prison. I wanted her
to have a home, with her own bedroom an' all."

The clouds have obscured the sun, and the light is dimmer
now in the front room.

"Can I, um, can I get you anything, a tea or a coffee or
something?" Nev says.

I don't answer, just shake my head.

"And your son, Jack, you said he went to Sladkovsky's?"

"Yes, when we were out of options. Jack had a few treatments, and then we stopped."

I don't know why, but I take out the photo of Jack I carry
around in my wallet and give it to Nev.

"Ah," Nev says, smiling. "I think I remember him from
your emails. He's a nice-looking lad. Can definitely see the
resemblance."

I take the photo back and look at it again. It was taken in
a children's playground, close to Regent's Park, just around
the corner from Dr. Flanagan's office on Harley Street. I feel

empty, as if I have been fasting: a gripy hollowness that cannot be filled.

A football hits the window again, and I can hear the glass shudder and bend. Nev does not even flinch. In the corner of the room there is a pile of folded clothes, and I can see that he is ironing his daughter's school shirts.

"So why did you stop then?" I say.

"Stop doing stuff for Sladkovsky you mean?"

"Yes."

"Do you want the truth?"

"It would be nice."

"I paid off the debt," Nev says, shrugging. "I was free. They dropped all them legal proceedings." Nev stops speaking and looks down into his lap. "Look, I... I really am very sorry, about what I've done, about what happened to your Jack."

It bothers me hearing him say Jack's name. It seems improper, as if Jack should only be spoken of in hushed reverence. Not by a stranger. Not by Nev.

"Did the money buy that then?" I say, nodding at a huge high-definition television in the corner.

"You gonna think I'm lying, but I actually won it. In a raffle, like."

"Right, Nev, because you'd never lie to me, would you? You'd never do that."

I shift in my seat. The foam in the cushions is old, and I am sinking into a gap in the middle. I look at Nev telling his sob story, his wiry body hunched over in his chair.

"Do you know how much hope you gave me? And not just me, but hundreds of other parents in exactly the same situation. You won't remember this, Nev, but I remember. I remember when I got an email from you. I was at our house in London, on the patio. I think I must have read it a hundred times. 'Good news,' you said. 'Another clean set of scans for

Josh.' Still today, I remember those words, because they meant everything to me. I used to read that email over and over again, on my computer, on my phone..."

I stop. There is nothing more to be said. I stand up to leave and Nev remains seated, motionless, crumpled in the corner. I walk over to him, and he thinks I am going to hit him and he cowers, sinks farther back into the cushions.

"You're pathetic, Nev. Absolutely pathetic." I want to punch him, to smash in his face, but I do not trust myself, scared that I would become unhinged, so I turn around and walk out. As I close the front door behind me, I can hear him crying.

Outside, the kids who were playing football are now huddled next to the car and I see him again, the boy I thought was Josh. Up close he looks different. His blond hair, which before seemed to shine, is greasy and unkempt. He has cold sores around his mouth, as if he has been sniffing glue.

"You like watching kiddies play football, do you, mate?" Josh says. He is older than I thought, only about half a head shorter than me. He is swigging from a big yellow can of energy drink, and spits some thick stringy spittle onto the ground. When I look at him now, he does not look anything like Josh—his face is much sharper, harder; his hair a different hue. Was it just wishful thinking, a trick of the mind?

"Fuck off," I say.

"Fack off," he says, imitating my London accent, and they all laugh, mimicking my southern vowels. "Bit far from home aren't you, mate," and the other kids cackle again and move closer as I walk to the car.

"Is that the one who gave you a hundred quid to suck him off, Gary?"

They all laugh, like a deranged Greek chorus. At the back of the group, I can see the two boys who told me where Nev lived, their baseball caps pulled down over their faces.

As I close the car door, the boys move closer, en masse, like a well-drilled regiment. My hands are shaking and I fumble with the keys, and have to grip the steering wheel to keep them steady. I screech away, hearing the chant of "Pe-do, Pe-do!" as the kicks and stones rain down on the car.

4

Subject: Re: Re:
Sent: Fri Jun 2, 2017 11:45 am
From: Rob
Recipient: naws09

Hello, hope everything is good with you and you're feeling a bit better. You asked in your last message why I took my son to Dr. Sladkovsky. Well, the short answer is because I'm stupid, because I was desperate, because I couldn't accept that my son was going to die.

I'm not making excuses. My wife, Anna, could see Dr. Sladkovsky was a fraud. She told me, over and over again, but I didn't listen. I treated her terribly and, understandably, she doesn't want anything to do with me. I wish I could make it up to her, do something about the pain I've caused, but I think it's too late now.

Other than that I'm fine. As ever, thanks for listening. How are you doing?

Subject: Re: Re:
Sent: Fri Jun 2, 2017 1:27 pm
From: naws09
Recipient: Rob

Hi, Rob. Not so bad, thanks, a little lost in my thoughts these days. (That happens when I don't do much but work and come home to an empty house.)

I wish so much I had my old life back. Sometimes I look at Facebook and see what I was doing that day three years ago, before this all happened. It makes me so sad to see my old routine: play center, my aerobics class, family days out. It's strange—a world that is very familiar but now is so distant.

I have this photo of my daughter, Lucy, in the bath. She is standing there with her goggles on, because she loved to wear goggles in the bath and stick her face under the water and blow bubbles. In the photo she has such a lovely expression on her face, almost a little glum or sulky, as if she's fed up with me taking photos. I can't stop looking at it. It's like I want to touch the photo, to climb inside it, to be back in that bathroom with her again. Anyway, sorry, this message has been all over the place. Probably not making much sense. Take care.

I have downloaded all of the messages to Nev from *Hope's Place* and organized them in a database. That way it is easier to go through them all, by location, by the year they were sent. I cannot exactly say why I am reading them. I know I am looking for something, but what? An explanation, as to how I fell for Nev, how I so readily believed Dr. Sladkovsky?

I recognize some of the names from *Hope's Place*. Thomas Banson. John Stevens. Murial Stenovic. Priya Davidov. It is quickly apparent that most of their children are now dead. I read their obituaries in local newspapers, about their love for Lego, their favorite fluffy slippers, their beloved Leicester City FC. There are eulogies on Facebook, shared hundreds of times, that speak of their children's resolve, their grace and humor right up until the end.

I was never interested in the people on *Hope's Place*. I did not care about their lives. I just read their posts to find out what treatments their children had received and how that might apply to Jack. I had no interest in the off-topic threads, their weekend plans and road trips, the word-association games they sometimes played.

I think I even looked down on them. Their bake sales and hashtags. The dolphin swimmers, I used to call them. The people who talked about being blessed, who praised every sunrise, who tried to convince the world—and themselves—that their child's cancer was really a gift.

Now I feel like I want to know them, all these desperate parents who poured their hearts out to Nev. So I read their stories. The forensics of how this came to be: the loss of appetite, the dizzy spells at school, how at first they thought it was nothing, just too much football on the weekend. In meticulous detail, as if they were testifying in court, I read about the day their child was diagnosed: whether the sun was shining, what the traffic was like that day, the smell of the receptionist's perfume, the feel of their clammy skin on the leather seats in the waiting room.

I read about their family holidays, the jobs they loved and lived for, their trips to the cabin on the lake. The things they did with their children, the days out at Peppa Pig World, the superhero birthday parties. I read about their hopes—a clinical trial, Vitamin-C infusions—and how quickly they were dashed. I read about their loss of faith, how they cursed a God that could allow this to happen.

They talked a lot about the "before." Before diagnosis. Before this all happened. Before Jamie got ill. Because now life was delineated differently. It was no longer "before we got married," or "before Jamie was born." There was now a new before and a new after. And I noticed just how much they needed to talk about this before, to resurrect this old life, because that was the world they wanted to return to. I understood why they told

Nev how much they used to have—the football tournaments, the canal-boat holidays—because then he might understand just how much they had to lose.

There was another reason why they told Nev everything. Because sometimes telling your story is the only way to stay alive.

Re: Newly diagnosed
by johnkelly» Mon Jun 5, 2017 8:05 am

Hello this has all happened so quickly. We have just received the devastating news that our beloved daughter has a tumor on her brain stem. They are still not sure what kind and we are in shock. She is only ten years old and is the captain of her school soccer team.

We haven't told any of our family yet and we have to wait to hear what the doctors say but we wanted to ask if anyone has any experience with tumors on the brain stem? What types of tumors do these tend to be? Can she still be cured? It's very difficult trying to find answers on this. Can anyone help us please?
John Kelly

Re: Newly diagnosed
by Rob» Mon Jun 5, 2017 8:30 am

Dear John,
So sorry that you're joining the club that no one wants to join. In answer to one of your questions, only pathology would truly show the tumor type and grade. I'm afraid I can't help you on your particular question about the brain stem, but I am sure that others will weigh in.

Please, please, try not to panic until you know exactly what you're dealing with. (I know that's easier said than done). And please try to stay off Google. There are many different types of tumors—and a lot of them are curable in children. Even in just the last few years, treatments for brain tumors have improved vastly. There is so much to be hopeful about.

Please let me know if I can help in any way and feel free to PM me any time on the forum if you want to talk. Thinking of you. Rob

Re: Newly diagnosed
by motherofdavid» Mon Jun 5, 2017 10:36 am

Don't really know how to start this but here goes. Our little boy James was diagnosed just over a month ago with Grade 3 Astrocytoma and we had some hope after diagnosis, some stories from this forum actually, and there was this clinical trial that James might have qualified for, but none of it has worked, nothing, and now they're thinking of stopping treatment because they're saying there's nothing else they can do.

This has just crushed us even though I think deep down I knew it was coming. How on earth can God be so cruel, James is only seven and they say he has probably a few months, maybe even weeks and I knew it was bad when he was diagnosed but thought we might at least have a year or two. I think my husband knew this all along but when the doctor came I have never seen him look so sad so broken. Our life has just gone and I don't know how I can carry on if we lose him and no one seems to know anything, whether there's anything now that can help and I just can't make sense of it, I am just broken.

Re: Newly diagnosed
by Rob» Mon Jun 5, 2017 11:02 am

Dear motherofdavid,
I'm so sorry that you have received this news. There are no

words to make it better. After going through this with my own son, I think there is no making sense of it and it is best not to even try, at least for now.

All you can do is cherish every moment you have together—as you say yourself, you don't know how long that will be.

I wish you and your family all the best. Please feel free to get in touch if you need to talk. I sent you a PM with my contact details and I'm here to listen any time.

Rob

Subject: Sorry
Sent: Wed Jun 7, 2017 12:05 pm
From: Nev
To: Rob

Dear Rob,

It's probably too late now and there's nothing I can say to you, but I just wanted to tell you again how sorry I am for what I've done. It was completely wrong of me and I have hurt you and countless other people.

I am trying to make amends and contacting all of the parents I have deceived. I have also been voluntarily to my local police station to give a statement about my role in all this. I realize, given the case against Dr. Sladkovsky, that I might face criminal proceedings. I will accept any punishment for what I have done and I deserve everything that's coming to me. I am worried about my Chloe but I have spoken to my sister and she said she could look after her if I had to go away for a while.

As I said, I don't expect forgiveness, but I do want you to know how sorry I am and if there was any way I could make it up to you, I would.

Best Wishes,

Nev

Subject: Re: Re:
Sent: Thu Jun 8, 2017 12:05 pm
From: naws09
Recipient: Rob

Hi Rob, just a quick note to say I was very happy to see you on Newly Diagnosed! I know it might not seem like such a big thing, but it has helped me so much. (That sounds terrible, I know. I don't mean to make it about *us* when of course it's about helping people going through an awful time, but well, I hope you know what I mean.)

If I can be philosophical for a minute, I suppose in each of us there is this need to give, to love, to share ourselves—and when we have children, we have this perfect vessel for that. A place we can put all of our love. When I lost my son, suddenly that was all gone. That love didn't have anywhere to go anymore. I think that's what I'm trying to do on Newly Diagnosed. Trying to help people but also trying to find a place for all my love (as selfish as I know that sounds).

Subject: Re: Re:
Sent: Thu Jun 8, 2017 12:15 pm
From: Rob
Recipient: naws09

Thank you. You expressed it perfectly. I want to write more later, but have to run out now. I'm a little confused from your last message. You said when you lost your son. Did you lose another child, as well as Lucy?

Subject: Re: Re:
Sent: Thu Jun 8, 2017 12:16 pm
From: naws09
Recipient: Rob

I wouldn't make a very good spy.

Subject: Re: Re:
Sent: Thu Jun 8, 2017 12:16 pm
From: Rob
Recipient: naws09

What do you mean?

Subject: Re: Re:
Sent: Thu Jun 8, 2017 12:17 pm
From: naws09
Recipient: Rob

My little slip, my giveaway.
It's me, Rob. It's Anna.

BEACHY HEAD

——

we were sitting in the sun having a picnic, looking down at the lighthouse and the rocks, and all you could talk about was the box, the kids takeout box from the chinese restaurant. god, that box, Jack, you were so besotted with it, wouldn't let it out of your sight. you even slept with it in your bed, still with the grease stains and prawn-cracker crumbs until mommy insisted we wash it out. i know what you loved about it, jack. it was the pictures of the balloons, the chinese lanterns, the humming birds flying into the burning sun.

5

The hall is dark apart from a spotlight on Anna. I am standing at the back of a conference room in a smart Mayfair hotel, cloistered by thick walnut doors. The people watching are sitting, straight-backed without moving, shadows in suits and patent shoes. Only Anna's face is visible. She is too far away, but her head is blown up on a big screen. She looks confident, austere, her hair tightly swept back off her face.

I think about the last few weeks we spent together. Drinking vodka behind drawn curtains; the smell of bleach; the washing machine on an endless cycle; Anna whispering to her mother in another room.

I listen, move a little closer to the stage. Anna is talking about "ethical accounting." After Enron, a need for the profession to regain the public's trust. That meant more than codifying good practices, she says, pulling up another slide. It was about bringing back the original—and now unfashionable—underpinnings of good, solid accounting.

The audience is clapping and Anna walks to the side of the stage, shaking hands with someone in the wings. The lights have now been turned on and the accountants start filing out, carrying folders of materials, their name badges on lanyards around their necks.

Anna is still speaking to people by the stage, and I watch as she kisses a smartly dressed older woman on the cheek. Slowly, they start to walk out, close but not touching. As she sees me, she makes her excuses and walks to where I am standing.

"Hello," she says. She does not smile but she does not frown. Something in between.

"Hi," I say, and I blush, and it is as if we are meeting for the first time. What is remarkable—so striking that I have to take a second furtive look—is to see how little she has changed, how beautiful she still is.

"You look very well," she says.

"So do you," I say, and I want to hug her but I don't, and keep my hands down by my side.

As we walk out toward the lobby, I steal a few looks at her again. Her hair is longer than I remember and she is a little thinner, toned, I assume from all the marathon running.

"Would you mind giving me fifteen minutes to say hello to a few people, and I'll meet you back here? Is that okay?"

"Of course," I say. "Are you sure that's enough time? I don't mind waiting longer."

"Have you been to an accountancy convention before, Rob?"

"No."

"I have," she says without smiling. "I'll meet you in fifteen."

I wait in the lobby, my hands clammy with sweat. After exactly fifteen minutes, Anna appears in her coat, carrying a laptop bag over her shoulder.

"I'm ready. Are you hungry?"

"I am a bit."

"There's a decent Thai place around the corner. Fancy it?"

"Sounds great."

For a few moments, we walk in silence. It is like the first time we met, at Lola's party in Cambridge, and how I was so desperately trying to think of something to say. "So how was the conference?"

"Oh, you know. Has to be done."

"Are you working here in London now?"

"Mostly. I'm just consulting. And you? Are you still living down in Cornwall?"

"Yes," I say, and we walk on in silence because, now, suddenly, I don't know what to say.

The restaurant is the sort of place we would have come to in our London lives, the type of light, finicky food we both used to like. We sit in a corner booth on austere wooden benches, the walls hemming us in like a crypt.

"It's strange to see you after all this time," Anna says. "I feel a bit nervous to be honest."

"Yeah, me too. Sorry, I'm being a bit of a freak. It is nice to see you, though."

"It is," Anna says. She smiles but it is a sad smile, and I don't know what it means. She looks down at her menu. "So are you ready to order?"

"Sure," I say, although I have barely looked. As I choose my food, I glance at her hands and notice that she is not wearing a wedding ring.

"I'm surprised you didn't know it was me," she says after the waiter takes our order.

"How do you mean?"

"Chatting on *Hope's Place*."

"Oh," I say. "I had no idea to be honest."

"Really?" Anna says, because she had always loved parlor games, charades. "I was convinced you would guess, especially after I mentioned the goggles in the bath."

"No, not at all. I really didn't. If you hadn't given yourself away, I wouldn't have known. Although, when I thought about it afterward, the name of your daughter, Lucy, did make sense."

Lucy, the name Anna had given to the second child we had lost.

The waiter puts down our drinks. A glass of wine for Anna, a water for me.

"I'm really glad you're not drinking anymore," Anna says after the waiter left.

"So am I," I say, but it stings a little. The drunk who doesn't like being told they are a drunk. There is a silence, a familiar silence. The silence across the kitchen table after Jack had gone.

"So," I say, taking a drink of my sparkling water and daring to look her in the eyes for the first time. "I know I've said it before, but I wanted to say sorry in person. I said some unforgivable things to you, about Jack, about the treatment in Prague. Unforgivable. I just lost it, with the booze, with everything. I know that's no excuse and I don't expect you to forgive me. But I do want to apologize. I really am so, so sorry..."

Anna pauses and then lets out a deep breath, as if she has been holding it in. "Thank you, Rob. It means a lot to me to hear you say that." Her tone was formal, still a little cold. "So, yes, I accept your apology."

"Thank you. That's very generous of you. Really."

Anna shrugged. "Life's too short, right? We know that better than anyone."

The appetizers arrive. Little spring rolls with whiskers of carrots protruding at the ends. Anna looks down at her plate, as if she is deciding whether to start.

"I won't lie to you, it hurt me a lot, when you said those things," Anna says. "About the clinic, about how we could have saved Jack and..." She stops herself and then wipes her mouth with her napkin. "Anyway, sorry, we don't need to go over all that again. I certainly didn't come here to berate you."

In recent weeks, more details have emerged about the clinic. Relatives and parents of former patients have come forward, many of them seeking compensation. A former nurse went to the media and revealed details about what the staff called "dosing up." They would give patients small quantities of morphine and steroids to simulate a clinical response to the immuno-engineering. I remember all the drugs Dr. Sladkovsky gave Jack—the little pots he used to bring, the pills I saw him slipping on Jack's tongue.

"It's ironic, isn't it," I say, "that after all the horrible things I used to say to you about the clinic and how it could have saved Jack and then, in the end, it was probably me…" I swallowed, my voice trailing off.

"Probably you what?"

"Well, that maybe it damaged him, that perhaps I cut his life short by taking him to Prague…"

Anna fiddles with her napkin ring and takes a sip of her wine. She looks at me, and I feel for a moment like one of her clients receiving counsel. "I do understand why you think like that," she says, "but you shouldn't. Really, don't do it to yourself."

"Why not?" I say. "With what we've learned about the clinic. It's more than possible."

Anna shakes her head and puts down her fork. "I have spent so much time over the last few years beating myself up, about what we could have done with Jack, whether you were right about Sladkovsky, whether we should have gone for treatment abroad, in Germany, or pushed more on that Marsden trial. But for what? Jack was dying, Rob. He would have died, no matter what we had done. The best specialists in the world told us that. Sladkovsky's or no Sladkovsky's, Jack didn't have a chance."

I swallow, drink some water, pick at a spring roll.

"The funny thing," Anna says, and I think I see the slightest hint of a smile, "is that Jack actually quite enjoyed the trip to Prague, being at the airport, on the plane."

I smile, remembering his little backpack and how it was too big for him but he insisted on carrying it. "He did, didn't he. He did always love going on the plane."

"Do you remember Crete? When they let him sit in the cockpit before takeoff?"

"I do. He absolutely loved it."

Anna is about to say something when the waiter arrives with the main courses. Little prawn sliders with coriander and tarragon. Cuts of beef bathed in chili. A laboriously arranged and dressed papaya salad. Anna is quiet, almost as if she thought she had said too much.

"Can I ask you?" I say, as we begin to eat. "Why did you get back in touch, on *Hope's Place*?"

Anna takes a bite of her crab cake, diligently chews and swallows, and then wipes her mouth. "Well, at first, I was just a bit worried about you. I didn't want you to kill yourself." She stops, puts down her fork, her brow furrowing as it would when she was perturbed by a crossword clue. "But it's a bit more complicated than that. If you must know, I think a part of me was hoping you would start talking badly about your wife, or ex-wife, or whatever I am. And then, for once and for all, I would know how horrible you really were and I could stop thinking about you."

Anna smiles and takes a deep sip of her wine and, for a moment, it is as if we have gone back in time, a cavernous Cambridge restaurant, our lives stretching out before us. "God, Lola would kill me now," Anna says, chuckling to herself. "She always says I'm far too honest... Anyway, my master plan didn't work, that was the problem. Because you didn't say anything bad about me in your messages. You only said nice things, and you seemed so genuinely sorry.

"It was more than that, though. I loved talking to you on *Hope's Place*. The way you wrote, how you explained things, talked about your feelings. Your messages really helped me. And it was what I had always loved about you, how we used to talk for hours, in bed, late into the night. Just the two of us. So...as I said, my plan didn't work, and I suppose that's why I'm here."

I dig my fingernails into my palms to stop myself from crying. "I'm so sorry," I say. "I'm so sorry I was horrible to you. It was disgusting what I did to you."

"Oh, Rob," Anna says. "You don't need to keep saying sorry. I do understand, you know."

"But I want to," I say, the tears welling behind my eyes. "I just…I feel I owe it to you."

Anna looks at me sternly. "If you say sorry one more time, I will walk out and leave you here with the bill."

I let out a little laugh. "Thank you," I say, "for being so nice. I don't deserve it."

"No, you don't." She gives me another stern look that turns into a smile and we sit, taking a breath, sipping our drinks.

"Can I ask," Anna says, breaking the silence, "how much do you remember about what happened? After Jack died, I mean."

"Not much," I say, a pang of shame that she is asking, the fear that I will hear more about the things I did. "It's a bit blurry, to be honest, just bits and pieces."

"Did you know that every night after Jack died, I set my alarm for midnight or one o'clock and got up to check on you?"

I didn't say anything, couldn't look her in the eye.

"Every night I thought you might die, choke on your own vomit or something." She stops, evaluates the expression on my face. "I'm not saying it to shame you. That's what you always thought. No, you were ill, Rob. You had a breakdown, and I just didn't know what to do. I tried to get you help, a place in a rehab clinic, but you refused.

"So that was that. I didn't know what to do, so, like you, I just withdrew into my own little world, as well. I worked long hours, I read my books, all my silly crime novels. And then when you started drinking even more, the arguments started, about every little thing—Sladkovsky's clinic, how I was always so cold, Jack's room. God, we spent so long talking about the room. You accusing me of clearing everything out. I just couldn't do it anymore."

I am confused and don't know what to say. I remember the boxes and bags, stacked up in the hall. "I thought we did clean it out."

"Rob," she says firmly, leaning forward across the table, "we didn't. We just didn't. One day, I took a couple of things out because I couldn't look at them anymore, and you started a huge argument with me and had it in your head that I was throwing things away. But I wasn't, I just wasn't. All those boxes and bags, they were mine. That was mine, the stuff I was taking to Lola's. I still have all of Jack's things, Rob. They're in my attic in Gerrards Cross."

I try to think back, to find a foothold somewhere, but I am slipping, losing my grip. She touches my arm across the table.

"Rob, I'm not saying this to hurt you or make you feel ashamed, but you were so drunk you couldn't even remember your own name. You didn't know what day it was. You couldn't remember the reason you walked into a room half the time."

I think Anna is about to cry. I can tell from the minute quiver of her cheek, the way she bites her lip, but she stops herself, steels herself.

"I hated seeing that. The man I loved, just destroying himself. I wanted to help you because I knew this wasn't the real you, and I felt like I owed you..."

"Why on earth would you owe me?"

Anna looks at me, intently, as if this is something she has thought about and wanted to say for a long time. "Do you remember Jack's Zoo? How you were the zookeeper and he was the boss, the zoo's owner, and he would always tell you what to do."

Jack's Zoo. We played that game for hours in his bed, making enclosures for the animals among the pillows and duvet, lining up Tiger, Monkey, and Ellie Elephant. And Jack, as the boss, would tell me which animals to feed, and then he would go to each one, asking them if they had enough food and inspecting their bottoms to see if they were clean.

"Yeah, I do," I say, smiling, and I remember the way Jack shouted "Zoo open!", his bedroom blinds casting warming licks of sunshine onto the floor. "He was so funny. So particular about certain things. The zoo had to be on the bed except..."

"The lion's cages," Anna says, finishing my sentence.

"Yes, exactly. For some reason, with the lions he felt it was okay to move the zoo onto the floor. With the two pillows for their cages."

Anna takes out a tissue from her bag and wipes her eyes. I still don't understand why she is telling me all this. Why would she feel that she owed me?

"He was always so happy with that game," I say, "he could play it for hours."

"And do you remember bath time? After he was dry and he was in his pajamas, and then you would hide. And he would come and look for you, and then you would jump out and Jack just thought it was the funniest thing and wanted to do it again and again. You two could play for hours like that."

Anna's face drops, and she looks sullenly down at the table. "I know that was never my strong point," she says. "I've never been particularly good at being silly. Even as a child, playing games, rolling around on the floor—it just doesn't come naturally to me. And this, Rob, all this is why I felt I owed you, because you were so good at that. You made Jack's life so wonderful. You made our home such a happy place for him, so alive with fun and laughter and joy—so much joy. God, all the games you invented—the dressing up, the rocket ships, the superhero stories, playing with your bloody helicopters in the back garden.

"Or when you played crocodiles with him and he was on the bed throwing pillows and teddies down at you on the floor. I tried it with him once and managed about ten minutes before my knees started to hurt, but you would keep going for hours. I just couldn't do that, not in the same way. And I'm so ashamed of that and wish I wasn't like that. But you, Rob—you made him smile hundreds of times every single day, every single minute. Jack just adored you, and you made his life so special, much more than I ever could have done. He was the happiest little boy right up until the end, and that was because of you, Rob, and I will never, ever forget that..."

Anna stops speaking and looks at me. "I'm sorry, I didn't want to make you cry."

I look down and realize that I am weeping, tears splashing onto my plate. Anna hands me one of her tissues from her handbag and gives me a moment to dry my eyes, to catch my breath.

"I still think about him every day," she says. "Where he might be, what he might be doing if he was still here..."

"He'd probably be in his room, wouldn't he?" I say. "Reading his books, or playing with his toys."

Anna smiles sadly. "I feel guilty whenever I hear about these kids with terminal cancer going to Disneyland or meeting celebrities," she says. "Or their parents organizing one of those flash-mob dances. I always think of Jack, sitting in his bedroom for his last few months, humming songs to himself."

"But, as you said, he was happy," I say. "I remember you saying in one of your messages how you were worried that you weren't a good enough mom, that you didn't care enough. Well, you know that's absolutely rubbish. You were a wonderful mom to him, Anna. You really were. Do you remember the birthday party and the Spider-Man cake you were up half the night making? He loved it so much. He was so happy that day."

"Yes, he did," Anna says sadly. "He was." She looks down at

her empty plate. "Shall we get dessert?" she says, as if she wants to change the subject. She is distant again, as if she feels that she has opened herself up too much and must take a step back.

For the rest of the evening, through dessert and another glass of wine for Anna, we don't talk about Jack—I think we deliberately don't talk about Jack—but speak about old friends, their kids, divorces, new lovers. We pay the bill, and I walk Anna back to her hotel and it is an odd moment, with no clear idea of when or if we will see each other again.

"Please keep in touch," I say, and we embrace awkwardly and she feels smaller than I remember, the jut of her collarbone palpable on my skin. I want to cry, but I feel as if all the moisture has been wrung out of my body. "I know I'm not allowed to say sorry again, but I am," I say. "I'm so sorry I hurt you."

"It's okay," she says, and we are still holding each other, but I sense that she wants to pull herself away.

Just as we are parting, Anna turns to face me, as if she has forgotten something. "Oh, I saw your website by the way. *We Own the Sky*. Your photos, they're just stunning. Really beautiful, and it's lovely to see all the places we went."

"You saw the website? How?"

"Er, it has your name on it, Rob. I Googled you. I know, I'm brilliant, aren't I?"

"I'm just surprised."

"Well, don't be. As I said, they're lovely, and it brings back such happy memories for me. Actually, if you must know, your website was how I kept tabs on you—well, apart from all the Facebook messages you sent my friends when you were drunk. Every time you posted a new photo I knew you were okay. I always told myself that when you stopped posting the photos, I would come and find you. But you didn't. Every week, every single week, you kept on putting up new ones, and I knew you were fine. I knew you were alive. You probably didn't realize, but I always commented on every photo."

The mystery commentator, the first ping I always received as soon as the panorama went live. *Beautiful. Lovely. Take care of yourself.*

"So you're swan09?"

"Indeed, I am," Anna says. "It wasn't just about keeping tabs on you, though. It made me so happy to see your photos, because that was the man I fell in love with. Someone who would build things, create things.

"Anyway, I'm rambling on," she says, taking a step back. She looks at her watch, still the same chunky Casio. "I've got to go. I've got to be up early tomorrow." And with that she is gone, disappeared inside the lobby of the hotel.

6

At the front of the hall cupboard are the four shopping bags stuffed full of Nev's letters. I take out the bags and go into the living room. Some of the letters have been bound together with ribbon and string, I presume by the man in Nev's old house. Others are haphazardly slung inside. They are dusty, some a few years old, the paper drying out and fading. Some are newer, whiter, the pen strokes on the envelopes more clearly defined.

I hesitate as I start to open one. I think I know what the letters will contain. Appeals from desperate people whose children were dying. Requests for information, pleas to be bumped up the patients' list. What was I supposed to do with them? Give them back to Nev? Write to them all and tell them that Nev is a fraud?

The Cedars
Firmtree Farm Road
Gedstone
Nr Barnstaple
Kent

Dear Nev,
I wanted to write to you to see if you could help us. I am writing on behalf on my grandson Antony, who has recently been diagnosed with an advanced brain tumor. We are potentially interested in receiving treatment at Dr. Sladkovsky's clinic...

I look at the date again. Six years have passed. I take another letter from the middle of the pile. It has an elaborate Indian postmark, a winged elephant flying above a river bend.

Dear Mr. Barnes,
I am sorry to bother You, Sir, but I am writing on behalf of my father, Engineer Bhagat. My father is very ill, very ill indeed, I might add. We have heard…

I read a few more, and they are all the same. I do not feel anger toward Nev, just a feeling that time and lives have been wasted. I sort through more of the letters, and can feel a chalky film of dust on my hands. After a while, I realize that the handwriting on some of the envelopes is the same. It is a neat script, by someone who has been taught proper cursive. It takes me a while to realize that the handwriting is Nev's. They are letters from him, addressed to people all over the world, that never arrived and were returned to sender.

I open one of the letters and a picture of Josh falls out. Even though I now know that it is not Josh, it still feels like Josh, and I so desperately want it to be Josh. The letter is long and I read it all. Nev was telling his correspondent about a trip to the zoo, but it is written as if Josh were seven or eight, an age he never reached, doing things older boys would do, riding the cable car on their own, swapping football stickers. Nev wrote in detail about how Josh loved the gorillas, how he wanted his dad to buy him a book from the gift shop. And then, when they got home, Nev described how they watched the sunset together, how Josh fell asleep in his arms, his gorilla book in his lap.

In another letter, Nev wrote about Josh's ninth birthday party and how he was overwhelmed that so many people came and what lovely presents he got, the Manchester United jersey, the tickets to Alton Towers. I open more of the letters, and they are all the same. Page after page describing Josh's life. Page after page describing a life that didn't exist.

It was more than the scam. I know that now. The Minecraft; the football matches they went to; the cliff walks as the sun was setting. Nev wrote the letters because it kept Josh alive. They were his love notes. And in that, Nev was no different from me.

Subject: Hello
Sent: Mon Jul 22, 2017 10:05 am
From: Rob
To: Nev

Dear Nev,
Thanks for your note and I appreciate your apology. I'm glad you're trying to make it up to people. I think that's the right thing to do.

Believe it or not, I do understand. I know how grief can do terrible things to people. And to be honest, I'm no better. I hurt my wife, Anna, very much and I am very ashamed of how I behaved.

I think what you did was wrong, but I do understand why you did it. You were desperate and doing what you thought was best for your family. You have lost two people you love in the most horrible way. No one should ever have to go through that.

The truth is that you helped me a lot when Jack was dying. You listened to me when I needed it and, despite everything that happened, you were a good friend to me.

I'm going to be up in your neck of the woods next week-end, at the Plover Scar lighthouse, to take some pictures, so if you'd fancy a coffee or something then do let me know. It would be good to meet.

I hope you and Chloe are well.
Rob

It is strange to walk through Hampstead graveyard with someone else. We walk closely, our arms touching, and there is something formal, funereal, about the pace of our walk—like the slow march of a ceremonial soldier. The graveyard always seemed like a wintery place—even in summer it was dark and dank, the trees forming a shroud, blocking out the light. Today, though, it is different. There is a lightness here, an orderliness, as if the place has been spruced up.

"I always knew you came here," Anna says. "The grave was always nice and tidy."

"When did you come here?"

"Normally Sundays. It seemed proper, like going to church. And you?"

"Early mornings, in the week."

"Hmm," Anna says. "I don't like it here much, if I'm honest. That probably sounds awful, but I don't find it to be a place of peace, or anything like that."

"Yeah, me too," I say, and we walk on in silence.

At Jack's headstone, we put down our flowers and stand in silence. The sandstone was a good choice. It is hardy, and will endure the weather. We look at each other, unsure what to do.

"Shall we get out of here?" Anna says. "Sorry. I just…"

"Yeah."

"I don't like saying goodbye or anything like that," Anna says. "I don't like even thinking that he's here."

"I know," I say. "C'mon, let's go," and we walk, quicker this time.

We go to a pub in Hampstead, one of the places I used to come to before I took the train back to Cornwall.

"Are you okay coming here?" Anna asks.

"You mean with the drinking?"

"Yes."

I laugh nervously. A little pulse of shame. "Yes, I am. But thanks."

"Did you talk to anyone about it?" Anna says quietly, as we are waiting at the bar. "The drinking I mean."

"No. I meant to, but I thought I would try to do it on my own. It's been difficult but, well, I'm managing so far."

Anna smiles approvingly. "Well, I'm very proud of you. I'm sure it's not easy."

"Thanks," I say, and I realize I don't like talking about my drinking because it makes me feel weak.

We order two roast dinners and two tonic waters and find a seat in a wood-paneled alcove.

"I see you're doing a lot more on *Hope's Place*," Anna says.

"Yeah," I say. "I enjoy it, if that's the right word. It's so sad, though, from the minute they post, you kind of know that for many of them, for their kids, there's probably no chance."

"Yes," Anna says, and then shakes her head. "Just like Jack. It was just too aggressive. He didn't stand a chance."

She looks away from the table. A couple with a small child comes in and sits at the table next to us. The mother fusses to get the child in a high chair, to take off his coat, to arrange his toys and sticker book in front of him. Anna smiles at the boy, and he smiles back and holds out a little plastic dog.

"To our beautiful little boy," I say, looking at Anna and raising my glass.

"To our beautiful boy," Anna says, and we softly clink our glasses. "To Jack."

We sit for a moment in silence, listening to the happy chirp and chink of Sunday lunchtime. I want to reach out across the table and hold Anna's hand, the way I used to make a small cocoon around her fist in our old, cold Clapham flat. But I don't. I keep my hands down by my side.

"I'm so sorry I was awful to you," I say again. "I just don't know how to…"

"Stop bloody saying sorry," Anna says, laughing a little, and she can't keep her eyes off the little boy, who is babbling and batting away the spoon his mother is holding out for him.

"Oh, there's something I wanted to show you," I say.

"Really? Exciting."

I reach down into my bag and pull out my laptop. I log on to the Wi-Fi and load up *We Own the Sky*.

"Ah, your website. Any new ones?"

"Yes, that's what I wanted to show you actually. Some photos. I think you'll recognize them."

"Excellent. Can I see?"

I pass the laptop to Anna, and she starts to scroll through the new photos. The view from our garden in Hampstead. A blinding shot into the sun from Jack's bedroom window. The lighthouse in Swanage, gleaming a bold and brilliant white. And then Greece, the panorama from our terrace; Jack, the human tripod.

"What, I don't understand. Did you take these?"

"No. They're Jack's, from his camera. The one we bought him for his birthday."

"Wow, they're amazing, they really are," Anna says, pulling the laptop closer. "That was a lovely day wasn't it, Swanage." She keeps scrolling through the photos as if she is looking for something in particular and then looks at me. "I thought we had lost the camera, though. You have it then?"

"I do, yes. I hope you don't mind."

"No, goodness, not at all. It was your thing. You boys. Going up tall buildings, taking pictures from the heath."

"Yeah, he loved it. There's something else I wanted to show you," I say, shuffling up next to her. "So, when I'm coding the

pages and uploading the panoramas, I write these little messages to Jack."

"What do you mean, messages?"

"They're just memories, things about Jack that I remember
from that particular place where we went. They were hidden
before, buried in the code, but I've made them all public now.
Look, if you mouse over the photo, the text comes up." I take
a deep breath. "I suppose it's all the things that I would say to
him if I could, if he was here now."

"Oh, Rob, that's so lovely."

"But look, this is what I wanted to show you. I made a version of the site for you. You just have to log in as you, and it
means that you can also add to them, add your own memories of Jack."

"Thank you, Rob, that's wonderful, but you didn't need to
do that…"

"I know I didn't need to, but I wanted to, because this has all
been about me, hasn't it? My sadness, my drinking, my grief,
and I let you down in the most horrible way. I didn't once think
about you, how all this affected you, how you were dealing
with things. It was just about me, and I'm so sorry for that…"

Anna is staring at one of the photos, one Jack took of the
two of us, wearing our raincoats on a Dorset beach.

"There was something you said the other day," I say, "that
made me feel so low. You said you were ashamed of how you
were with Jack, that you wished and regretted that you hadn't
done more and I understand that, I really do. But it's not true,
because he adored you, he really did. Fathers and sons are one
thing, but it's different with a mother. He needed you in a special way, a way he could never need me.

"Do you remember in the mornings sometimes, the times
he slept late and we were already downstairs in the kitchen and
he would come, still sleepy, his hair standing up, and he al-

ways wanted his mom first, to come and rest his head on your lap. Never me. He always had to go to you first. And I always loved that. I loved watching the way he so obviously cared so much about you."

I can see Anna's bottom lip begin to quiver, so I put my arms around her. She doesn't pull away and buries her head into my neck.

I have a sudden and desperate urge to be with her, to know her once again, to discover the person she had become, the person she'd been even before we had first met. Because that was love. To feel sorrow that you had no part in someone's past. To be with her when she was washing paint pots, or running through sunflower fields, or sitting at her desk, trying to make sense of her sums.

That Christmas when we went to Suffolk to visit her parents, Anna took me to her secret place. We were bored, wanted to escape the house, so we went for a walk. It was, she said, the place she would come as a child when she wanted to be alone.

We walked deep into the woods around her house, until we came to a dense thicket of trees and shrubs. It seemed impenetrable, but Anna said there was a way through, a way she had to learn. She went first and I followed, twisting and turning, getting down on our hands and knees. After the last part where we had to crawl, we came to a huge clearing, the trees and shrubs forming an awning, as if it had been hollowed out by a giant machine.

She came here to read, she said, to escape her parents. She would bring a blanket and some fruit and cheese and stay here all day. It was pristine, untouched, a place where no human apart from Anna had been, and I don't think—then and now—I had ever loved her more. I wished I could have seen her as a child, her knees pulled up to her chest, needles of sunlight pricking through the canopy of branches and leaves.

I pull her close to me and kiss the top of her head, and it is inadequate as a gesture, but I do not know what else I can say or do.

"Did you see this one?" I say, pulling over the laptop, wanting to divert her, to make her feel better. She clicks on a photo of Beachy Head, the day we had a picnic.

"Aw, I remember that day. The weather was just perfect." She looked at the photo again, as if she is remembering something. "Rob, I just don't know what to say, they're so lovely. God, that box from the Chinese, I remember that, how he used to sleep with it."

Anna closes the laptop. "I'm sorry, though. I can't look at them here, or I'll be an absolute mess. More to the point, I had forgotten what a huge geek you are."

"We all need a project, right?"

"Right. So are you working on something new?"

I smile nervously, not sure whether to mention it or not.

"What?" Anna says, looking at me sideways.

"Well, don't laugh, but I'm actually still trying to do something with my drones."

Anna smiles at me, as if she was a teacher reprimanding a naughty but favored child. "I think you just need more time, Rob, more time to perfect it. How long has it been now, nearly ten years?"

Her eyes sparkle and, because we are still a little brittle with each other, she nudges me to let me know she is joking.

"Fuck off," I say, smiling back at her. "It's gonna be huge."

"Actually, that reminds me, I have something for you," she says, opening her handbag and rummaging around inside.

"Here it is," she says to herself and hands me a small flash drive. "It took me a while, as I couldn't bear to look at them for so long. But I finally went through all my old photos and videos of Jack. There's something in particular you'll like on

there. Something I watched, and then the name of your website suddenly made sense."

"How do you mean?"

"Just take a look. You'll like it. There's a lot of the Greece
holiday on there, as well. Jack loved that holiday, every single
minute of it."

"Yeah," I say, "he did."

Jack, my boy. Our boy.

On the train back to Cornwall, I settle at my table with a
coffee and open my laptop. I plug in the flash drive Anna has
given me and see that she has made folders: Birth, Christmas
2010, Christmas 2012, Spain, Brighton.

I click through every folder, every photo. Jack's first Christmas dinner, little slices of things he didn't eat on his Mickey
Mouse plate, his paper hat pulled down over his face. Jack making a happy lion's face in a ball pit; Jack pretending he was in
prison, smiling at me through the bars of his cot.

There is a video of Jack's Zoo, and I cannot stop myself grinning. I watch as we lined up the animals on his bed and made
a hollow mound out of the duvet—a cage, Jack said, for the
monkeys. And then Jack kissed my neck, a kiss so tender and
so full of love, it makes me gasp.

There are two videos remaining that I don't think I have ever
seen. They are from the house in Hampstead, taken in the summer, the year before Jack's diagnosis. We were buoyed with wine
and good friends, and kids were running madly and perilously
around the garden. Jack was being boisterous, and Anna wanted
me to have a word with him. So I did, but with perhaps a little
too much wine, I started tickling Jack and soon he was laughing hysterically, and we were both rolling around on the grass.

A tear falls, then two, three, and they do not stop, but I
don't care who can see me crying on the train, because I am

watching us all, sun-kissed with happiness, nothing tainted in our little world. This was our before. Our wondrous before.

I click on the second video and the time stamp shows it is from the same night, after the guests were gone, as the sun was going down. It was a holiday and our neighbors were doing the same and having a barbecue. They were louder, younger, without children, and it sounded from the noise like they were a little drunk.

Jack was shouting at the moon, charging around the backyard with Little Teddy and a toy plane. There was suddenly a huge burst of laughter from next door and Jack looked at me, wagged his finger and said, "naughty, naughty" and narrowed his eyes, just like he did when he saw a dinosaur with bared teeth or a knobbly scary tree in a book.

Jack ran back to the patio and pressed his head onto my knees and then looked up at me and asked who was making the noise.

"They're our neighbors," I said, "they live next door." Then a pause, Anna saying something inaudible off camera.

Jack looked up at me with his big wide eyes and asked what neighbors were and I said, "Well, we own this house, and they own the one next door."

And then he asked, "But what about the yard, who owns that," and I said, "Well, we own our yard and we own the house and the patio and everything you can see around us."

"Everything," he said, opening his hands wide as if he had caught the biggest fish.

"Yes, everything," I said. "The trees, the walls, your bedroom window, the roof with the birds."

The camera shakes slightly, as Anna, out of sight, attempts to stifle a laugh.

Jack looked up at the sky and then at me. "Dad," he said, pointing at the red sunset and the moon and the streaks of airplane dust, "do we own the sky, as well?"

EPILOGUE

———

The sky is tenuous, as if it is going to break, and I know that I will have to leave soon. For now, though, the garden at The Rockpool is too inviting. The sunlight is blazing, and it is the first time in a long time that it has felt this hot.

The benches and tables are full of people, scattered haphazardly under the trees. Children run in through the wide-open doors, dodging, running rings around the bar staff. Bags of potato chips are fanned open on tables for families to share.

I am taking advantage of the Wi-Fi to work on my new project. One day, I was reading an article in the *Guardian*. It was about a little boy with a terminal disease who was using a camera to document his last few months. I remember looking at this boy's photos and thinking just how much they reminded me of Jack's. It was their sense of wonder about ordinary things, the shapes and colors we had become so accustomed and indifferent to: the vivid, bright blue of a pen lid; the ribbed texture of a teddy bear's nose; the digital red glare on the display of an infusion pump.

So I started Sunflowers—the name had been Anna's idea— and I asked tech companies to donate high-end cameras to children who were terminally ill. We offered free photography lessons to the children, at their homes, on the wards, so they could learn the fundamentals of form and technique.

I started small but was soon overwhelmed. Parents, relatives— sometimes dying teenagers themselves—emailed, asking if we could send them a camera. When they wrote, they always said the same thing: they wanted to document and capture their worlds, the worlds they knew they were leaving behind.

They knew how people saw them: bald-headed, sickly, dependent on others. And that wasn't how they wanted to be remembered. Because even though their worlds had shrunk, to the confines of their bedrooms, a hospital ward, there was still so much life they wanted to capture, to breathe in: a flock of seagulls zooming past their window; a board game lovingly laid out on their hospital bed; the day they sat with their family and watched the crimson sunset set the sky alight. These were the things they wanted to leave behind. And these were the things they wanted us to never forget.

I finish my coffee, zip up my coat and leave the café. The wind is getting stronger and people are starting to move inside, and I know it is time to go. I put my backpack over my shoulder and head up the path toward the cliffs. The air is almost intolerably muggy now, the storm threatening on the horizon. In the distance, there are flashes of lightning over the ocean and, as the wind picks up, I can hear gentle rumbles of thunder.

At the top of the hill, I leave the path and walk toward the cliff edge. In the distance, I can hear an engine stutter, failing to start, and somewhere, on one of the farms, the frenzied, infectious barking of dogs.

At first it seems like it might be a light shower, that the storm will just graze us, but then there are two giant claps of thunder and the downpour begins. The rain beats down on my head, slaps my skin raw, my raincoat sticking to me in the heat.

I stand still, looking out to sea, its swirls and whitecaps like impressionist brushstrokes. I am shivering now, but not with the cold.

The wind has picked up, and I know the time is right. I take off my backpack and dig deep for the party balloons and the can of helium. I choose a blue one, blow it up, and then write on the balloon with a black marker.

Dear Jack,
We own the sky.
Lots of love, Mom and Dad

I move as close as I can get to the edge of the cliff and wonder if I should say some kind of prayer, but I just think of how Jack would have loved it up here: the blustering rain, the wind whipping through the overgrown grass like a scythe.

He was always excited by bad weather. I smile, thinking of him charging around on a rainy Brighton beach, and then let go of the balloon. It doesn't go far and starts heading down the incline toward the edge of the cliff and the rocks beneath.

And then it stops—perhaps some turbulence or an opposing gust of wind—and hangs in the air, and for a moment I think it is going to plummet down into the sea. What is amazing is how still it is, an inertia I don't understand, as if it is being held in place by invisible hands.

I walk toward the balloon and, just as I am starting to clamber down the steeper section of grass, it is picked up by the wind, darting and diving, zigzagging up into the air.

I watch the balloon fly out across the gray sea until it is just a speck on the horizon. I watch it until I am sure that finally it is gone.

★ ★ ★ ★ ★

ACKNOWLEDGMENTS

———

I couldn't have written or published this book without my agent, Juliet Mushens. It was her advice and unrelenting editorial input that turned my unstructured manuscript into a novel. Since our first conversation on the phone, she has always been my biggest champion and I couldn't wish for a kinder, more understanding, kick-ass agent. Thanks also to Nathalie Hallam at Caskie Mushens for all of her help and support on some of the less thrilling aspects of publishing.

I also couldn't have wished for better editors—Sam Eades at Trapeze and Liz Stein at Park Row Books. Since they first read the manuscript, their advice and reshaping have been invaluable. They have helped me trim and expand and shape and it has been more than a pleasure to work with them. Also, a big thanks to the copy editors, Joanne Gledhill and Cathy Joyce, for ironing out all the inconsistences, fixing my terrible punctuation and changing some of the more oblique Britishisms.

The book would never have gotten off the ground without the wonderful comments and suggestions on the first draft. So huge thanks to Kathryn Baecht, Andrew Gardner, Ruth Greenaway, Rob McClean and Nicole Rosenleaf Ritter. Thanks also to Jessica Ruston for her wonderful, extensive critique, which really helped me hone the manuscript. And thank you to Andrew Rosenheim, who gave me a chance on an earlier project, which convinced me I wanted to write long-form.

To all my friends and family in the UK and the Czech Republic, my colleagues at Radio Free Europe/Radio Liberty, all the love, support, tolerance of my "jokes," but also, practically, the time to write. You always said to me, you have to get better, I know you'll get better—and that was enough. I couldn't have done any of it without you.

And to my two boys, Tommy and Danny. You are my world, my everything, but please stop hitting me in the balls.

ABOUT THE AUTHOR

———

Born in the UK, Luke Allnutt is a writer and journalist based in the Czech Republic. He is married and has two young boys. *We Own the Sky* is his first novel.

thank you for all the laughs and support over the years. Cancer is generally pretty awful but you all helped me get through it. Special thanks to "the lads," as my mum would say. To all of you—in particular, Daniel Easton, Michael Howard, Ben Mellick, Neil Okninski and Glenn Woodhams—who, week in, week out, came to meet me for a beer before each round of chemotherapy. You turned something frightening and horrible into something lovely. I will never forget it.

Speaking of cancer, thanks to my amazing doctors who saved my life, Professor Paris Tekkis and Dr. Andrew Gaya, who have been what every doctor should be: compassionate, patient and always willing to listen to my panicky questions. The same heartfelt thanks go to all the amazing nurses and support staff at the London Clinic and Leaders of Oncology.

I must also thank everyone in COLONTOWN, an online community for those affected by colorectal cancers. It has always been a wonderfully supportive place and has helped me a great deal.

To my parents-in-law, Miroslav Jirák and Iva Jiráková, who, especially when times were tough, helped out more than they ever could know and have been just the best grandparents to our boys. Without their support (and endless help looking after the children), I could never have written the book.

To my sister, Ruth, thanks for all the love and support, not in the least for help answering all my nervous medical questions!

To Mum, thanks for all the love and for always believing in me, as a son and as a writer. You always had a quiet confidence in me and that is the best gift you can give someone. You are the best mum in the world and I am so lucky to have you.

To Dad, thanks for being a wonderful father and for teaching me, without ever saying a word, to never give up. I just wish you could be here now.

Most of all, to my wife, Markéta, who has given me so much: